Westward Hearts

Westward Hearts

MELODY CARLSON

HARVEST HOUSE PUBLISHERS
EUGENE, OREGON

Cover by Koechel Peterson & Associates, Inc., Minneapolis, Minnesota

Cover photos © Koechel Peterson & Associates, Inc. / iStockphoto / Thinkstock

Back cover author photo Ruettgers Photography

WESTWARD HEARTS

Published by Harvest House Publishers
Eugene, Oregon 97402
www.harvesthousepublishers.com

Library of Congress Cataloging-in-Publication Data
Carlson, Melody.
Westward hearts / Melody Carlson.
p. cm. — (Homeward on the Oregon Trail ; bk. 1)
ISBN 978-0-7369-4871-5 (pbk.)
ISBN 978-0-7369-4872-2 (eBook)
1. Widows—Fiction. 2. Women pioneers—Fiction. 3. Overland journeys to the Pacific—Fiction. 4. Oregon National Historic Trail—Fiction. 5. Women pioneers—Fiction. 6. Wagon trains—Fiction. I. Title.
PS3553.A73257W47 2012
813'.54—dc23

2012002080

Printed in the United States of America

12 13 14 15 16 17 18 19 20 / LB-CD / 10 9 8 7 6 5 4 3 2 1

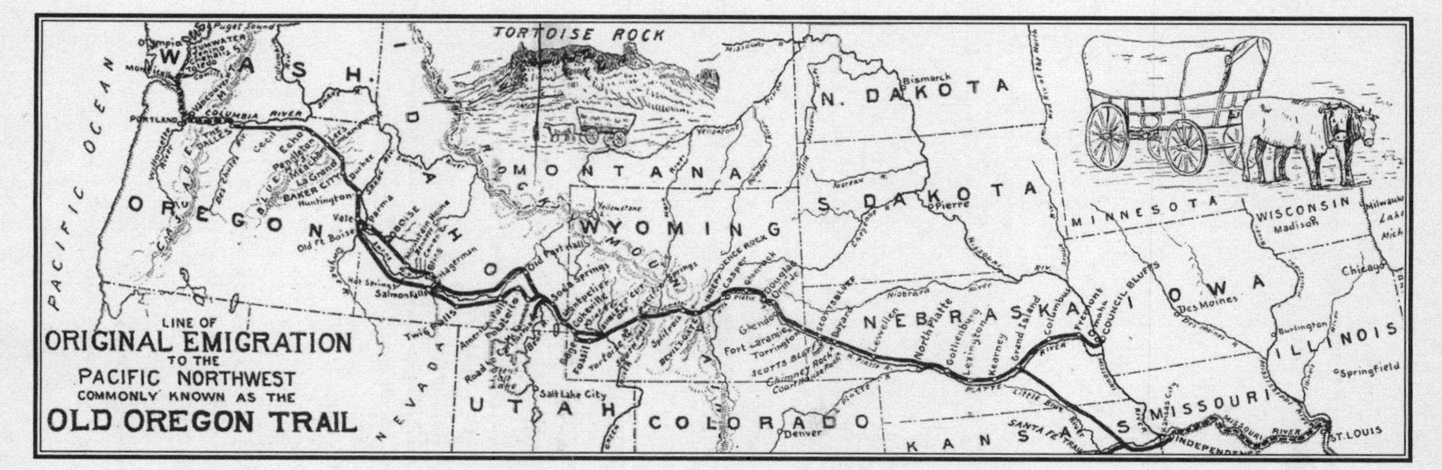

LINE OF
ORIGINAL EMIGRATION
TO THE
PACIFIC NORTHWEST
COMMONLY KNOWN AS THE
OLD OREGON TRAIL
TORTOISE ROCK
PACIFIC OCEAN
WASH.
OREGON
IDAHO
MONTANA
WYOMING
N. DAKOTA
S. DAKOTA
NEBRASKA
IOWA
MINNESOTA
WISCONSIN
ILLINOIS
MISSOURI
KANSAS
COLORADO
UTAH
NEVADA
Olympia
Puget Sound
PORTLAND
COLUMBIA RIVER
THE DALLES
Echo
Pendleton
La Grand
BAKER CITY
Huntington
Vale
Parma
BOISE
Old Ft Boise
Hagerman
Salmon Falls
Twin Falls
Old Fort Hall
Soda Springs
Montpelier
Cokeville
Salt Lake City
Bismarck
Pierre
INDEPENDENCE ROCK
Casper
Douglas
Fort Laramie
Torrington
SCOTTS BLUFF
Chimney Rock
Bayard
Lewellen
North Platte
Gothenburg
Lexington
Kearney
Grand Island
Columbus
Fremont
Omaha
COUNCIL BLUFFS
Des Moines
Madison
Milwaukee
Chicago
Burlington
Springfield
ST. LOUIS
INDEPENDENCE
Kansas City
MISSOURI RIVER
SANTA FE TRAIL
Denver
PLATTE RIVER

Chapter One

December 1856

Elizabeth Martin sat up and blinked in the pitchy darkness. What had disturbed her dreamless slumber? With pounding heart, she shoved back the warm layers of quilts and reached for the woolen shawl at the foot of her bed. Wrapping it snugly around her flannel nightgown, she pushed her feet into her sheepskin slippers and tiptoed down the hall to peek into the children's bedroom. Quietly listening, she waited until their even breathing assured her they were both still sleeping peacefully.

She crept down the stairs, treading lightly on the creaking steps until she finally stood motionless in the front room. Holding her breath, she listened intently to the sounds of the night. But other than the ticking of the mantel clock and the whistling of the winter wind outside, the farmhouse remained silent. Even old Flax, faithful friend and watchdog, appeared unconcerned as he snoozed blissfully on the braided rug in front of the glowing coals of the fire.

Stooping down, she set a couple more logs on top of the last remnant of red embers. She hoped they would catch and burn until morning. Blowing onto the hot cinders, she watched as flames flickered to life and then licked up the birch's papery bark. Without even moving, Flax opened an amber eye, peering up at her with canine interest.

"Sorry to disturb you," she whispered as she stroked a silky golden ear. "You didn't hear anything, did you?"

His tail thumped contentedly in answer. Just the same, she gazed up at the long shotgun mounted above the mantel, wondering if she should take it down…just in case. But standing, she slowly shook her head. No, there was probably no need for that. She was confident that it was loaded and that she was fully capable of firing it—and wouldn't hesitate to if necessary. Less than two weeks ago, she'd shot at a small pack of coyotes that had threatened to invade the chicken coop. But she suspected that tonight's intruders were simply products of her own imagination. Otherwise Flax would have barked. Or Brady would have tapped quietly on her door. Despite his sixty-some years, his hearing was as sharp as ever. The freed slave was her dependable hired hand. She didn't know what she'd do without him.

Just to be sure, she went over to the front window and, barely moving the lace curtain back, peered out into the farmyard. Thanks to a bright half-moon and the freshly fallen snow from earlier in the evening, she could see that all was a picture of perfect peace out there. No sign whatsoever of intruders. No farm animals stirring. She didn't even spy any tracks of wild critters in the blanket of new snow. Brady's little cabin looked equally undisturbed and somewhat picturesque with a thin layer of snow coating its shake roof. All was obviously well, and she knew she would be wise to return to her own bed while it still retained a margin of warmth.

But she was fully awake, and despite being worn out from a long day of holiday baking as well as her usual farm and household chores, she knew that sleep would not come easily to her now. It never did at times like this. Besides that, returning to her empty bed was always much more unsettling in the middle of the night than when she retired at her usual bedtime, not long after she'd tucked the children into their beds and listened to their prayers. At first it had seemed strange to turn in with the chickens and the children, but over time she'd convinced herself these early bedtimes conserved kerosene and candles and firewood, especially during winter, when the nights were so long. Oh, she knew the real reason for her juvenile bedtime…even if she couldn't admit it to anyone else. It was a clear-cut case of plain old loneliness.

More than three years had passed since she'd lost James. In the beginning, everyone had promised her it would get easier with time. Sometimes her mother still reminded her of this. And in the bright and shining light of day, Elizabeth believed her. It had gotten a tiny bit easier over the years. But at times like this, awakened in the middle of the night and experiencing her solitude, the rules changed.

Elizabeth's usual loneliness turned into a deep black pool in the night. Pulling her down, holding her under, it sometimes made simply breathing a struggle. Alone in the darkness, her grief felt as fresh and intense as if it she'd only just lost him. And she knew the ache in her heart would never heal. How could it? But eventually morning would come. She would go through her daily paces, and sometimes she would even laugh and smile, moving forward one day at a time. But nights were difficult.

She sat down in the rocker by the fireplace, and staring blankly at the flickering flames, she began to pray. It was her usual prayer, painfully familiar to her, and she hoped God didn't grow weary of her pleading. She always began by asking God to help her to bear her grief with grace and with strength. Then she asked him to make her wise enough to parent Jamie and Ruth with dignity and mercy. Finally she asked God to grant her peace—that lovely perfect peace that surpassed understanding. And for the most part God had generously given it to her, at least in the daytime.

Recently, however, even in the light of day, that particular sense of peace seemed to be lacking. She couldn't quite put her finger on where it had gone or when it had started to fade, but she felt certain that something had changed. Or perhaps it was simply a result of winter. The cold and ice and snow had come earlier than usual this year. Certainly, that could make anyone uneasy. At least that was what she had tried to convince herself.

But when she was being perfectly honest, like on a night such as this, she had to admit that something was definitely amiss. In all truthfulness, these stirrings had begun early in the fall. Her unsettling sense of discontentment, as if something—and not just her beloved departed husband—was missing from her life. Deep down inside of her, similar to a festering splinter or a stone bruise, something was disturbing her.

"You're just ready for a new relationship," her mother had happily told Elizabeth after she'd confided this sense of restlessness several weeks ago.

"A new relationship?" Elizabeth had been confused.

"It's only natural that a young woman such as yourself should want a good man by her side." Then, as was her habit, Elizabeth's practical mother had begun to list the eligible bachelors and recent widowers within a twenty mile radius. This was followed by all the recent gossip tidbits her mother had overheard in town that week. And finally, her mother had ended by declaring that Howard Lynch was the perfect man for Elizabeth. "You know how he lost his wife and little girl to cholera too. Gladys Barton told me that he's been very lonely of late."

"That's not what's troubling me," Elizabeth had declared. "I'm not looking for a man, Mother. It's something much bigger than that. A restless sort of stirring deep inside of me. I can't even describe it properly."

Of course, that had worried her mother. She'd even felt Elizabeth's forehead, thinking she might have a fever. "But remember, you have Jamie and Ruth," she had said with concern. "Those youngins depend on you. Even if you're discontent in some way, you do have your children to keep you going. Don't forget them."

As if Elizabeth could ever forget them. "I love Jamie and Ruth more than I love my own life," Elizabeth had reassured her. "You know that, Mother."

Smiling in a knowing way, her mother had gently patted her hand. "It is simply a season, my dear. All women suffer from these afflictions at times. Don't fret, this too will pass."

But as Elizabeth stared into the fire tonight, she wasn't convinced this would pass. Something inside of her knew this was more than just a female problem or a seasonal stirring. And certainly not a desire to remarry. It was much bigger than those things. Elizabeth was fairly certain that this longing was related to an old dream that she and James had nurtured early in their marriage. Back when the children were small, she and James would sit right here in the evenings. Relaxing in their chairs that flanked this very fireplace, together they would discuss this dream as they planned for a future that was exciting and adventurous and challenging.

It had been a very big dream, but when James was alive, it had seemed realistic and possible. However, cholera changed everything in 1853. The dream had died when Elizabeth had buried her husband and stillborn baby.

But in recent weeks, this old longing had been trying to return. It had been sneaking into her dreams, whispering into her ear, and waking her in the middle of the night—as it did tonight. But the dream was unsettling now. It felt too big for her. Too big for her children. And for the most part she wished it would go knock on someone else's door. And yet...there was a small part of her that was still intrigued by this dream. Probably because of the way it made her feel connected to James.

Sometimes, she almost felt as if James was the one waking her in the middle of the night. That he was sitting with her by the fire, filling her mind with these strange ideas in the wee hours of the morning. She could never admit this to anyone—certainly not her mother—but sometimes she almost felt as if she were being haunted by her dearly departed husband. No, "haunted" was the wrong word because she never felt frightened. It was more as if he were sending her messages.

Even now she could imagine him sitting in his chair across from her, smoking his pipe, smiling with confidence as he encouraged her to pursue the old dream. She sensed him assuring her that this was the right path for her and the children. And sometimes, in the quiet of the night, she almost believed it too.

But common sense always came with the morning, and in the light of day she always realized how impractical, impossible, and slightly insane it was to entertain such wild imaginings. So for days, she would dismiss this crazy dream altogether. And other than that fleeting sense of discontent, which came and went, she would move smoothly through her life. But then a night like tonight would sneak up on her. And suddenly the dream seemed like a real possibility, and a part of her felt as if she almost wanted it to come true.

But another part of her, that protective maternal part, was hesitant and careful and slightly afraid. After all, her children were dependent on her. Common sense must prevail. And so as she watched the flames flickering and crackling, she once again asked God to direct her, to help her to lead her children on the path that was best for all of them. And if somehow this dream was truly best for them, if it was the direction God wanted them to take, he would have to show her the way and lead her. Otherwise, she would simply stay put.

Chapter Two

"Ruthie, hold still," Elizabeth told her daughter as she plaited her hair, trying to contain the wispy golden strands into one smooth braid down her back.

"I'm too excited to hold still." Ruth's feet continued to dance. "I want to get to Grandma and Grandpa's. I can't wait, Mama."

"If you don't stop squirming, I'll have to start all over again, and it will take us even longer to get on our way."

"But Grandma said to be there by two," Ruth pointed out.

"And we will get there by two, if you'll just stop wiggling."

"The carriage is hitched and ready to go." Jamie came into the house, stomping the snow off his feet by the kitchen door.

"Did Brady check it for you?" Elizabeth asked.

"He said I did just fine." Jamie pointed to the kitchen table, loaded with boxes and packages. "Do you want me to take these out now?"

She nodded as she reached for the red satin ribbon. "Thank you, son. And be careful with that small white box. It's breakable."

"I know," he said importantly. "It's the vase for Grandma."

"The one with the pink rosebuds," Ruth added. "To go with her dishes. I picked it out of the catalog. Remember?"

"We all picked it out," Jamie said as he hefted up the biggest crate, the one containing the pies that Elizabeth had baked the day before.

"Be careful with that one too," she warned. "Place it where it won't get jostled about. And keep those tea towels tucked snugly over the top."

Jamie sniffed and then smacked his lips. "Don't worry, Ma. I'll put this one in a real safe spot."

"And did you already take that pecan pie out to Brady?"

"I did, Mama, and he said to thank you for thinking of him."

"And you took him his Christmas present as well?" Elizabeth had ordered the old man a new heavy woolen coat from the catalog. His other one had been looking threadbare.

"I gave it to him. He said he wouldn't open it until Christmas morning though."

"Thank you, son." She turned back to Ruth, securing the shiny ribbon midway down the long braid.

"I wonder what I'll get for Christmas," Ruth said dreamily.

"Remember, honey, Christmas is about *giving* gifts," Elizabeth told her. "Not just receiving them."

Ruth's forehead creased in concern. "But we *always* get gifts for Christmas, Mama."

"Yes, I know." She fashioned the ribbon into a nice big bow. "But I just don't think you should *always* expect them."

Ruth looked unconvinced.

"There." Elizabeth patted the backside of Ruth's red and white gingham party dress. "All done. You look very pretty, Ruth Anne."

Ruth smiled at her, but then her smile faded as she pointed to Elizabeth's dress. "Why don't you wear a pretty dress, Mama?"

Elizabeth shrugged as she smoothed the black taffeta skirt. This had been her "good" dress for the past three years, and it still had plenty of wear left in it.

"Cora May's mama quit wearing widow's weeds a long time ago."

"Widow's weeds?" Elizabeth looked curiously at her daughter.

"That's what Cora May calls them. And she said her mama never wears black anymore."

"Well, that's fine for her." Elizabeth reached for her coat.

"And Cora May told me her mama sewed herself a new dress to wear for Christmas, and she made Cora May one to match. Cora May said the fabric is exactly the color of a blue jay."

"That sounds very pretty." Elizabeth patted Ruth's head. "I'm very happy for Cora May and her mama."

"But Cora May's papa died the same time as my papa."

It seemed clear that Ruth had been giving this subject some thought of late. "Yes, Ruth, I know."

"But you still wear black, Mama."

Elizabeth sighed. "Yes, I do."

"But why, Mama?"

"I don't know…I suppose it's because I'm so used to it."

"But don't you think colors are pretty?"

Elizabeth smiled and then nodded as she put on her winter hat, which was also black. "Yes, I do think colors are pretty. But are you forgetting that this is Christmas Eve and we need to get to Grandma and Grandpa's? So run and get your coat. And don't forget your scarf and mittens. It's cold out there."

Before long they had everything, including the dog, securely loaded into the back of the carriage, and as usual of recent times, Jamie insisted on driving. Elizabeth didn't argue, but also as usual, she sat next to him just in case. For a boy of nearly twelve, he was as responsible as they came. And yet she knew he was still a child. And even though he sometimes strutted around the farm like a little rooster, trying to be the man of the house, she didn't want to put too much upon him too soon. Childhood was fleeting enough without being rushed through it.

"Can we sing Christmas songs?" Ruth asked as the carriage rumbled down the drive, cutting new tracks through the thin layer of fresh snow.

"Certainly." Elizabeth nodded as she adjusted the muffler more snugly around Ruth's neck, making sure to keep the cold draft out. "You get us started."

Soon they were singing "Jingle Bells," including all the verses Jamie and Ruth had learned in school. And before they knew it, they were there, unloading the carriage in front of Elizabeth's parents' home.

"Merry Christmas!" Elizabeth's father said cheerfully as he burst out of the house, bounding down the front steps with energy that belied his age. Not that he was so old, although Elizabeth knew that he'd be fifty-five in a few weeks. But Asa Dawson was a big man and full of life and kindness. Due to his size, he could easily intimidate anyone, but when he grinned he reminded Elizabeth of an overgrown puppy dog. He bent down to hug each of them, wishing them all a happy Christmas. Then, spying the largest crate, he lifted the towel and peeked inside. "Well, well. I reckon I better help you with this one."

"It's the pies," Jamie told him as he helped Flax jump down onto the ground.

"Mmm-mmm…I might just have to sneak that apple pie out back." He winked at Jamie. "Your grandma banished me from the kitchen and I'm about to starve to death."

"Oh, Father." Elizabeth laughed as she picked up the present for her mother. "Are Matthew and Violet here yet?"

Asa shook his head as he opened the door for them. "Matthew went to pick her up some time ago. I thought for certain they'd be here by now."

"There you are!" Elizabeth's mother came over to greet them.

"About time you children got here. Now come over here and get warm by the fire."

"Look at the Christmas tree!" Ruth exclaimed. "It's almost as tall as Grandpa!"

"It's beautiful." Elizabeth smiled as she unbuttoned her coat. Being in her parents' home on Christmas Eve always took her back to childhood days as if nothing had changed over the years. But of course, she and Matthew had grown up. And she had children of her own. And Matthew was engaged to be married in the spring.

She stood by the fire, watching as Jamie and Ruth arranged the presents beneath the tree, carefully placing them and sneaking surreptitious peeks at the other gifts. The two whispered secrets to each other, clearly intrigued with the magic and mystique of Christmas that only children understood. After warning the children not to get too curious and reminding Jamie to let Flax in the house, Elizabeth left them to their fun and headed to the kitchen to help.

"This bird is done," her mother announced. With her face reddened from the heat radiating from the big black cookstove, she stood straight, rubbing the small of her back with one hand. Clara Dawson was a strong woman both in spirit and in body. Reaching for some kitchen linens to protect her hands, she reached into the hot oven, carefully extracting the large roasting pan.

"I thought Violet and Matthew would be here by now," Elizabeth said as she tied on one of her mother's old aprons.

"They were supposed to be here." Clara set the pan on top of the stove and wiggled a drumstick on the golden-brown turkey. "Everything is ready."

"I didn't see Matthew's carriage on the road." Elizabeth picked up a wooden spoon to give the gravy a stir. But it already looked creamy and smooth.

"That's odd. He's been gone for several hours, and he promised not to be late."

Elizabeth shrugged, acting unconcerned. After all, Matthew was a grown man. He'd turned twenty-two last summer, and besides helping Elizabeth with her farm, he'd begun building a house for himself and Violet on the back forty beyond the creek. She knew her "little" brother was perfectly capable of getting himself to town and back. "Perhaps he stayed to visit with Violet's family?"

"Perhaps. But he knew we planned to eat around two. It seems you'd have spotted him on the road into town. Did you see any carriages at all?"

"I saw the Perkins' wagon headed for town. But nothing besides that, at least that I recall." Elizabeth set the wooden spoon down. "But I was probably paying more heed to Jamie's driving skills than to other holiday travelers."

"I sure hope Matthew didn't have a problem. I suggested he use the sled this morning, but your father said there wasn't enough snow for the skids yet."

"There were still some bare spots on the road."

"But was it slippery? Perhaps his horse stumbled and the carriage slid off the road." Her brow creased with worry. "Was it icy?"

"No, Mother. It's so cold that the snow is dry and crunchy. Not bad at all. Otherwise I wouldn't have allowed Jamie to drive. I must say, he did a fine job of it too."

"That boy is growing up so fast." Clara pushed a graying strand of hair from her damp forehead. "Seems like only yesterday that Matthew was his age." She shook her head and sighed. "Time sure passes...one day your children are tugging on your apron, and the next thing you know they have children of their own." She laughed. "Oh, my!"

Elizabeth studied her mother as she spread some butter over the turkey breast and then covered it with linen to keep it moist. Sometimes she forgot that this worn and gray-haired woman had once been young and vibrant. Or that, just like Elizabeth, she'd mothered small children, watched them grow up, and now complained that it all had happened too quickly. Elizabeth couldn't imagine her children being fully grown or leaving her, but suddenly she wondered if one day she would be just like her mother. It didn't seem possible.

"*Uncle Matthew!*" Ruth's happy cries echoed through the house.

"Sounds like they're here now," Elizabeth told her mother.

"Thank the Lord! Let's start putting dinner on the table before it gets cold, Lizzie. Your poor father's been complaining that he's as hungry as a springtime bear."

Elizabeth was just filling a warmed bowl with potatoes when her father came into the kitchen with a confused expression. "*Clara?*" he said in a tone that told Elizabeth something was amiss.

Her mother stopped scooping dressing from the turkey. "What is it, Asa?"

"Matthew." He shook his head and then glanced over his shoulder with a frown.

"What's wrong, Father?" Elizabeth set the half-filled bowl of potatoes down and went to her father. "Is Matthew all right?"

"I'm not entirely sure," he said quietly.

"What happened?" Clara asked with concern.

"I honestly don't know." Asa scratched his head. "Matthew stormed into the house with a sour expression. Didn't say a word to me or to the kids. He just marched up the stairs, went into his old room, and slammed the door."

"Oh, my!" Elizabeth exchanged glances with her mother.

"And Violet?" Clara asked. "Is she out there now?"

"Violet wasn't with him."

"Oh?" Clara put a hand to her cheek.

"I'll go talk to Matthew." Elizabeth untied her apron.

"Yes, that's a good idea." Asa nodded eagerly. "I'm sure Matthew will talk to you, Lizzie."

"What about dinner?" Clara held her hands up. "It's going to get cold."

"Give us a few minutes," Elizabeth called as she hurried away.

"What's wrong with Uncle Matthew?" Jamie asked her as she walked through the living room.

"I don't know," she admitted.

"He looked angry," Ruth said in a worried tone.

"I'm on my way to talk to him." Elizabeth paused on the stairs. "You two go and ask Grandma if she needs any help getting dinner on the table." Then she hurried on up and quietly tapped on the door to Matthew's bedroom, the same bedroom that had been his when they were children. "Matthew?" she called. "It's me. Can I come in?"

He made what sounded like a "humph," and she decided to take that as a yes. "I'm sorry to intrude," she said as she let herself in. With slumped shoulders and hands hanging limply between his knees, Matthew sat in a straight-backed chair, staring out the window with a blank expression as if she weren't even there.

"What has happened?" she asked.

He didn't answer, and she sat down on the edge of the narrow bed. "Please, tell me what's wrong, Matthew. Does it have to do with Violet?"

He turned and glowered at her. "*Violet is dead.*"

Elizabeth felt a surge of panic rush through her, and tears filled her eyes. "Violet is dead?" She choked on a sob. "Oh, Matthew, I'm so sorry! How did it—"

"She's not actually *dead*." His hands balled into fists and his blue eyes turned dark and stormy. "But she's dead to me. I never want to hear her name again."

Elizabeth stood and, going to him, placed a hand on his shoulder. "Tell me what happened, Matthew," she said gently. "You only have to tell me once. And if you wish, I'll never speak of it again. But we're your family, Matthew. We deserve to know what is going on. *Please.*"

He made a growling sound. "Fine." He turned to look at her, still smoldering. "I went to fetch Violet—I mean, *that woman*—I went to get her, and I was informed that she wasn't there. I asked her mother where she'd gone, and Mrs. Lamott acted funny."

"*Funny?*"

"She started saying strange things about Vi—about her daughter. She was talking in circles and wringing her hands. And it just made no sense whatsoever."

Elizabeth just waited.

"Finally, Mrs. Lamott told me that her daughter had gone with Walter."

"Walter?" she questioned. "*Walter Slake?*"

Matthew nodded grimly as he stood. Pacing back and forth in front of the window, slamming a fist into his palm, he looked as if he wanted to slam it into something...or someone. Probably Walter.

Elizabeth was truly shocked. Walter Slake had been Matthew's best friend since childhood. His parents owned the farm just down the road, but Walter had left the farm in order to work at the bank in Selma several years ago. He'd happily exchanged overalls and work boots for fancy suits and shiny shoes. He even drove around town in a fine new Rockaway carriage with lanterns. She could just imagine Violet sitting prettily by his side in it.

"I don't understand, Matthew. Where did they go? To Walter's folks'?"

"No." He stopped pacing and shook his head. "That's what I thought too. Vi—I mean *that woman*—she *ran off* with Walter."

Elizabeth gasped. "Ran off? With Walter?"

He nodded with an expression that reminded her of when he was a boy, trying not to cry over some big disappointment. His chin trembled, and she could tell he was on the verge of tears.

"Are you absolutely certain about this?" She studied his pained face. "I'm not questioning you, but...it's just so hard to believe. Do you know for a fact that it's true?"

"I heard it from her mother, Lizzie. Oh, she was sorry. Real sorry.

And she was embarrassed too. But she said those words herself. Mr. Lamott was so angry at Walter and Violet, he couldn't even speak."

"She truly ran off with Walter?" Elizabeth was still trying to absorb this outlandish news. It sounded like something she would overhear about somebody else, one of those hushed but lively conversations that transpired between certain folks while shopping in the mercantile. It sounded like plain old mean-spirited, small-town gossip. She sighed as she realized that was exactly what it would soon be. Small-town gossip.

"Yes." He slumped back down onto the chair. "My fiancée left me to run off with my best friend."

"Oh, Matthew!" Elizabeth didn't know what to say.

"Mrs. Lamott said they were headed to Frankfort and that Walter was going to get a bank job there. And of course, she assured me that they were going to get married too." He turned to stare out the window again.

"Oh, Matthew..." She sighed, wishing she had a way to make this better, to take the sting away. "I'm so sorry."

"I took off after them. Drove about ten miles out of Selma as fast as I could. And then I stopped and asked myself, what's the use? Even if I did catch up with the two scoundrels, which was unlikely, what could I do to make this right? I sure don't want to force a woman who doesn't love me to become my wife." He grimaced, letting out a low groan. "And so I turned around and came home. Really slowly. The horses appreciated that."

Elizabeth had no words. The truth was she had never been overly fond of Violet Lamott, and right now she wanted to throttle the silly girl. Oh, Violet was certainly pretty and witty and spirited. But she had always seemed somewhat frivolous and selfish to Elizabeth. An only child, she had been spoiled and indulged by her doting parents. However, Elizabeth had no intention of saying as much to her brother. Not now. Probably not ever.

He was wringing his hands now. "I just don't understand how it happened. Or *when* it happened. And why I didn't see it coming." He shook his head. "With my own best friend too…"

She went over to stand by him. She felt as protective of him now as she had on his first day of school long ago. She'd been twelve and he'd been six, and the first time one of the bullies had even looked cross-eyed at her baby brother, she had intervened. Of course, it wasn't long before Matthew was big enough to fight his own battles.

"I don't know exactly how you feel, Matthew, to lose someone like that. But I do know how it feels to lose the love of your life." She reached up and pushed a strand of light-brown hair off his forehead. "And I'm truly sorry. I know how badly that hurts. You didn't deserve it."

He continued to gaze out the window with a hardened jaw, but she noticed a shiny tear slipping out the corner of his eye. But before it reached his cheek, he used a tightened fist to wipe it away. "I'll get over it. In time."

"Do you want me to tell Mother and Father for you?"

He just nodded.

She squeezed his shoulder. His big strong shoulder. Her baby brother, all grown up and now brokenhearted. Life was strange sometimes. "Do you think you'll be joining us for Christmas dinner?" she asked quietly.

He shook his head with misty eyes. "I—I don't think so."

"All right."

"Give them my apologies, please?"

"I'll do that. And I'll bring a plate up for you."

"Thanks, but I'm not hungry." His voice was gruff with emotion.

"I know it's hard to believe this right now, but you will get past this, Matthew. You're strong. And you'll be stronger for it too."

He nodded but didn't look convinced. Knowing there was little more to do right now, she left, quietly closing the door. As she went downstairs, she wondered how she would tell her children and her parents. Gathered around the fully set dining room table, they looked up at her with expectant faces.

"What's wrong with Uncle Matthew?" Jamie asked.

"Is he sick?" Ruth queried with an anxious tremor in her voice.

"No, he's not sick," Elizabeth assured her as she went to her chair. She knew her family had a fear of sickness—and for good reason too.

"What is it then?" Clara asked with a furrowed brow.

"Matthew is sad," Elizabeth told her as she sat down. She looked evenly at her parents. "He sends his apologies that he can't join us for dinner." She placed her napkin in her lap and made a forced smile for her children and then nodded to her father. "Maybe you should go ahead and say grace before the food gets cold."

As Asa said the blessing, Elizabeth prayed for a way to explain Matthew's broken heart in a way that both generations could understand. As he said amen, she had a plan of sorts. Then, as her father began to carve the turkey, she began to speak.

"There has been a change in plans," she said slowly. "Matthew and Violet have decided not to get married after all." Her mother let out a little gasp, and Elizabeth continued. "These things happen sometimes," she said calmly. "People change their minds about things. And Violet has decided to go to Frankfort."

"Who is Frank Fort?" Ruth asked with wide eyes.

"Frankfort is a big city," Jamie declared.

"Bigger than Selma? Big as Paducah?" Ruth asked. "Paducah is a big city."

"It's certainly the biggest city you've ever seen," Elizabeth assured her.

"And our county seat," Clara pointed out.

"But Frankfort is lots bigger than Paducah," Jamie informed his sister with authority—as if he'd actually been there. "And it's the capital of the whole state of Kentucky. Don't you know that yet, Ruth?"

Ruth ignored him, directing her question to her grandfather instead. "Where is Frankfort?"

"It's northeast of us a spell." With a grim expression, Asa laid some turkey on his wife's plate.

"Will Uncle Matthew go to Frankfort too?" Jamie asked.

"No," Elizabeth told him. "Matthew is staying here."

"Is Violet going all by herself?" Ruth was confused.

"No." Elizabeth looked across the table at her mother, who appeared as confused as Ruth. "Walter Slake is taking her there."

"*Walter?*" Holding the carving knife in the air like a torch, Asa gave his daughter a shocked expression, and Clara dropped her fork. They all jumped as it clanged loudly against the plate.

"Why is Walter taking Violet to the big city?" Ruth asked.

"Because Walter and Violet have decided they want to get married," Elizabeth said plainly. "It seems that they both want to live in Frankfort after they get married."

"But what about Uncle Matthew?" Ruth asked. "Who is going to marry him?"

Elizabeth made a stiff smile. "Don't you worry about that, Ruthie. Your Uncle Matthew is a *fine* young man. Honest and hardworking and smart and *fine*. The girls will probably be lining up to marry him."

"Can I marry him?" Ruth asked hopefully.

The grown-ups chuckled.

"No," Jamie said sharply. "You're not allowed to."

Ruth frowned. "But I love Uncle Matthew."

"You can't *marry* your uncle," Jamie scolded. "Don't be such a silly goose."

"*Jamie.*" Elizabeth shook her head with disapproval. "Manners, please."

"I just don't understand." Clara shook her head. "How did all this happen?"

"How do you *think* it happened?" Asa said in a grumpy tone.

"Well...I..." Clara sighed and then slowly shook her head. "I...I suppose it's for the best. It's an ill wind that blows no good."

"Anyway..." Elizabeth continued calmly for the sake of the children. "Uncle Matthew might be sad for a few days or even longer. So let's all be kind and understanding to him. And it is best if we don't talk about Violet or any of this. Not at all." She glanced at her parents now. "Uncle Matthew doesn't even want to hear Violet's name spoken. It will only make him sad."

"That's just fine and dandy by me." Asa flopped some turkey meat onto Elizabeth's plate with a grim expression. He was obviously disturbed by this news.

"And now I'm going to fill Matthew a plate of food. Even though he's sad, he still needs to eat." Elizabeth reached for one of the empty plates that had been set for Matthew and Violet, but her mother beat her to it.

"Let me do that," Clara insisted as she grabbed a plate and began heaping it with potatoes.

Elizabeth nodded. "But I'll take it up to him."

"Poor Uncle Matthew," Ruth said sadly.

"We'll have to do our best to cheer him up." Elizabeth gathered a napkin and silverware. "But not until he's ready to join us." She stood and picked up the heavy plate of food.

"Give him our love." Clara sighed.

"Of course." Elizabeth turned to leave the room.

"Can we still have Christmas?" Ruth asked meekly.

Elizabeth paused, but to her relief, her father laughed heartily and merrily. "Of course, we can still have Christmas, little Ruth. As I live, we will not let the likes of Walter and Violet rob us of that pleasure. Now, let's enjoy this fine meal your grandmother has prepared for us."

Chapter Three

Despite Elizabeth's announcement that she wanted to clean up after dinner by herself, Clara would not hear of it. "Please, Mother," Elizabeth urged, "you worked hard to make a lovely meal. Now I want you to put your feet up."

"Nonsense. We will do it together," Clara insisted. "Just like we always do."

So while Asa took the children out for an after-dinner walk and to check on a mare that was with foal, Elizabeth and Clara began washing the dishes.

"Fetch some more hot water, will you?" Clara pumped more fresh water into the big stone sink while Elizabeth filled a kettle with steaming water from the reservoir on the side of the stove.

"Remember the old stove?" Elizabeth asked as she carefully poured the hot water into the sink. "And how you had to heat water in a kettle on the top?"

"Yes, I must admit that this new cookstove does make life easier." Clara smiled. "But it took a while to convince me of it."

Elizabeth pumped cold water into the empty kettle now. "I remember how upset you were when James and I delivered it for your forty-fifth birthday."

"Oh, I wasn't upset exactly. It was simply that I was rather attached to my old stove. My goodness, I'd had it since you were a baby."

"But it was falling apart." Elizabeth opened the reservoir, pouring in the cold water, which would soon be hot. She never appreciated these stoves more than when doing dishes.

"Yes, well, I suppose we older folks can get a bit set in our ways."

Elizabeth picked up a linen towel and continued with drying. "This Haviland china is so pretty, Mother. And you still have almost a full set of it too." She set a rosebud-trimmed plate on the growing stack in the center of the worn pine table. She knew she was trying to make small talk...anything to keep the subject away from having to talk about her brother.

"Yes, but only seven dinner plates. Just enough to set the table today. Although as it turned out, we didn't need the plate for Violet."

"And Father got the china set for you for your tenth wedding anniversary?" Elizabeth asked to distract her. "How long ago was that, Mother?"

"You know good and well how long ago that was." Clara frowned as she handed her daughter another dripping plate. "We celebrated our thirtieth anniversary last June, Elizabeth Anne. I know what you're doing, child."

Elizabeth wiped furiously on the plate. "I'm just admiring your china, Mother. I wonder how difficult it would be to find a plate to replace the one that got—"

"What did your brother say to you when you fetched his plate, Elizabeth? I know you're keeping something from me. Please, while Asa and the children are occupied outdoors, tell me what is transpiring right here under my own roof. If you don't spill the beans, I will go up and ask Matthew to—"

"No, Mother, please don't trouble Matthew just now."

"Then speak, daughter." She handed Elizabeth a bowl.

"Matthew has gotten a rather strange idea into his head, Mother."

"I suspected as much." Clara vigorously rubbed fresh soap into the dishrag. "Is he going to take off for Frankfort and demand that Violet return with—"

"No, Mother, nothing like that." Elizabeth pushed a strand of hair away from her cheek as she considered her words. Perhaps it was best to simply lay it out there. "As a matter of fact, Matthew has set his mind in the opposite direction."

"The opposite direction?" Clara frowned. "*West?*"

Elizabeth nodded.

"Oh, my goodness!"

"I know he is only responding to the pain he feels right now. He's hurting badly, and he's not thinking clearly."

"West..." Clara shook her head with a stunned look.

"He feels so humiliated by what Violet and Walter have done to him. As if he can no longer hold his head up in this town. It's so unfair too because it's not even his fault. But who can blame him when you consider how folks will talk."

"I'm sure some tongues are flapping already." She handed Elizabeth a platter. "Poor Matthew."

"I told him that good decisions are not made in haste."

"Wise advice."

"But he seems bound and determined to leave, Mother." Elizabeth decided not to hold back now. "He even started to pack his bags."

"He's packing his bags?" Clara looked horrified. "Matthew would head west in the middle of winter? Surely, you're not serious. That's not only foolhardy, it could be deadly as well."

"If it's any comfort, I suspect he was being melodramatic. He's so distraught...it's as if he feels he must do something."

"But heading west in winter?" She pursed her lips. "Even if he's brokenhearted, surely the boy's got more sense than that."

"I know, Mother. I think I convinced him to wait."

"How can you be sure?"

Elizabeth made a sheepish smile. "When he wasn't looking, I sneaked his bag out of his room. I hid it beneath your bed."

Clara chuckled. "Well, that might slow him down a bit." Her concerned look returned. "But not for long if he's really determined. Oh, dear, what will we do to prevent this?"

"I'm not sure, but I did get him to promise to join us this evening…to celebrate Christmas Eve with his family. He agreed he would come down later. He also promised not to leave on Christmas Day. I told him that was heartless."

"Well, that is some consolation."

They continued to work side by side, and other than the quiet crackling of the stove and clinking of dishes, the kitchen was silent. Elizabeth knew that her mother was worried about Matthew. She was likely plotting some way to delay him from making a foolish journey. Meanwhile, Elizabeth was torn—unsure whether she should disclose the plan that was slowly piecing itself together in her mind. However, she felt concerned for her mother. How much more distress could this poor woman take?

Finally, Elizabeth decided to speak. "Remember when I told you how I was feeling unsettled recently?"

Clara shrugged as she dipped a pot into the gray soapy water. "We need more hot water."

Elizabeth reached for the kettle, quickly filling it. "You thought perhaps I was in need of a new husband or suffering from feminine moodiness." She slowly poured the hot water into the sink.

"Yes?" Clara peered curiously at her.

"Well, I think it's something more than that, Mother."

Clara took in a deep breath, as if bracing herself for more bad news.

"As I was talking with Matthew, encouraging him not to make this big decision in haste, I began to wonder…"

"Wonder? About what?" Clara waited.

"About an old dream."

"What old dream?"

Elizabeth twisted the damp linen towel in her hands. "Of going west."

"Oh..." Clara turned back to the sink, busying herself with scrubbing a cast-iron pot.

"Remember how James and I often spoke of this very thing? Of joining his brother John and his family out West?"

"But that was before—"

"I know, Mother. But I keep getting this feeling. It's as if James is telling me to go." Elizabeth poured out the rest of her story, confessing to her mother about how she often woke in the middle of the night, and how she was beginning to feel that a better life might be waiting for them out West. "You know as well as I do that my small farm can barely support a family, and when Jamie is—"

"Yes, but you have your hands *full* with that small farm," Clara pointed out. "And even more so if Matthew leaves."

"Not if the children and I go with him."

Clara clutched a hand to her chest and closed her eyes as if in pain. "Lord have mercy!"

"I don't mean right now, Mother. But maybe in the springtime. We would have to journey west to Missouri and join a party of—"

"Elizabeth Anne!" Clara's eyes flashed with fear. "You cannot be serious. First I lost the twins to cholera, and then your brother Peter. Now you're saying I'm going to lose my only two surviving children and my grandchildren as well? You must be jesting!"

"I don't really know anything for sure, Mother. And I certainly didn't mean to upset you like this. I only want you to understand what has been on my mind of late. I tried to tell you once before."

Clara stared at Elizabeth with widened eyes. "I am flabbergasted, Elizabeth. I had no inkling you harbored such wild imaginings!"

"I'm nearly as confused and perplexed about this as you are. I'm simply trying to be honest with you, although I realize I must sound strange."

"Strange, indeed." Clara turned back to the sink.

Elizabeth regretted her words. What had she been thinking? And to say such a thing on Christmas Eve—and after Matthew's troubles. She cleared her throat. "I'm sorry, Mother. Please, don't take this too much to heart. It's entirely possible that this is nothing more than a silly old dream. Something that James and I conjured up long ago and that is best forgotten."

"I should say so."

Just then Asa and the children burst into the kitchen.

"Penny had her foal," Ruth said with glistening eyes. "We got to see it, Mama!"

"Oh, my!" Clara dried her hands and looked at Asa. "But isn't it too soon? Is the foal well?"

"I thought it was early. But it seems Penny knew what she was doing. The foal—a fine-looking colt—is healthy." He chuckled. "Healthy as a horse."

"His coat is fuzzy," Ruth told them. "And his eyes are brown."

"And he stood up almost right away," Jamie said. "He's a strong one."

"What will you call him?" Elizabeth asked her father.

"Jamie picked a name," Asa told her.

"Copper," Jamie declared. "He's the same color as Penny."

Elizabeth nodded. "Perfect."

"Can I go and tell Uncle Matthew?" Ruth asked.

"Not just yet," Elizabeth said. "But he promised to join us for dessert. You can tell him then." She exchanged glances with her mother and suspected they had just shared the same thought—they hoped Matthew hadn't snuck out already.

"Now that we worked off that fine dinner, I'm ready for a great big wedge of apple pie," Asa announced. "And maybe a small piece of pumpkin too."

"Not yet," Clara told him, shooing him and the children from the kitchen. "We aren't even finished in here. Unless you are offering to help, be on your way."

Elizabeth handed a tin plate of table scraps to Jamie. "Go feed this to Flax, son. He deserves a Christmas dinner too. Then let him run outside a bit before it gets dark."

"Go check on your brother," Clara told Elizabeth after the children left. "Make sure he's not sneaking away."

Elizabeth nodded as she untied her apron and hurried up the narrow back staircase and tapped quietly on Matthew's partially opened door. Alarmed that he had already left without saying a word to them, she pushed open the door to see that her brother was sleeping soundly on his bed. Various clothes and shoes and miscellaneous items were strewn about his room, as if he had tired of attempting to pack without the aid of a bag and had given up. Feeling a mixture of guilt and relief, she quietly closed the door and tiptoed back down the hallway. Her trickery had delayed his plan for the time being and perhaps longer. But what could they do to keep him around until spring?

Chapter Four

Matthew didn't come down until after the children had gone to bed. Even then he was sullen and quiet. "Pecan pie," Elizabeth said as she set a generous slice topped with heavy cream on the table in front of him. "Your favorite."

He just shrugged as he picked up the fork, holding it loosely in his hand.

"Want some coffee to go with that?" Clara offered.

"Sure he does," Elizabeth answered for him.

"You've had a rough day, son." Asa leaned back in his chair, taking a long pull from his pipe.

Matthew stuck his fork into the pie without responding.

Elizabeth took the chair closest to him and, feeling protective, began to chatter about the new colt and what a beauty he was going to be.

"He's got running legs," Asa said. "And he's all yours, son, if you want him."

Matthew looked at his father with an empty expression. "Thanks, Pa, but I don't want him."

Asa tossed an uneasy glance at Elizabeth, as if he expected her to fix this somehow.

"Well, you might change your mind on that once you see the colt," she said lightly. "He's truly a fine—"

"Can't take a horse that young to the frontier." Matthew took a bite of the pie, chewing noisily.

"*Wh—what?*" Asa sat up in his chair, coughing and sputtering. "What are you saying?"

"I'm going west, Pa." Matthew looked evenly at his father.

Clara set a cup of coffee on the table and then sat down across from her son. Deep frown lines creased her forehead as she rested her chin in one hand. "Surely you're not planning to leave until springtime, are you?"

"I'd leave today if I could." With eyes downward, he took a sip of coffee.

"Are you serious?" Asa looked dumbfounded.

Matthew set the cup down with a clink. "I am."

"Because of that flibbertigibbet Violet?"

Matthew's eyes narrowed.

"Matthew and I discussed this earlier," Elizabeth said quickly. "As you know, James and I had intended to go to the Oregon Territory one day. We wanted to join his brother John and his family out there."

"Yes, yes." Asa waved his hand. "That was before...well, you know...*before.*"

"I know. But I have been thinking about it lately, Father. I have been wondering if it still might be the right thing for me to do...for the children and me."

"Have you lost your ever-loving mind?" Asa set his pipe down with a thud. "A lone woman and her young children out on the Western frontier? With savages and wild animals and infidels around every corner? Elizabeth Anne, if I didn't know better I'd say you've lost your good senses. You cannot possibly be serious."

Elizabeth glanced toward the stairs, hoping that the children were fast asleep by now. This wasn't a conversation she wanted them to be privy to. "I know it must sound strange to your ears, Father. But it was our dream…James' and mine…and I think perhaps it is a dream that should not have died."

Asa got up and began pacing back and forth in front of the fireplace with hands in the air, expounding on all the dangers in the West. "I read the accounts in the newspapers," he told her. "It's no place for a lone woman. And I would wager that no self-respecting trail master would allow a widow woman and her children to join his party."

"You are missing one important point," Matthew said quietly. "I would be traveling with Elizabeth and the children. She wouldn't be alone."

"But…but…*this is absurd!*" Asa sat back down, blowing out a frustrated sigh. "Completely absurd."

"Asa," Clara said quietly. "Maybe we should let Matthew and Elizabeth speak for themselves and explain their thinking on this matter."

"Are you suggesting that you approve of this harebrained idea?" Asa shook his finger at her. "We've already lost Peter—do you wish to see your only other children and your grandchildren banished to the wilderness?"

"Certainly not." She firmly shook her head. "But they are entitled to their opinions. I should like to hear more."

"*Why?*" Asa demanded. Now he turned to Elizabeth. "And why, pray tell, would you embrace such folly?"

She took in a deep breath, steadying herself. "James and I used to talk of our future, Father. We wanted a change. We knew that our farm was small and that the land was worn out from too many years of tobacco."

"And then you became abolitionists," Asa reminded her. "Getting rid of your slaves didn't make farming any easier."

She nodded. "I know. But we didn't regret it then, and I don't regret it now. Especially after reading Harriet Beecher Stowe's book last summer."

"And thanks to *Uncle Tom's Cabin,* we followed your lead." Clara pointed at her husband. "Asa, you know good and well that it was the right and Christian thing to do. So don't be complaining about it now, even if it does make farming harder."

"Peter had been considering going west," Matthew told his father in a quiet tone.

"That's true," Elizabeth agreed. "He and James spoke of it many times. He didn't like that so many newcomers were moving to Kentucky."

"I do recall him expressing frustration over how Selma was changing...growing too fast." Clara got a wistful look. "Perhaps it's unfortunate he didn't go west before the cholera outbreak." Her brow creased. "But we discouraged him then..."

"Many families are going west," Elizabeth continued. "Each year, it seems that more farms are being divided...more farmers are struggling to get by. Look at you, Father. Your farm has been divided so many times, there's hardly enough land for Matthew to support a family anymore."

"That's only because you children are third generation in these parts." Asa waved his hands. "When your grandparents came to this land there was plenty to go around."

"That's what we're saying, Father. There was enough *before*, but what about future generations? And right now our government is offering 320 acres of prime agricultural land. Beautiful and rich land, free for the taking. Can you imagine such bounty?"

"But this is our home," Asa insisted. "Your ancestors carved out a fine way of life right here. We have good solid houses, big barns, well-bred livestock, corrals and fencing and wells...You have a nearby town and friends and family. A church, a school, a community. We are comfortable, are we not?"

"Yes, Father, we are comfortable. But what is there for Jamie and Ruth to look forward to here?"

Asa frowned. "I don't know what you mean."

"I'm glad Kentucky is enough for you, Father, but what if Matthew and I and the children need more?"

He shook his head. "What more could you want?"

"John and Malinda wrote letters describing the beautiful and fertile land in the Oregon Territory. They say anything can grow there. Livestock thrives, roaming free year-round. They wrote of rivers and streams full of fish. Forests with abundant timber. Serene lakes and a majestic ocean. It's a new land...and it's a future."

Asa ran his hand over his head in frustration.

"Think about this, Father. What if your ancestors hadn't decided to go west? What if they had been content to stay in England?"

"They had cause to come here. Remember, they came for religious freedom."

"But what if they hadn't come, Father? What if they had stayed behind? Would you be happier there?"

Now he looked confused.

"I want an adventure," Matthew declared.

Asa shook his finger at Matthew. "You want to run away!"

Matthew slammed his fist onto the table so soundly that the teacup jumped on the saucer. "What if I *do* want to run away? It's my life. Should I not have the freedom to do as I choose? What about life, liberty, and the pursuit of happiness?"

Now the room grew quiet, but Elizabeth could tell that emotions were not only sitting on the surface but raw as well. There were still words left to be said, but it was getting late.

"Father and Mother," she said gently, "I never meant to introduce this controversy on Christmas Eve. And I am sorry if it grieves you to think your only two living children are considering such an adventure. But when Matthew told me he wanted to leave, I couldn't sit silently. I knew I had to express my true feelings."

"Elizabeth Anne," Asa asked slowly, "are you honestly telling me that you think you are strong enough to endure the rigors and hardships of traveling for months? That you are capable of making a home for you and your children? That you can provide for them? Out there in the wilderness?"

"John and Malinda are there," she reminded him. "And James' parents too. They've all settled in a fertile valley just a day's travel from the Pacific Ocean. They have already started a school and a church. And their description of the climate sounds ideal. I suspect if I write to them, they would have land already picked out for me to settle on by the time I got there. So you see, it isn't as if I would be alone when I arrive."

"And I would be there to help her too," Matthew pointed out in a voice that sounded more like the brother she knew and loved.

Elizabeth looked directly at him. "It could be a grand adventure."

He nodded. "I am in need of a grand adventure."

"Oh, my." Clara shook her head. "I am in need of bed."

"Yes," Elizabeth said. "It's late. Again, I apologize for putting you two through this tonight. It had not been my intention."

Asa stood, helping his wife to her feet. "Don't you worry," he told her in a conspirator's tone. "They will probably have changed their minds about this by morning."

Elizabeth just laughed.

"I do have one question," Clara said before leaving. "Do you two plan to tell anyone else about your outlandish ideas?"

Elizabeth glanced at Matthew, and he simply shrugged.

"Because there is the Christmas service at church tomorrow. And then there's the annual gathering at your grandparents' home afterward. Do you plan on mentioning this to anyone tomorrow?" Clara looked truly concerned.

"I don't even plan on attending either of those functions," Matthew said.

"But Matthew, it's Christmas." Clara frowned.

"I do not blame him in the least," Elizabeth said. "You know how conversations will go."

"She's right," Asa agreed. "Matthew doesn't need to be subjected to that."

Matthew stood to face his mother. "Please, make my apologies to the grandparents."

Clara simply nodded.

"And I will not say a word about our migration plans," Elizabeth assured her.

Clara sighed in relief and then bade them both goodnight.

"Mercy!" Elizabeth said after their parents were out of earshot. "I had not planned on any of that."

Matthew threw a couple more logs on the fire and then sat down in his father's chair, stretching his legs out in front of him with a quizzical expression, as if their conversation was still sinking in. "Are you really sincere about this, Lizzie? Would you truly take Jamie and Ruth on the Oregon Trail like you said?"

She thought hard about her answer. "I have been praying for God to lead me in regard to this strange dream," she said quietly. "If I am convinced that God is the one doing the leading, then yes, I would go to Oregon."

He just nodded.

However, Elizabeth also knew that she would never have broached this volatile topic, especially on Christmas Eve, if not for her brother's unexpected broken engagement. Common sense told her there was still a chance that Matthew might change his mind about going west after the initial shock of Violet's coldhearted betrayal wore off. Perhaps in a week or two. And she certainly hoped it would wear off because Violet Lamott hardly seemed worth such emotional pain and suffering. If that were to happen, and if Matthew decided to forgo this trip, Elizabeth wondered if she would continue to pursue this somewhat foolhardy dream. Was she strong enough to attempt something like this on her own steam? And yet, if she didn't go, she might be sorely disappointed too. Truly, it was best to leave it in God's hands.

Chapter Five

As promised, Elizabeth did not breathe a word of her westward dreams on Christmas Day. Instead, she was polite and congenial, if not slightly bored, as she visited with her female relations following the Christmas service at church. And certainly it was better to be with the women than to be subjected to the heated political argument going on in the next room. As usual, the debates were over secession and Northern oppression and slavery and abolition and all the other controversial topics of the day. Elizabeth had opinions on all these issues, but she knew the men would not care to hear them. Nor was she inclined to express them.

And to be fair, it wasn't that cooking or sewing or child rearing were of no interest to her. Normally, she engaged in these housekeeping conversations. It was simply that she was distracted. Instead of listening to Aunt Belle describing her latest quilt-top pattern,

Elizabeth secretly daydreamed of how she was about to embark on an exciting journey. Fresh ideas for this adventure had been fueled by reading one of her father's newspaper stories. She'd discovered it the night before after everyone else had gone to bed. As a result she'd stayed up until she finished it.

The story was written by an explorer who had crossed the continent four times! And it included a dramatic engraving of an overland crossing through the mountains. The author certainly did not downplay the hardships of such travel. But at the same time, he painted such a romantic and vivid picture of the vast and ever-changing landscape, the Indians, and the interesting characters he'd met along the way that Elizabeth felt somewhat enchanted by the time she'd gone to bed.

So much so that all she could think about during the Christmas gathering at her grandparents' house in town—although she feigned interest in Cousin Phoebe's recipe for candied yams—was her eagerness to get back home and open up the "dream box" that she and James had used to store letters and lists and all the information they had gathered about Oregon. She could not wait to reread them.

At last the party was wearing down, and Elizabeth could tell that Jamie and Ruth were worn out, so she thanked her grandparents for their hospitality and said her goodbyes to aunts, uncles, cousins, and finally her parents.

"I realized at church this morning that your talk of going to Oregon was only an attempt to help your brother," Clara whispered to Elizabeth as they walked outside together. "You are a good sister, Elizabeth."

Elizabeth tried not to register her surprise at this comment. Did her mother truly think that all that was said the night before was only to lift Matthew's spirits? If so, perhaps it was for the best.

"Merry Christmas, Mother." She kissed Clara's cheek and then turned to herd the children and the dog into the carriage. "Take the reins," she told Jamie. "But not too fast."

As Jamie drove the carriage home, Elizabeth imagined him behind the reins of an ox team towing a heavy prairie schooner behind it. Or would that be too much for a boy his age? Perhaps she would ask Matthew to look into this for her, assuming Matthew was still interested in Oregon. And if he was not…well, she didn't have to think about that yet.

Ruth slipped her mittened hand into Elizabeth's. "You seem happy, Mama. Did you have fun today?"

She squeezed Ruth's hand. "Yes. It was a good day. Did you enjoy playing with the cousins?" Most of the relatives were second and third cousins—offspring of Clara's siblings. And most of them were older than Ruth.

Ruth's expression was hard to read. "I wanted to play with Victoria…but…"

Elizabeth could tell something was wrong. So she waited.

"Are we rich, Mama?"

"Rich?" Elizabeth laughed. "Is that what Victoria told you?"

Ruth nodded. "But she said it in a mean way."

"Some of our cousins think we're rich," Jamie said quietly.

"We are not rich," Elizabeth declared.

"But we have more land than most of the cousins," Jamie said.

"That's true. But it's because your father's family had more land. The cousins at Great-Grandma and Grandpa's house are a different side of the family. Those are your grandma's folks. Do you know how many brothers and sisters Grandma Dawson has?"

"How many?" Ruth asked.

"There were fourteen children in Grandma's family," Jamie answered.

"Fourteen?" Ruth sounded shocked. "Is that true, Mama?"

"It's true. Grandma had eight brothers and five sisters. But not all of them are alive now. And some of them moved away. But many of them live in town."

"Like Victoria," Ruth said.

"Yes. The reason I'm telling you this is to explain why they might think we're rich. With so many children in Grandma's family, they had less land and fewer farms to share."

"But Grandma and Grandpa have a nice big farm," Ruth contended.

"Yes, but that came from Grandpa's side of the family. And that farm used to be bigger, but it's been divided too. Not as much because Grandpa only had two brothers." She didn't tell them how much larger the farm had been fifty years ago. She wasn't even sure why she was telling them this now, but that she wanted them to understand. She knew there was land envy among some disgruntled family members, and although it was unfair, she did understand. But it was unfortunate that cousins like Victoria were unkind.

Elizabeth thought about James' brother and wife again. John and Malinda had five children. The youngest, as far as she knew, was around four now, and the oldest was probably thirteen. If Elizabeth took the children to Oregon, they would have several school-age cousins living nearby. And there would be plenty of land for everyone. Not that she planned to mention this to her children. Not yet anyway.

"Looks like we left just in time," Elizabeth said as snow began to fall. She put her hand on Jamie's arm. "But don't try to hurry. We'll be just fine."

Jamie just nodded, keeping his gaze straight ahead and the reins secure in his hands. So much like a man...and yet he was still a boy.

"Can we sing Christmas songs again?" Ruth asked.

"Certainly!" And so, as Jamie carefully guided them toward home, they all sang Christmas songs. But by the time they pulled in front of the house, the snow was falling hard and fast.

"Hello, hello!" Brady called as he rushed out to help. Wearing his new coat and a big grin, he helped Elizabeth and Ruth down from the carriage and carried their bags up to the door. "Let me take care of the horses for you, Mr. Martin," he said to Jamie.

"Thanks, Brady." Jamie handed him the reins and then pulled out a box to carry into the house.

"I made you a fire, ma'am," Brady called as Elizabeth reached the top of the porch steps.

"Thank you, Brady!" she called back.

"Thank *you,* ma'am!" He jutted a thumb toward his new coat. "Nice and warm!"

"You're more than welcome," she called as she opened the door.

It wasn't until household chores were done and the children put to bed that Elizabeth pulled out the "dream box." She hadn't opened the small oak box in nearly a year...not since she'd slipped the last letter from John and Malinda into it. And even then, she hadn't taken time to reexamine the rest of the contents. Until now, the items in that box had seemed both mocking and threatening. But now, sitting by the crackling fire, she opened the box and removed everything, one by one, laying them out on the side table by the chair. Letters and lists and addresses and advertisements...all pertaining to an overland journey and the final destination of the Oregon Territory.

Perusing the papers, she knew she should consider going to bed because the morning would come soon, especially considering her late night the previous evening. But she did not feel the least bit sleepy. Instead, she felt compelled to read all she could about what was beginning to feel like an impending journey.

She was just reading Malinda's most recent letter, written in the summer of 1855, when she heard a noise.

"Mama?"

"Jamie?" She blinked in the dim light, spotting her son at the foot of the stairs.

"My tummy hurts."

She dropped the letter and rushed over to him, immediately putting her hand to his forehead to see if he was feverish. Ever since the cholera, she had been extremely careful about sickness. However, his head did not feel hot.

"Come over here." She led him over to the fire and lamplight, where she examined him more closely. First she checked his skin for any sign of a rash. Then she had him stick out his tongue. "You look all right. Where exactly does your stomach hurt?"

He put his hand on his midsection and groaned.

"What did you eat and drink today?"

Now he began to list off all that he'd eaten, and the list went on and on…finally ending with chess pie. "I had two pieces," he confessed.

"Oh, my." She touched his forehead again and then smiled. "No wonder you have a stomachache."

He peered over at the box and papers spread across the table. "What's that?"

"Oh, just letters and whatnot."

He picked up a supply list and frowned.

"How about if I make you some warm peppermint milk for your tummy?"

He nodded. "That might help."

She picked up a woolen blanket, draping it over his shoulders like a cape, and tucked him into the chair by the fireplace. "Don't get chilled," she warned as she lit another lamp, taking it with her. "I'll be back in a few minutes." As she went to the kitchen she realized he would probably be curious about the papers she'd been studying. But as she stoked the coals in the cookstove, she realized that perhaps it wasn't such a bad thing. After all, Jamie was almost twelve. If she took on this daunting challenge, which was still uncertain, she would need his full cooperation.

When she returned with a mug of warm peppermint milk, Jamie was setting one of the letters back down. "Here you go," she said as she gathered up the papers, placing them back in the oak box.

"Why are you reading those?" Jamie asked as he leaned back in his father's chair.

Elizabeth sat down, pondering her answer. "Uncle Matthew and

I were discussing something yesterday," she began. "Something that your father and I had considered doing a long time ago."

"Going to Oregon?"

"Yes." She didn't know why she was surprised. "But we were only talking about it. And mostly because Matthew was so sad."

"About Violet and Walter?"

She nodded.

"I never liked Violet very much." He took another sip.

"I wasn't too fond of her either. But Matthew was."

"Does Matthew want to go to Oregon?"

Elizabeth considered this. "I'm not sure. He seems to want to go, but it's possible he's simply looking for a way to escape."

"Because of Violet?"

"Maybe. It was unkind of her to run off like that, especially with his best friend."

"I'll say." Jamie shook his head with a wise look that belied his youth. "I would never do something that low-down to a friend. Not even to an enemy."

"You are a good man." She smiled and then pointed to her own upper lip. "With a milk mustache." He wiped it off, and she almost wished he hadn't. It looked so like a little boy. And now she wondered about how much she should burden him with.

"Pa wanted to go to Oregon."

"We had been making plans." She closed the box. "But that was before…"

He nodded to the box. "Those letters make Oregon sound like a great place."

"But it's a long, long way away."

"How far is it?"

"About two thousand miles."

His dark eyes grew wide.

"And a prairie schooner can only travel about twelve miles a day. Some days even less."

Now his brow creased. "That's more than a hundred and sixty."

She nodded. "I know."

"About five months," he said somewhat absently.

"Your arithmetic is good."

"I've read about Thomas Jefferson in history," he told her. "His dream was to make our country bigger by opening up the West. And I've read about men who explored the West. The Lewis and Clark expedition."

She smiled. "You're getting a good education."

"Why didn't we go to Oregon with Uncle John and Aunt Malinda?"

Elizabeth wasn't sure how much to say now. But if Jamie was going to be her right-hand man, he deserved to know. "I was with child," she confessed. "Your father worried that the journey would be too difficult. As it turned out, I lost the baby anyway."

"You mean because of the cholera? When you and Pa and Uncle Peter got sick?"

She shook her head. "No, the cholera came nearly two years later."

Jamie frowned. "You mean you lost *two* babies?"

She nodded sadly.

"Oh..." Jamie looked troubled, as if he was trying to grasp all this.

"You weren't even school-age when I lost that first baby, Jamie. There was no reason for you to know about it." She peered at him. "How's your tummy doing?"

"I think the milk is helping."

"Oh, good." She felt a rush of relief. "You know how I always get worried if I think someone I love is getting sick."

"How did you and Pa and Uncle Peter get cholera?" he asked. "I know you went on a trip. And Ruth and I stayed with Grandma and Grandpa. But that's about all I know. What happened, Ma?"

She thought back to that time. "It was late summer," she began, "and we'd had a pretty good harvest of corn, and your father and uncle wanted to take it to Paducah to get a better price." She sighed. "And to look at wagons..."

"What kind of wagons?"

"Your father was thinking about going to Oregon again. Planning for the upcoming spring."

"Oh."

"I wanted to go with them to Paducah. I thought it would be fun to do some shopping and city things. It sounded like an enjoyable trip. And it was. We sold the corn for top dollar and did some shopping. We went to the theater and stayed in a fancy hotel. The next day we looked at wagons. Your father had almost decided on one, but Uncle Peter had heard about a wainwright down by the river. It was a family-owned business with some innovative-looking prairie schooners, and we spent the whole afternoon with them. We had no idea there was a cholera outbreak. We ate with them and drank lemonade..." She sadly shook her head. "Later on, we realized that the lemonade had probably been contaminated...infected with the cholera. But how would we know?"

"The lemonade made you sick?"

"Not the lemonade, but it was likely in the water they used to make it. Thinking back, I remember that I didn't like the taste of it. But I thought perhaps it was just me. So I didn't drink too much. But it was a hot day, and your father and uncle were very thirsty. I'm sure they had plenty of lemonade. It wasn't until we came home the following day that we realized something was wrong...very, very wrong."

Jamie's expression was so serious that Elizabeth felt badly. Perhaps this was too much to put upon a boy. What had she been thinking? How could she turn this around? "So..." she pointed to the oak box. "What did you read in there?"

He admitted to reading letters and the supply list.

"What did you think?"

He brightened. "Could we really do that, Ma?"

"You mean go to Oregon?"

He nodded eagerly. "Could we?"

She pressed her lips together.

"It would be so exciting. Traveling like that, seeing new places, exploring new land…like a real adventure!"

She couldn't help but laugh. "It would certainly be that."

"I could help drive the wagon," he offered.

"Yes, I'm sure you could." She looked at the clock. "But it's very late now, Jamie. Is your stomach better?"

He nodded, setting the empty mug on the table.

She tapped the box. "I've been giving it serious thought, son. And I must admit it sounds exciting to me too."

"Really?" He looked hopeful.

"So, there's something you can do to help."

"What?" His eyes lit up.

"Ask God to lead us, son. Pray about it. If it's the right path for us to take, God will have to show us. And if God shows us, I will gladly go."

"I'll do that. I promise. I'll pray about it a lot."

"Good." She stood and reached for his hand. "You get back to bed, and you can pray about it tonight."

"I will, Ma." He scurried toward the stairs. "Right now."

Encouraged by his enthusiasm, she tossed a couple more logs on the fire, blew out one of the lanterns, and headed up to her own chilly bed.

Chapter Six

Thanks to Jamie's exuberance about the possibility of becoming Western explorers, Ruth soon figured things out. "Is it true, Mama?" she asked the next evening as the three of them sat around the dining table together. "Are we going to Oregon to live with Uncle John and Aunt Malinda?"

Elizabeth exchanged a glance with Jamie and then smiled. "I honestly don't know, Ruthie. But if you want to pray about it with us, maybe God will show us his answer."

Ruth looked around the room. "If we went to Oregon, would we ever come back here again?"

"I...uh...I don't really know for sure. But if we went to Oregon, we would have to sell this house and the farm. Sometimes people come back, but it's a very, very long trip."

"How long?"

"More than a hundred and sixty days," Jamie told her.

Ruth's blue eyes got big.

"We would leave in the early springtime," Elizabeth explained. "And we would travel until the early fall."

"Would we still go to school?" Ruth asked.

Jamie laughed. "No, silly."

"We would still do lessons," Elizabeth explained. "We would take your schoolbooks and work on reading and writing and arithmetic."

"And we could learn a lot of things on the Oregon Trail," Jamie said with eager authority. "About animals and birds and plants and all sorts of interesting things."

"That's true." Elizabeth got an idea. "Perhaps we could write about what we see. And we could draw pictures. We could make books about it."

"That sounds like fun," Ruth said happily. "I'm going to ask God to send us on the Oregon Trail."

As Elizabeth washed the dinner dishes, she felt slightly overwhelmed—as if she had truly gotten the wagon ahead of the horse—and she hoped she was not mistaken to get her children's hopes up like this. At the same time, she knew this was a good life lesson. Just because one wanted to do something did not make it right. Her children needed to see for themselves that God was able to lead and direct them. To add emphasis to this, she looked in the family Bible for a particular scripture, something she planned to read to them at bedtime.

So it was that after the children were tucked in and their prayers were said, Elizabeth opened the big black book to Proverbs and read these words: "*Trust in the LORD with all thine heart; and lean not unto thine own understanding. In all thy ways acknowledge him, and he shall direct thy paths.*" She looked from one bed to the other, making sure they were listening. "Do you know what that means?"

Ruth looked uncertain.

"It means we should trust the Lord," Jamie answered.

"That's right." She nodded. "It also means we don't have all the answers, so we shouldn't lean on our own understanding. But if we acknowledge God—if we believe him and listen to him—he will direct our paths. He'll show us which way to go."

"On the Oregon Trail?" Ruth asked hopefully.

"If that's the way he wants us to go." Elizabeth closed the Bible. "Or he might show us that we need to stay right here."

Both of the children looked dismayed by this.

"So it's up to us to trust God and pray for him to lead us." She smiled and stood. "And whichever way God shows us to go, it will be the best way." She kissed each of them, and with the Bible in one hand and the lantern in the other, she told them goodnight and slipped from the room.

The topic of the Oregon Trail came up a few times in the following days, but as the week progressed, Elizabeth knew that Jamie and Ruth were distracted with the planning and preparations for their annual New Year's Eve supper. It was a tradition that James had originally begun early in their marriage, something his parents had eagerly passed down to him. But even after his parents and John went to Oregon, and after James' passing, she had continued this hospitality at the insistence of her children. It involved a lot of work, including roasting a pig out in the farmyard, which Brady took responsibility for. There were also treats to bake and other chores to tend to. Still, it was an evening that family and neighbors and friends had grown to appreciate over the years, and Elizabeth felt it was a lovely way to welcome the new year.

As usual, Elizabeth's mother came early in the day in order to help with food preparation. But when she arrived, she seemed to be in a bit of a fluster. "I told the children to empty my carriage for me," she told Elizabeth as she hurriedly peeled off her hat and gloves.

Then, tugging Elizabeth with her, she led her to the spare bedroom in the back of the house, closing the door behind them.

"What in the world is wrong?" Elizabeth asked with concern.

"Oh, my word! I don't even know where to begin." Clara sat down on the edge of the bed, waving her hand in front of her face as if she was too warm, although the room was chilly from having been closed off.

"Tell me," Elizabeth urged. "Is someone ill? Is it Father? Matthew?"

"No...no, not exactly." Clara took in a deep breath. "I had a dream."

"Oh." Elizabeth nodded, sitting down in the chair across from the bed. This didn't seem too serious. "What sort of dream?"

"Oh, dear!" She shook her head. "A very bad dream. I almost hate to say the words out loud, dear."

Elizabeth didn't know how to respond. "Then perhaps you shouldn't."

"No, I must tell you. I'm afraid I'll burst if I don't confide in someone." She took in a deep breath and began. "There was a war—or so it seemed, although I heard no gunshots. But it was right here in Selma...I could tell a very bad battle had occurred because there was row upon row of dead soldiers, lying throughout the streets, right in the middle of town. And there were flies buzzing around them and blood everywhere...oh, my, it was so gruesome!"

Elizabeth's hand went over her mouth. "That's horrible, Mother."

"I know—believe me, I know." Clara looked at Elizabeth with frightened eyes. "But it gets worse."

"How can it get worse?"

"I was walking among the dead, and I saw Matthew lying there too."

Elizabeth felt a rush of panic. "But—but it was only a dream, Mother."

Clara shook her head grimly. "But sometimes dreams have meanings."

"Or else they are simply bad dreams. Perhaps you ate something that disagreed with you before going to bed."

"Sometimes dreams are warnings."

"How do you know?"

"Because I've had this happen before." Clara looked truly disturbed, first wringing her hands and then fanning her flushed face.

Elizabeth was confused. "How so? What are you saying, Mother?"

"I never told you this..." Clara pulled a lace-trimmed hanky from her sleeve, using it dab her forehead as if she were perspiring.

"Told me what?"

"The dream I had before you and James and Peter went to Paducah that summer."

Elizabeth cringed. "What sort of dream?"

"It was about Peter. To be honest it seemed nothing much at first. Certainly not anything like last night's dream."

"Tell me what it was."

"I dreamed Peter was sleeping peacefully in his bed. And then someone reached down and placed two silver coins over his closed eyes." She shuddered.

"You dreamed he was dead?"

"That's what it seemed to be..." Clara looked on the verge of tears. "At the time I passed it off as a foolish dream. It wasn't until you children returned home and were sick with cholera that I realized it had been more than just a dream. Of course, it was too late by then. I never told you—or anyone for that matter. What was the use?"

"So do you honestly believe your dream is warning you that Matthew is going to die in some untimely fashion?"

"I know it must sound fantastic, but I'm terribly worried."

Feeling frustrated and overwhelmed, Elizabeth tried to make sense of this. "But Matthew isn't going to war. He's not enlisting in any sort of army...*is he*?"

"No, not that I know of. But there has been fighting in Kansas. Your father told me of it."

"Perhaps that's what's behind the dream. You were worried about Kansas, and you've been worried about Matthew. Certainly…that makes sense."

"It was more than that, Elizabeth. This war happened *right here*. And there are many people, including your father, who truly believe war is coming."

"That may be true in some places, like the deep South. But this is Kentucky, Mother. We are in the middle. I'm sure we will remain neutral."

Clara shook her head. "I don't know."

Elizabeth let out a long sigh. "I really don't know what to say, Mother. And really, I need to get busy. There's so much to be done today."

"Yes, yes." Clara slowly stood. "I know, I know. I just needed to tell someone…I needed to get it off my chest."

Elizabeth put a hand on her mother's shoulder. "I don't know what to say to you. But since war is not imminent and since Matthew isn't joining any army, at least that we know of, I don't see any real cause for concern right now."

"I know you're right. But it was so upsetting." She shuddered again. "It seemed so real."

Now Elizabeth hugged her. "It will be all right, Mother. Don't think on it anymore. Just come and help me with the bread pudding. No one makes it quite as tasty as you do. And I need to get the shortcake rolled out."

As they worked together in the kitchen, no more was said of Clara's strange dream. However, those images now felt etched into Elizabeth's imagination, almost as if she had endured this nightmare herself. What did it mean?

Fortunately, the house grew busier, and she was too distracted to fret. And before long, guests began to arrive. Busily tending to them, Elizabeth was unable to dwell on her mother's strange dream. However, she felt dismayed that her brother hadn't come. And the party wasn't as merry as it should have been. She understood his reasoning, but she missed his cheerful fiddle playing just the same. No one lit up a party quite like Matthew Dawson. And it grieved her to think he was home alone...still feeling hurt and betrayed by that senseless Violet.

Shortly after midnight, guests began thanking her for her hospitality and excusing themselves to their carriages, and Elizabeth, worn out as well, kissed her children goodnight and sent them to bed. Her father was asleep by the fireplace, but her mother, fussing about the front room, still looked anxious and upset.

"It was a good gathering, don't you think?" Elizabeth said as she gathered up some punch cups.

Clara nodded. "Yes...very nice crowd. Good food."

"Do you and Father wish to stay over? I opened the door to the guest room. It should be warmer by now."

Clara looked at Asa, who was now snoring loudly. "If I wake him, he'll probably insist on going home and sleeping in his own bed. Although that might be best since Matthew is home alone."

"How is Matthew anyway? Besides telling me about the dream, you didn't mention how he's faring."

Clara picked up some dishes. "He's still hurting...and humiliated...and angry. Poor boy. But at least he's keeping himself busy."

They carried the dishes into the kitchen. As usual, some of the women had helped with the cleaning up, so it wasn't too daunting. "I'll tend to these in the morning," Elizabeth said as she set the cups on the table.

"I didn't tell your father about my dream," Clara said quietly.

"Maybe that's for the best." Elizabeth shoved some more pieces of wood into the cookstove. "It was rather disturbing."

"Don't I know that!" She shook her head. "But I do believe it has pushed me to make up my mind."

"Make up your mind about what?" Elizabeth closed the iron door with a clang.

"If you and Matthew decide to go to Oregon, I will no longer oppose you. It may be in Matthew's best interest to be on the other side of the continent. I may not be happy about it, but I will not stand in your way if you choose to go on the Oregon Trail."

"Oh?" Elizabeth smiled at her mother. "I appreciate that. But if it's any comfort, I have made no such decision."

"But Matthew seems determined." Clara picked up a piece of a broken shortcake cookie, popping it into her mouth.

"What do you mean by determined?" Elizabeth took the other part of the broken cookie, nibbling on it.

"I mean he's been working out in the barn. He got the notion that he can outfit one of the farm wagons into a prairie schooner. Not only that, but he is working on some new innovations."

"Are you serious?"

"Very. He's been sawing and hammering. I took a peek at it while he was in the house, and I must say I was quite impressed. Matthew rigged up a long narrow box that's attached alongside the wagon, but it folds down into a workbench or table of sorts, and there are places to hang and store pots and pans and cooking utensils behind it while traveling. But when it's up, you hardly notice it. Very clever indeed."

Elizabeth nodded. "That does sound handy."

"I suggested he cut a hole in the board to hold a tub. It could act as a sink for washing up."

"That sounds like a good idea, Mother."

Clara waved her hand. "Well, if one is going to live like that for months on the dusty trail, one should be as comfortable as possible. Don't you think?"

"I couldn't agree more."

"Elizabeth?" Clara lowered her voice.

"Yes?"

Clara got a sly expression. "Be honest with me now…don't try to spare my feelings." Now she looked doubtful. "Do you think your father and I are too old to make an overland journey to the Oregon Territory?"

Elizabeth was shocked but tried not to show it. "Too old?" She considered this for a moment and then slowly shook her head. "I don't think so. You are both hard workers, and you're in good health. I think if you truly wanted to go, you would be just fine." She studied her mother carefully. "Do you want to go?"

Clara shrugged. "I suppose I'm simply thinking out loud."

"Have you spoken to Father about this?"

"Oh no, of course not! He would say I've gone daft."

Elizabeth laughed.

"Two old grandparents bungling along down the Oregon Trail with a bunch of young whippersnappers...it does sound a bit batty."

"Not necessarily. You and Father have a lot to offer in the way of wisdom and experience. I know that if Matthew and I should decide to take this venture on, I will sorely miss your sage advice and your..." Elizabeth felt a wave of sadness now. "And your friendship too, Mother!"

"Oh, Elizabeth." Now Clara began to quietly cry. Elizabeth wrapped her arms around her mother, holding her close and longing to assure her that she wasn't really going to leave Selma or Kentucky or her family. However, she just wasn't sure that was true. And so she held her tongue.

Chapter Seven

Everything seemed to move so quickly in the first week of the new year that Elizabeth wondered if she could possibly keep up. It started with an unseasonably warm spell that melted all the snow and ice within a day and consequently flooded the nearby creek, turning much of the farm into a lake. The ground on the road was so soft and muddy that she kept the children home from school. But the weather wasn't the only thing changing. One evening, just before suppertime, Flax began to bark as if he heard an intruder, and Elizabeth looked out the window to see a horse and rider in front of the house. Upon closer inspection, she was pleased to see it was her brother.

"You stay here," she told the dog as she slipped outside to greet Matthew.

"The parents were afraid your house might be underwater," he said as he came onto the porch, where they both stood surveying the large brown pond that had once been her barnyard.

"I'm not concerned." She pointed to the water. "In fact, it seems to be receding. Tell them not to worry. But I do appreciate you checking on me."

He nodded as if satisfied, but didn't appear to be leaving. "Well, my mind's made up, Lizzie."

"Made up about what?"

"I'm going to Oregon, sis. Come early spring, I'll be on the Oregon Trail."

"Are you in earnest?"

He looked westward with a longing in his eyes. "I'm ready for it." He adjusted the brim of his hat against the bright rays of the sinking sun. "Well, I'm not actually ready, but I'm working on it."

"Mother told me about your invention."

He brightened. "I did some reading up, and it seems you don't have to buy a prairie schooner. You can outfit your own wagon. That is, if you've got a sturdy one. And I figured I won't need to haul as many goods as a full-size family would. Anyway, I've been doing some reading and making some modifications, and if I do say so myself, the wagon is looking pretty good."

"So you really plan to do this?" She could hardly believe it. "In the spring?"

He nodded. "And I want you to understand that I don't expect you and the children to go just because I'm going. Not unless you truly want to...and unless you know it's the right thing to do."

"Oh, my..." She shook her head.

"What?"

"Well, the last time the children and I prayed about this—and, believe me, we've been praying about it a lot—but the last time—"

"You mean Jamie and Ruth know you're considering this?"

"They most certainly do."

"What were you about to say, Lizzie? About praying with the kids?"

"I was going to tell you *how* we prayed." She took in a deep breath. "We asked God to show *you*, Matthew, because we have all decided we want to go. But we also decided we would not go unless God showed you first."

He shook his head in a confused way. "Well, I don't rightly know that God showed me…but I do know I'm going, sis. My mind's made up."

"Can you stay for supper?"

He shrugged. "Don't see why not."

Naturally, Jamie and Ruth were thrilled to have Uncle Matthew as their supper guest. After Elizabeth asked the blessing, she invited Matthew to tell the children about his plans for the upcoming spring. His announcement had barely left his mouth when a loud *whoop* erupted from the Martin house—so loud that Elizabeth wondered if Brady would come running or if her parents might have heard it as well!

"Does this mean we're going too?" Jamie's brown eyes gleamed hopefully.

"Well, I don't know…" Elizabeth glanced nervously at her brother.

"We prayed that God would show Uncle Matthew what to do, Mama." Ruth beamed at her uncle. "If he's going on the Oregon Trail, we should be going too."

Matthew held up his hands in a helpless gesture. "Now, I don't want to take responsibility for your ma's decision," he told them. "It's a big decision. And she's got to do what she thinks is best for ya'll."

"Let's put it to a vote," Jamie suggested eagerly. "That's how democracy works."

Matthew chuckled.

"All right." Elizabeth nodded. "Let's put it to a vote—just for the fun of it."

"Should it be secret ballot?" Jamie asked with a serious expression.

"You bet," Matthew told him.

"Wait until after supper," Elizabeth told him.

Throughout supper, the children quizzed Matthew regarding his plans to go to Oregon. Ironically, Matthew was now taking the role of expert, although Elizabeth felt sure that she probably knew more about these matters than he did. After all, she and James had begun looking into this many years ago. However, she appreciated his enthusiasm, and it was clear that he'd done some investigating. She was also relieved to see him excited about something.

After the supper dishes were cleared, Jamie brought in four slips of paper and a pencil. "If you want to go to the Oregon Territory, write down 'go,'" he instructed. "If you want to stay here in Kentucky, write down 'stay.'"

Matthew chuckled as he took his paper. "Well, ya'll know what my vote is. But I'll play along just the same."

Elizabeth sat looking at her blank piece of paper for a long moment. She knew this vote wasn't going to become law, but she wanted to vote sincerely.

"Here you go," Matthew handed her the pencil they were sharing.

As she looked in his eyes, she remembered her mother's dream, and a cold chill ran down her spine. She couldn't bear to lose her little brother to a war. Not after losing James and Peter. It was hard to believe that war could really intrude upon their gentle community, but she couldn't pretend it was impossible.

"Come on, Mama," Ruth urged her.

Elizabeth wrote down her vote and handed the pencil to Ruth, and as soon as she printed her response, Jamie printed his and gathered up the slips. Sitting at the head of the table, he opened the first one and began to read. "One vote for go." He opened the next. "Two votes for go." He continued until it was clear that the vote was unanimous. "Everyone wants to go to Oregon!" he proclaimed victoriously.

"Does that mean we're going, Mama?" Ruth looked hopeful. "Truly going?"

Elizabeth gave Matthew a nervous smile and then turned back to her children. "Is that what you two really want?"

They both nodded eagerly.

"Well, it's always what your father dreamed of…for us. It was what we'd planned to do…" She closed her eyes, realizing that she felt calm and peaceful inside, as if this was exactly the right decision for them. "So it looks to me like we will be going."

Jamie and Ruth both jumped up and began dancing about the room. And it wasn't long until their enthusiasm pulled Elizabeth and Matthew to their feet and they were dancing too.

"Are you going to tell Mother and Father?" she asked Matthew when it was finally time for him to leave.

He shrugged. "You want me to wait?"

She shook her head. "No, you go ahead and tell them if it comes up." She considered confiding to him about what their mother had said recently, asking if she was too old to go to Oregon. But she thought better of it. Mother could speak for herself if she wanted to.

"There's a lot to get done before we go," Matthew told her.

"Yes. We will have to sit down and make plans." She still wondered if she could do this. So much was at stake now. "I'll have to ask Thomas Barron if he still wants to buy the farm. James had promised to sell to him if we left."

"I bet he'll jump on it. It'll more than double his acreage. And his wife will probably be eager to move into your house. It's so much nicer than their cabin."

Elizabeth knew that was true. She also knew, despite her father's claims that she would never find such comforts out West, she would be perfectly happy to leave this all behind. She couldn't even explain exactly why. She simply knew it was time to move on. And she was ready to go. Above all else, and as strange as it might seem to anyone else, she could sense James cheering her and the children on. They were going west!

Elizabeth wasn't terribly surprised to spot her parents' carriage pulling up in front of her house the next morning. Fortunately, the standing water had receded, and although the ground was still soggy, the children had already ridden Molly to school. She didn't usually let them ride a horse to school, but the idea of them slogging through the mud made no sense. Besides, she realized it would be prudent for them to both get more comfortable on horseback. Jamie was an experienced rider, but Ruth still had room for improvement.

"Hello," she called out to her parents, watching as her father helped her mother from the carriage. Brady came hurrying from the barn, giving Asa a hand with the team.

"Elizabeth!" her mother exclaimed. "Matthew tells us that you have decided to go west. We wish to get to the bottom of this."

"Come in, come in." Elizabeth opened the door. "The coffee is still—"

"We did not come for coffee," Asa said in a stern tone. "We came to talk some sense into our daughter."

Casting a concerned glance toward Brady, who didn't yet know of her plans, Elizabeth ushered her parents into the house. "Please," she said to her father. "Brady doesn't know yet and—"

"You're worried about Brady?" He frowned. "What about us?"

She patted her father's shoulder. "I'm plenty worried about you, Father. But Brady is dependent on me, and I—"

"Brady is a good man. He'll have no problem finding employment," Clara assured her as she peeled off her gloves.

"We'll be happy to have him work for us." Asa hung his hat on the hall tree and began to remove his coat.

"Elizabeth!" Clara blinked and opened her eyes wide. "You're not wearing black!"

Elizabeth looked down at her calico dress. "Well, there's some black in the print. But you're right, it's mostly violet." She sighed. "Ruthie had been begging me to put away my widow's weeds."

"Good for her." Clara briskly handed Elizabeth her hat. "But that is not what we came to discuss."

"That's for sure and for certain." Asa shook his head glumly.

Elizabeth felt guilty as she led the way to the kitchen. She knew her parents were hurt by this news, but what could she do to soften the blow? Soon they were seated around the table with three mugs of hot coffee and a plate of leftover doughnuts between them.

"There's really not much to say," Elizabeth quietly told them. "We have decided to go with Matthew to Oregon."

"Just like that?" Asa shook his head.

She gazed sadly at her parents, wishing there was an easier way to do this. "The hardest part by far will be leaving you two."

"Yes...well, that is precisely why I insisted your father and I pay you a visit this morning." Clara spoke in an uncertain tone that didn't sound quite right. "In order to discuss this a bit further."

"Not that it will do much good." Asa picked up a doughnut and peered into the hole as if looking for something. "Seems to me she's already made up her mind, Clara."

"It seems that way...." Clara looked intently at Elizabeth now. "But I am not going to take this lying down."

Elizabeth blinked. "What exactly did you have in mind?"

"I refuse to sit idly by as my only two living children and my two precious grandchildren trek to the ends of the earth...perhaps never to be seen again." She pulled out a handkerchief, dabbing her eyes, although Elizabeth didn't detect any tears. "There is only so much an old woman can take."

"You're not an old woman," Asa insisted. Now he pointed a finger at Elizabeth. "See what you've done to your poor mother."

"I'm so sorry." Elizabeth patted Clara's hand with a curious look. Either Elizabeth was mistaken or her mother was up to something.

Clara turned to Asa now. "It seems our hands are tied. Apparently the only thing left to do is to pack up and go with them."

Asa's heavy brows arched. "*Go with them?* Have you lost your senses, woman? You want to go with them? At our age?"

Clara tilted her head to one side. "But you just said I'm not an old woman, Asa."

"Well, you aren't. Not exactly, anyway. But you cannot be serious."

She gave him a stern look. "I am serious. If the children insist on doing this, I must insist on going with them."

He blinked. "You can't possibly mean what you're saying, Clara."

She nodded firmly. "I do mean this. Matthew and Elizabeth... Jamie and Ruthie...they are all I have."

"You have me," Asa said meekly.

She put her hand on his cheek. "I know, dear. It would be terribly hard to leave you behind. But there are four of them...and only one of you. So tell me true, Asa, could you honestly sit by and watch them leave—perhaps never to be seen again?"

"Well, I...uh...I don't know for sure."

"You used to be a strong and adventurous man, Asa. You loved hunting and fishing and riding the horses." Clara squeezed his arm. "I hate to say it, but you've let yourself get a little soft."

Now he lifted his arm, flexing his muscle with a determined look. "I am not soft!"

She squeezed again and then chuckled. "No, I see you're not. That's what I'm saying, Asa. There's a lot of life left in you—and in me. Why shouldn't we want to have an adventure together? And with our children and grandchildren? Certainly, you don't want to spend the rest of your days sitting in your rocking chair, do you?"

He frowned. "Well, no...of course not."

"So why shouldn't we go? What is stopping us?" She looked directly into his eyes. "You're not scared, are you?"

"Scared?" He rubbed his chin thoughtfully. "No, no…I'm not scared. But I've read a lot about the Oregon Trail. It's a grueling trip, Clara. Full of perils and pitfalls and dangers."

"So you are scared?"

"No." He shook his head. "I am not scared. But are you sure you're capable of such a strenuous journey?"

She sat up straighter, narrowing her eyes. "You doubt me?"

"No, no…I'm not saying that, dear. But have you given this serious thought?"

"I have thought of little else since Christmas Eve."

Asa looked at Elizabeth now. He appeared to be just as stunned as she. "What do you think about this?"

She paused to consider her words. "I think…well, if you and Mother know this is the right thing for you…I mean, if you truly believe God is leading you in this direction…then I would love nothing more than for you to join us on this adventure."

He frowned with uncertainty. "You don't think we're too old?"

She smiled. "I think you and Mother have so much to offer in the way of experience and wisdom and knowledge."

He nodded. "That's true."

"And if there are tasks that are difficult along the trail, you will have Matthew and me and the children to help. And you are both strong and in good health."

"That's true," he said again.

She reached out and grasped both their hands. "I want whatever is best for you."

"And I want the good Lord to lead us," Asa said quietly.

"Maybe he is leading us," Clara suggested. "Remember the scripture…'A little child shall lead them'? Perhaps our children are leading us."

Asa nodded thoughtfully as he turned back to Clara. "You truly *want* to do this?"

She nodded with misty eyes. "I do, Asa."

He took in a deep breath and finally smiled. "Then so do I."

Elizabeth could hardly believe her ears. "You do?"

His smile turned into a grin. "There's so much to be done." He stood. "I need to look into wagons, and we need to start deciding what to take. We'll have to sell our farms and get organized."

"I have lists," she told him.

He laughed. "Oh, I have lists too, Elizabeth."

"You do?"

He nodded with a sly look. "Surely you don't think that I was going to let you and James and the children go off without being informed of what you were up against. I've been gathering information and reading up on the Oregon Trail for years." He reached for Clara's hand. "Come on, wife, we have work to do."

Clara tossed Elizabeth a surprised but pleased expression. "Thank you for the coffee and doughnuts," she said lightly.

"Certainly," Elizabeth replied, still half dazed as she walked them to the door. "And when the ground gets dry enough, I suggest you start walking every day, Mother. Perhaps you could walk over here and back."

"Every day?" Clara pulled on her gloves.

"That's nothing compared to how much you'll be walking on the trail," Asa told her.

"But I thought I would ride in the wagon," she said.

He chuckled. "Well, you can do that if you like."

"It can be a rough ride in a wagon," Elizabeth explained as she walked them outside. "Not like our carriages, Mother. Many women prefer to walk alongside the wagons."

Clara tied her bonnet strings beneath her chin and nodded. "Fine, then. I will begin walking daily. I've always enjoyed a good invigorating walk. I've heard that it's good for the vital organs."

Elizabeth smiled and waved as her parents drove away. Flax chased their carriage down the driveway and then happily trotted back, his tail wagging. "Come on, boy," she called. "Let's go inside."

As she closed the door, she felt torn. On one hand, she could not be happier to think that they would all be doing this together. On the other hand, what if this trip proved too grueling for her parents? What if some unexpected calamity befell them? Would she feel responsible? Would she blame herself?

Instead of worrying about something she had little or no control over, Elizabeth decided to pray. Standing in front of the parlor window, she thanked God for how he had led her, and she then asked him to guide her parents' decision. If there was reason for them to remain here in Selma, she prayed God would stop them from going...that he would direct them away from this before it was too late to turn back. But she hoped with all of her heart that wouldn't happen. More than anything, she wanted her parents in Oregon with her.

As she went into the kitchen, she realized she needed to share this good news with John and Malinda. Wouldn't they be surprised to hear that not only she and the children were coming west, but the rest of her family as well! Malinda's last letter had mentioned how their little town grew a bit bigger each year as new citizens arrived from the East or babies were born. She would be so pleased to learn that their population was going to increase by six this year.

However, Elizabeth knew it would take some time for her letter to reach the other side of the continent. And it was doubtful she would hear back from Malinda before it was time to depart on their trip. But John and Malinda were experienced with life in the West, and perhaps they would know points along the way where they might send correspondence to Elizabeth. She hurried to James' old writing table, and opening a new bottle of ink, she began to plan the words she would pen to her relatives—words of hope and joy and great expectations!

Chapter Eight

It didn't take long for the folks in Selma to stop gossiping over the broken engagement of Matthew Dawson and Violet Lamott. Even talk of Walter Slake, who'd been renamed Walter Snake, subsided some. Elizabeth knew this was because their friends and neighbors had something more scintillating to discuss. The talk of the town now revolved around the news that the Martins and Dawsons planned to migrate west come spring. Some folks thought the family courageous, but others thought they'd lost their ever-loving minds.

"Have you sold your farm yet?" Oliver Thorne asked Elizabeth as she did some shopping at the Thorne Mercantile. Elizabeth knew that the store owner was well aware of the status of her negotiations.

"Thomas Barron has made me an offer," she informed him. "I expect we'll come to an agreement soon."

His dark brows arched as he measured off ten yards of moss-green calico. "You sure you know what you're doing?"

"I don't quite know what I'll use this fabric for just yet, but I'm sure it will be useful in Oregon. It's certainly pretty enough. Perhaps it will become dresses for Ruthie and me."

He cleared his throat. "I'm not speaking of the dry goods, Mrs. Martin."

Of course, she knew that. She was simply being coy.

"I can't fathom why you and your family are making this move." He used what he probably assumed was a paternal tone. "I've done a fair amount of reading on the subject, and I can assure you, I would never dream of taking my wife and children out to that savage wilderness. Do you have any idea what it's like out there in the Wild West? Are you prepared for what you'll encounter?"

"I'll admit that I don't know everything there is to know about traveling that far west," she confessed. "But I've been studying up on it for years. And as you know, my in-laws have all relocated there. From what they've written me, it's a wonderful place to farm and raise a family."

"But a lone woman, traveling through Indian country?" He frowned as he snipped a straight line through the fabric. "Seems mighty perilous to me."

She gave him a tolerant smile. "I won't be alone, Mr. Thorne. Didn't you hear that my parents and my brother are going as well?"

"Certainly, I heard that…but still, you being a widow woman with two youngins…well, if you ask me…" He shook his head. "Just don't seem right."

She pointed to a bolt of blue gingham now. "I think I'd like ten yards of that one too, please."

"That's a lot of cloth," he said as he reached for the indigo blue. "Looks like you're going to be mighty busy."

"As you can imagine, we're trying to stock our wagons with useful items—things that won't be easily procured once we set out on our journey. As a result, I expect you'll be seeing a fair amount of my mother and me in your store for the next few weeks. We have quite a list of goods to purchase."

His eyes lit up as if he was counting his profits now. "Well, I reckon it's a challenge to fully outfit a wagon."

"It certainly is." She examined one of the large storage tins, testing the lid to see that it fit snugly and thinking it would be practical for staples. "Fortunately, we'll be taking three wagons. That allows us to take more. But we're planning carefully, making the best use of the space and weight."

"Does that mean you're driving your own wagon?" He folded the gingham into a neat bundle.

"I am."

He looked skeptical. "I've heard an oxen team can prove a challenge, even for a strong, experienced man. How do you expect you'll manage that by yourself?"

"Matthew and my father will drive the heavy wagons, and they'll be pulled by oxen teams. I'll drive a lighter wagon with a horse team. We've chosen our most dependable plow horses to do the job. I don't see that it will be much of a problem. In fact, I think Jamie might even be able to handle driving some." She made a confident nod. "We reckon it'll be handy to have horses once we get to the Oregon Territory."

"I suppose that makes sense."

"You know, Mr. Thorne, the Oregon Territory will be a wonderful opportunity for smart businessmen like yourself someday." She paused from picking out buttons to look him in the eyes. "For anyone with a spirit for adventure, it could be quite a profitable move."

He made a nervous laugh. "Don't you go trying to lure me out on some harebrained quest, Mrs. Martin. My wife would sooner have me tarred and feathered than to entertain such a notion."

Fortunately, more customers had come into the mercantile, and Elizabeth was allowed to browse and shop in peace for a few minutes.

"Elizabeth Martin!" exclaimed a female voice. "I thought that was you."

Elizabeth turned to see Mary Franklin approaching. The two had gone to school together as children but had never been close friends. Truth be told, Elizabeth had never cared for Mary and partly for good reason. However, she was determined to take the high road with Mary now. "Good morning," she said cheerily. "It's been a long time."

"Indeed, it has." Mary peered curiously at Elizabeth. "Is it true what I've been hearing lately?"

Elizabeth braced herself. "I suppose that would depend on what you've heard."

"Did Violet Lamott jilt your younger brother?"

Elizabeth made a stiff smile. "The engagement is off."

"And is that why you and your entire family are fleeing to the West?" Mary's eyes were still as piercing blue as Elizabeth remembered, but her previously auburn hair was now the color of a faded board, and she had gained a considerable amount of weight.

"It's true my family and I are venturing to Oregon," Elizabeth said lightly. "Perhaps you remember my late husband's younger brother, John Martin?" Elizabeth not only knew that Mary would remember John but also thought she might still regret that John had not proposed marriage to her. Mary had been smitten by John as a youth. "John and Malinda and their five children as well as the elder Martins have all settled quite happily in the Oregon Territory," she continued. "They homestead in a lovely green valley just a day's travel from the Pacific Ocean." Elizabeth put several spools of thread into her shopping basket. "Malinda writes me that the climate is so mild, their livestock graze year-round."

"So it is true. You are leaving."

Elizabeth nodded as she browsed through the sewing notions. "We plan to depart Selma in just a few weeks."

"This is so sudden!"

"If James had lived, we surely would have been in Oregon by now." Elizabeth looked evenly at Mary. "So truly, it is not so sudden."

"But to pick up and leave like this?" Mary frowned. "I can only imagine how distressing this must be for you, Elizabeth. Such a demanding journey...for a woman your age...it's inconceivable."

"Nonsense." Elizabeth dropped a spool of white cord into her basket. "I'm looking forward to this trip as a great adventure. So is the rest of my family." She glanced around to see that other shoppers were listening in. "And if you'll excuse me, there is much to be done. But if I don't see you again before we leave, I wish you well, Mary." She made a genuine smile now. She did wish Mary well, especially since she had heard that Mary's marriage to an older wealthy man was not a very happy one. Elizabeth reached out to squeeze Mary's gloved hand. "And if you are truly worried for the welfare of my family and me, I invite you to keep us in your prayers in the upcoming months."

"Well, yes, of course." Mary nodded quickly.

Elizabeth made a few more selections, fended a few more neighborly inquiries, and finally decided to take her mother's advice and defer the bulk of her shopping for Paducah and Kansas City. Merchandise was cheaper in Paducah because it was located on the Ohio River. It would also save time because no one would know her there. However, once in Kansas City, prices would probably jump much higher. And who could predict whether they would have all that was needed to complete a successful overland journey?

This very subject had spawned a lively debate among their family the previous week. Without consulting Elizabeth or her mother, the men had decided that they should do all their purchasing in Kansas City, including wagons and livestock and all their supplies. "That way we can travel up river unencumbered. We won't be carrying all our worldly goods with us," Asa had explained.

"We'll just jump off the riverboat in Kansas City and get whatever we need there," Matthew added. "And off we go."

"What if they don't have everything we need?" Elizabeth queried.

"Oh, sure they will," Asa told her.

"But what about our own things?" Clara protested. "I've already begun to box up what I wish to take with us to Oregon. Are you saying I must leave it behind?"

Asa frowned. "Well, I suppose we could take some freight with us on the river."

"Wouldn't that mean we'd need to take a wagon from home?" Elizabeth questioned.

"I suppose..." Asa scratched his chin.

"And how would we dispose of the wagon before getting on the boat?" Clara frowned.

"We could sell it."

"So we would sell our perfectly good wagon, probably at a loss, and then turn around and buy new ones, perhaps not as well built as the wagons we left behind but most likely at a premium price?"

Asa and Matthew exchanged uncertain looks.

"And what about the wagon you were working on?" Elizabeth challenged her brother. "It sounded like it was coming along nicely. Mother said you got it rigged up to hold a sleeping hammock beneath it and a number of other improvements. You probably won't find a wagon outfitted like that in Kansas City."

"Yes...but it's smaller than the usual prairie schooner. I decided I want a bigger one."

"But it would be easier to drive a smaller one," she said.

Asa pointed at her. "Probably just the right size for you to drive, Lizzie. That wagon would be relatively easy to handle with a dependable team of horses."

"What about getting our wagons in Kansas City?" Matthew insisted.

"Think about it," Elizabeth told him. "Wouldn't it be much simpler and cheaper to utilize our own sturdy wagons right from our own farms? And to outfit them here with our own tools and supplies, items we've trusted and used for years?"

Asa nodded. "That does make sense. I don't like the idea of getting out on the trail with shoddy tools and equipment."

"I've read time and again that careful preparation is the key to success on the Oregon Trail," Clara told them. "I say we take our own wagons and livestock."

"And that gives us more time to plan carefully and to load them properly," Elizabeth persisted. "And that way we will know exactly what we have before we get to Kansas City. We won't be scrambling to find everything we need or settling for low quality. Think about it, Father. How would you like to be out on the trail and have a poorly made wagon breaking down on you?"

"You make a good point," Asa agreed. "But it will cost more to transport them on the riverboats. And I'm not sure about transporting livestock."

"Maybe we could get some of our livestock in Kansas City," Matthew suggested.

"But would it be dependable livestock?" Clara challenged.

"Do you want to be out on the trail with an unruly team of oxen?" Elizabeth asked. "Or an animal that's in poor health? We know our livestock."

"That's a valid point too," Asa concurred.

So it was decided they would use some of their own livestock, including their most dependable horse team, to get their fully outfitted prairie schooners up to Paducah and loaded onto the riverboat. If needed, they would purchase additional oxen and horses in Kansas City. In the meantime, there was much to be done and only a few weeks left to do it.

As Elizabeth drove the carriage home from town, she wondered what she would miss most about Selma. It was unrealistic to think she would miss nothing. But at the moment, with dreams of a great adventure to occupy her thoughts, it was hard to think of much else. Certainly, she would miss their church…and the children's school. And, she realized as she pulled in front of the house, she would miss Brady too.

"Hello, Missus Martin," he called out as he came to help with the horses.

"Hello, Brady." She smiled as she reached for her shopping basket. "There are some parcels in back, if you wouldn't mind bringing them into the house for me."

"Yes, Missus."

Elizabeth knew that Brady had been sad to hear her news. However, he had not been terribly surprised. James had told Brady years ago, back when he'd given him his freedom papers, about their plans to go west. Even then, Brady had claimed he was too old to make that journey. That was why James had promised Brady that when the farm was sold, he would make a written provision for Brady to remain as a farmhand for the rest of his days. Fortunately, this was one of the details that Thomas Barron had agreed to. The particulars that were still in discussion had more to do with furnishings and farm implements. Thomas Barron seemed to feel that since Elizabeth could not take everything with her, she should include them with the price of the house and farm.

"Thomas Barron is a shrewd businessman," her father had told her a few days ago. "How about letting me handle this negotiation for you?"

Elizabeth had been relieved to pass this on to him. There was enough to occupy her without dealing with Thomas Barron as well. However, Thomas Barron's greediness had motivated her to do something she hadn't considered before. And it was why the front parlor was now piled high with boxes. As Elizabeth began going through her household goods, she realized that many of these items, things she had accrued from James' grandparents and the original property owners, might be useful to others, so she had offered the surplus to her church. Pastor Kincaid had kindly accepted her donation and already had a group of eager church women who promised to put her donations to good use for missionaries both in America and abroad.

Going through James' things wasn't easy, but the task was long overdue. However, as she went through his clothing, she felt relieved that she had not gotten rid of anything. At the rate Jamie was growing, it wouldn't be long until he would be big enough to wear some of these things. So she packed away the items that seemed most suited for Oregon. And when she found James' gold pocket watch, she decided to put it on a chain to wear around her neck. Not that it would be so important to know the time out on the trail, but it would be a comfort all the same.

Then, as she sorted through the attic, she realized that some old pieces, like James' grandmother's spinning wheel, might prove valuable in the Oregon Territory as well. Hence, she was acquiring an interesting accumulation of items. She would invite her mother to peruse it with her. Together they would decide what should stay and what should go. All in all, despite the extra work, Elizabeth was enjoying this process.

As were the children. Every day, when they got home from school, after their chores and supper were finished, they read together through geography books as well as first-person accounts of traveling overland to the West. They studied maps and the calendar to make timelines, and Jamie did the arithmetic to determine how many days each stage of the journey would take. It was educational and interesting and exciting.

"We're going to be on a riverboat for fifteen days?" Ruth asked with wonder.

"Perhaps longer," Elizabeth explained. "It depends on the current of the river."

"And we'll be on three different rivers," Jamie told Ruth as he traced his finger up the map. "First the Ohio River, then the mighty

Mississippi, and finally, for the longest river trip, the Missouri—all the way to Kansas City."

"And then all the way across here?" Ruth traced her finger from Kansas City to the Pacific Ocean.

"Your finger travels fast," Elizabeth told her. "But that's the longest part of our trip. We probably won't arrive in Fort Vancouver until September." Elizabeth pointed to the spot on the map and reiterated her father's plan. "From there we will travel by ship on the Pacific Ocean down to a place called Cape Arago."

"How long will we be on a ship?" Ruth asked with wide eyes.

"About a week, I think your grandpa said."

"And then we'll see Uncle John and Aunt Malinda and Grandma and Grandpa Martin," Jamie announced. "And our new home."

Elizabeth nodded, trying to appear confident. However, she realized there was still the chance that her letter might not reach her in-laws. Despite Jamie's admiration of pony express riders, she suspected that mail was sometimes lost and sometimes stolen. For that reason, she had decided to write several letters, and she planned to send them from various points along the way. After investing so much effort and expense into this monumental overland journey, she did not want to catch her in-laws by surprise.

Chapter Nine

As their departure day drew closer, Elizabeth wondered how she ever imagined she could have accomplished this feat on her own. And she was ever so thankful that her brother and father were helping out with the wagons as well as handling most of the travel arrangements. Between overseeing the selling of their properties, sending numerous telegraphs and letters, and making a couple of trips to Paducah to secure various traveling supplies, Matthew and her father seemed to be managing this trip with intelligence and enthusiasm.

"I got the Barrons to agree to a fair price that includes most of the furnishings and farm implements," Asa informed her one morning. "I'm certain they realize they are getting the best part of the bargain. But that comes from selling property with short notice."

"Yes...it's too bad we hadn't started this last summer."

He grinned. "Well, as I just reminded your mother, we aren't getting any younger. There's no time like the present."

She laughed. "How true."

"Now, I came here to warn you that there was one little condition in the selling price. Mrs. Barron insists on being allowed to walk through your house one more time."

"One more time? She's already seen it dozens of times. And now it's rather...well, look at it, Father." Elizabeth waved her hands toward the disheveled parlor.

"I don't believe she's coming to inspect your housekeeping, Lizzie. She knows you're preparing to leave."

"Well, I suppose it shouldn't matter so much. Except to my pride." She pushed a box with the toe of her boot. "And I'll ask Brady to move some of these crates out to the barn." She pushed a strand of hair away from her face and sighed loudly.

"You're not having regrets, are you?" He peered curiously into her eyes.

"No, Father." She made a tired smile. "Not at all. In fact, I am counting the days until we leave. I'm so eager to be done with this and on our way. So are the children."

He patted her back. "I told your mother that all this sorting and sifting and cleaning and packing and moving of things will make us all stronger—more fit and ready for the physical demands of the journey ahead."

"I'm sure you're right. But I must admit I'm looking forward to a peaceful and relaxing riverboat trip."

"I just hope we don't all get too fat and lazy on that leg of the journey." Asa frowned. "I told your mother that we will have to get out and walk around the decks for our daily constitutional."

"Yes, that would be wise."

"Well, I'd best let you get back to your chores and packing," he said. "And I s'pect Mrs. Barron will soon be here."

Asa's wagon had barely left when Mrs. Barron arrived in her carriage. Flax greeted her with loud barking, but Mrs. Barron did not appear to appreciate the welcome. Wearing a feathered hat and a frown, she came onto the porch where Elizabeth was waiting.

"Don't mind the dog," Elizabeth told her. "He thinks he's just doing his job."

"Yes, well, your father told me I could come and look around again." With her head held high and dressed as if she'd been invited for a tea party, she walked into the house and immediately began to look around.

"I apologize for the disorder," Elizabeth said as she followed her into the parlor. "I've been using this room to sort through—"

"Does this stay with the house?" Mrs. Barron pointed to a rug that Elizabeth had rolled up and pushed against the wall.

"Actually, I had planned to take that. I thought it would be useful on the trip and when we get there."

"It seems too nice to take to the wilderness."

"I felt it would be a comfort to have some special pieces," Elizabeth told her. "Although it's difficult to choose. And the wagon is only so big."

Naturally, this seemed like an open invitation for the older woman to advise Elizabeth on what should go with her and what should remain with the house. Elizabeth was tempted to ask Mrs. Barron on what she based these opinions—had she read much about the Oregon Territory? But it became more and more obvious that Mrs. Barron only had her own tastes and desires in mind.

Finally, Elizabeth felt she couldn't tolerate one more question as to the age and condition of another piece of furniture, or why Elizabeth should not take the ladder-back dining room chairs to the wilderness.

"I invite you to walk around as much as you like," Elizabeth finally told her. "If you have specific questions, feel free to write them down." She handed her a slip of paper and the stub of a pencil.

"But I have much to do in preparation for our upcoming trip, so if you'll please excuse me."

Mrs. Barron appeared slightly miffed by this, but Elizabeth suspected she would be even more insulted if Elizabeth remained with her and honestly spoke her mind, which she was sorely tempted to do. Instead, she went back to the kitchen, where she was carefully wrapping dishes between linens and packing them into a small barrel. She hoped she would finish before Mrs. Barron popped in and insisted that those dishes were too fine to go to the wilderness!

Elizabeth realized that wagons had to be packed carefully and that too much weight in the wagon could determine the fate of the journey. So she was being careful. But at the same time, some items simply seemed necessary to family life. However, she had heard stories of some pioneers being forced to unload wagons along the way. Usually it was the large pieces of furniture left behind—headboards, cabinets, even pianos! She'd also heard of some Mormons returning to the Oregon Trail after settling in Utah in order to collect the valuable pieces of debris from alongside the trail. Whether fact or hearsay, she thought it was clever.

At the same time, she hoped that she and her family would pack their wagons sensibly enough not to endanger themselves or be forced to cast off family heirlooms to be salvaged by strangers later. It was bad enough letting Mrs. Barron walk through her house, picking at her furnishings like a vulture. Elizabeth consoled herself with the thought that Mrs. Barron would soon be someone from the past.

"I do not see how you can simply pick up and leave like this," Mrs. Barron said as she came into the kitchen and glanced around. "Not that I'm complaining. You know that Mr. Barron and I have hoped to purchase this property for some time." She sniffed. "Although I did expect it would be in slightly better condition than this."

Elizabeth put the lid on the barrel and looked up. "It usually is in better condition. And I promise you that when you and Mr. Barron take occupancy, it will be in apple pie order. It's just that you caught me at a bad time." She waved her hands. "So much to do. I'm sorry the house doesn't look as tidy as you would like."

"I do have some questions." Mrs. Barron held up her piece of paper.

"Feel free." Elizabeth moved the kettle to the center of the stove. "Perhaps you would like some tea."

Nearly two long hours later, Mrs. Barron was finally on her way... and somewhat satisfied with Elizabeth's answers, although the greedy woman clearly wanted everything she could get her hands on. If Elizabeth had been forced to endure one more "You're taking *that* to the wilderness?" question she might have canceled the entire transaction. The mere idea of that pushy woman becoming the lady of this sweet old house grated on her so badly that she was tempted to announce the house was no longer for sale. Of course, she could not do that. And so for the sake of her parents and brother and her children, she had bit her tongue.

But truly, the sooner this was all over and done with and the sooner they were on their way, the happier she would be. Her one consolation was that this house had been in James' family, and James had always wanted them to go to Oregon to join the rest of his family. So despite her ill feelings, Elizabeth prayed that God would bless the Barrons with this house. The sooner the better.

On Saturday, Elizabeth and the children headed for her folks' house for dinner. "Grandpa told me he has a surprise for me," Jamie told Elizabeth as he drove the carriage.

"What about me?" Ruth asked with dismay.

"I don't think you're old enough for Grandpa's surprise," Elizabeth told her.

"Do you know what it is?" Jamie asked.

Elizabeth just smiled and unbuttoned the top of her coat.

Although it was early February, the weather was unseasonably warm. If this held out, they might be setting out on the Oregon Trail sooner than usual. However, the weather was always unpredictable this time of year.

"Just think," Jamie said eagerly. "One week from now we will be leaving Selma for good."

"Just one week?" Ruth's eyes lit up. "And we'll get to go on the riverboat?"

"We'll spend one day in Paducah, shopping for some supplies. And then we'll board our first riverboat." Elizabeth could hardly believe how quickly the past few weeks had flown by. With the departure date so near, she felt a mixture of nervousness and excitement. Was this really happening?

Her father was waiting for them on the porch with a twinkle in his eye. "Ruth, you go inside and help your grandma," he instructed. "Elizabeth and Jamie, you come with me." Then he led them back behind the barn, where he had set up what appeared to be a shooting range of sorts. Elizabeth knew that Asa planned to teach Jamie how to shoot, but she was surprised when her father presented Jamie with a very large gun. "This is a Colt shotgun," Asa told Jamie. "But not any ordinary shotgun. This is a revolving shotgun with four chambers, which means you have four shots."

"Oh, Father." Elizabeth frowned. "That's too much gun for a boy."

"Please, Ma?" Jamie looked longingly at the long gun.

Asa winked at Elizabeth. "I'm fully aware that this gun's a little big for Jamie, but he'll grow into it. Besides, you can both use it if need be. I ordered the thirty-inch barrel, which is the shortest they make. It's an excellent gun, patented in 1850, but only made available this past year. I was lucky to get my hands on one." He turned back to Jamie. "And I expect you to treat it with great respect, son."

Jamie nodded as he smoothed his hand over the sleek wood stock. "Is it really mine? To keep?"

"That's right." Asa grinned. "I s'pect we'll want to do some hunting on the trail. And it's possible you might need it to protect your family someday."

Elizabeth was still uneasy. "Are you sure he's old enough to handle a firearm like this, Father?"

Asa laid some ammunition on the board he'd set up as a table. "Of course he's old enough, Lizzie. I was Jamie's age when I got my first gun. But it was nothing like this beauty." He handed it over to Jamie now. "That stock is walnut."

Elizabeth hoped he was right. "But why did you want me to come out here?" she asked. "Shouldn't I go help Mother with—"

"No." Asa firmly shook his head as he removed a square piece of gray wool cloth to reveal a smaller gun. "I want you out here as well. You're both going to learn how to shoot."

"I know how to shoot," she told him. "I've fired James' shotgun dozens of times."

"But do you know how to shoot this?" He handed her the handgun.

"What is it?"

"This is a Colt Dragoon. Forty-four caliber with six shots."

She felt the weight of it in her hand. Much smaller than a shotgun or rifle, but still heavy. Now she lifted the gun up, peering down the barrel like she would do with a shotgun. "Like this?"

Asa chuckled. "Not exactly." He lowered her hand, extending her arm slightly. "Keep the gun level and aim at the center of the target. Your eye should help to align your hand."

"Do you really think this is necessary?" she asked.

"According to Captain Brownlee, the wagon master we are signed up with, it is not only necessary, it's required. All adults must bring their own firearms and be capable of shooting."

She looked at Jamie. "But he's not an adult."

"Not officially, but he'll be with you in the wagon. He needs to know how to handle a gun. And you may be capable of shooting a shotgun, but there's plenty you don't know. Today we're going to practice until both you and Jamie are sure shots. But before we start shooting, I'm going to make sure you both know how to clean and care for your guns. Then we'll work on loading them. No use in having a good firearm by your side if you don't know how to load it."

They spent an hour just learning how to clean the barrel with oil and a plunger and how to load the rounds and how to store everything safely and properly. They never even got around to shooting before Ruth came out to call them to dinner.

"What are you doing out here?" she asked curiously.

"Learning about guns," Jamie said importantly.

"I want to learn about guns too," she insisted.

"Not until you're older," Asa told her.

Ruth frowned.

"Grandpa's right." Elizabeth slipped her arm around Ruth's shoulder. "Guns are very dangerous. I was much older than you the first time I learned to shoot."

During dinner, all the talk around the table was about the upcoming trip. Matthew showed them the canvas water buckets he'd found in town.

"Why not just use a regular bucket?" Jamie asked.

"Because these are lightweight and don't take much space," Matthew explained. "We have to do all we can to keep the wagons from being too heavy."

And so they continued, planning and debating and going over what remained on the lists, deciding what should go and what should stay and what supplies they should procure in Paducah and what should wait until Kansas City.

"I say we buy only perishables in Kansas City," Clara finally said. "We can get everything else in town or in Paducah. Although I heard that Thorne's has weevils in their flour. So I say let's wait for Paducah for that."

"Maybe we should get the rice and beans there too," Elizabeth suggested.

"Let's plan on it. And while you were working on your guns, Ruthie and I made up some saleratus," Clara told her.

"What's that?" Jamie asked.

"It's what makes biscuits fluffy," Ruth said with authority. "You mix baking soda and baking powder, right, Grandma?"

"That's right."

"So if we shop the food staples in Paducah, we need to make sure we've got plenty of time to transfer everything into our watertight containers and secure it all in the wagons before we get on the river."

"Speaking of secure," Asa said with uncertainty, "Vernon Griggs was just telling me about a family that did like we're planning. They transported their wagons by riverboat only to discover, once they were on the trail, that someone had stolen provisions and tools from their wagon while they were on the river."

"I'll stay with the wagons and guard them," Matthew offered.

"The whole time?" Elizabeth was skeptical.

"Someone will have to be around to tend to the stock," he said. "I figured I'd do it."

"And I can help," Jamie offered.

"Maybe we fellas can take turns," Asa suggested.

"Anyway, we'll figure it out," Matthew assured them. "For sure and for certain, we are not going to let some scoundrel pilfer from us before we even get on the trail."

After dinner, Elizabeth offered to help her mother clean up, but Asa wouldn't hear of it. "The most important thing right now is for you to learn to shoot."

Clara nodded soberly. "Your father is right."

So Elizabeth followed her father and Matthew out, where the two men both worked with the novices. And after a couple of hours, both Elizabeth and Jamie knew how to load and shoot.

"I want you to practice at home every day before we go," Asa instructed Jamie as Elizabeth and Ruth were getting into the carriage. "By the time we're on the trail, I expect you and your ma both to be sharpshooters."

Elizabeth just laughed, but Jamie nodded as if he planned to do it. And, to be fair, he was a pretty decent shot for a boy his age. She just hoped this trip wouldn't make him grow up too fast.

Before going home, Matthew insisted on showing Elizabeth and the children his progress on the wagons. "I got the canvas covers put on two of them," he explained as they went into the barn. "TJ Sawyer helped me put the bows in."

"Where are the bows?" Ruth asked.

"These are the bows." Matthew patted an arched piece of wood that supported the heavy white canvas. He did some maneuvering with the edge of the covering, and suddenly it was transformed into an awning of sorts, allowing more air into the wagon.

"That's clever," Elizabeth told him.

"TJ showed me how to do that too." Matthew seemed pleased.

"You sure got plenty of ways to store stuff on the outside of the wagon," Jamie observed as he opened a trunk-like box in the rear of a wagon.

"The more we can store outside, the more room we got inside. Besides that, you want some items handy, like tools or cooking pots." Matthew squatted down and pointed to the bottom of a wagon. "And you see all that black tar down there? You know what that's for?"

"Is it to protect the bottom of the wagon?" Jamie asked.

"Well, that too. But I sealed 'em up real good, so when we go through water, they should be as tight as a boat."

"We're going to take our wagons in the water?" Ruth's eyes grew big.

"We'll have to cross some rivers and streams to get to Oregon country," Matthew explained. "But don't you worry, Ruthie, these schooners will hold up just fine. I even tried one out in the pond just to be sure. Watertight."

"You're doing a wonderful job on these wagons," Elizabeth told him. "I don't know what we'd do without you."

"I just want to be sure we're in good shape when we head out, Lizzie. From what I've read, that trail can be real rugged."

Chapter Ten

Finally the big day was here. At the crack of dawn, and following a family prayer for traveling mercy, three fully loaded covered wagons rolled out of the Dawsons' farm and headed toward Selma. Matthew's sturdy wagon, pulled by four oxen, led the way. This was followed by Elizabeth's smaller wagon, pulled by four strong horses. Asa and Clara's full-sized prairie schooner, also pulled by a hefty team of oxen, brought up the rear. Tethered to the backs of these wagons was a variety of livestock, including three spare riding horses and three cows.

The plan was to get additional teams once they arrived in Kansas City. But traveling on the relatively smooth, flat road to Paducah didn't require the same kind of strength that crossing the prairie, mountains, and rivers would.

"We're like a short wagon train," Ruth proclaimed as they rumbled along the road to town.

Elizabeth just nodded. She felt an unexpected flutter of nerves as she tried to remember if there was anything they'd forgotten, something important they'd left behind. Oh, she knew there probably wasn't—they'd gone over the lists many times. And even if something had been overlooked, it was too late to turn back now. The Barrons had taken occupancy of her farm two days ago. She and the children had been staying with her parents because the new owners of their farm wouldn't arrive until next week. The past couple of days had been spent tending to the final details and helping to pack and repack the wagons.

During the past several weeks, Matthew had built dozens of sturdy pine storage crates, all the same height and made to fit snugly in the boxes of the wagons. These were filled with goods and marked accordingly. And some were built with drawers that could be opened to retrieve necessary supplies. Then these crates had been arranged and rearranged to create a high raised platform, where feather mattresses and bedding could be unrolled and layered to create a bed when needed. Matthew had opted for a hammock beneath his own wagon. Besides that, they had a large canvas tent that Asa had insisted was necessary.

Matthew and Asa had come up with the final plan for packing the wagons, and Elizabeth thought it was rather ingenious. Most of the crates in Elizabeth's wagon contained items for setting up housekeeping in Oregon. Consequently, most of these things wouldn't be needed on the trail. This allowed her wagon to be less disturbed and to be available for the children or her mother to rest while traveling. It had various furnishings wedged along the sides as well as pieces, like the ladder-back chairs, that could be removed during stops. They had tried to take everything into consideration.

Her parents' wagon had Matthew's drop-down kitchen board attached to one side, and this wagon was loaded with whatever was needed for cooking and had easy access to crates that would soon contain the food supplies they planned to purchase in Paducah. Once filled, it would be a heavy load too. But as Matthew had pointed out, half of their food would be gone and the load lightened when they went over the mountains.

Meanwhile, Matthew's wagon contained all of the precious tools and guns, as well as many other everyday supplies that would be needed on the trail, including an interesting selection of wood, metal, and leather pieces that Asa had decided would be useful for repairs. Consequently, this wagon was probably the most valuable one, and because of the firearms, it would need to be guarded most closely during their river travel.

Asa had taken charge of stowing the cash from the sales of their farms. More than half of it, money they would need once they got to Oregon, was stored in a safe box that he and Matthew had rigged up in the bottom of Asa's wagon. Without knowing what to look for, no one would ever guess what was beneath those boards. Besides that, it was now covered by boxes and crates. The rest of the cash, their much-needed travel money, had been divided between the four adults, where most of it was securely hidden in money belts. This money had to cover the costs of supplies in Paducah, riverboat tickets and freight charges, expenses in Kansas City, and finally their ocean passage fares. It would take what seemed like a small fortune to get the six of them to their new home. Still, Elizabeth believed it would be worth it. She prayed that it would.

"Flax is happy," Ruth told her. "He's all snuggled down in the bed I made for him in the corner of the wagon."

"How are the chickens doing?" Elizabeth asked Jamie, who was sitting on the side of the wagon where they'd hung several crates of chickens.

Jamie crooked his neck to see. "They're bouncing up and down a little, but they look just fine, Ma."

"We're on our way," Elizabeth said as she clicked the reins. For now, she was driving the team. It was a new experience to be pulling a covered wagon like this. But she knew that before the day was over, she would let Jamie try his hand at it too.

"This seat is real nice, Mama." Ruth patted the padded seat beneath them. "Lots better than a hard old board."

"I hope we still feel that way a few months from now." It had been Elizabeth's idea to use spare blankets and quilts to create a padded bench. She'd folded several of them to match the length of the wooden wagon bench. Then she'd wrapped a couple of the old buckskins that had been hanging in the barn over the top of the blanket pad, securing the skins tightly around the bench with small brass tacks to protect the blankets. All in all, it was fairly comfortable. Still, it wasn't as fancy as her parents' wagon, where Matthew had managed to rig a padded carriage seat for his mother's comfort.

They were about a mile out of town when Elizabeth noticed that her father's wagon was slowing down considerably.

"Why is Grandpa stopping?" Jamie asked.

Elizabeth pulled back on the reins and slowly pulled on the brake. "I don't know."

"Is he broken down?" Ruth asked with concern.

"Is that *Brady* up there?" Jamie craned his head to see better. "By golly, it is, Ma. It's Brady, right there on the road."

"Oh, my!" She handed Jamie the reins. "I'd better go see what's wrong."

She climbed down and hurried over to where Brady and her father were talking.

"Brady?" She peered curiously at him. "What are you doing out on the road this early in the morning?"

"I'm leavin', ma'am."

"Leaving?"

Asa grimly shook his head. "Brady says he's not happy working for the Barrons."

"Oh, dear." Elizabeth frowned. "I'm so sorry, Brady."

"Not your fault, ma'am. Them Barrons, they make their own troubles."

"But where are you going, Brady?"

"Don't know for sure, ma'am. Just away." He peered down the road and then shrugged as if it didn't matter.

Matthew joined them, looking on curiously.

"You know you're welcome to come with us to the West," she told Brady. "I've told you that before."

"I know that, ma'am." He frowned. "I feared I was too old...and I feared I'd be killed by Injuns. But now I'm thinking Injuns might be better than them Barrons."

Matthew chuckled, and Elizabeth exchanged glances with her father. He nodded soberly, as did Matthew. It seemed to be clear.

"Brady, we would be honored if you decided to come to the Oregon Territory with us," she told him. "You know we consider you as family."

His face brightened. "Thank you, ma'am."

"So you'll come with us?"

He still looked unsure. "You don't think I'm too old?"

"Aw, Brady, you're not that much older than me." Asa patted him on the back. "And we all know you're a good hard worker."

"That's true 'nough. I sho' am." He nodded.

"Everyone has to pull his weight on the trail," Matthew warned.

"I got no problem with that. I reckon I druther drop dead with you folks than be back there peeling taters in Missus Barron's kitchen." He glumly shook his head. "That woman seems to think she bought me when she bought that there house."

"Brady!" Elizabeth suddenly noticed he was only carrying a small bundle, as if he'd left in a hurry. "Did you remember to bring your papers?"

He patted his chest. "Oh, yes, ma'am. They be right here on my person."

"Oh, good." She smiled in relief. "I'm so glad you're going with us."

"Why don't you ride with me," Matthew said to Brady. "I'd appreciate the company."

Brady's face broke into a happy grin. "I reckon it's true then. I'm going to Oregon!"

They loaded back into their wagons, and as they continued on their way, Elizabeth told the children the good news.

"I heard Mrs. Barron talking to Brady," Jamie quietly confided to her. "Before we left for Grandma and Grandpa's. You wouldn't even talk to a stray dog that way, Ma."

Elizabeth just shook her head. "Well, I'm glad it worked out like this. God must have known we needed Brady with us."

"Can we sing songs?" Ruth asked. "Traveling songs?"

"You get us started," Elizabeth told her. And so, rumbling along the town road in the gray dawn morning, they sang "Oh, Susanna."

As their small wagon train made its way into town, Elizabeth felt a tinge of sadness. She spent her whole life in these parts, and she suspected the time would come, maybe months from now or maybe sooner, when she would miss Selma and Kentucky. It seemed only natural. She sighed as they passed the children's school and then their church with its white steeple.

Because it was early and a Saturday, not many people were out and about, but Harvey Fortner, at the feed and seed, glanced up as he hoisted a big bag into the back of a wagon. He grinned at them. "Wagons, ho!" he called out as he reached for another sack.

Elizabeth waved and Jamie tipped his hat…and on they rumbled through town. Elizabeth had just been into the feed and seed last week, gathering up dozens of packets of vegetable and flower seeds to use for her garden in Oregon. These were safely packed in the crate that contained her fabrics and linens. It still amazed her to think of what her new home might be like…one day. Right now it seemed a distant dream. First they had many, many miles to travel and many, many days to pass. And she was no fool—she knew that it would not be easy. Her simple prayer was that they would make it. All of them.

After several hours of travel, they stopped for a midday meal. Clara and Elizabeth had packed a basket of sandwiches wrapped in brown paper and two jars of fruit preserves, which they shared together alongside the road. During this break, Clara checked some of the food crates, curious to see how her other carefully packed preserves were faring. Fortunately, not one jar had broken. Clara knew they would need to be consumed early in their journey or risk perishing, but she had not wanted to leave the carefully preserved foods behind.

"How long until we get to Paducah?" Ruth asked as they were loading back into the wagons.

Elizabeth laughed. "We'll get there when we get there. And if I were you, I wouldn't fret over how long any part of this trip will take."

"We'll be there before dark," Asa promised as he helped Clara into the wagon.

"Will we sleep in our wagon tonight?" Ruth asked Elizabeth as they began to rumble along again.

"Not tonight."

"Why not?" Ruth sounded disappointed now.

"Because your grandmother preferred we stay in a hotel."

"But I want to sleep in the wagon," Ruth protested.

"Trust me, dear daughter, you will have plenty of nights to sleep in the back of the wagon once we're on the Oregon Trail. Until then, you should just count your blessings."

"Uncle Matthew said he and Brady are going to sleep with the wagons tonight," Jamie informed her. "Can I stay with them?"

"I don't know…let me think about that." The idea of Jamie sleeping in the back of a wagon parked in a busy town like Paducah was a bit unsettling. Still, she knew that there would be many new challenges to face in the upcoming months. Perhaps she should simply get used to it.

It was just getting dark when they arrived in Paducah. They took the wagons directly to the livery stable that Asa had reserved with a telegram a couple of weeks ago. Then Clara took Ruth across the street to the hotel where they'd reserved rooms, and the fellows began to remove harnesses and yokes and see to the comforts of the livestock. Elizabeth, wanting to do her part, began to fill a feed bag.

"I'll do that, ma'am." Brady set down a harness and took the grain bucket from her.

"Looks like you folks must have quite a trip ahead of you," one of the stable hands said. "Going west?"

"We are," Asa confirmed as he tossed some more hay in front of the horses.

"Why don't you head on back to the hotel," Matthew told Elizabeth. "We can finish up from here."

"I want to do my share," she informed him. "The other livestock still need—"

"I'll help tend to them," Jamie told her in a grown-up–sounding voice. "And I'll take care of Flax too."

"We got plenty of hands here," Brady told her.

Asa nodded. "Go on ahead of us, Lizzie. You ladies can get yourselves some supper at the hotel and put our little Ruthie to bed. She looked mighty tired to me."

"What about you?" she asked.

"We'll get ourselves a bite to eat as soon as we finish up here. And don't you worry about Jamie. I'll get him safely to your room when we're done."

And so, feeling fairly tired and somewhat hungry, she decided to take her father's advice without protesting.

"It seems that life will be much simpler once we're actually on the Oregon Trail," Elizabeth told her mother as the three of them sat down at one of the dining tables.

"I s'pect it'll be simpler in some ways…harder in others." Clara smoothed a hand over the checkered tablecloth. "But it was a good day, don't you think?"

"Are you too worn out?" Elizabeth asked with concern.

Clara laughed. "Not at all. I enjoyed the trip."

"So did I," Ruth echoed.

The waitress came and began telling them their choices, and all three of them decided to have the fried chicken supper.

Elizabeth felt relieved. "And once we get on the riverboat, it should be somewhat relaxing."

"What's a riverboat like?" Ruth asked.

"The last time I was on a riverboat was about ten years ago," Clara told her. "But I will never forget it." She waved her hand and lowered her voice. "This hotel is very nice, but the riverboat your grandpa and I went on was even fancier. There were thick carpets and beautiful chandeliers and fine furnishings...Oh my, was it nice."

Ruth's eyes grew large. "Will our riverboat be like that?"

"I don't know for sure. But I guess we'll take what we get," Elizabeth answered.

"Well, your father booked our passage," Clara told Elizabeth. "If we don't care for the conditions, I suppose we'll let him know the reason why."

When their food came, Elizabeth said the blessing and thanked God for their safe journey thus far. Then, as they ate, they made plans for where they would shop in the morning. And just as they were finishing up, Asa and Jamie came in.

"Matthew and Brady insisted on staying with the wagons, and they're keeping Flax for their watchdog," Asa informed them.

"What about their dinner?" Clara asked with concern.

"Matthew had helped himself to a jar of peaches when we left, but we promised to bring them both some dinner."

"Here, take our table," Elizabeth said as she laid her napkin down.

"I recommend the fried chicken," Clara said as she stood.

"And I got an idea," Asa said as he sat. "Why don't you girls share a room tonight and Jamie can stay with me. That way you can set out to do your shopping whenever you want, and Jamie can help Matthew and me get the wagons over to the docks."

"But don't you need me to drive my wagon?"

"We got a plan all worked out," Asa assured her. "Starting first thing in the morning, we're going to take one wagon at a time. That way we can all help with the loading and make sure we get everything secured and the animals all settled in."

"But what about the provisions we still need to buy?" Elizabeth reminded him.

"That's right," Clara agreed. "We need to get them safely packed before—"

"We got that all figured out," he told her. "We'll park our wagon right in front of McCall's General Store. From what we hear, McCall's has the best prices in town. You gals can take your time and get what you need. Then get it all loaded by noon or thereabouts, and that will be the last wagon we take to the boat."

"Sounds like a good plan." Once again, Elizabeth wondered how she ever would have carried out a trip like this without the help of her father and brother. Thankfully, God must have known how much she needed them.

They finished their shopping before noon, easily finding everything that was on their list and many things that were not. "I hope we didn't buy too much," Elizabeth said as they packed the dried foods in airtight containers and stowed them into the pine crates.

"I don't see how we could possibly have too much food," Clara said as she secured a lid onto a tin. "If you're worried about the extra weight, most of it will probably be consumed by the time we reach the mountains."

"That's true." Elizabeth poured a bag of beans into a tin. "And we can always share with other passengers."

"Or use it to trade with."

"That's a lot of beans," Ruth said as she folded one of the empty burlap bags. "Are we really going to eat all of them?"

Elizabeth chuckled because she knew Ruth didn't care much for beans. "The list said to bring fifteen pounds of beans per person. We bought 120 pounds total, which was a bit more than needed, but like your grandmother said, we probably can't have too much food."

"And all that flour..." Ruth shook her head in wonder. "I never saw that much flour all at once. Will we really eat that many biscuits?"

"The list said 150 pounds of flour for each traveler," Elizabeth reminded her. "When we have time, we'll sit down and do the arithmetic on all of these things just so you can see how much it really is."

"I'm glad we hadn't done our shopping before Brady joined us," Clara said as she handed Elizabeth another bag of rice. "We might have run short."

"I don't think we'll ever run short," Ruth said. "All this food is filling up your wagon, Grandma." Ruth crawled to the back of the wagon to make room for Elizabeth as she filled another container.

"Well, I'd rather run out of almost anything but food." Clara pounded the lid of a crate firmly into place. "The men will hunt and fish along the way, but you can't always depend on that. Even though it's a lot of work, it's best to be prepared."

They continued working for nearly an hour and were finally closing the tailgate when Asa and Jamie came ambling down the boardwalk toward them. Elizabeth blinked at her son, imagining that he was growing up right before her eyes.

"We got the two other wagons all loaded onto the boat," Asa informed them. "Matthew stayed with them."

"To make sure no one steals anything," Jamie explained. "And Brady's tending the livestock."

"Matthew was worried about the firearms going missing," Asa told them. "Some disreputable types were milling around down there. But the captain assured us that once the hold was fully loaded, it would be locked down tight as a drum, and unless we're at port, no one is allowed in that part of the cargo area."

"But it's not locked up where the livestock stay," Jamie explained. "You're allowed to come and go down there as much as you like, in order to take care of your animals. But Brady has offered to stay with them for the whole trip."

"Brady's going to stay with the animals?" Elizabeth frowned.

"He said he preferred that to sleeping on the colored deck," Jamie told her. "And he already got a nice bed made of hay. And I got him some blankets from the wagon. And I told him we'd bring food to him."

"Oh..." Elizabeth nodded. Perhaps being with the animals was preferable to sleeping next to strangers on a crowded deck.

"And Brady asked me to put his savings in my safe place for him," Asa told her. "I also assured him that we would all continue to pay him a fair day's wage for a fair day's work. And he was much obliged, but he asked that we keep an account for him and then settle up when we get to Oregon."

"Thank you, Father. I had meant to extend that same offer to him."

"And Matthew and I will help him with the animals too," Jamie assured her. "And Brady said that Flax can stay down there with him. But I'll take him out for walks on the deck."

"Sounds like you have everything all figured out," Elizabeth told them.

"Now, unless you ladies have more shopping to do, I'd like to get this wagon down to the boat too," Asa said. "Matthew is holding us a place, but we can't keep him waiting."

"We've gotten everything on the list," Clara told him.

"And then some," Ruth added.

"Would you rather walk or ride?" Asa called out as he climbed into the wagon seat.

"How far is the dock from here?" Clara asked.

"Less than two miles."

"I think we should walk," Elizabeth decided. "But does that mean we have to carry our bags with us?" They had packed special bags of clothes to be used on the riverboat trip, but they weren't exactly light.

"No, we'll have those sent to your cabin for you," Asa told her as Jamie climbed into the seat beside him. "You ladies will share a cabin on the ladies' side of the boat."

"Ladies' side?"

"Oh, yes." Clara nodded. "I remember now. Unless you have a bridal cabin, which is quite expensive, the men and women have separate areas."

"Hold on there," Asa called out as he reached into his jacket pocket. "Don't forget these." He leaned down to hand Elizabeth the tickets and then gave them some quick directions to the dock. "You can't miss 'er," he said with a grin.

"She's called the *Princess Annabelle*," Jamie called out as Asa released the brake on the wagon and gently snapped the reins.

"*Princess Annabelle*," Ruth repeated with wonder as they began to walk. "What a pretty name."

As it turned out, the riverboat was just as pretty as her name, tall and white with two levels of cabins above the water's surface and an enormous red paddle wheel on the back. Crew and workers buzzed about the boat like bees on a hive, loading and unloading and cleaning and helping.

"This does look nice," Elizabeth said as they paused on the dock to admire it.

"Come on, Mama," Ruth urged, "let's get on."

Feeling like royalty, Elizabeth took Ruth's hand and looped arms with her mother, and the three of them marched up the gangway and onto the boat. "I hope this doesn't spoil us," she murmured.

Clara chuckled. "Might as well enjoy it while we can."

"Oh, my!" Elizabeth exclaimed as they went into a large room on the first deck. Carpeted with floral red rugs and furnished with red velvet chairs and couches, it was far more luxurious than she ever imagined.

"Look at the lights," Ruth whispered.

"Gas," Clara explained.

"Look at that." Ruth pointed to an enormous pastoral oil painting that filled up a whole wall.

"Very pretty." Elizabeth nodded and then glanced at a pair of women walking past them. One was dressed in an elegant periwinkle blue velvet gown. The other wore a similar dress in a russet tone.

"And look at the ceiling!" Ruth pointed to the ornate moldings. "Is that real gold, Mama?"

"I don't know for sure."

Ruth continued to gush over the furnishings, and Elizabeth turned to her mother. "Look how finely the passengers are dressed," she quietly told her. "I feel like a hayseed in comparison."

"Perhaps we should go to our cabin and freshen up," Clara suggested.

Just then a steward appeared, asking if they needed directions. Elizabeth showed them their tickets, and they soon found themselves standing in a lovely stateroom, furnished similarly to the rest of the boat.

"I can sleep here." Ruth flopped down on the velvet-covered couch by the window. "You and Grandma can have the big bed."

"Here are our bags," Clara announced.

Before long, they had unpacked and freshened their dresses. "If I had known we were going to be traveling in such style, I would have packed more festive clothes," Elizabeth said as she rebraided Ruth's hair. "I had no idea."

"What few festive clothes I brought are packed in the bottom of one of those crates," Clara said. "I suppose we shall just have to make do."

"If anyone asks us, we will simply tell them we're pioneers." Elizabeth laughed as she tied a blue ribbon around Ruth's braid. "Frontier women, about to go on a great adventure."

"Let's go out and have an adventure right now," Ruth suggested.

"You two go ahead," Clara said. "I think I will simply enjoy a little adventure right here on this nice little couch."

Elizabeth could hardly believe they had a little more than two weeks to spend on this lavish riverboat. It just didn't seem right. What if they became so spoiled by these luxuries that the deprivations of the Oregon Trail seemed much worse by comparison? What if they all became soft?

"Let's walk around the decks," she told Ruth. "We need to keep ourselves strong for the trip ahead."

Ruth didn't complain. But as they walked around the riverboat, going up and down stairs and around the various decks, Elizabeth began to see that there were all sorts of influences aboard this boat. And she suspected that many of them were not particularly good.

"Excuse me, ma'am." An officer stopped her as they came around a corner. "You and your little girl should not be down here."

"Oh?" She blinked. "We were just trying to stretch her legs."

"Stretch them on the upper deck," he sternly told her.

She nodded. "We'll do that. Thank you."

By the time they returned to the cabin, she had decided that under no circumstances would Ruth be allowed to roam freely on this boat. She'd seen enough debauchery, including drunken men and ill-clad ladies, to convince her that a riverboat was not a wholesome place for children. She would make certain that her father and brother understood this in regard to Jamie too.

In fact, despite the glitter and glitz of the *Princess Annabelle*, Elizabeth would be greatly relieved when this portion of their journey came to an end. She looked forward to being on the Oregon Trail more than ever now. She imagined the wagon train, where people would be decent and hardworking—like herself and her family. They would have a sense of kinship and purpose, like a big family. Perhaps they would have a church of sorts or at least sing hymns and pray together. Compared to this riverboat, it would be heavenly.

Chapter Eleven

Fortunately, Elizabeth discovered that when she and the children stayed to their own deck, there was much less riffraff to rub elbows with on the *Princess Annabelle*. Certainly, there were some who looked to be gamblers, but they were well dressed and relatively polite, and they didn't usually emerge until later in the day. The same was true with some of the questionable ladies. As a result, Elizabeth created a schedule for how they spent their time.

She insisted the children get up early, and while the boat remained fairly calm and quiet, they would walk around the upper decks with Flax and their grandmother for at least an hour. During this time, they would discuss the river towns they were passing by and consult with their map. Jamie was sometimes excused from this activity when he joined Matthew and Brady in caring for their livestock below.

Following their constitutionals they would have breakfast, and after attending to their various chores on the boat, which included washing their clothes and cleaning their cabins, they would then settle themselves at one of the big round tables in the dining hall and do their schooling.

Elizabeth had purchased all their books from the school in Selma, and she intended to keep Jamie and Ruth on track throughout the upcoming months. "But if you get ahead of your lessons during the boat trip," she promised, "we might not need to have school every day while we're on the Oregon Trail." The idea of an early vacation from studies seemed incentive enough, and the children worked hard. Besides, they soon discovered that the schoolwork was a good way to fill the time.

Elizabeth focused much of their schoolwork on their travels. Whether it was arithmetic, geography, or writing, she tried to relate their studies to their journey. They calculated mileage and dates. They wrote poems about the landscape and rivers. They drew maps of Kentucky and Missouri, including the Ohio River, where their journey began, and then the mighty Mississippi River, which they navigated for nearly one hundred miles, and finally, after passing the large city of St. Louis less than halfway through their riverboat trip, the Missouri River.

After their schoolwork was done and following another constitutional around the upper deck, usually with Flax joining them, they would all have an early supper. Then Elizabeth and Ruth would retreat to the cabin for reading or drawing or writing in their journals until bedtime. Meanwhile Jamie would take Brady his supper and help with the livestock for an hour or so before joining Elizabeth and Ruth in the stateroom.

Elizabeth understood that Matthew and her parents enjoyed staying up later, mixing with the other travelers, absorbing the color, and enjoying the music. The riverboat became louder and livelier after stopping in St. Louis, and sometimes Elizabeth felt she was missing out on some of the fun. But for the most part, she was content to remain with the children in the stateroom.

However, there were times when she found some of the grown-ups' activities a bit disturbing. It hadn't taken long to realize that gambling, drinking, and flamboyantly dressed women could spell trouble. Not that her family participated in that sort of thing. At least she hoped not…although she couldn't be absolutely sure about her brother. It made Elizabeth uneasy knowing about such goings-on, and she was thankful to have her children safely with her. And eventually her mother would grow weary of the noise, and Asa would take Jamie back to his cabin for the night.

Traveling by riverboat wasn't an ideal existence, but Elizabeth reminded herself it was getting them ever closer to the jumping-off place. And before long, it would simply be a memory.

"Six more days," Elizabeth announced toward the end of February. They had just sat down to their schoolwork, and she was studying the map and the calendar, secretly wishing that they were closer to Kansas City by now. "We will pass by Booneville today," she said absently. The children simply nodded, focusing on the lessons in front of them. It was clear that the charm of riverboat travel had worn off with the children as well as with her. Even her parents seemed bored and restless. And Matthew was growing concerned that the livestock could be suffering from lack of exercise. It seemed that all of them were eager to begin the next part of their journey.

"Are you part of that family that's going to the Oregon Territory?" a tall, dark-haired woman asked Elizabeth.

"Yes," Elizabeth told her. "We're the Martins." She introduced herself and the children.

"Pleased to meet you. I'm Florence Flanders." She extended her hand. "My kin and I are headed for Kansas City and the Oregon Trail."

"I'm so pleased to meet you." Still clasping Florence's large, rough hand, Elizabeth stood and looked directly into her gray eyes. She looked to be a few years older than Elizabeth. "Do you have children too, Florence?"

"My friends call me Flo. And I sure do have children." Flo nodded toward the door. "Them being so excited to explore this big ol' boat, I ain't even sure of their whereabouts now."

"Oh..." Elizabeth tried not to appear too concerned.

"We all boarded last night from Columbia. It was pert near midnight when we got on, but I insisted everyone go direct to bed. Now I s'pect them youngins are running about the place like a buncha wild Injuns."

"Mama says the riverboat is no place for children to run unattended," Ruth proclaimed like a wise little old lady.

Flo laughed. "Oh, well, I'm sure no harm will come of it."

"It's just that there are some...well, shall I say unsavory types on this boat." Elizabeth made an apologetic smile.

Flo nodded. "I know just what you mean. We noticed some of them unsavory types when we boarded." She frowned. "Two gamblers got into a big ol' brawl. Land sakes, I thought for sure that one of them was going to be killed right before my own eyes!"

"Oh, my!" Elizabeth was shocked. "And they say they don't allow gambling."

"Well, the cap'n threw them both off."

"He threw them overboard?" Jamie asked with wide eyes.

"No, he made 'em get off while we were still docked in Columbia. But I've heard tell of folks bein' thrown off, right into the Missouri River—that is, if they're overly misbehaving," she said somberly.

"What ages are your children?" Elizabeth asked, mostly to change the subject.

"My eldest is eighteen and the baby just turned eight."

"I'm eight," Ruth said proudly.

"Same age as my Tillie," Flo told her.

"You have a girl? And she's eight like me?" Ruth's eyes lit up.

"I'm sure she'll be pleased to meet you." Now Flo turned to Jamie. "And my boy Walter, he's eleven. I'll wager that's about your age."

"I'll be twelve soon," he told her.

"How many children do you have?" Elizabeth asked.

"Five altogether," Flo told her. "Mahala's nearly eighteen and Ezra's sixteen but big as a man. Hannah's thirteen but dependable. And, as afore mentioned, Walter and Tillie." She waved to a large bearded man just coming into the room. "And that there's my Bert. Come on over here and meet our new friends," she called to him.

After introducing Elizabeth and the children to Bert, Flo inquired about Elizabeth's husband.

"I'm a widow," Elizabeth told her.

"A widow?" Flo's thin brows arched. "You're taking youngins to Oregon country all on your own?"

Elizabeth quickly explained about her brother and parents.

"Oh, well, that's a relief. For the life of me, I cannot imagine how a lone widow and youngins would fare on such a journey." She shook her head. "I still can't fathom how my Bert talked me into this scheme. But the youngins were raring to go. And then, of course, there's the lure of free land."

Before long, the Flanders' children began wandering in, and the schoolwork was set aside as more introductions were made. Ruth and Tillie seemed to hit it right off. But Walter and Jamie barely spoke. Then Jamie spied his grandpa and asked to be excused to go help with the livestock. "I promised Uncle Matthew and Grandpa I'd help with the livestock this afternoon. Grandpa wants to walk them around some. We'll do it every day until we get to Kansas City—so they can stretch their legs."

"That's a very good idea," Elizabeth told him. "You run along now."

"Walking the livestock?" Flo looked confused. "Are you folks working for your passage on the river?"

"No..." Elizabeth smiled. "Jamie is helping to tend our own animals. And I'm afraid this long trip might be taking a toll on them. As far as I'm concerned, we won't deport from this boat one day too soon."

"You're transporting your own livestock by riverboat?" Bert rubbed his chin. "That musta cost someone a pretty penny."

"We're farmers," she explained. "And I suppose we're rather attached to our animals. Also, bringing our own teams allowed us to bring our loaded wagons from our homes."

"You got fully loaded prairie schooners on this here riverboat?" Flo asked in disbelief.

Elizabeth nodded. "Yes. We debated over this a fair amount among ourselves. But eventually it seemed the best plan. Hopefully we won't regret it."

"Surely y'all know you can purchase whatever you need in Kansas City." Bert studied her with a creased brow. "You jus' jump off the boat and there are wagons and teams and tools and mos' anything you want. Right there. You load 'em up and head on out. Nice and neat. That's what we plan to do."

"Yes, my brother might have agreed with you on that, but as I said, we were already farming our land and fairly well set with livestock and wagons and such. It seemed senseless to sell everything and then be forced to purchase the exact same things all over again." She smiled at him. "Tell me, Mr. Flanders, how do you make your living?"

"Bert is a blacksmith," Flo said proudly.

"Now that's a wonderful skill to bring on an overland journey. I do hope that you folks will be joining our wagon train. My father and brother would be so glad to know a blacksmith is in our party. We'll be traveling with Captain Brownlee."

"Captain Brownlee?" Flo repeated the name thoughtfully. "Do we know what party we're going with, Bert?"

He scratched his head. "Nah, we'll figure it out when we get there."

Now they began to discuss their final destination, and it seemed that the Flanders had not completely made up their minds about that either.

"'Ceptin' we do want to go all the way west," Bert assured her. "From what I heard, the best land is way out there in the far West, and we don't plan to settle for less than the best." He grinned at his wife. "Do we?"

Flo shrugged as if uncertain. "I jus' want a nice patch of lush green land and some big ol' shade trees to sit under. I s'pect that's not too much to ask for…once we get out West."

"I don't think that's too much to ask," Elizabeth assured her. "From what I hear, there's plenty of that to go around."

Chapter Twelve

When it was time to unload the wagons and livestock, Elizabeth was more thankful than ever that Brady had come with them. The task ahead seemed daunting, and an extra pair of hands would be invaluable. It was somewhat reassuring that her father and brother appeared unconcerned. They had decided to hold back from unloading, allowing anxious passengers, including the Flanders family, to rush from the boat like scared rabbits. Dashing off in pursuit of prairie schooners and teams and supplies, they gave the distinct impression that there might not be enough to go around. This made Elizabeth somewhat uneasy.

And with the unseasonably warm day and spring sunshine, Elizabeth worried that some of the wagon trains might already be hitched up and ready to roll away on the prairie by now. They all knew that the only thing stopping overland travel was the lack of good grazing land for livestock. And the only thing stopping good grazing land was bad weather. Despite it being late March, they hadn't had bad weather for nearly a week now.

Asa's plan had been to bide their time today, waiting until things quieted down on the riverboat so they could unload their wagons and livestock in a controlled and careful manner. It had seemed a good plan last night, but standing here in the sunshine today, Elizabeth felt her patience wearing thin.

"When can we get off?" Ruth asked as the three women watched from an upper deck.

"Soon, I hope." Elizabeth peered down to where a large piece of machinery was slowly but steadily being unloaded from the cargo hold. "I told Grandpa we'd wait until he gave us the go-ahead."

"And then will we go on the Oregon Trail?" Ruth asked.

"Not right away," Elizabeth told her. "First we have to find our group."

"How will we find them?"

"Your grandpa has it all figured out," Clara assured her. "Don't you fret."

Elizabeth patted the note in her skirt pocket. Her father had given her the names and details of where they would eventually meet up with their group this afternoon. Finally, after the unloading appeared to have slowed down significantly, Asa called up to announce they were about to start hitching up the teams. "It won't be long now," he promised.

"Do you need me to help with the wagons?" Elizabeth called back.

"No." He shook his head. "But we do need you womenfolk to disembark now. Like I told you last night, I want you to go on ahead of us. Follow the directions I gave you. Get to camp and find Captain Brownlee. Tell him we'll be there soon, and ask him where we should park the wagons for the night. Then you head back on down the same road, and we shouldn't be more than an hour or so away. You can lead us into camp, Lizzie."

Taking Ruth's hand in hers, Elizabeth nodded to her mother. "Here we go." They walked down the gangway, and as happy as she was to be finished with the *Princess Annabelle*, Elizabeth gave the boat a quick salute before they happily continued on their way. Once they were on the dock, Elizabeth pulled the paper from her pocket, peering at the hand-drawn map. "Looks like we go that way." She pointed to her right.

"The ground feels funny." Ruth stumbled, and Elizabeth gripped her hand more securely.

"Oh, my!" Clara tipped to one side. "I'm afraid we need to get our land legs beneath us now."

"Land legs?" Ruth looked confused.

"From being on the boat," Elizabeth explained. "Remember how you felt it rocking when we first got on it? And how you had to get used to it? Now you need to get used to the solid ground again." Tucking her note securely into her pocket, she grabbed her mother's hand too. "We'll help steady each other." They laughed as they tottered along, slowly making their way down the dock and onto a crowded street.

"Look at all the people," Ruth said as they began to make their way through the throng.

"Just like a herd of cattle." Clara sniffed. "And nearly as smelly."

Ruth laughed.

Elizabeth looked at the frantic people scrambling about from stores to vendors, some carrying bags, some looking lost. "I'm so thankful our wagons are already loaded," she said to her mother.

Clara just nodded. "I hope the livestock are fit enough to get the wagons and the men off the boat safely."

An unwanted image flashed in Elizabeth's mind—confused horses getting spooked and an overturned wagon. Someone could be hurt. She stopped walking, and looking at her mother and Ruth, she said, "Let's pray for them to get safely off the boat." And so, standing right there in the middle of a busy street, the three of them bowed their heads and prayed. Feeling somewhat consoled as they said amen, Elizabeth looked up and saw the name of the street ahead. "That's Oak Street," she told them. "We're supposed to go north there."

"Which way is north?" Ruth asked.

Elizabeth looked back toward the river and then at the sun's angle, finally pointing to her right. "That way."

They walked past more stores and through more crowds of people, and the farther they got from town, the more covered wagons they saw. There were hundreds of them—some parked, some on the move.

"My word," Clara said. "Will you look at all those prairie schooners!"

"All that white canvas reminds me of when the sky is full of clouds," Elizabeth observed.

"I think it's pretty," Ruth said.

"We go down this street for about a mile," Elizabeth told them. "Then we should come to a road. We take a left on it and stay on that road for another mile."

"Two more miles to walk?" Clara sounded surprised.

"There'll be a lot more of that once we start on the trail," Elizabeth reminded her.

After a good hour, they finally found a sign that gave Elizabeth hope. "Read that," she told Ruth.

"Captain Brownlee's Party Ahead," Ruth proclaimed.

"That's our party," Elizabeth told them.

"How many wagons do you suppose will be in our group?" Clara asked.

"Father said it would be around fifty."

"Fifty wagons!" Ruth's eyes got wide. "That'll be a long train."

"I doubt that they'll all be going to the far West," Elizabeth explained as they walked through the camp. "But just imagine," she said quietly, "these people you see right now—out here working on their wagons, mending harnesses, feeding their animals, fixing food, doing their washing—these same people will become our neighbors, Ruth. Like a big traveling town."

"You women lost?" a heavyset older woman demanded as she approached them, wiping her hands on a grubby apron.

"No, but thank you," Elizabeth replied. "We're looking for Captain Brownlee."

The woman scowled. "Where's your wagon?"

"Oh, don't worry about that," Elizabeth assured her. "Do you know where I can find Captain—"

"Are you *signed up* for this wagon train?" the woman asked with a skeptical expression. "Because this wagon train is already more than full up. And we're about ready to go. You can't just sashay in here with a pretty smile and expect to join up at the eleventh hour."

"I beg your pardon." Elizabeth stood to her full height, several inches taller than this rude woman. "I am here to see Captain Brownlee. If you don't know his whereabouts, will you please excuse—"

"Can I help you?"

Elizabeth turned to see a long-legged man swinging gracefully down from a tall Appaloosa. With his dark shaggy hair and fringed buckskins, she thought for a moment that he was an Indian. But upon closer inspection, she thought perhaps she was wrong. "Excuse me?" she said to him.

"Can I help you?" he said again.

The portly woman stepped in between them now. "These women just showed up and they seem to think they're gonna join our wagon train," she told the dark-haired man. "But, as you can see, they ain't even got a wagon. I was just trying to find out if they were lost or something."

"Are you lost?" the man asked Elizabeth.

"I don't believe I am," she told him. "My father has been in contact with the captain."

"What's your father's name?"

"Asa Dawson," Clara said importantly. "I am Mrs. Dawson. And I assure you that my husband Asa has—"

"Ah, the Dawson party." He nodded. "We have the Dawsons down for two wagons. And we're still waiting for the Martin party."

"I am the Martin party," Elizabeth told him.

His dark brows went up. "You're traveling by yourself?"

"No good'll come of that," the nosy woman declared. "A lone woman on a—"

"I'm not alone," Elizabeth told her.

"That's right," Ruth declared. "Mama's not alone. Me and my brother are going with her."

"A lone woman with youngins!" The intrusive woman shook her head and grumbled. "Nothing but trouble."

"Elizabeth is not traveling alone," Clara said to the woman. Then she turned to the man. "She has her parents and her brother as well."

"And Brady," Ruth said importantly. "And Flax too. He's our dog."

The man looked slightly amused but then grew more serious as he turned back to Elizabeth. "Who is driving your wagon?"

"I am," she told him.

He frowned. "Do you know how to drive a team?"

"I do." She looked evenly at him. He might have been a few inches taller than her, but she felt she could stand up to him. "I assure you I will not be a problem."

"What will you do when you break down?" the woman asked. "You know how to change a wagon wheel? Can you fix a broken axle?"

"Her father and her brother and Brady will help her," Clara told the woman.

The man frowned and then looked over her shoulder. "And where's the rest of your party, ma'am? And your wagons?"

"They're unloading them from the riverboat."

"You brought your wagons by boat?" Now the woman actually laughed.

Ignoring her, Elizabeth turned back to the man. "You know our names, but we don't know who you are."

He nodded. "My apologies, ma'am. Name is Eli Kincaid. I'm the scout for this wagon train."

Now Elizabeth explained about coming ahead of the wagons. "My father wanted me to find out where they should camp the wagons. I was going back to meet them on the road and direct them. We're concerned for our animals. They were more than two weeks on the river and—"

"You're bringing stoved-up animals with you?" The woman pursed her lips.

Elizabeth was fed up with this woman, but trying hard not to show it. "I'm sorry," she said tersely. "But I don't even know you. I am trying to talk to Mr. Kincaid about our arrangements, and I do not see how that has anything to do with you."

"Nothing to do with me?" It was clear this busybody was mad now. "I'll have you know that everybody on this here wagon train has something to do with everybody else. If you are the weakest link, and I'll wager you are, you could put the rest of us in serious peril." She shook her finger at Elizabeth. "If this train gets slowed down by folks trying to take care of you and your youngins, you'll be putting all of us in danger. And if you don't respect that, you don't belong here."

Elizabeth blinked, trying to gauge her words and not wanting to set a bad example for Ruth. "I do respect that. But you don't know me, and you have no right to judge me."

"That's right," Clara said. "Elizabeth is a very responsible woman. She's been running her own farm. And, like we keep trying to tell you, she is *not* traveling alone. She has her whole family backing her."

"Why don't you let me handle this, Gertrude?" Mr. Kincaid smiled at the older woman, revealing a nice even set of white teeth. "We appreciate your concern for the well-being of this train, but you can best serve by tending to your own campsite." He nodded over to where a couple of adolescent boys were having a knife-throwing contest, using a bucket on the side of a wagon as a target. To Elizabeth's relief, the woman huffed off.

"Thank you." Elizabeth let out a little sigh.

"Gertrude tends to speak her mind. But she's not a bad person."

"No, I don't expect she is. But right now I'd like to go meet the wagons and direct them. Where would you like them to park, Mr. Kincaid?"

"I don't cotton much to 'mister.' Just call me Eli."

"Fine." She nodded. "Where would you like my family to camp our wagons and livestock?" Elizabeth looked around the already crowded camp. "And when do you expect the wagon train to depart?"

"I'm not sure of the exact day yet, but it's getting closer. I'm leaving first thing in the morning to see how the grasslands are looking. Everyone thinks just because the sun is shining, we should be on our way. But weather can be misleading. My best guess is that we still have a week for the grass to get tall enough." Now he walked them over to the edge of the other campers to show them where they should park the wagons. He also told them a few rules of the wagon train, which sounded just like common decency to Elizabeth.

She thanked him, and after he left, she and Clara and Ruth walked through their campsite, picking spots for the wagons and a larger area where they could pen up the livestock by running ropes between the trees. "Why don't you two rest here." Elizabeth pointed to a log that looked like it might double as a bench. "I'll go find the men."

As she walked past Gertrude's campsite, Elizabeth still felt slightly rankled at the intrusive woman. She wondered what made a person act so persnickety and mean. Elizabeth hoped they wouldn't cross paths too much during their travels. With a wagon train this size, it seemed a realistic expectation. Now she thought about Mr. Kincaid, or Eli as he preferred. A bit rough around the edges, but he seemed nice enough. And he was well spoken and appeared kind and trustworthy. And yes, she had to admit to herself as she walked back toward town, he was handsome in a rugged sort of way.

Chapter Thirteen

It was late in the day by the time all three wagons were parked in the space allotted to them. Now the process of setting up camp was begun, and there was much to do. But first Elizabeth wanted to check on the animals.

"I'm glad we stopped off for hay and grain today," Asa told her as they worked together to remove a yoke. Despite having Brady's additional help, Elizabeth still felt responsible to contribute to the feeding and care of the livestock. And right now, thanks to Gertrude's acidic comments, she was particularly interested in the condition of her own team, which to her relief seemed to be fairly good.

"Good old Beau," Elizabeth said as she stroked the sleek black neck of her most beloved horse. She reached around to attach the feed bag. Percheron draft horses were still relatively rare in this country, a French breed that James had invested in a few years before his death. At the time, he had intended to purchase a colt and a filly in the hopes of raising Percherons, but the breeder had surprised him by sending a gelding and a mare instead. James had complained at first, even threatening to return the horses, but they were such beautiful animals, Elizabeth had encouraged him to keep them.

As it turned out, the Percherons were the most dependable draft horses on the farm. They were not only strong and intelligent but also exceedingly handsome. Elizabeth had even considered breeding Bella, the mare, with another one of her draft horses in hopes of securing mixed Percherons for the future. Perhaps she would pursue this further in Oregon.

"We can take care of this," Asa told her. "If you'd like, you could help Clara with supper. I know we're all hungry as bears."

She nodded. "I'm sure Mother will appreciate some help. I just wanted to see the horses for myself. They look to be in decent shape."

"Decent enough. But we will keep working them every day until we leave here. We want them in tip-top condition for the journey."

"And you'll shop for more?" She ran her hand over Bella's smooth back, wondering what months beneath the yoke would do to this fine mare. Elizabeth hoped they would have enough stock to give Bella and Beau breaks along the way.

"The man we bought feed from is going to show us some stock tomorrow. He told me he has a pair of draft mules that are well broken in and good with horses."

"You've always been a good judge of horses." She ran a hand through Jamie's dark curls as he stooped to lay down a harness. "You look tired, son."

He stood up straight. "I'm not tired."

She instantly realized her mistake. Jamie was working with the men and probably wanted to be treated like one. She simply nodded. "I'll go see to supper now." She chuckled to herself as she returned to the wagons. By the time they reached Oregon, Jamie would probably be a full-grown man. Or at least he would think he was.

"How's it coming?" she asked as she joined her mother by the fire.

"I got some things unloaded," Clara told her. "And Ruthie's been bringing us water." She pointed to the big kettle on the grill over the fire. "I've got some heating."

"Here's more water," Ruth said as she carried the canvas bucket over to them, sloshing some of it over. "Oops."

"Let me help." Elizabeth took it from her. "Are we using these for holding water?" She pointed to a storage barrel attached to the side of the wagon.

"Yes. The one with the spigot is for water."

After she poured the water into the barrel, she glanced around the various boxes and storage bins that were piled around. "What can I do to help?"

"I've got beans soaking and some bacon to go with them. I thought we might throw in some tomato preserves, and I've chopped an onion. Do you want to make some biscuits?"

"Certainly." Elizabeth frowned at the folded metal box that was supposed to act as an oven. "I'm curious to find out if that contraption really works. Do we set it directly over the fire, or will that be too hot?"

"That's my best guess, but I reckon we'll learn as we go, Lizzie."

Elizabeth unfolded the portable oven and made room for it by the kettle.

"Well, at least if you burn the biscuits, we'll have berry jam to put on them," Ruth said cheerfully.

"And tomorrow we can shop for some fresh foods like butter and eggs," Clara said. "I know perishables won't last long on the trail, but it might be nice to start out with them."

As Elizabeth mixed the biscuits, she called to her mother. "This is like a real trail supper, isn't it?"

"It sure is. I just hope the fellas won't be too disappointed."

Elizabeth laughed. "If they don't like it, you can tell them to go hunting and fishing."

"Not much they can hunt or fish around these parts."

"Want me to get some more water?" Ruth offered.

"Sure," Elizabeth told her. She appreciated Ruth's enthusiasm but wondered how long it would take for the newness of camp to wear off.

"Look for more firewood too," Clara called to her.

"Is supper ready?" Jamie asked as he came over to join them. "I'm starving."

"We're working on it," Elizabeth told him. "You can help by getting some chairs out for us. And that folding table that Matthew made. I think I saw it hanging on the other side of Grandma's wagon."

"And when you're done with that, go see if you can find more firewood," Clara called from where she was setting a pot on the fire.

"Can you get out some lanterns too?" Elizabeth called to Jamie. "It'll be getting dark soon."

Their campsite wasn't perfect, the beans were a little tough, and the biscuits were slightly scorched, but as they sat around after supper, eating fruit preserves and drinking coffee with the campfire crackling and kerosene lanterns burning cheerily on the table, Elizabeth thought it was rather a homely sight. "Our first night in a real camp," she said quietly. "It's rather exciting, isn't it?"

"It'll be more exciting when we're out on the Oregon Trail proper," Matthew told her.

"More coffee?" Clara offered as she used a cloth to pick up the enamel pot. "There's at least two cups left."

"I'll have some of that." Asa held out his cup.

Ruth stood up suddenly. "Will you play the fiddle for us, Uncle Matthew?"

"Oh, I don't know."

"Come on," Elizabeth urged as she tossed another piece of wood onto the fire.

Brady held up his harmonica. "I'll play some too," he offered. "If Mr. Matthew will get out his fiddle."

"I'll sing," Ruth said.

Before long, they were all singing along and clapping to Matthew's fiddle and Brady's harmonica. Elizabeth noticed that some of their fellow campers were wandering by, watching them from the shadows. She was tempted to invite their neighbors in, but it was late, and she needed to get their wagon ready for bed. She didn't want to keep Jamie and Ruth up too late because tomorrow would be a busy day. However, she reminded herself, there would be plenty more times to invite others to join them—about six months' time.

Elizabeth could hear people stirring outside while it was still dark, but judging by the gray light in the eastern sky, dawn was not far off. She had not slept well. Sharing a bed with both Jamie and Ruth had been cozier than expected. Plus there were the strange night sounds, and Flax, tethered beneath the wagon, had barked a few times. Probably, like her, just getting used to the new surroundings.

She lay there for a while, imagining she was going to snag a few more minutes of sleep. But eventually her stiff back got the best of her, and longing to stretch, she wiggled her way out of bed. Trying not to disturb Ruth in the tight space and dim light, she managed to pull on her shirtwaist and skirt. Then, crawling out of the wagon and stepping onto the barrel they'd placed to use as a step, she proceeded to button and fasten her clothing, hoping that no one was watching.

This getting dressed and undressed in the covered wagon was proving more of a challenge than expected. And she wondered if she would eventually opt to sleep in her clothes, just as Jamie had insisted on doing last night. According to her son, that's what men did out on the trail. She planned to ask her mother about this later.

She was just buttoning up her shoes when Matthew ventured past her with a load of firewood. "Morning, sis," he said. "How'd ya sleep?"

"As well as can be expected," she told him, "when you're sleeping with children."

He chuckled. "We can rig up a hammock for Jamie if you like. He could sleep with Flax underneath the wagon."

Elizabeth had been opposed to this idea before. "We'll see," she muttered as she attempted to smooth her hair back into a presentable bun.

"I reckon it'll get easier when we get our routines down some," he told her. "Out on the trail." He knelt down to stack the wood by the fire pit in front of his parents' wagon. "Hankering after some coffee. Any chance you can make some?"

"You make the fire and I'll make the coffee."

"I thought we should get an early start today. Lots to do, and from what I heard, this wagon train could be taking off any day now."

"Oh, I don't know about that." She opened the water spigot to fill the coffeepot with a bit of water and, giving it a quick rinse, dumped it out.

"What do you mean you don't know?"

"I met the scout yesterday. He sounded a little uncertain." She filled the pot up full. "He was heading out today to see how the grass was growing."

"But the weather's been good for a week. I'd think the grasslands would be good and lush by now."

"Eli said it might be nearly a week until it's time to leave."

"Eli?"

"That's his name. Eli Kincaid. And he seems like a smart man. I'm sure he knows what he's doing."

"Did you meet Captain Brownlee yet?"

"No." She turned the handle of the grinder round and round.

"We did." He lit a small pile of twigs with a match, blowing to get it going.

"Why do they call him captain? Is it because he's in charge of the wagon train?"

"No, it's because he was a captain in the US Army. Fought in the Mexican–American War."

"Oh." She poured the grounds into the basket, secured the top, and then took it over to where the fire was just starting to catch. "Does he seem like a good man?"

"He does to me. Pa said he came with high recommendations. He's led a wagon train to Oregon every year since leaving the military. I reckon that's about eight expeditions. So he should know what he's doing."

Elizabeth could hear others stirring now. "Matthew, I got to thinking about Brady last night," she said quietly. "I know you rigged him up a hammock to sleep in, but he brought so little with him. I think we should get him some extra pairs of boots and spare clothes and whatnot. But I'm not even sure what he might need."

"Want me to ask him?"

She nodded. "Yes. Then make me a list with sizes. Mother and I can get it while we're in town."

"I'm sure glad Brady decided to come like he did. I didn't realize how much we needed an extra man round here."

Elizabeth tried not to feel insulted by this. She knew that Matthew was probably bearing an unfair share of the workload already. And as much as she wanted to be useful with the horses and wagons, it probably made more sense for her to help with the women's chores...the cooking and washing and mending and such.

She already had bacon sizzling on the cast-iron griddle and was just mixing up pancake batter when her mother got up. "Sorry to have slept in," Clara told her as she buttoned the front of her knit jacket. "Chilly out here, isn't it?"

"Go warm yourself by the fire." Elizabeth handed her the bowl of batter. "I'm going to check on the children."

"Jamie's already up," Ruth said sleepily. "He and Flax went to get some firewood."

Elizabeth thought the idea of the dog helping gather wood was almost as entertaining as Jamie doing chores without being told to. "Well, you get yourself dressed and come out and help Grandma and me with breakfast."

Ruth yawned. "I slept good, Mama. I like camping."

Elizabeth smiled. "I'm glad to hear it."

They ate breakfast in shifts. First the men so they could work the teams for a while, getting them into shape for the trail. After that, Asa and Matthew would head to town to look at more draft animals. Brady offered to stay behind to keep an eye on the animals as well as their camp.

"I appreciate that," Matthew told Brady, nodding to his wagon. "You know what we got in there. And until we're on the trail, I don't care to leave it unattended much." He turned to Clara. "I don't expect we'll be home until supper, Ma."

"And I'm guessing we'll be plenty hungry by then." Asa grinned as he pulled on his felt hat.

Now Matthew handed Elizabeth a list. "Here's what you asked me for...for when you go shopping today."

She tucked it in her skirt pocket and then mixed up more pancake batter for her mother and Ruth and herself. With the fellows taken care of, they enjoyed a leisurely breakfast and then spent the next couple of hours getting their campsite into better shape. Ruth even found some wildflowers to put in a jar of water, which she placed on the tablecloth that she'd spread over the table.

"Very pretty," Elizabeth told her as they anchored the corners of the tablecloth with lanterns to keep it from blowing off.

"It feels good to get our housekeeping in order around here," Clara said as she strung a clothesline between their two wagons and hung some damp kitchen linens over it.

"We'll need to do laundry in the next day or so," Elizabeth pointed out. "It would be good to set out with that behind us."

"I agree. But today we'll do our best to stock up on food," Clara declared. "And tonight we'll have a supper that everyone will enjoy."

"Let me take the leftover bacon and hotcakes to Brady to eat for his midday meal." Elizabeth picked up the tin plate she'd covered with a piece of cheesecloth. "And then I'll be ready to go."

"What will we eat for our midday meal?" Ruth asked.

"I s'pect we'll find something to eat in town," Clara said.

Elizabeth found Brady with the livestock. He was trimming Beau's hoof. "Here's something for your dinner," she told him. "I'll set it here on this stump."

"Thank you, ma'am."

"And I hope you don't mind...I'm going to pick you up some things in town. Things that you'll need before this trip is over."

"Is that why Mr. Matthew asked me my shoe size?"

She smiled. "Yes. They say this journey can wear out three pair of boots."

He shook his head in disbelief. "Three pair of boots."

"We are all so glad you came with us, Brady. I hope you don't regret it." She carefully considered her next words. "Because if you have any second thoughts...if you think you'd be better off to stay behind...it's not too late to say so."

"Are you worried I'm not pulling my weight?"

"Not at all. The truth is we really need you, and I want you to go with us. But I also want you to know you are free to choose whatever is best for you. *Free*, Brady. And you have the papers to prove it."

"Well, I think it's too late, ma'am. I'm afraid I already got the fever."

She felt a rush of panic. "Fever? Are you feeling ill?"

He chuckled. "Not that kinda fever, ma'am. I think I got the *Oregon* fever. I want to see this new country too. Besides, you folks is like my family. I don't intend to stay behind."

She smiled. "Oh, that's such a relief. I just wanted to know you were coming with us because it was what you wanted."

"It's what I want, ma'am. You can be sure of that."

"You have a good day, Brady. We'll be off to town now." Feeling greatly relieved, Elizabeth walked back to the wagons. That was one of the concerns that had been nagging at her in the middle of the night last night. And she was glad she'd asked him about that. She knew this trip was going to be hard on all of them, but due to Brady's age as well as his skin color, it might be particularly hard on him. She planned to do whatever possible to keep it manageable. And she felt certain Matthew and the rest of her family were of the same mind.

Most of all, she was very happy to hear Brady was going with them for the very same reasons they were going—because he wanted to see this new country and because he felt like they were his family. That meant more to her than anything.

Chapter Fourteen

Thanks to Brady, the women wound up riding to town in Elizabeth's wagon. Before they could leave, he hurried over and insisted on hitching up the horses for her.

"You be doing these animals and your menfolk a favor," he assured her. "They need to be worked some. And town's a good spell from here. Besides that you need to get used to driving this wagon." He nodded with what seemed like pride. "It's not every woman can drive a team like this, ma'am. But it does take some work."

As Elizabeth maneuvered the wagon out of their campsite and through the grounds where so many other prairie schooners, livestock, and other animals were set up, she realized that Brady was right. This was good practice for her. And the team did need to be worked. It was much more challenging than just driving down a straight, even road.

By the time she got into town, her arms were a bit sore from all the stopping and going. But she figured it was a good sore and she'd best get used to it. "This is a busy, busy place," she said as she stopped to wait for a group of people to cross the street.

"I never saw so many people in my whole life," Ruth said.

"Or wagons," Clara added.

"I wonder if we'll even be able to find much to buy," Elizabeth said as she pulled the wagon up to where another wagon was leaving in front of a mercantile. "See how many people are shopping? You'd think there'd be nothing left."

However, once inside the mercantile, they discovered plenty of things to buy. Unfortunately for most of the shoppers, the main staples, like sugar, flour, rice, and beans were running low. But eggs, butter, and other perishables still seemed to be plentiful. They also stocked up on potatoes and onions and pickles as well as a number of other items they hadn't found in Selma or Paducah. "I'm glad Brady talked me into bringing the wagon," Elizabeth said as they loaded their purchases in the back.

"We never could have carried all this back to camp." Clara hefted a bag of potatoes up to Elizabeth, who was arranging things in the back of the wagon.

"Look, Mama." Ruth was pointing at a store window.

Elizabeth peered out the back of the wagon to see. "What?"

"*That!*" Ruth ran to the window of a music store and pointed at a beautiful wooden guitar.

"Oh?" Elizabeth wasn't sure what to make of this.

"Can we get that for Jamie?"

"For Jamie?" Elizabeth stowed the last parcel beneath the bedding.

"For his birthday," Ruth insisted.

Elizabeth eased herself down from the wagon.

"Jamie told me he wants a guitar," Ruth explained.

"When did this happen?"

"On the riverboat. Remember? We saw those men playing music.

Jamie liked the sound of the guitar, and he told me he wants to learn to play too."

Clara went over to peer at the guitar in the window, and Elizabeth, now curious, went to see for herself. "His birthday is only a week away," she admitted as she looked at the shiny amber instrument. It really was beautiful. "Are you sure your brother really wants a guitar?"

Ruth nodded eagerly.

"But he doesn't even know how to play."

"I know, but he wants to learn, Mama. Maybe Uncle Matthew can teach him."

"Uncle Matthew plays the fiddle."

Ruth just shrugged. But then she began hopping up and down, pointing at the guitar. "Look, it has our name on it, Mama!"

"What?"

"Down in that hole. Look!"

Clara and Elizabeth both bent down to peer inside the hole in the front of the guitar. Illuminated by the sun coming in the window, Elizabeth saw it too. "My word!"

"Well, that settles it." Clara stood up straight, nodding firmly. "That's what Jamie is getting for his twelfth birthday. Let's go."

Elizabeth started to stop her but then wondered why. Instead, she and Ruth followed her into the music store, where without further ado Clara asked the salesclerk to remove the guitar from the window.

"It's beautiful," Elizabeth said as she ran her hand over the sleek front of the guitar.

"That's spruce and rosewood," the salesclerk told them. He pointed to the glistening circle. "And that's abalone and ivory. This is a real nice instrument, ladies. Made by CF Martin in Nazareth, Pennsylvania."

"That's our name too," Ruth told him. "Martin."

He smiled. "Maybe you're related."

"Maybe." She nodded. "What does CF stand for?"

"Christian Frederick."

"My brother's name is James Theodore," she told him. "He'll be twelve on his birthday."

"Is this guitar too nice for a boy his age?" Elizabeth asked with uncertainty.

"Not if he is a musician." The clerk pointed to the guitar. "CF Martin started making musical instruments when he was only fifteen."

"Goodness." Clara shook her head.

"I began playing piano when I was six," the clerk told them. "And Mozart was a musical genius as a child. It's possible that your boy is a protégé too."

"I'm sure you're right," Clara said with confidence. "And I wish to purchase this CF Martin guitar." Before they left the music store, the savvy clerk talked Elizabeth into purchasing spare guitar strings, a music book, a tuning pipe, and a case.

Elizabeth knew the gift was extravagant and probably much too fine for the Oregon Trail, but she was glad her mother had gotten it. She just hoped that Ruth hadn't gotten mixed up about this. It would be a sad waste if Jamie had no interest in a guitar.

Next they went to a haberdashery. There, Elizabeth pulled out the list Matthew had made for her and handed it to a clerk. "We need sturdy, serviceable clothes that are fit for the Oregon Trail and a working man."

Before long, the clerk had a good-sized parcel wrapped up for Elizabeth, and Clara had even selected a few items for Asa. With their purchases made, they were ready to go have some lunch.

"This has been fun," Ruth said as they finished up their lunch with pie. "But I'm ready to go back to our wagon train now."

Clara and Elizabeth laughed.

"I like camping," Ruth said in defense.

"I'm glad you do," Elizabeth said as they got up to leave. "And I hope you still feel that way a few months from now."

Clara wanted to look in a dry-goods store before they left. "Just to see if they have anything new or interesting," she told Elizabeth. "This might be our last chance…"

Although Elizabeth felt like Ruth about returning to their camp, she knew her mother was right. It might be the last time they'd see a store like this for a very long time. And so they walked around the store and managed to find a number of things that they felt would be useful on the trail and in the far West.

"Now I'm ready to go home," Elizabeth said tiredly. The crowds and noise and busyness were starting to wear on her nerves.

"Home?" Clara sounded startled.

"Home to our wagon train," Elizabeth clarified as she released the wagon brakes and shook the reins, clicking her tongue. "Home is where the heart is, Mother."

"Let's sing," Ruth said happily.

Elizabeth pretended to be enthused as they sang, but she was really trying to stay focused on driving the wagon. There seemed even more wagons and horses and shoppers than this morning. If she never had to come back to Kansas City again, she would be only too happy. After what seemed like several hours, but was probably only one, she was turning the wagon by the sign that said Captain Brownlee's Party. "Here we are," she said with relief. "Almost home."

As they went past the entrance, Gertrude came out and peered curiously at them. Elizabeth, not wanting to make an enemy of this woman, just smiled and waved. "Good afternoon," she called out in a cheerful tone. If nothing else, Gertrude should be pleased to see that Elizabeth not only had a wagon and a team but that she could drive them too.

But Gertrude simply scowled.

Elizabeth suspected that nothing would please that woman. She hoped they would be distanced well apart in the train.

Brady must have heard them coming because he was ready and

waiting, eager to help Elizabeth park her wagon between the other two. It took a little maneuvering, but eventually they got it right.

"I'll take care of the team," Brady told her.

"Thank you. And we'll start on supper."

It wasn't long until the others arrived. As promised, they brought additional oxen as well as a pair of sturdy-looking draft mules. Elizabeth went out to inspect the livestock, but she could tell at a glance they weren't as good quality as their own animals. She wanted to question her father on this but couldn't think of a gracious way to ask.

"I know what you're thinking, daughter." Asa frowned.

"Really? What am I thinking?"

"These animals are second-rate."

She studied him. "Are they?"

"Second-rate compared to our stock. But compared to what's out there...well, they're far and above superior."

She shook her head grimly. "Imagine if we had not had the foresight to bring our own teams from Kentucky."

"I don't like to think of it." He sighed. "The wagons for sale were pretty picked over too. And the prices...*oh, my.*" He rubbed his chin. "The riverboat trip and the additional freight costs weren't small, that's for sure. But compared to what we would have paid out here, I'd say it was more than equitable. And I'm not even talking about quality now."

"I'm glad to hear that, but I should go help Mother with supper."

Asa made an uneasy chuckle. "I s'pect you can't wait to tell your mother about this. I hope you womenfolk won't be rubbing our noses in this."

She laughed. "Not at all, Father. But you can't blame us for being happy. And, if it makes you feel any better, we will be feasting tonight."

He smacked his lips. "That makes me feel much better."

Naturally, Clara enjoyed a good laugh over this recent turn of events, but she promised not to gloat over it. "Better to simply be thankful," she said as she turned the ham spit over the fire. "And now I must ask your permission to break a rule," she said quietly.

"Break a rule?" Elizabeth was confused. "You mean a wagon train rule?"

Clara chuckled. "No, nothing like that." She glanced around. "I know that Jamie's birthday isn't until next week, but right now we have more free time on our hands, and I would so love to give him his birthday present early."

Elizabeth nodded knowingly. "So he could learn to play some before we're on the trail?"

"Wouldn't that be nice?"

"I do believe that's a good idea, Mother."

"You don't mind?"

"Not a bit. It seems certain that we'll be on the trail by his birthday. No telling how exhausted we'll be by then. Why not celebrate now?"

They worked happily together, enjoying the variety of foods they'd found in town and putting together what turned out to be a veritable feast of ham, potatoes and gravy, green beans and bacon, buttermilk biscuits, and cherry cobbler with cream for dessert. Once again, the biscuits were scorched in places and a little underdone in others. But the cobbler, cooked in the cast-iron dutch oven, appeared to have turned out just right.

"You may not have known, but this is a celebration dinner," Clara said as she dished out the cobbler.

"What are we celebrating?" Matthew asked.

"Well, it's a little bit early..." Clara winked at Ruth, the prearranged signal that Ruth was to go and fetch the guitar case from the back of their wagon. "But Jamie has a birthday next week, and we decided to celebrate it tonight."

Jamie looked surprised. "My birthday?"

"Yes," Elizabeth told him. "I hope you don't mind."

He just shrugged.

"Here you go," Clara handed him a hefty serving of cobbler.

Ruth came out carrying what looked like a large burlap bag. As she got closer, she began singing "Happy Birthday" loudly. Everyone else joined in, and Jamie looked slightly embarrassed by this unexpected attention.

"This is from Grandma and Grandpa," she told her brother as she held out the sack.

"And you and your mother too," Clara reminded her.

Ruth nodded. "Yes. Some of it is from us too." She pushed it toward him. "Open it, Jamie."

Jamie reached for the bag and slowly opening it, reached inside. But before he pulled it out, his brown eyes got big. "What is this?" He pulled out the case and set it on his knees, fumbling with the latch. Finally, he opened the case, and Elizabeth thought his eyes were going to pop out of his head. "A guitar!" he cried. "A real guitar!"

Everyone laughed and clapped as Jamie attempted to play the instrument, although it sounded as if he had some work to do. Or perhaps just some tuning.

"There are a few other things in the bag," Elizabeth told him. "To help you learn to play."

"And I'll try to help you too," Matthew promised. "Although the guitar is probably a lot different than a fiddle."

Jamie happily thanked everyone, and after they finished dessert, the women cleaned up while Jamie and Matthew attempted to tune the guitar. Finally, after everything was cleared and put away, the fellows decided to have another musical session. Tonight Matthew played the fiddle, Brady played harmonica, and Jamie played the guitar as best he could. As Elizabeth tapped her toes to the music, she knew that not every night on the Oregon Trail would be this merry or energetic. She knew that there would be hard times ahead...times when no one would feel like singing. But for now, she intended to enjoy it!

Chapter Fifteen

The next two days passed without incident, but it was clear that fellow travelers were getting antsy. "When will we leave?" were the four most common words throughout the Brownlee camp. The problem was that no one seemed to know the answer. However, there were rumors circulating that other trains were departing. And this led to more anxiety as the waylaid travelers imagined that all the prairie grass would be devoured by the other trains before their train even made it out. The other big question was, where was Captain Brownlee? It seemed that no one had actually seen him.

"I know that Captain Brownlee knows what he's doing," Asa assured their camp at breakfast on the third morning of waiting. "I have complete faith in him."

"Have you ever met him?" Matthew asked with impatience.

"Not in person. But we corresponded with letters."

"You mean when you sent him your money?" Matthew asked.

"I did send him half of our payment," Asa admitted.

"What if Brownlee isn't even here?" Matthew questioned. "What if, after all our work to prepare for this trip, Brownlee has simply taken our money and run? What if we're sitting here while everyone else is on their way?"

"Hello to the camp!" boomed a loud voice.

They all looked to see a tall man wearing a dark-blue jacket approaching. "Is Asa Dawson here?"

"I'm Asa." He stood and went to meet the man.

"I'm Captain Brownlee."

Elizabeth nudged her brother with her elbow.

"Pleased to make your acquaintance," Asa told him, taking a moment to introduce the rest of his family. "We were just speaking of you."

The captain chuckled. "Not sure I care to hear what you were saying. I know that many of the emigrants are growing impatient. But I come with good news."

"Would you like some coffee?" Asa offered.

"Or some breakfast?" Clara added. "We have eggs and sausage."

His brows arched. "*Eggs and sausage?*"

"And hotcakes with jam and butter," Ruth said eagerly.

"And grits too." Elizabeth held up what was left in the pan.

"Well, well…." He rubbed his gray beard thoughtfully.

"I'll fix you a plate," Clara said as Asa offered him a chair.

"I'm making my rounds with all the wagons this morning," the captain explained. "Meeting everyone and letting them know that we'll leave at dawn two days from today. It's nearly two weeks earlier than last year. And that's right providential. An early start is always a good sign. My scout assures me the prairie grass will be ready by then."

"We heard that some trains have already left," Matthew said.

"That's true." The captain nodded as he chewed a bite.

"I was just assuring my son that you're experienced at these expeditions," Asa said somewhat apologetically. "I'm sure you know the best time to depart, Captain."

"I like to think so. If a party leaves too early, the stock suffers from too little food. Believe me, all sorts of trouble can result from malnourished animals by the end of the journey. Timing is everything in a successful overland trip."

Asa gave Matthew a knowing look. "Well, we're farmers, Captain, so we do understand the importance of caring for our livestock."

"I noticed you have some fine-looking animals." The captain forked into a piece of sausage. "And I can see you've taken care in preparing your wagons."

"Matthew was in charge of outfitting the wagons," Elizabeth told him.

"Nice work, son."

"Thank you."

He ate the last bite of his hotcake and then smiled at Clara. "Thank you for the fine breakfast, ma'am." Now he turned back to Asa. "As head of this family, I commend you. I wish all the emigrants were as well prepared as you. Unfortunately, that never happens."

"We saw a lot of folks scrambling to get wagons and teams in Kansas City this week." Asa shook his head. "I just hope they make it all the way out West."

"I do everything I can to ensure they do, but it's a rugged trip." He stood. "And that reminds me. A family wishes to join our party. They say they met you on the river. Flanders is the name."

"Oh, yes," Asa told them. "The blacksmith and his family."

"We can always use another smithy." Captain Brownlee's brow creased. "So, you recommend them?"

Asa looked conflicted. "Well, I barely know them, but they seem like good folks. And as you said, another blacksmith would probably be handy."

He nodded. "There will be a meeting today at four o'clock. Up on the knoll by the creek. If you don't know the time, just listen for the bell clanging. I expect all the travelers to attend." He tipped his faded brown hat and went on his way.

"Well, I reckon that answers your questions," Asa said to Matthew.

"I like the captain," Jamie declared.

"He does instill confidence." Clara picked up his empty plate.

"Two days from today," Elizabeth said happily. "And we'll be on our way."

Suddenly there seemed much to do, and everyone went about doing it. By three thirty, according to Elizabeth's watch, they all headed up to the knoll.

"I tied Flax to your wagon," Jamie told Matthew as they walked. "To be the watchdog."

"Good thinking," Matthew told him.

Although they arrived early, several dozen others were already congregated on the knoll. A short man banged on an iron triangle to make a loud clanging sound, and more families joined them. Most of the families looked to have children the ages of Jamie and Ruth…and older. To Elizabeth's surprise, there were a few couples who appeared much older than her parents. Some families looked well-off, and others seemed a bit down on their luck. It was quite an assortment.

Eventually the captain arrived, placing himself on the top of the knoll so that everyone could see him. By now Elizabeth estimated there were around three hundred people gathered. Quite a crowd, but they quieted down when they saw the captain was ready to speak. First he welcomed them. Then he went over the rules of the wagon train, which were not much different from the laws of the land, except that instead of a court of law, the wagon council would be the enforcer, and the punishment would be executed promptly. Most of the rules, especially in regard to carrying adequate supplies and firearms and care of draft animals, were familiar and simply common sense. But Elizabeth was glad that the crowd listened attentively.

"We will average fifteen miles a day except for Sundays, when we only travel for half a day. We water our animals when we stop to eat. Every man eighteen or older will take turns at guard duty. If a guard falls asleep, he will walk behind the wagons for a day." He paused. "Now I have mentioned the wagon council to you. I run my train like I run a regiment. I am the captain, but because we have more than sixty wagons on this train, with a total of two hundred eighty-seven people, I have divided the train into units. Each unit has about twelve wagons, and I will appoint one councilman to oversee each unit. My council is as follows."

He now proceeded to read the names of five men, and to Elizabeth's surprise, her father's name was among them. "These five council members will each have a list of about twelve wagons. These will be your traveling units for the duration of the trip. Councilmen can be changed only by my approval and a democratic vote of the unit. The units are numbered and will proceed in numerical order, which will rotate every Sunday."

The captain held up some pages. "Will all the councilmen please come forward?" After the men joined him on top of the knoll, the captain asked if any of them wished to decline this responsibility. After none refused, the captain made them raise their right hands and proceeded to swear them in. Elizabeth could see the pride and pleasure in her father's face as he vowed to do his duty as a councilman. Now the captain handed the newly appointed councilmen lists of names, and one by one they read them. Elizabeth listened closely as her father read. None of the names sounded familiar except for the Flanders.

"It will be up to the heads of the families to locate their councilman and introduce themselves," the captain told them. "Find your councilman's campsite before the day is over, and he will inform you as to where your unit will be gathering. Then I want all the units assembled in camp together before sundown tomorrow. That'll give you a chance to get acquainted." Then he thanked everyone for their patience, asked a blessing on their upcoming journey, and asked for the councilmen to remain afterward to meet with him for further instructions.

"Can you believe it?" Elizabeth said to her mother as they walked back to camp. "Father is a councilman."

"Asa will be a good councilman." Clara smiled. "He is a natural leader."

"Did you hear that the Flanders are in our group?" Matthew said. "That means we'll have a blacksmith close by."

"And Tillie," Ruth said happily.

"I'm gonna gather up some kindling." Brady pointed to an area where someone had been chopping wood but had left smaller pieces scattered all about. "I saw it there this morning," he said. "If'n no one wants it, we can put it to use."

"Good idea," Matthew told him. "I'll bring back something to carry it with."

"I like that we're in units of twelve wagons," Clara said as they neared their camp. "It will make it easier to get acquainted."

"If each wagon had four people, that would be forty-eight total," Jamie said.

Elizabeth patted his back. "Good multiplication."

"If there were six in each family, it would be seventy-two," he said.

"How does he do that so fast?" Ruth asked.

"Because he's older." Elizabeth reached for Ruth's hand, giving it a squeeze.

"And I made a decision," Jamie told her. "About my name."

"About your name?" Elizabeth turned to look at him.

"I'm too old to be called Jamie," he said. "That sounds like a baby."

"Oh..." She just nodded.

"And James is a good name, but it sounds like Pa's name to me."

"It was your father's name."

"I want to be called JT," he proclaimed.

"For James Theodore," Ruth said. "JT. I like it."

"JT," Elizabeth said slowly. "It sounds very grown-up."

"It's a good name," Matthew said. "I'm pleased to call you JT."

"Is that all right with you?" Jamie asked his mother.

She smiled. "Will you be upset if I sometimes forget and call you Jamie?"

He seemed to consider this. "Nah, mothers are allowed to make mistakes like that."

Clara laughed as they came to their wagons. "How about grandmothers?"

"Don't worry," he told her. "I'll still come if you call me Jamie."

"Come on, *JT*," Matthew called. "Let's grab some buckets and go give Brady a hand."

The women were just starting in on supper when Asa returned. He was all smiles. "I'm honored to be picked a councilman," he told them as he sat down by the table. "But it's a fair amount of work too."

"Do you want to decline?" Elizabeth asked.

"No. Not at all. I just don't want to let anyone down." He glanced around their campground. "Where are the fellas?"

Elizabeth explained about Brady and the kindling.

Asa frowned. "I would have thought I'd seen them on my way."

"I'm sure they'll be along—"

Just then they heard Jamie yell, "Grandpa! Come quick! Uncle Matthew needs you!"

Asa got up and took off.

"Ruth, you stay with Grandma," Elizabeth called as she ran after them. Passing her father, she was nearly catching Jamie when she saw a group gathered up ahead.

"This n----r stole my wood!" a red-faced man was yelling.

"Like I just told you, the wood is for everyone," Matthew yelled back. "It was left behind. We were just picking it up."

"I told my boy to come back and get that."

"It's been lying there all day," Matthew told him.

Elizabeth pushed her way through the onlookers, seeing that Brady was being held with his arms pinned behind his back by a young pimply-faced man. "What's going on here?" she demanded.

"You stay outta this," the red-faced man yelled at her. "Nonna your business."

Elizabeth walked over to Brady, looking the young man directly in the eyes. "You release him right now!"

"Pa?" the kid said.

"You hold tight!"

"You heard the woman," Asa huffed. "Let that man go."

"Pa?" the kid said again.

"Let him go," Asa said more firmly.

"Hey, that's one of the councilmen," someone said.

"Let him go! *Now!*" Elizabeth yelled right into the kid's face. The kid let him go, stepping back like he was worried Elizabeth was going to hit him.

"Is he your slave?" The red-faced man pointed a finger at her.

"Brady is *not* a slave," she said loud enough for everyone to hear. "He is a free man. And he's traveling to the Oregon Territory with my family and me."

"Where's his papers?" the red-faced man demanded.

"His papers are in a safe place," Asa told him in a calm but firm tone.

"I'll bet he's a runaway," the man said. "I'll bet we can turn him in for a reward."

Now Matthew stepped closer, glaring at him. "Brady is a free man. And you and your boy better keep your hands off of him. You hear?"

"He was stealing my wood!"

"That wood was there for the taking and you know it. You and your lazy boy left a mess behind, and it was up for grabs. The truth of the matter is that you were just spoiling for a fight, weren't you?"

Matthew shook a fist in his face. "But if you want a fight, don't go picking on an old man."

Elizabeth was ready to intervene but knew that would only aggravate her brother, and he seemed aggravated enough. She glanced at Asa, but he tossed her a warning look and just watched as the two men glared at each other.

"All right," Asa finally said with authority. "I think you folks have seen all there is to see, and I'm sure you have better things to do. Brady here is a free man, and we have papers to prove it." He pointed at the still angry man. "Now I don't want to have to report you to the captain before we've even hit the trail, but I know he don't take kindly to this kind of behavior."

The man said a foul word, and now Asa stepped up and, backed by Matthew, grabbed the man by the arm. "Seems to me you weren't listening to the rules today." He looked at the onlookers. "Anyone else listen to the rules? You all recall any rules prohibiting the use of coarse language or cussing in this community?"

"It's a finable offense," a woman called out.

"That's right." Asa nodded then turned back to the man. "Who's your councilman?"

"I dunno," the man mumbled.

Asa tilted his head to one side. "Well now, that is troubling. First you're caught picking a fight. Next you're caught swearing. Now you can't recall who your councilman is? I think you could just about get yourself thrown off this train before you're even started."

"Our councilman is Harris," the kid said quickly. "But, please, don't kick us off the train. We sold everything we own to come. My ma and the rest of us need to get to Oregon Territory. Please, sir. I'm sorry. I just did what my pa said to do."

Asa looked kindly upon him. "Well, you seem like a good boy. How old are you, son?"

"I'm eighteen."

"You think you're old enough to keep your pa in line?"

The boy looked perplexed.

"Eighteen's old enough to do guard duty," Asa told him. "How about you practice by doing some guard duty on your pa?"

The man growled, and the boy made an uneasy shrug. "I reckon I can try."

"I expect you to help keep him in line until he figures out the rules for himself."

The young man nodded.

"In the meantime, I will let Harris know about the infraction. What's your pa's name?"

The boy told him their names and, with his father in tow, quietly left. And now the crowd slowly dispersed as well.

"Come on," Elizabeth said to Brady. "Let's go back to camp."

"No," Matthew sharply told her. "Brady and I still want to get that wood. No sense letting it go to waste."

"That's right." Asa nodded to Brady. "You fellas get that wood, and I'll go speak to Harris about this matter."

As much as Elizabeth wanted to protect Brady and take him back to camp with her, she understood. This was a matter of male pride, and she had interfered. She turned to her son, but remembering he too was part of the "men's club," she refrained from grabbing his hand and dragging him back to camp with her. Instead, she considered her words. "I suppose you'll want to help the men with that wood, JT."

He gave her a lopsided grin, and she could tell he was pleased that she'd remembered to call him JT. "Don't be late for supper," she called as she left.

Before long she was back at their campsite, dramatically retelling the whole story for the sake of her mother and Ruth. "Father handled it so perfectly," she said finally. "I was very proud of him."

"Poor Brady." Clara dropped a peeled potato into the water. "I figured we'd run into some folks like that. I'm glad the men were around to defend him."

"I just wish I hadn't jumped in like I did," Elizabeth admitted. "But I was so mad."

"I probably would have done the same thing," Clara said.

"Me too," Ruth declared. "Nobody should be mean to our Brady just because he's colored."

"Well, your grandpa set them straight," Elizabeth said. "But I don't see how I can be expected to hold my tongue if something like that happens again. Woman or not, I will not sit idly by when there's injustice going on."

"It's not easy being a woman in a man's world," Clara said.

"This is our world too," Elizabeth reminded her.

"But you still have to respect their manly pride," her mother counseled.

Elizabeth sighed as she tied on her apron. "So I'm expected to be able to drive a team and fix a broken axle and protect and provide for my family just like a man, but at the same time I still have to play the little woman?"

Clara chuckled as she dropped another potato in the water. "I reckon it's a fine line, Lizzie. A fine line that only a strong, wise woman can walk. You'll figure it out."

Chapter Sixteen

It was Ruth's idea to make sugar cookies. "We can give one to every person in our unit," she explained to Elizabeth and Clara. "When they come to see Grandpa after dinner tonight, we'll surprise them with cookies." But she was a little concerned when Grandpa informed her that 37 people were in their unit.

"That's a lot of cookies." She looked at the bowl of dough she was stirring. "The recipe said this makes three dozen. How many is that, Grandma?"

Clara paused from slicing carrots. "That's a JT question."

"I'll help you." Elizabeth poured a handful of beans on the table. "You know that a dozen is twelve. Now just make three piles of twelve and count them."

Ruth did as told. "Thirty-six!"

"So it's almost enough dough?"

Ruth scooted one more bean over. "There. Thirty-seven."

"So you just make a few of the cookies a tiny bit smaller," Clara told her. "And you should have enough dough."

"The real trick will be getting them to bake right in our funny little oven," Elizabeth said. "First let's see if I can bake some cornbread without scorching it."

Thanks to some good coals and Ruth's diligent watching, the cookies turned out pretty good. "Maybe we'll put you in charge of the baking from now on," Elizabeth teased as she helped Ruth remove the hot baking sheets from the oven.

"Hello, Dawsons and Martins," called a woman's voice.

"Welcome, Flanders!" Asa got up to greet them, shaking Bert's hand.

"I made cookies," Ruth called out with excitement. "One for each."

Tillie came over to see. "Your ma lets you cook on the fire?"

Ruth nodded with a flushed face.

"With supervision," Elizabeth clarified.

"We don't let Tillie near the fire," Mahala, the oldest girl, told Elizabeth. "Too dangerous."

"Ruth really made those?" Hannah asked.

"She did," Clara told them. "Ruth helps us with all the cooking."

Tillie's lower lip stuck out. "Ruth is lucky."

Hannah laughed. "You think doing kitchen chores is lucky?"

"We'll start you on peeling potatoes if you promise not to cut yourself," Mahala told her.

Ruth counted out seven cookies on a plate and took them to Bert. "Here you go, Mr. Flanders," she said proudly. "One for each member of your family."

He thanked her, sharing the cookies with his brood. Then he chatted with Asa for a while, both of them smoking their pipes congenially.

"I'm glad you were able to join our party," Elizabeth told Flo. "Have you decided where you're going to settle yet?"

Flo just laughed. "I don't know for sure. Maybe we'll go all the way to the Pacific Ocean with you folks."

"If we don't run out of supplies first," Mahala said in a slightly bitter tone.

"Oh, Mahala." Flo frowned. "Always expecting the worst. Ever since she turned eighteen she's been acting like an old woman. I swear it won't be long till her hair turns gray."

"That's 'cause Mahala keeps worrying that she'll be an old maid," Hannah teased.

"A pretty girl like her?" Elizabeth smiled at Mahala. "I don't think so."

"She's too picky," Hannah said. Then she flitted over to where Matthew and JT were making music.

"From what I hear, there are more than enough men to go around in the West," Flo said quietly to Elizabeth. "I s'pect she'll find herself a man out there."

"There seem to be plenty of young fellows on this wagon train too." Elizabeth tried not to think about her encounter with the young man earlier.

"I think Mahala's already got her eye on someone," Flo confided to Elizabeth, nodding over to where Mahala was wandering toward the music makers. "She mentioned to me how your brother was both good-looking and smart."

"Oh?" Elizabeth tried not to look surprised. The idea of Mahala and Matthew had never occurred to her. "How old did you say Mahala is?"

"She turned eighteen last fall."

Elizabeth simply nodded. Certainly old enough to be considered marriageable.

"Have you met the Mullers yet?" Flo asked quietly.

"I don't believe so."

"That Gertrude..." Flo looked around to be sure no one was listening, but most of the children had drifted over to the music.

"Gertrude?" Elizabeth suddenly remembered the outspoken woman from their first day here. Her name was Gertrude.

"Gertrude is the wife," Flo said. "And, take it from me, she is one piece of work. And truly, I am a woman who can get along with most anyone. But that Gertrude..." She shook her head. "She's as prickly as a porcupine. And less manners than a polecat."

"I...uh...I think perhaps I did meet her." Elizabeth sighed. "She's in our unit?"

"She most certainly is. We parked our wagon by theirs the first day we got here, so we've been *neighbors*. And that Gertrude, well, she just picked us apart right from the get-go. First she tells me our team is no good, and then she swears our wagon won't make it over the plains in one piece. I just wish she'd mind her own business and let us be." She shook her head. "And those boys of hers are perfect hoodlums." She lowered her voice. "Well now, speak of the devil."

Elizabeth looked up to see Gertrude and the rest of her family coming into camp. Unsure of what to do, Elizabeth decided to just wait for her father to take the lead.

"Welcome," he hailed as he went to meet them, introducing himself to the husband, a pale, mousy man about half the size of his wife.

"I'm Henry Muller," he quietly said, "and this here is my bride, Gertrude."

Flo and Elizabeth exchanged amused glances.

"I go by Gertie." She shook Asa's hand. "And these are our children. Otis here is the oldest, just turned seventeen. That's Horace, he's fifteen. And Albert, the quiet one, he's twelve. And that there is MaryLou, the baby."

"I'm not a baby," the yellow-haired girl declared. "I'm ten years old."

Ruth, bless her heart, carried another plate of cookies, this time for the Mullers. "These are for you," she told Gertie. "One for each member of your family."

Gertie tilted her head to one side. "Didn't I meet you already?"

Ruth nodded politely. "You met me and Grandma and Mama that first day when we got here."

Now Elizabeth knew it was her turn to be hospitable. "Welcome to our camp." She smiled at Gertie as she linked her arm in her father's. "As you know, Asa is your councilman, but he's also my father."

Gertie seemed to be at a loss for words as Asa introduced the Mullers to the rest of his family. Then another group entered the camp, and soon Asa was distracted by a young couple—very young. But they seemed sweet.

"I'm Paddy McIntire," the young man said with a strong Irish accent. "And this is my wife, Fiona. We've only been in this fine country a few months. But we're on the way to the West for land." He sighed. "Aye, land…won't it be grand?" He nodded over to where the music was playing. "I've got me a fiddle," he told Asa. "And a drum as well. Fiona and I love music."

"I hope you'll join us for some sing-alongs," Asa told him.

"Aye, t'would be a pleasure. And won't we have a grand time of it too?"

A family named Schneider arrived. The parents spoke broken English with strong German accents, but the school-aged children, Anna and Jonas, spoke good English and had perfect manners. Jonas was the same age as Jamie and, after politely thanking Ruth for the cookie, went directly to where the music was being played.

The next two families were from Boston, but with so many people now crowding the campground, Elizabeth didn't manage to catch all their names. However, between the two families there seemed to be six or more adolescent children and three wagons. And it appeared the families were old friends. It also appeared that the Bostonians were rather wealthy and, although she didn't like to pass judgment, they had a slightly superior air about them, as if they felt above the other emigrants.

"I heard that one man's a lawyer and the other's a merchant of some sort," Flo told Elizabeth.

"It figures they'd wind up in our group," Gertie said in her usual disgruntled way. "More greenhorns here than you can shake a stick at."

Elizabeth noticed an older couple on the fringes, and eager to escape Gertie, she made her way over to welcome them. Quiet and polite, they introduced themselves as Horace and Jane Taylor. "We are missionaries," Jane explained to Elizabeth in a somber tone. "Our mission is to go to the West to save the heathen Indians."

"Oh..." Elizabeth didn't know how to respond. "Is it just you and your husband, or do you have family traveling with you?"

Jane shook her head. "It's only Horace and myself. The Good Lord chose to keep us childless. I suppose that is so we could be of help to others."

The campground grew lively and loud with animated discussions, children roughhousing, Flax barking occasionally, and music. Everyone seemed to be having such a good time that Elizabeth wondered how late their guests would want to stay. Surely they'd be concerned for children's bedtimes.

"Mama?" Ruth held up a plate of cookies. "There are still four cookies left. Did I count them wrong?"

"Have you given one to everybody?"

She nodded. "And our family each had one after dinner."

"Why don't we ask Grandpa if a wagon is still missing?"

So they went to Asa, and he pulled out his list to find out that, sure enough, one group had not shown up. "That would be the Morrises," he told Ruth and Elizabeth. "Ruby and Jess and—"

"You talking about the Morrises?" Gertie interrupted.

Asa showed her the list. "These four haven't shown up yet."

"I doubt they will," she told him. "Matter of fact, that wagon should be kicked off of the train by now."

"What do you mean?" Elizabeth asked.

"I mean that those Morrises, if that's even their name, are a bunch of no-goods. And if they haven't been kicked off the train by now, they'll get kicked off soon enough."

"But the captain never mentioned this." Asa frowned. "Are you sure of this?"

"I'm sure they're nothing but trouble."

Elizabeth looked at Asa. "Do you suppose it's the man and the boy from the woodpile?"

"No. Wrong name." Asa shook his head. "Besides, they weren't in our unit."

"Well, believe me," Gertie said, "you don't want them Morrises in your unit neither. They are good-for-nothings and—"

"Hello, hello," called out a woman who was coming their way. Even in the dimly lit camp, Elizabeth could see that her hair was red and she had a happy bounce in her step. The other woman looked less enthused, and they were both trailed by a thin and reluctant-looking young man. "We finally made it."

"Oh, Lordy." Gertie rolled her eyes as she lowered her voice. "Here comes them no-goods now. Mark my word, these folks are nothing but trouble."

Elizabeth gave Gertie a stiff smile, but she'd had more than enough of this sour woman. "Excuse me." Now she hurried over to the smiling redhead. "Hello," Elizabeth said warmly, grasping her hand. "Are you here to meet my father? He's the councilmen for unit five."

"Then we *are* in the right place after all." The woman's eyes twinkled as she elbowed the brown-haired woman with her. "And you thought we were lost. But I heard the music and laughter down here, and I said this must be the place. I'm so glad I was right."

"Welcome to our camp." Now Elizabeth led them to her father and Gertie. But just as Elizabeth began introductions, Gertie simply walked off.

"She's not overly fond of us," the redhead confided. "But it's a real pleasure to meet you folks. I'm Ruby Morris and this here is Doris." Now she pointed out the sulky young man who was remaining along the sidelines with a book in his hands. "That's Jess over there. And we left poor Evangeline back at the wagon. She wasn't feeling too smart."

"I hope she's all right," Asa said with concern. "Nothing contagious?"

"Probably just something she ate," Doris explained. "Evangeline's got an awful finicky stomach."

"Oh, well, maybe my wife can be of some help. She's got all sorts of remedies. Let me go ask her." Now Asa left.

"We're from St. Louis," Ruby told Elizabeth.

"We passed by there on our way," Elizabeth said. "What a big city!"

"Oh yes, and getting bigger all the time." Ruby nodded. "We'll surely miss some about that river town, but what I won't miss is how big it was getting. That makes it lots easier to part ways."

Now Clara came over to join them, inquiring about the ailing Evangeline. "I have some peppermint and chamomile and bitters and a few other things."

"She's probably sleeping by now," Ruby assured her. "Maybe she'll feel better by morning."

"If not, you feel free to come around." Clara smiled at Ruby. "I've been so relieved to see I'm not the only older woman on this train. I was a little worried." She nodded toward Doris. "Is Doris your daughter?"

Ruby smiled. "We've been together for so long that I think of her as my daughter. But, no, we're not related. Not by blood."

"When Ruby told me she was going west, I insisted on coming with her," Doris said. "It sounded like a great adventure."

"That's what I think too," Elizabeth said. "A great adventure."

"It was really Jess' idea to go west." Ruby nodded over to where the young man was now seated by the fire. Leaning over, he was attempting to read his book by the firelight. "Jess wants to be a farmer, of all things." She shook her head. "Can you imagine living in a city like St. Louis and dreaming of being a farmer? But Jess has been reading up on farming for years now. Not sure if books are much help when it comes to growing things though."

"We're farmers," Elizabeth told her. "Maybe Jess would like to talk to us about farming."

"Oh, I doubt that," Ruby said. "Jess is as shy as they come."

"And a bookworm to boot. Always got a book in hand." Doris shook her head as if that were a bad thing.

"Certainly, there are worse things than reading." Elizabeth smiled at Ruby. "I know I'm always pleased to see my children with a book."

"You must be proud of your son's interest in reading," Clara said to Ruby.

Ruby waved her hand. "Oh, I'm not Jess' mother."

"Ruby is Jess' aunt," Doris explained.

"And guardian," Ruby added. "That's how I got talked into this whole crazy venture in the first place. I couldn't allow Jess to head out into the wilderness all alone. That would be irresponsible."

"Well, I'm glad you came along," Clara told Ruby. "It's encouraging to see a few older women making this trip. I suspect we'll have lots in common to chat about."

Ruby chuckled. "Well, you just never know."

"Tell Jess that we brought some books with us too," Elizabeth said. "It was difficult deciding which ones to take and which ones to leave behind. But he is welcome to borrow some if he likes."

"My husband, Asa, brought along a fine selection of books too," Clara said. "I'm sure he'd be happy to loan them."

"You are both exceedingly kind." Ruby smiled happily. "You make us feel right at home."

"And if Jess wants to talk to someone about farming, you tell him to come by," Clara said. "Believe me, Asa can talk for hours on the subject. He probably has some farming books with him too."

Ruby chuckled, exchanging a glance with Doris. "Well, I doubt Jess will take you up on that offer, but it's right generous of you all the same. I'm much obliged."

Elizabeth tried to be cordial to all their visitors, but some of them, particularly Gertie Muller, made it difficult. And Elizabeth let out a sigh of relief when the Mullers finally made their departure. However, she did enjoy the cheerful company of Ruby and Doris. And, before they left, she insisted on sending some leftover ham and potato soup for Evangeline. "It will be just the thing for an upset stomach," she assured them.

"Thank you kindly," Ruby said. "You are truly a good soul, and it's an honor to travel with you and your family."

"I expect we'll be fast friends by the end of this trip," Elizabeth assured the two women. "I look forward to getting better acquainted with you." She and Clara watched as the women went over to Jess, who still had his nose in the book.

"I'll encourage Matthew to spend some time with that boy," Clara said quietly. "He might just be lonely. And Matthew might be just the ticket to bring him out of his shell some."

"That's a good idea, Mother." Elizabeth looked over to where Asa was still holding court with some of the men. Their expressions looked intense, as if the subject matter was of a serious nature. She paused for a moment, straining to hear, and suddenly she realized they were talking about Indian attacks. She felt a chill rush through her, and the hairs on her arms stood up. Surely they weren't expecting any trouble like that on this trip, were they? All the Indians she'd known much about, back in Kentucky, had been relatively peaceful.

Feeling uneasy, she looked about the shadowy campsite, trying to spot her children. And finally, she simply called out for them. To her relief, they came running, but still feeling anxious, she opened her pocket watch and proclaimed it time for bed. She knew she was being overprotective, but she just wanted them safely by her side.

Chapter Seventeen

It took most of the morning for the wagons to rearrange themselves into their camp units. But by midday, all twelve wagons in unit five were circled in the east meadow. The men were tending to the livestock, and Clara had gone over to check on Evangeline. Meanwhile Elizabeth and Ruth were getting dinner started, and JT, finished with his chores, had sat down to play to them on his guitar.

"Your brother is going to be a pretty good guitar player," Elizabeth told Ruth as she dropped some carrots into the pot.

"He can play 'Skip to My Lou' real nice," Ruth told her.

"It was a good idea you had at the music store that day." Elizabeth patted Ruth's head. "I'm going to get some sugar and some baking things from Grandma's wagon. Will you keep an eye on that pot for me? Give it a stir now and then to keep the lamb from sticking."

"Sure, Mama."

As soon as Elizabeth climbed into her parents' wagon, she heard Flax barking from where he was tied on their wagon. Then she heard a man's voice calling out a greeting. JT hushed the dog, but before Elizabeth could see who was there, Ruth welcomed him in a sweet, friendly tone.

"Hello, Mr. Kincaid," Ruth said. "How are you today?"

"I'm just fine and dandy, Ruth. But we're friends, so you better call me Eli."

Without speaking, Elizabeth poked her head out, curiously watching from the back of the wagon. Eli, dressed in his usual buckskins, was peering down in the pot.

"What you got cooking here, little lady?" he asked.

"Mama's making lamb stew for dinner." Ruth gave the pot a generous stir with a big wooden spoon.

"Smells mighty good."

"You can join us if you like," Ruth offered. "We always have plenty."

He chuckled. "Well, that's right hospitable of you, little lady, but I have some rounds to make. Is your grandpa nearby?"

"He and Matthew are seeing to the livestock, but they said they'll be back in time for dinner."

"Who's that I hear playing the guitar?" Now Eli cocked his head to one side.

"That's my brother, Jamie," Ruth said proudly. "I mean, *JT.*"

"You calling me?" Now JT came around the corner of the wagon with his guitar in hand. Elizabeth could tell by his face he was surprised to see Eli there. She supposed they hadn't met yet.

"Who are you?" JT asked with wide eyes.

Now Ruth politely introduced them, and Elizabeth couldn't have been prouder of her daughter. "Eli is the scout for our wagon train," Ruth told her brother. "Me and Mama and Grandma met him on our first day here."

"Pleased to make your acquaintance," Eli told JT.

"What does a scout do?" JT asked.

"A lot of things. Mostly I take care of the train by helping to find good grass for the livestock and game for hunting and drinking water for everybody."

"Do you look for Indians too?" JT asked.

Eli nodded. "I keep an eye out for anything I think might be a threat."

"That's sure a big knife." JT pointed to the knife sheath hanging from Eli's belt.

"It's a bowie knife." Eli pulled it out. The shiny blade glinted in the sun. "You probably know all about these knives since Jim Bowie hailed from Kentucky."

"Yeah, I heard of Jim Bowie before." JT was obviously impressed. "My grandpa and uncle have hunting knives too. But not as big or nice as this one."

"Do you have a knife?"

JT reached in his pocket to pull out his pocketknife, showing it to Eli.

"That's a good knife too. But I wouldn't want to go in the wilderness without a real bowie knife. Some folks think a bowie knife's more valuable than a gun. I reckon if I had to choose between them, I'd go with the knife."

"You'd pick a knife over a gun?" JT looked skeptical.

"If I was out in the wilderness, I would." Now Eli pointed to the guitar. "That's a real handsome guitar, JT. Is it yours?"

So JT told him about getting it for his birthday.

"But it wasn't really his birthday. Not yet anyway," Ruth explained. "That's not for a few more days."

"I got it early so I could start learning to play before we were on the trail proper," JT told him.

"And he's getting real good at it too," Ruth said with sisterly pride. "He can even play 'Skip to My Lou.'"

"I only know three chords so far," JT admitted. "And I'm not even sure if I'm doing them right or not. But I keep trying."

"Let's hear you play your three chords." Eli slipped his knife back into his sheath.

"Right now?"

"Why not?" Eli sat down on a stump by the fire, folding his arms in front of him.

JT sat down on the stool next to him, and after getting his fingers arranged, he began to play hesitantly. After a bit, Eli reached over and gave him some pointers on how to hold his fingers and how to strum.

"You know how to play guitar?"

Eli nodded. "Sure do."

Feeling guilty for eavesdropping, and because her back was starting to ache from being hunched over, Elizabeth decided it was time to make an appearance. But first she gathered up the sugar and flour and saleratus. Then, trying to make a graceful exit from the wagon, she casually walked back over to the cooking area.

"Hello, Eli," she said as she carried the ingredients over to the kitchen board alongside her parents' wagon.

"Oh, hello." Eli looked up from where he was showing JT something on the guitar. "I didn't know if any of the grown-ups were around."

"Matthew and Brady are rotating the livestock to a new pasture, and my father's helping Paddy McIntire with his team. Paddy isn't very experienced with driving yet."

Eli frowned. "Don't know why folks decide to go west when they don't even know how to properly drive a team."

"I'm sure Paddy can learn to drive."

Eli's brow creased as if he was unsure.

"Eli knows how to play the guitar," JT told her. "He just showed me how to play an A chord."

"Thank you for helping," she told Eli. "My brother plays fiddle, and he's trying to help JT, but—"

"But a fiddle's not the same as a guitar," JT finished.

"Maybe we can play music out on the trail sometime," Eli told JT. "That's the best way to learn, just playing with others."

"Sure, I'd like that." JT nodded eagerly. "Anytime!"

Now Eli looked at Elizabeth. "Can you give your father a message for me?"

"Certainly."

"Tell him we'll be by around three o'clock for weapons inspection."

"Weapons inspection?"

He nodded then tipped his hat. "Your father will understand."

"All right." For the sake of the children, she tried not to look as alarmed as she felt.

"Do you want us to save you some stew?" Ruth offered.

Eli grinned. "That's mighty tempting, little lady, but I don't want to be any trouble."

"It's no trouble," Elizabeth assured him.

Eli nodded. "Well, then I might just take you up on that offer. If it tastes half as good as it smells, it might be the best meal I've had in days." His blue eyes twinkled as he smiled at her, and to her surprise, an unexpected warm rush ran through her. And it had been chilly all day.

It was past two by the time they started cleaning up the dinner things, but Elizabeth set a generous tin bowl of stew by the fire to stay warm. She wasn't sure if Eli really intended on eating it, but she hoped he would.

"Why are you having a weapons inspection?" she quietly asked Asa as he was laying his guns out on the table.

"As you know, part of the agreement for traveling with this wagon train is that each wagon must carry adequate firearms. Partly for hunting purposes and partly for protection..."

"Protection from what?" Even though she knew the answer, she couldn't help but ask.

"Wild animals...and the possibility of an Indian attack."

"Is that very likely?"

"Not very. But our preparedness is critical to our success, Lizzie. You know that."

She nodded. "Yes, I suppose I do. It's just that now that we're so close to actually leaving...well, I just want to be sure."

"Are you having second thoughts?" His brows arched.

She glanced over to where Ruth was happily helping Clara wash dishes and then over to where JT was bundling firewood for the trip. She shook her head. "No, Father, I know we're doing the right thing."

"The reason we're having the inspection is to be sure that all the firearms are in good working order and that everyone knows how to maintain them." He plunged a cleaning rod down the barrel of his shotgun. "We also want to be sure that everyone is comfortable using their weapons."

Now Flax began to bark, announcing that others were coming into their camp, carrying various weapons with them. It was somewhat startling to see all these guns in one place, almost as if they were getting ready for battle. "I guess I should go get my own guns," she said quietly.

"And Jamie's." He cleared his throat. "I mean, JT's."

As Elizabeth went to fetch the guns, she experienced an unwanted and frightening vision—her only son crouched behind the wagon with his rifle as a war party of Indians galloped toward him. She shook her head. That was ridiculous. Unrealistic. First of all, JT would never be alone like that. The wagon train was filled with grown men, all of them fully armed. And everyone knew that tales of Indian attacks were always exaggerated and sensationalized in newspapers, all for the purpose of thrilling the readers.

When she returned with her guns, still wrapped in the quilt

she'd packed them in, a couple dozen fellow travelers were gathering around Captain Brownlee. Eli was standing nearby and, to her surprised amusement, had the tin bowl of stew in his hand. Probably Ruth's doing. But as Elizabeth got closer to the group, she felt stunned. She couldn't remember ever seeing so many guns in one place before. JT was standing next to Matthew, watching on with youthful curiosity as the captain thanked them all for coming.

"As you know, we'll be leaving tomorrow morning," he said. "But before we're officially on the trail, I insist on seeing that every wagon is properly armed. You all signed an agreement with me, but over the years I've learned to take nothing for granted. And as you know, I'm a military man. I take this weapons inspection very seriously. Any traveling party unable to hold up their end of the bargain will not go with us." He cleared his throat. "I've already removed two wagons from this expedition."

Faces in the crowd went from mild interest to concerned angst. Even Elizabeth felt anxious. Her gun skills were far from polished. She was fairly comfortable with the old shotgun, and her father had taught her how to clean and maintain guns, but the rifle and handgun were still relatively new to her. What if she didn't measure up to the captain's high expectations?

"You might find this hard to believe," the captain continued, "but emigrants are about as likely to die from an accident as from an Indian raid."

"What kind of accidents?" Bert Flanders asked.

"There's the usual drowning and snakebite death…" The captain looked evenly around the group. "But more commonly is from a gun."

"Are you saying emigrants shoot each other?" one of the adolescent Bostonians asked.

"Not usually." The captain shook his head. "Although it has happened on occasion. More likely, an emigrant hasn't properly cleaned his gun. Or he's misloaded it. Or the gun goes off accidentally. This is why Eli and I will be looking at your weapons and asking you some questions. Now if we could form two lines, we'll begin our inspections. Everyone over the age of eighteen will please fall in."

Elizabeth started to get in the captain's line, but seeing Gertie heading that direction, she decided to go for Eli's line instead.

"I really don't know much about guns," Flo quietly confessed to Elizabeth as they stood in the back of the line together. "Bert's real good with firearms though. And he took some time to teach Mahala how to shoot last fall." Flo looked at the handgun she was holding and frowned. "I sure hope I don't let anyone down."

"Do you know how to load it?" Elizabeth asked.

"Oh, sure. Bert's been helping me with that part. And I know how to clean it too. It's just the shooting part that worries me."

"Well, I don't think the captain is going to make us shoot," Elizabeth assured her.

"No, it doesn't seem like it." Flo sighed. "And he already checked our ammunition and food supply when we got here. Otherwise, he wouldn't let us join the train."

Now Ruby, Doris, and Jess came over to stand in line with them. "Evangeline is feeling better," Ruby told them. "But she's still resting. I hope the captain won't mind she's not here."

"I'm sure he'll understand." Elizabeth pointed at the women's impressive-looking handguns. "And you look sufficiently armed. But I know you're from the city. Do you really know how to shoot?"

Ruby laughed. "We most certainly do."

Doris held up her gun now, narrowing her eyes and taking aim at a stump. "Bang," she said. "You're dead." Then she blew the end of the barrel and lowered the gun, and the women laughed.

"And you know how to load and clean them too?" Elizabeth quizzed them.

"No worries there either," Doris assured her.

Ruby jerked a thumb over her shoulder. "And Jess is a real good shot with that rifle too."

"It's those Boston folks that worry me," Doris confided. "I heard Lavinia Prescott saying how she'd never touched a gun in her life."

"And her husband don't look like he'd know one end of the gun from the other," Flo said quietly.

Elizabeth looked at the Bostonians standing together in the captain's line. "But at least they have some fine-looking guns. I'll bet they're brand-new."

"Probably never even been fired," Flo said. "I was hoping to have more confidence in my fellow travelers."

"Well, maybe they can learn," Ruby said. "If they're half as smart as they're dressed, it shouldn't be a problem."

Again the women laughed. And now Clara came over to join them. She had a small rifle in hand. "Asa told me I can't get out of this," she said a bit nervously. "I hope they won't make us shoot."

"You're a good shot, Mother." Elizabeth patted her on the back. "And you know how to clean and load. Really, you have nothing to worry about."

The line slowly shortened, and when Elizabeth finally reached the front, she let her mother go ahead of her. "That way you can go put your feet up for a while before supper."

Clara laid her gun in front of Eli, and Elizabeth listened from behind her as Eli asked some basic gun questions. He asked how much black powder she used for one shot and where she kept the powder and how often she cleaned it. Eventually he seemed satisfied, and Clara turned around and smiled. "Now, that wasn't too bad."

Elizabeth just nodded as she moved forward with her quilted bundle. She laid it on the table as if it were a sleeping baby, a little embarrassed. "I suppose I should have left the quilt behind."

"That's actually a good way to protect the guns from moisture," he told her as she unrolled it to reveal the first rifle.

He examined the firearms and asked her the same questions he'd asked her mother. "Are you a good shot?" he said finally.

She shrugged. "I'm all right."

"What about Brady?"

Now Elizabeth felt nervous. Was this a trick question? She knew that some people would throw a fit to see a Negro man with a gun. It could be just the sort of problem that would get her family removed from the wagon train. "What do you mean?" she asked quietly.

"I haven't seen Brady at the weapons inspection. Does he have a gun? Can he shoot?"

She glanced around to see if anyone else was listening, but she was the only one left in the line. Feeling extremely uneasy, she looked directly into Eli's eyes, wondering if she could trust him.

"I need to know the truth, Mrs. Martin."

"The truth is..." She bit her lip then lowered her voice. "After my husband passed...I was alone on the farm." She cleared her throat. "What I'm trying to say is that Brady knows how to use a gun."

Eli just nodded. "Will he be carrying a gun?"

Elizabeth hadn't actually given this any thought. "Should he be?"

His brow grew thoughtful. "Not unless he's out hunting. But if he's driving your wagon, he should have a gun nearby...within reach."

"That's not a problem."

"And he should be comfortable with loading and everything else that I've quizzed you about. Are you confident of his skills?"

"I am." She nodded firmly. "And I'll ask my father to help with this."

"Good."

She sighed. "Is that all?"

"For now."

She began to wrap up her guns again, but she could feel him watching her, and her hands felt clumsy as she tried to hurry up the process. Finally she stopped and, looking at him, she realized that he was watching her with what seemed amusement.

"Am I entertaining you?" she asked with mild irritation.

He stood and smiled. "I'm sorry. I was just trying to imagine you a few months from now."

She continued wrapping the guns, finally getting the bundle secure enough to pick up. "How do you imagine I will be?" She stood up straight with the heavy bundle in her arms, looking defiantly into his clear blue eyes.

"I imagine you will be tougher and dirtier with a little more grist to you."

"Grist?"

"I'm curious, Mrs. Martin. What do you intend to do in the Oregon Territory?"

"Farm."

He just nodded, folding the paper that he'd been writing his gun inspections notes on and slowly standing. "You make a fine bowl of stew, ma'am."

"Thank you," she murmured.

"Thank *you.*" He grinned. "And I wish you an uneventful journey."

She wasn't sure how to respond to that. And so she simply thanked him again, and shifting her bulky bundle of guns to the other side, she headed back to her wagon. But as she set the bundle inside, her face felt flushed and warm. Strange…it was a cool and damp day. She hoped she wasn't coming down with something.

Chapter Eighteen

At last, at last—they were finally on their way! Elizabeth had felt a mixture of jubilance, high anxiety, and impatience when her wagon started to roll that morning. Unit five was currently occupying the tail end of the train, so they didn't actually pull out until nearly eight. However, she and JT and Brady had gotten the team hitched and ready to go at the "crack of dawn," just as her father had instructed. After that, JT noticed that Ruby and Jess, whose wagon was behind them, were struggling to hitch up their own team, and he went over to offer his assistance. Elizabeth couldn't have been prouder of her boy. Asa went over to supervise but soon returned to assure Elizabeth that JT had gotten it just right. "He's a smart lad."

Then, with their wagons hitched and packed and ready to roll, they'd all consumed a standing breakfast of cold cornbread and bacon and hard-boiled eggs—prepared to jump into their wagons at any moment. But the wait, almost two hours, had seemed endless. Naturally, they were all antsy to be on their way. However, Asa made good use of their extra time by reading from the family Bible—he read the scriptures about Abraham and Sarah setting out on the desert—and then he asked God's blessing on their first day of travel.

To start the journey, Elizabeth had decided to drive her own wagon with her children at her side and the dog in the back. Brady was riding alongside Matthew with the understanding that he'd take her place behind the reins after they stopped for dinner. After that, she and the children would walk or ride horses until they finally stopped to make camp for the night. However, she soon realized that driving the wagon wasn't nearly as fulfilling as she'd imagined, especially in the rear of the train, where it was exceedingly dusty. Just the same, the children's spirits were high, and at Ruth's insistence, they sang some songs. The pace seemed slow, but Elizabeth understood why that was. What she didn't understand was why they stopped several times. Would it always be like this?

A misty spring rain began to fall by midmorning so that Elizabeth had to pull the tarp awning out over their heads to protect them. Then JT fetched a blanket that they shared over their shoulders. However, the moisture did help to settle the dust some, and Elizabeth knew it would be advantageous to the prairie grass as well. As they continued to roll along, it felt good to be out in the open again. The days spent on the river and then in the wagon camp had felt a bit close and crowded. But looking from the right to the left, from north to south, and seeing nothing but rolling grasslands was refreshing.

All was peaceful and green with a wide stretch of cloudy sky for as far as the eye could see. Bucolic and serene. Even the rain-scented air smelled fresh and clean. And the team seemed energetic and happy to plod steadily along. Perhaps they smelled the sweet meadow grasses, or perhaps they were simply glad to be finally going somewhere. All in all, despite the jostling ride, it was a most pleasurable experience.

However, by the time the wagon train slowly ground to a halt at midday, the travelers were eager to get out of the wagon and stretch their legs. Elizabeth's back ached from the bumpy ride, and the children needed a break.

"Stay together," she warned them. "And don't wander far from the wagon. And watch out for snakes, JT."

She rubbed her back as she went up to the team. "Good work." She began to undo the harness from Beau's neck. "I'm sure you've worked up a thirst."

"Me and JT can see to the animals," Brady offered. "If'n you want to go help your ma with dinner."

She thanked him and headed up to her parents' wagon, curious as to how her mother had fared. To Elizabeth's relief, Clara was in good spirits.

"Oh, don't get me wrong," she said as she struck a match to some twisted paper and held it to the kindling she'd already stacked. "My backside's a little sore. I s'pect it'll take some getting used to."

"That carriage seat Matthew rigged up for you should help some." Elizabeth opened up the kitchen board, letting it down to discover that everything was now coated with dust. "I plan to walk this afternoon in case you care to join me." She wet a rag and began wiping out a skillet. Soon the children joined them and were put to work getting water and firewood. Everyone had chores to do and seemed happy to do them. Elizabeth just hoped this helpfulness wouldn't wear off before this trip ended. She didn't even want to think about how many days and miles still stretched ahead of them. Mostly she was thankful that they were finally on their way.

Everyone was in good spirits when they eventually sat down for their midday meal of beans and ham and biscuits. "Nothing fancy," Clara said apologetically. "But at least it's hot."

"And we got coffee." Matthew held up his cup.

"And we'll have something more interesting for dinner," she assured them. "I still have a few things packed on ice. And there's corned beef and a smoked ham yet too."

"But eventually the menu will become more limited," Elizabeth warned them. "Unless you guys do some hunting or fishing."

"You sure won't hear me complaining about food," Asa told them. "I just got a close look at what some of our fellow travelers will be eating today. I was checking on how our unit fared." He shook his head grimly. "And I'm glad I'm not dining at their tables right now."

"What are they having?" Elizabeth asked.

He chuckled. "Let me just say this. Our Bostonian friends appear to be somewhat lacking in their cooking skills."

"What was wrong?" Clara asked.

"To begin with, they couldn't get their fire going. I helped them a bit. Then I mentioned how you brought some catalogs along to use for fire starting purposes, as well as for some other purposes. Now I'm afraid you might need to hide those catalogs of yours, Clara. Precious tender."

They all laughed.

"But what were they cooking?" Elizabeth asked.

"Well, they thought they were cooking beans." He chuckled. "Problem was that Lavinia didn't know she had to soak the beans overnight. She thought she could just pour them into the pot and cook them."

"Bostonians who don't know how to make beans?" Matthew hooted.

"Seems they left their cooks back in Boston," Asa explained. "None of their womenfolk know much of anything about cooking. I doubt they've ever cooked on an open fire before."

"We'll have to go help them at suppertime," Clara said to Elizabeth.

Elizabeth nodded. "As much attention as you men placed on guns, I suppose we should have spent some time talking about cooking. It's been an adjustment for us too. But I figured the other women knew what they were doing."

"Lavinia admitted to me that they'd been getting food in town almost every day. Buying bread from the bakery and food that was ready to eat."

"Do they have adequate food for the trip?" Clara questioned.

"Oh, sure. They got everything on the supplies list just like we did. The problem is they don't quite know what to do with it now."

"Well, be assured, we'll help them," Elizabeth told Asa. "At the very least, we could send Ruthie over." She winked at her daughter. "You could teach them a thing or two about baking."

Ruth nodded eagerly. "I'm happy to go help them, Mama."

"I'm sure you are."

They were just finishing up their meal when Captain Brownlee came by on horseback. "Everyone doing all right in unit five?" he called out to Asa.

Asa saluted him and then nodded. "All's well in unit five."

The captain tipped his head. "Good to hear. We had a few minor breakdowns. That was the reason for those delays. Harness trouble in unit three. A hitch problem in unit two. But we should be ready to roll in about an hour or less."

After the captain left, Clara grinned at Asa. "I'm glad you didn't tell him about Ruby's challenges."

"No need to," Asa told her. "JT's promised to continue assisting their wagon as needed."

Now Elizabeth nudged her father. "You didn't mention the cooking problems with the Bostonians either," she teased.

He laughed. "Oh, Lizzie, I don't s'pect the captain wants to hear about that sort of troubles. Not just yet anyhow."

After dinner, JT and Brady took over driving Elizabeth's wagon, and she joined Clara and Ruth in walking alongside the wagons. It was interesting to be far enough away to see the full length of the train.

"It's really rather picturesque," Elizabeth said as they trekked along. "If I were a painter, I'd like to paint it just now."

"It's like a town on wheels," Clara said.

"Wouldn't it be fun if the wagons were all stores," Ruth suggested. "We could buy cakes from the bakers and candy and hair ribbons from the mercantile."

"Speaking of cakes, JT's birthday is just two days away. Will we try to bake him a cake?" Clara asked. "I have some cocoa powder tucked away for special occasions."

"Can we have a party?" Ruth asked hopefully.

"Why not?" Elizabeth nodded.

So, as they walked, they made plans for a birthday celebration for JT. Elizabeth wasn't sure how many of these plans they would carry out. It was quite possible that after three days on the trail, they would all be worn out. But it passed the time to talk about it. After a couple of hours, Clara returned to riding in the wagon, and Ruth decided to join her grandparents. Curious to test her own stamina, Elizabeth continued to walk. By the time the wagons began to slow and finally stop, she was thoroughly worn out. Seeing that the units were being rearranged into camp circles, she sat down on a boulder and just watched.

Some folks were obviously more skilled at driving teams than others. And it was one thing to keep a wagon going in a straight line but something else to get the wagon pulled into a circle. However, after about half an hour, the wagons seemed to be settled, and the teams were being released from their harnesses. Feeling slightly guilty for just sitting, Elizabeth forced herself up from her stone seat and made her way over to unit five, where Clara was already getting their cook fire started.

"Do you think I should check on the Bostonians?" Elizabeth asked. "Make sure they're getting their fire started?"

Clara reluctantly handed her the catalog. "Just take a few pieces."

Elizabeth nodded. "Precious tender."

"Can I come?" Ruth asked.

"Why don't you stay and help Grandma to get supper started," Elizabeth suggested. "If I need you, I'll call out."

Elizabeth wasn't sure how she'd be received by the Bostonians, but she was determined to offer them a hand. She hadn't really met them properly, perhaps because she sensed they were a bit standoffish. Or perhaps because she'd been too busy. But if they'd really eaten uncooked beans for lunch, she thought it was about time.

"Hello," she called out as she approached their wagons, where the men were still struggling to remove harnesses and yokes from one of the oxen teams. At the rate they were going, it might take them some time. But one of the women came over to greet her. "You're Asa's daughter, aren't you?"

"Yes. I'm Elizabeth Martin." She extended her hand.

"I'm Belinda Bramford," the young woman said. Now an older woman was joining them. "And this is Lavinia Prescott."

Elizabeth grasped her hand too. "My father mentioned you were having some challenges with cooking over an open fire." She held up some catalog pages. "Would you like some fire starter?"

Lavinia nodded eagerly. "I was just telling my daughter Evelyn that I was tempted to start tearing up one of my books." She sighed. "But it seems a shame to burn a perfectly good book."

"You'll have to teach your children how to gather little twigs along the trail. When the weather gets warmer, dry grass will work too. You can bundle them into fire starter bundles and put some lard on them." She walked over to where one of the girls was bent over the fire, blowing so hard that Elizabeth was surprised she hadn't fainted by now.

"This is Evelyn," Lavinia said. "She was certain she could get the fire going."

Elizabeth bent down to help Evelyn. "I've been trying to figure out who goes with whom in your families." She stood and looked at Lavinia. "You're Mr. Prescott's wife, right?"

"Yes. Hugh is my husband."

Now Elizabeth looked at Belinda. She'd seen her riding next to Mr. Bramford, although she seemed a bit young. "So are you Mr. Bramford's wife?"

Belinda giggled. "No. I'm his daughter."

"Oh." Elizabeth glanced around their camp. "Where's your mother?"

"Belinda's mother, also my best friend, died several years ago," Lavinia said quickly.

Elizabeth slowly nodded. "I'm sorry."

"But your father mentioned that you're a widow," Lavinia said with interest.

Elizabeth nodded. "That's true."

"You're brave to take this trip without a husband," Belinda told her. "I'm sure I never would do that."

"I have my family with me," she reminded them. "And it had always been my husband's dream to go to Oregon. His family is already there."

"It was my father's dream too," Belinda said.

"And William talked us into coming with him," Lavinia explained. "But I'm starting to wonder if we really knew what we were getting into."

Elizabeth looked at their citified clothing and wondered too. "My family and I are farmers, so we're accustomed to a more rustic lifestyle." She looked at the fire, which was starting to burn. "I thought perhaps I could help you with dinner."

"Really?" Belinda looked hopeful. "Wouldn't that be wonderful, Lavinia?"

Lavinia's eyes lit up. "Any assistance would be most appreciated."

As Elizabeth helped them, showing them how to make biscuits and how to use their own collapsible oven, which was actually higher quality than her mother's, she also helped them to put their outdoor kitchen into better order. As she worked with them, she met the other children. Between the two families, there were six offspring. Three young men and three young women, all in their mid to late teens and energetic. If many hands truly did make light work, the Bostonians should fare well.

"With these three girls, you should have no problem preparing meals," Elizabeth told Lavinia. "Once you get more order and figure things out."

Lavinia still looked flustered, and her patience often seemed to run thin, especially with Evelyn. She looked even more frazzled with the dusting of flour across one cheek. "I'm not sure I even know how to get organized. I can manage a retail establishment, but I seem to be useless with food preparation. And this cooking over an open fire..." She held up both hands. "What in the world have I gotten myself into?"

"My mother and I will help you." Elizabeth promised. Now she looked at Belinda. This girl seemed to be the fastest learner of the group. "I have an idea. Why don't I take Belinda back to my camp with me? She can see how my mother runs her kitchen, and then she can return to help you to run your own."

Lavinia nodded. "I suppose that would work. Someone needs to teach them how to cook. Perhaps the girls can take turns visiting your camp while we're preparing meals. They could provide labor in exchange for cooking lessons." She made a helpless sigh. "I just never realized how difficult it would be. I've always had cooks and household help." She frowned at Elizabeth. "And I don't mean slaves. My family have been abolitionists for as long as I can remember."

Elizabeth bit her tongue. This was not the time to get into that discussion. Not with all the hungry people about...people who'd put in a hard day's work without even having a decent midday meal. "Well, it looks as if you have things under control." Elizabeth gave Lavinia and the two girls a few more pointers, and then, feeling that they were off to a fairly good start and promising to come back to check on her, Elizabeth took Belinda back to her own camp, where

Clara and Ruth were well into their own supper preparations. Clara liked Elizabeth's idea of labor in exchange for teaching, and she quickly put Belinda to work peeling potatoes. As they worked, they talked.

"After my mother died, I tried to learn how to be more useful in the kitchen," Belinda told them. "My mother was such a good cook. Oh, she always had kitchen help, but she was in charge of our meals, and they were always wonderful. I thought I could do it too. But then Dad hired a full-time cook so that I could apply myself to my schooling. He said there would be plenty of time for cooking later."

"It looks like later has come," Clara said lightly.

"What made your families want to make this trip?" Elizabeth asked Belinda.

"For as long as I can remember, my dad has dreamed of going to the far West."

"My daddy dreamed of that too," Ruth told her.

"Everyone thought it was odd," Belinda confided. "I mean with him being a lawyer and all. And no one would guess to look at him that he's really an explorer at heart."

"That's just like my brother," Ruth said eagerly. "He loves explorers. He's always talking about Lewis and Clark."

"My father loves reading about their expedition too." Belinda paused from peeling a potato. "It's what he's always wanted to do, and now we are doing it."

"So are we!" Ruth beamed up at her new friend.

"What part of the West are you going to?" Clara asked.

"I'm not sure. Somewhere near the coast I think."

"We're going to live near the coast too," Ruth told her. "Maybe you'll be near us."

"Oregon is a big place," Elizabeth told Ruth.

"But they might be near us," Ruth persisted. Elizabeth could tell that Ruth was quite enamored by the pretty, friendly girl. "It would be fun to be your neighbor."

Belinda smiled down at Ruth. "I would love to be your neighbor."

"Speaking of neighbors, I should probably go back to your camp to see how Lavinia is faring," Elizabeth told Belinda.

Unfortunately, the Bostonian cooks were floundering again. According to Amelia, Evelyn and Lavinia had gotten into a big argument over how to properly make coffee, of all things. Now Lavinia was in her wagon fuming, and Evelyn and Amelia were trying to finish making supper on their own.

"Goodness gracious! However will you people survive this expedition if you can't work together?" Elizabeth scolded the girls. "And you have a family of *how many* people to feed?"

"Nine," Amelia meekly confessed. "And those men and boys eat a lot."

"Clearly, there's no time to squabble and fuss." Elizabeth took over now, putting a slab of bacon into a cast-iron pot and shooting orders at the two girls. "Amelia, you peel the outside skin off of that onion and chop it into small pieces. Evelyn, you get out some rice and another pot." Thankfully the girls didn't argue with her. In fact, they seemed to enjoy being ordered about, even laughing about it and calling her Captain Elizabeth as they scurried around the camp. She even made certain that they both knew the correct way to make coffee on the campfire.

"Light a couple of lanterns," Elizabeth called to Amelia as she helped Evelyn roll out the biscuits. "It's getting too dark to see back here."

"Something smells awfully good," a male voice said from behind her. "Lavinia, you must be improving your culinary—"

She turned to see one of the Bostonian men approaching, but he stopped in his tracks, blinking in surprise.

"Why, you're not Lavinia at all. Am I in the wrong camp?"

"No." She smiled with a meat fork in her hand. "I'm Elizabeth Martin, and I came to help out."

"Oh, yes, I remember now. You're Asa Dawson's daughter."

She pointed the fork toward the wagon. "I believe you'll find your wife in the wagon."

He tilted his head to one side, and Amelia giggled as she set a lantern next to Elizabeth. "Lavinia's not *his* wife," she quietly explained. "This is my father. William Bramford."

"Oh." Elizabeth shook her head. "I'm as confused as you are. I thought you were Mr. Prescott."

Amelia pointed at the other man now coming into camp with a couple of young men. "That's Uncle Hugh. *He's* Lavinia's husband."

With a confused look he joined them, and more introductions were made. "So tell me, where *is* my wife?" he asked Elizabeth.

Again she pointed to the wagon. "My father was concerned that your camp was having some...uh, cooking challenges." She made an uneasy smile. "He thought I might be able to lend a hand around here."

Hugh grimaced. "Word travels fast."

Elizabeth looked back at Mr. Bramford. She knew some explaining was in order. "So you see, my mother and I thought we could help out. Right now, your daughter Belinda is at my camp learning some things about cooking. I'm helping out here."

"Sort of an exchange program?"

She shrugged. "I suppose you could call it that." Noticing the cooking fire was dying down, she pointed to the sparse stack of wood beside it. "Do you suppose your boys could gather us some more firewood, Mr. Bramford? And more water as well?"

"Captain Elizabeth has spoken," Amelia teased.

"At your service, ma'am." He made a mock salute and then turned and called to the boys.

Elizabeth looked back at Evelyn. "I wonder if you might coax your mother out? She really needs to learn to do these chores too."

"My mother is not speaking to me."

"I'll get Lavinia," Amelia offered.

"Good luck," Evelyn snipped.

Elizabeth continued working and giving orders, and eventually, despite Lavinia's absence, Elizabeth proclaimed that the meal was done. It wasn't the caliber that she and her mother had been preparing lately, but it smelled tasty and appeared edible. Much better than the uncooked beans they'd suffered through for dinner. And there was plenty to go around and perhaps even enough for leftovers tomorrow. She hoped they would appreciate it.

She moved the coffeepot away from the flame. "I'll go tell your other daughter that it's suppertime over here," she told Mr. Bramford.

"You might not be able to tear her away from your camp now that she's seen what real cooking looks like." Mr. Bramford chuckled and the others laughed.

"Well, I hope your own supper will be somewhat tolerable, Mr. Bramford."

"Please, you've slaved over our fire and cooked our meal. Just call me Will."

"Fine. But if you'll excuse me, I'll take my leave."

"You could stay here and eat with us, Captain Elizabeth," Amelia suggested in what seemed a sincere invitation.

Elizabeth smiled at the girl. "Thanks for the offer, but my family is expecting me."

"I wish they were expecting me too," Evelyn teased.

As Elizabeth made her exit, several more food-related jokes were made, all at Lavinia's expense, and it was likely the poor woman heard every one from the not-so-private confines of her wagon. Elizabeth just shook her head and hurried toward her wagon. To think this was only the first day of this trip. She hoped cooking would get easier for the Bostonians before long.

Chapter Nineteen

The next couple of days passed as uneventfully as the first one. The weather remained cool with intermittent showers, which thankfully fell in the evenings, sometimes accompanied by lightning storms that boomed through the prairie. And there continued to be occasional delays in traveling due to various breakdowns. Captain Brownlee assured them this was all quite normal and unfortunately inevitable.

"We hope to get the kinks out early on," he told Asa when he stopped to check on the status of unit five at the end of the day. "The second week usually goes smoother."

Elizabeth was helping with her team this afternoon, not because Brady couldn't handle it but simply because she just wanted to give Beau and Belle a thorough grooming and inspection. She wanted to check their hooves and their hocks and make sure they were in good shape and ready for the upcoming week.

"Some of the wagons in my unit had problems too," Asa told the captain as he led a pair of oxen over to the grazing area. "The Prescotts just about lost a wagon wheel this morning. That was a close one, but my grandson noticed it was wobbling. And then the McIntires kept having trouble with their team this afternoon. Turned out they put the yoke on wrong." He chuckled. "But they're learnin'."

The captain nodded. "Most of the greenhorns will be old hands come June. Course, that's when the traveling will get rougher." He ran a hand over Beau's back now. "That's a mighty fine team you got there, Elizabeth. Handsome pair of horses."

She smiled as she ran the currycomb over his coat. "They're strong and smart too. Called Percherons, and they came from France."

"All the way from France?" He shook his head. "Well, it's reassuring to see you taking good care of 'em. I hope they make it all the way west without trouble."

Elizabeth's smile faded, but she just nodded. "Thank you. So do I."

"Now, being that tomorrow's Sunday, everybody can enjoy a little reprieve, including the stock." He turned to Asa. "We don't pull out until one tomorrow."

"I nearly forgot it was Saturday." Asa coiled a lead rope, setting it by the yokes. "And that reminds me. Today is my grandson's twelfth birthday."

The captain went over to where JT was picking a rock out of a mule's hoof. "Congratulations, son. What will you do to celebrate?"

"My grandma's making a chocolate cake." JT stood up straight, smiling at the captain. "And I'd be obliged if you and Eli would stop by our camp and share a piece with us." Now JT glanced at his mother as if to be sure it was all right.

She grinned back at him then turned to the captain. "We would be honored to have you join us. But not just for cake, Captain. Please, come for supper too. We've got a roast and all sorts of other good things that we need to cook. Our ice pack is only good for another day or so. So unless our men have luck with hunting or fishing, our menu will soon become much less interesting."

"Well, I got to hand it to you folks, you do make eating a pleasure." The captain smacked his lips as he clapped JT on the back. "I'd be delighted to come for your birthday, JT. Thank you."

After Elizabeth finished up with her horses, she left the rest of the stock to Brady and JT to tend and hurried back to her camp to tell her mother about their unexpected supper guests. "I hope you don't mind," she said as she washed her hands and reached for her apron. "I think it'll make JT happy."

"Don't mind a bit. I wish we could invite all our neighbors," Clara said. "Course that might not be too practical. Asa says we have around forty people in our unit. I s'pect that'd be quite a crowd to feed."

"Maybe we can have a big potluck supper sometime," Elizabeth suggested. "That might be fun."

"A chance to eat someone else's cookin'." Clara chuckled. "Although I'm not sure I'm ready to sample Lavinia's just yet."

Elizabeth frowned. This was the first evening since they'd started on the trail that she and Clara weren't helping their Boston friends. And none of the Boston girls were having cooking lessons at their camp kitchen. As much as Elizabeth liked the chatty girls, it was nice just having their own family again. "I hope the Bostonians are faring all right," she said absently as she washed the cabbage.

"Belinda came by and offered to help," Clara said. "I told her that she might be more useful at her own camp since we planned to do our own cooking tonight."

"She was disappointed to leave," Ruth said sadly.

"Oh, well, that's because she likes working with you, Ruthie." Elizabeth pushed some hair away from Ruth's eyes. "But they need Belinda back there. She's turned out to be the best cook of the bunch."

"Ruth wants to put the icing on the cake," Clara told Elizabeth.

"That's a fine idea. I think she should make the icing too."

"I don't know how to make icing, Mama."

"Then it's high time you learn." Elizabeth laughed. "After all, you don't want to end up like Lavinia now, do you?"

Ruth giggled. That had been their private joke when anyone complained about cooking. They'd say, "You don't want to end up like Lavinia, do you?" Poor Lavinia, besides being a useless cook or perhaps because of it, she seemed to suffer from a case of nerves that often incapacitated her. Clara had begun to suspect it was simply her way of escaping the kitchen chores.

For supper, they spread the table with a checkered cloth, and although Elizabeth wasn't sure if both Captain Brownlee and Eli would attend, she asked Ruth to set enough places for them. Ruth was just setting a small bouquet of meadow flowers in the center of the table when Ruby Morris entered their camp. "I don't mean to intrude," she quietly told Elizabeth. "I know it's JT's birthday today, and he was so kind to help Jess with hitching up the horses these last few mornings." She pushed a small parcel toward Elizabeth. "Well, we just wanted him to have this."

"Oh!" Elizabeth wasn't sure how to react. "But everyone should be helping everyone on this journey. There's no need to—"

"We *want* to," Ruby insisted. "JT is a fine boy, and Jess and I were both grateful for his help." She glanced over her shoulder. "Some folks are not so charitable. And we know we're tinhorns, but we truly appreciate JT's generosity."

Elizabeth smiled. "Well, then thank you. I'll see that he gets this." As Ruby hurried back to her own camp, Elizabeth was curious as to the content of the small package. She knew as well as anyone that with limited packing space, everything they had brought was considered precious. She checked the pocket in her skirt to be sure that James' watch, safely wrapped in a handkerchief, was still there. She had decided several days ago that JT was old enough to have his father's pocket watch.

To JT's pleasure, both the captain and Eli came to his birthday dinner. And with the surplus of good food and exciting conversation, Elizabeth could tell that they were all having an enjoyable time.

"I can't remember the last time I had chocolate cake," the captain said as he stuck his fork into a generous slice.

"This one turned out a bit lopsided," Clara said apologetically.

"But it should be tasty," Elizabeth said. "And since we're almost out of eggs, it might be some time before we see a real cake."

"Unless our chickens start laying again," Ruth said hopefully.

Clara laughed. "I doubt that's going to happen. I don't think they much like the bumpy trail."

After dinner, as was their custom, JT was presented with his birthday gifts, starting with a book from his grandparents and two red bandannas from Ruth.

"This is from Ruby and Jess," Elizabeth said as she handed him the small package. "It's their way of saying thank you for how you've helped with their team."

He unwrapped the package to reveal a silver belt buckle. "Wow." His eyes grew wide. "This is really nice."

"You be sure to thank them," Elizabeth said and instantly wished she hadn't. "I know you will." Now she handed him her own gift. "Happy birthday, JT."

He peeled the white handkerchief away to reveal the gold pocket watch and then turned to Elizabeth with a shocked expression. "Pa's watch?"

She nodded. "I know he'd want you to have it."

JT seemed uneasy.

"You're proving every day that you're nearly a grown man, son. I know you will take very good care of it."

He nodded slowly. "I'll sure try."

"And if you want to keep it in a safe place during the trip, you let me know," Asa told him.

Next the captain gave JT a silver dollar, and then Eli presented him with something wrapped in brown paper. To Elizabeth's horror, it was a large hunting knife. It wasn't nearly as big as Eli's or even her father's or Matthew's, but it did seem overly large for a boy. It also seemed extravagant. She wasn't sure she approved.

"Thank you!" JT slowly removed the knife from its sheath to examine it.

"That's a fine knife," Asa said with appreciation.

"Looks like a bowie," Matthew added.

"It looks very sharp," Elizabeth said with concern.

"My pa told me that twelve is the age of accountability." Eli glanced at Elizabeth and then back to JT. "That means you are expected to think and act like an adult." He smiled. "From what I've seen, you are already fairly accountable, JT. And, like I told you the other day, a man needs a good knife out in the wilderness."

"Thank you so much," JT said again. "I'll use it with respect and care."

"I know you will," Eli assured him.

"I got something for you too," Brady said a bit shyly. Now he held out a small wooden box with the initials JTM carved on the top.

"Thank you, Brady." JT opened the lid. "This is really handsome. Did you carve it yourself?"

Brady nodded.

"It's beautiful," Elizabeth told Brady.

"Thank you, ma'am."

"This is the best birthday I've ever had," JT told everyone, thanking them all again.

"And now I think we should continue the celebration with some music." Matthew was already pulling out his fiddle, and JT went to get his guitar. But after he tuned it, he handed it to Eli. "Would you play some?"

Eli looked uncertain.

"I'd sure like to hear you play," JT encouraged.

Soon Eli and Matthew were playing some lively tunes. And JT urged Brady to pull out his harmonica and join them.

"Do you mind if I go over and thank Ruby and Jess for the belt buckle?" JT asked Elizabeth as she was making a fresh pot of coffee.

"Of course not." She poured the freshly ground grinds into the basket.

"Invite all of them to come over and enjoy the music and some coffee, if you like," Clara suggested. "Sorry there's no leftover cake to offer them."

It wasn't long before Ruby, Doris, and Jess, led by JT, came over to listen to the music. Jess, as usual, lurked on the sidelines, but Elizabeth could see him tapping his toes. And then, to everyone's surprised pleasure, Doris enticed the captain as well as Asa and Clara and then JT and Ruth out to the open area to dance.

"We need another couple to form a square," Doris called as she clapped her hands to the music.

"Come on, Elizabeth." Ruby grabbed Elizabeth by the hand, and with the square formed, they all began to dance. Elizabeth hadn't danced in years, but it didn't take long for her feet to remember the steps. And by the time they finished the first set, a small group of onlookers had gathered along the sidelines.

"Come on," Doris hailed them. "There's room for more."

"Bring some more lanterns so we can see," Asa called out. "Then ya'll come out and join us, and we'll do the Virginia reel."

With more dancers arriving, including all the Bostonians, Elizabeth was surprised to find that her dancing partner had been replaced by Mr. Bramford. At first she was uncomfortable with this arrangement, but with all the teenagers and her own children having such fun, she decided to set aside her inhibitions and simply enjoy herself.

After several dances, she was ready for a break. "Thank you, Mr.

Bramford," she told him politely. "That was exhilarating, but I think I should go make some more coffee."

"Please, call me Will," he said as he followed her over to the campfire.

She just nodded, pausing to watch as Matthew, Brady, and Eli continued to play a boisterous tune. Matthew's brow was perspiring, and she wondered if they were in need of respite. Then, seeing that there was still coffee in the pot, she offered some to Will and then filled three more cups, which they carried over to the musicians, holding them up invitingly. They all nodded and, after they finished their song, seemed relieved to have a break.

Although the dancers expressed disappointment when the music stopped, Paddy McIntire offered to go and fetch his own musical instruments as did a couple of others, and before long a complete new ensemble of musicians was playing enthusiastically. Elizabeth watched happily as her children mixed with the others. Sometimes Ruth danced with her friend Tillie Flanders. Sometimes she danced with her brother. And JT seemed to be the most sought-after partner of the girls his age. Even the older Bostonian girls took their turns with him. He seemed to be growing up right before her eyes.

Before the evening ended, Elizabeth had danced with a number of partners as well. And not only her father and brother and son either. But she was most surprised when Eli Kincaid asked to be her partner. As they were dancing a second reel, Elizabeth burst into unexpected giggles. For some reason it struck her as terribly funny when she considered how shocked she would have been just one year ago if she could have imagined herself right at this moment. Elizabeth Martin, dancing out here in the middle of the prairie with a man dressed in fringed buckskins, no less. Imagine being out here, surrounded by people who until recently had been nothing more than strangers to her. How completely unpredictable—and delightful!

Chapter Twenty

They woke to the misty drizzle of rain the next morning. Elizabeth could hear it dripping down the sides of the canvas, steady and dismal. As she and Ruth dressed, everything inside the wagon felt cold and clammy and damp. "We'll get the fire going," Elizabeth promised Ruth as she helped her into a cardigan sweater, "and we'll dry out and warm up." But with wet kindling, a fire proved a challenge. Fortunately her parents had their fire going, and the three of them sloshed over to join them.

As the men tended to the livestock, Elizabeth, Ruth, and Clara hovered beneath the awning that extended over the kitchen area, trying to catch some heat from the fire and do some cooking. But by the time breakfast was fixed, the drizzle had turned into a deluge, and small puddles of water were pooling over the same area where there had been lively dancing and merriment the previous evening.

"As you know, I invited everyone in our unit to join us after breakfast today," Asa said as they were cleaning up. "I thought we could have us a little church service." He nodded to Matthew. "You think you could accompany some hymns? Something easy to sing, like 'Amazing Grace' or 'Rock of Ages'?"

Elizabeth pointed to a growing puddle. "I wonder if anyone will brave the rain."

Asa frowned up at the slate-colored sky. "I hadn't counted on this weather. If this keeps up, I won't be surprised if no one comes."

"Well, if anyone comes, I'm willing to play," Matthew agreed. "But maybe JT and Brady can help out too."

"How about if we rig up a bigger awning?" Asa suggested.

"I've got some extra canvas tarps in my wagon," Matthew told him.

So as the women cleaned up after breakfast, the men put up an awning, arranging it so that most of the rainwater ran into a water barrel, which would alleviate the need to carry water from the creek in the evening. Having this somewhat protected area actually made their camp feel more habitable, and with the campfire burning nearby, it almost gave an illusion of being dry and warm. Around ten o'clock, Matthew, JT, and Brady began to play music, and it wasn't long until several families came over to join them, huddling together beneath the awning.

The Flanders were all present and most of the Bostonians, except for Lavinia. Even some of the Mullers attended, including Gertie, who had been noticeably absent last night. And finally the Taylors joined them. Mr. Taylor had on what looked like a freshly brushed black frock, and his wife had on a shiny black satin bonnet that was spotted with rain. Both bore pious expressions and carried Bibles, reminding Elizabeth of how the older couple planned to be missionaries in the West. She sure hoped they didn't intend to preach to the group today.

Asa warmly welcomed everyone, and several familiar hymns were sung with surprising enthusiasm. Then Asa opened his Bible. "I will be reading from the Gospel of Matthew," he told them. "Chapter thirteen, verse forty-four." He cleared his throat. "*Again, the kingdom of heaven is like unto treasure hid in a field; the which when a man hath found, he hideth, and for joy thereof goeth and selleth all that he hath, and buyeth that field.*" He closed the Bible, and Elizabeth could tell that people were surprised. They had probably expected him to read a lot more. But she was well acquainted with her father's ways.

"Those words were spoken by our Lord Jesus," he told the listeners. "But as a farmer I can appreciate their meaning. You see, I understand the worth of land. To me good land is like a valuable treasure. It's precious. Because I understand this, I was willing to sell all I own. I was willing to leave my worn-out land back in Kentucky. I sold my home and most of my possessions. Just like you good folks, all I have left is what's packed into a wagon." He nodded to the covered wagon behind him. "I gave up everything in order to go west—to the promised land. I did this because I felt hopeful that I was going to a land much richer and much more fruitful than the land I'm leaving behind." He looked at their attentive faces. "I s'pect you folks did the same. You gave up something in order to get something that you hope is better. Am I right?"

Everyone nodded, even Gertie Muller, although her face still looked like she was sucking on a lemon, and Asa smiled. "So you see, this is just what the Lord Jesus is talking about. God's kingdom of heaven is like the treasure in the field. And our Lord says we must give up something—something we value greatly—in order to secure our places in God's kingdom of heaven. So let's all bow our heads now." He waited a moment and then began to pray. "Dear Lord God Almighty, we ask you to show us what it is that we need to be willing to give up in order to receive your kingdom of heaven. For some of us it will be pride. For some of us it will be an earthly distraction. For others it will be doubts and disbelief. Whatever it is that is keeping us from receiving the riches and glory you have for us, we ask you to show us. And we ask you to help us to give it up and lay it at your holy feet so that we might have treasures that never perish. Amen." Now Asa nodded to Matthew and he began to play "Rock of Ages." Brady and JT played along as best they could, and everyone sang along, but Elizabeth could tell that the Taylors knew the words better than anyone and were pleased to sing loudly.

After the song ended, people continued to stand around, visiting among themselves about the weather and whatnot. But Elizabeth could tell that not everyone was pleased with her father's short and simple service, including Gertie Muller and, it seemed, the Taylors as well. Mrs. Taylor spoke up first, directing her question to Asa. "Is that all?"

He tipped his head to one side as if he didn't understand. "All what?"

"Is that all you're going to do for church this morning?" she persisted.

"*Jane,*" Mr. Taylor warned quietly.

"I'm sorry," she continued. "But I'm accustomed to a much longer service. More scripture reading. More prayers. More preaching. I do not see how you can possibly call that a church service. Surely, it wasn't more than ten minutes altogether."

Asa looked directly at her. "The good book says where two or more are gathered, the Lord is there in the midst of them. There is nothing said about how much time must be spent in the gathering."

"I thought Asa's sermon length was perfect," Will Bramford declared loudly. "To be honest, my family and I have been neglectful of our church attendance in recent years." He turned to Asa, shaking his hand. "I found your words to be refreshing and encouraging. Thank you very much, sir."

Several others chimed in with similar praise, shaking his hand and then excusing themselves. But Elizabeth could tell their compliments were making her father uncomfortable. Finally, only the Flanders, Mullers, and Taylors remained.

"I have a question for you, Asa Dawson," Gertie Muller said loudly.

He nodded at her. "Go ahead."

"It appears to me that if you're setting yourself up to be both our councilman and our pastor, you ought to be paying a mite more attention to some of your wayward flock." She narrowed her eyes and then jutted her thumb back to where Ruby's wagon was parked behind Elizabeth's.

"What are you saying?"

"I'm saying those women in that wagon are not the kind of women we should be associating ourselves with." She stepped forward now, glaring directly at Asa. "And I'm saying that the kind of carrying on that took place over here last night was not Christian or proper. Not to mention it was an unwholesome influence on my boys."

"We were having a birthday celebration for JT," Asa told her. "Naturally, everyone in our unit was welcome to come. You and your family were invited and—"

"You were *dancing!*" She spat out the last word like it was filth.

Asa nodded. "That we were. Playing music and dancing and merrymaking. It was a celebration of my grandson's—"

"It was an evil and disgusting display." She grimly shook her head. "Plum wicked."

"Oh, Gertie." Flo frowned. "What on earth are you blathering about?"

"I'm speaking about sinful pleasures," Gertie said bitterly. "No good will come from it neither. Next thing, ya'll will be drinking and gambling too." She shook a finger in front of Asa's nose. "I plan on reporting you, Asa Dawson. I'm going to demand that you be replaced or else my wagon gets moved to another unit. I plan to speak to Captain Brownlee this morning."

"Captain Brownlee was one of our guests last night," Elizabeth calmly told Gertie. "Both he and Eli Kincaid came to our celebration."

Gertie's eyes narrowed and she pointed to Ruby's wagon again. "I am not going to tolerate this wickedness for one more day. That is a wagon of ill repute, and I will insist that it be removed from the wagon train or Captain Brownlee will refund my deposit immediately. I signed a contract with that man." She pointed to her children now, two of the younger ones who had come with her. They looked slightly frightened by their mother's fury. "My children are being exposed to sin and corruption, and I will not keep quiet about it."

"Those are strong words," Asa told her. "As councilman of this unit, I must insist that you keep those kinds of accusations private. I suggest that you go and get your husband right now, and we will all go speak to Captain Brownlee together."

Asa excused himself and proceeded to briskly walk Gertie and her children back toward their wagon.

"My word!" Flo put a hand over her mouth.

"I don't know what makes some people so mean," Clara said sadly.

"And I thought we'd had such a nice service too," Elizabeth added.

"There are bound to be troubles along the path to righteousness," Mr. Taylor said solemnly.

Mrs. Taylor took Clara's hand now. "Please, tell your husband that if he needs help with next week's Sunday worship service, my husband will be more than happy to take care of it for—"

"Jane, please," Mr. Taylor interrupted.

"What is the harm of offering your assistance, Horace? You are an ordained man of the cloth. Asa Dawson is not. Besides, it's plain to see he has a lot more on his hands than he realizes." She frowned at Ruby's wagon. "Do you suppose there's any truth in Gertie's accusations?"

"Of course, not!" Elizabeth told her.

"Thank you for coming," Clara told the Taylors. "I will convey your offer to help with church services to Asa."

The Taylors excused themselves, and now only a handful of

women and children remained. "I suppose I better go help Bert to pack up the wagon and hitch the team," Flo said. "Come on, kids." She winked at Clara and Elizabeth. "But you be sure to let me know how this all turns out."

"Why was Mrs. Muller so angry?" Ruth asked as they were packing up the kitchen things.

"I think some people just like to be angry," Elizabeth told her.

"And some folks don't know how to be any other way." Clara shook her head as she wiped a pot dry.

The rain continued throughout the morning. Shortly after one the wagons started to roll, and Elizabeth, holding the reins, said a silent prayer that her team would have no mishaps along what was sure to be a muddy trail. She knew her horses were sure-footed, and so far the mules had been reliable. But weather could play havoc with animals, and she prayed that the afternoon would go smoothly. She had seen her father coming back to the wagon, but by then everyone was so busy getting ready to leave that she never got to find out about his conversation with the captain. However, she knew she'd hear the details later. Probably over supper.

JT had opted to ride on horseback today, and Brady was riding with Matthew, so it was just Ruth and Elizabeth. "Why don't you go and rest in the back of the wagon," Elizabeth suggested after Ruth laid her head in her lap. She knew the little girl was worn out from staying up too late the night before. "I know it's bumpy, but at least it's drier back there."

Ruth didn't argue, and now it was just Elizabeth driving the wagon and cringing each time a hoof slipped in the mud. Fortunately, none of the horses had stumbled yet. At least the pace was deliberately slow. Sometimes they came to a complete halt, and she imagined that one of the wagons ahead was having a problem. By now there were many trails cutting through the prairie, and she tried to follow the one that seemed the least rutted. But at this plodding pace they'd be fortunate to make three miles before evening. Still, it was better than going too fast and risking animals. And preferable to not moving at all.

Elizabeth tried not to think of how many wet, miserable days might be ahead of them. They'd been blessed with gentle spring weather thus far, but it wasn't quite April yet. She'd heard stories of wagon trains hit by tornadoes or pelted with hailstones the size of plums. There was no way to know what conditions might greet them down the road. At the same time, she reminded herself that they'd barely begun this journey. To start fretting over uncontrollable things like the weather was senseless.

As the train came to another halt, Elizabeth noticed the Muller wagon up ahead on one of the adjacent trails. As usual, Gertie was driving with her daughter MaryLou by her side. And as usual, Gertie's husband, Henry, was nowhere to be seen. Matthew had confided to Elizabeth that Henry often slept in the back of the wagon while they were traveling. She glanced back in her own wagon to see Ruth nestled on the feather mattress and quilts with her doll cradled in her arms and Flax snuggled up next to her. They were the sweet picture of peace, at least while the wagon was stationary. How anyone could sleep back there with the bumping and rocking and rolling was a mystery to Elizabeth. She'd have to be seriously ill to endure that kind of torture. Perhaps Henry Muller wasn't too well. So far, she'd barely seen the slight man, and she couldn't even recall him uttering a single word—not that he could get one in edgewise around his loquacious wife.

Not for the first time, and not unlike Ruthie, she wondered why Gertie Muller was so cantankerous. Of course, it couldn't be easy traveling with four loud children and a husband who looked incapable of doing something as basic as swinging an ax. But the two older boys looked fairly strong, and with Gertie ordering everyone around, it was likely that chores got done eventually. But it couldn't be much fun. And for Gertie to claim that dancing was sinful and to say mean things about Ruby and the others—well, Elizabeth didn't even like to think about it.

As the wagons began to move again, she decided to think about something happier, something to lighten her spirits in this drizzling rain. And so she let her mind wander back to the dancing they'd all enjoyed last night. It had been such a pleasure to see her children, her parents, and even Matthew dancing and laughing and having a good time. She still couldn't fathom why Gertie wanted to paint it all in such a twisted way.

And yet Elizabeth had to admit—at least to herself—that she had felt slightly guilty to begin with. But that was entirely different from Gertie's brand of guilt. Elizabeth's discomfort was simply because it had been the first time she'd danced since being widowed, and for some reason, it hadn't seemed quite proper. Not at first. Of course, it had been nearly four years since she'd lost James, so she really shouldn't have been overly troubled by this. It just felt odd.

Elizabeth had never loved anyone except James. And she'd loved him since she'd been sixteen. Perhaps even before that. She had always imagined they would spend the rest of their days together. Even now, all these years later, she found it hard to believe she could ever love another. And yet, if she were completely truthful with herself, she had to admit that she'd felt a strange stirring inside of her last night. It had been a faint, almost imperceptible feeling when she'd danced with Will Bramford, a small flutter to see him watching her in a certain way. But there was no denying that the feeling had become even more pronounced when she'd danced with Eli. She'd attributed her flushed cheeks to the exertion of dancing, but she knew the warm rush had begun with the sensation of Eli's hand supporting her back as he guided her through the dance steps, the touch of her hand in his. It had been unsettling...but pleasant.

However, it had been somewhat disturbing too. Although they danced several times, it had seemed that Eli had barely looked at her. He'd been polite and congenial, but not with the devoted sort of attention that Will had bestowed upon her. And to her disappointment, Will had insisted on having the last dance with her. She would have preferred to dance with Eli. But the gentleman in buckskins had simply tipped his head and handed her over as if he didn't even mind. Then he went back over to join the other musicians. And throughout that final dance, she tried to act nonchalant as if she were perfectly happy with her dance partner. Why shouldn't she have been? Will Bramford was a perfect gentleman, well spoken and intelligent. An attorney at law, he'd received his higher education from Harvard.

Yet, even as she appeared to enjoy Will's company, she kept trying to get a sneak peek at the tall handsome man in the fringed buckskins. And that aggravated her. Perhaps it was Eli's apparent disinterest toward her that made him so attractive to her. Perhaps that sense of elusive distance made him seem safe to her. And yet... she had definitely felt a stirring last night. In fact, just thinking of it gave her a warm rush now. Despite the chilling rain, her cheeks grew flushed, and she was glad no one was around to see. She suddenly felt embarrassed for how she'd allowed her imagination to run away with her just now. Truly, it was plum foolishness to dwell on such things. Did she think she was a schoolgirl again? A giddy youth like Evelyn or Belinda or Amelia?

She would rather stew over someone as disagreeable as Gertie Muller than obsess over Eli Kincaid. Indeed, Gertie was a hard one to figure. The cranky woman seemed determined to make everyone in their unit just as unhappy as she was. But why? Perhaps it was simply that misery loved company. Elizabeth's parents planned to pray for Gertie. And Elizabeth knew if she were truly a good Christian woman, she would be praying too—for Gertie and for the welfare of Gertie's whole miserable family. And perhaps in time, Elizabeth might reach the place where she could do that with genuine sincerity. But for the time being, it was unlikely. Every time she thought about Gertie Muller, she felt angry. And if she'd had her druthers, she'd put up with this foul wet weather for days on end rather than be subjected to Gertie Muller's foul disposition for just a few minutes.

Chapter Twenty-One

Asa was quieter than usual at supper. He didn't mention why, but Elizabeth suspected it was because of Gertie Muller. But then, everyone seemed a bit gloomy. Perhaps that was simply a result of the drizzly rain, which seemed to show no signs of quitting. Consequently, everyone decided to call it an early night.

"Are you sure you're warm enough in the hammock under the wagon?" Elizabeth asked JT for the second time.

"It's real dry," he assured her. "I've got plenty of blankets, and Flax keeps me nice and warm."

"All right then. You sleep well, son." She pulled her head back into the covered wagon and secured the canvas door. She picked up her journal, which she'd planned to write in as she usually did each evening. But not thinking of much to write about the dreary and dismal day, she simply put away the book and pen, blew out the lantern, and climbed into bed with Ruth. They'd already said their bedtime prayers, and she thought Ruth might already be sleeping. But as she tucked the quilt more snugly around her little daughter, Ruth spoke up. "Mama?"

"Yes?"

"Why did Gertie say Ruby's wagon has ill repute?" she asked in a tiny but worried voice. "Is it because Evangeline is terribly ill? Like when you and Pa got cholera?"

"No, it's nothing like that, Ruth."

"Then what does it mean?"

Elizabeth wondered how to answer. "Sometimes folks say things about other folks, Ruth. Things they don't know for sure. Sometimes mean things."

"Like gossip?"

"Yes. Exactly like gossip."

"Gossip is sinful, isn't it?"

"It sure is. And it's hurtful too."

"Why is Gertie so mean?"

"I don't know for sure, Ruth. But sometimes people are mean to others because they're unhappy inside."

"Grandma said we should pray for Gertie."

"Yes...she did say that."

And then, without further ado, Ruth began to pray again. "Dear heavenly Father, please bless Gertie Muller. Please help her to be happy in her heart so she won't be so mean to everyone all the time. Amen."

"Amen," Elizabeth echoed. Then she leaned over and kissed Ruth on the forehead. "You are a sweet and fine girl, Ruth Anne Martin."

The next morning was just as wet and rainy as the previous day. After a slightly soggy breakfast, they loaded up the hitched wagons, and the dreary slogging through the mucky rutted trail continued. Just like the day before, there were numerous breakdowns due to the slick mud and, as a result, many delays along the way. After the midday meal break, Elizabeth asked Brady if he would like to drive her wagon for her. "And perhaps JT can help," she told him. "He needs the practice."

"You gonna walk in this rain, ma'am?" Brady said with concern.

"No. I plan to ride Molly."

"You're going to ride in the rain?" Ruth asked.

Elizabeth nodded. "I'm weary of watching the team trudging along in this mud," she told her. "I'm in need of a break. Even if it's a wet one."

"Can I ride too?" Ruth asked.

Elizabeth frowned. "I'd prefer you stay in the wagon…warm and dry."

Clearly disappointed, Ruth's lower lip jutted out.

"But I have an idea you might like."

"What's that?"

"Maybe you can invite Tillie Flanders to ride with you."

Ruth's eyes lit up. "Oh, can I, Mama?"

"Sure. Just make sure you girls clean the mud off your shoes before you get on the bed."

Elizabeth went into the wagon, changing into her split riding skirt, layering on a wool sweater, and topping it with James' old barn jacket. Its well-worn oiled surface would repel the elements. She exchanged her prairie bonnet for one of James' old felt hats. She might not look very feminine, but the wide brim would help to shed some rain. Besides, who would even notice her appearance on a gloomy day such as this?

She had just gotten Molly saddled up when the wagons started to roll again. Tillie Flanders had been thrilled with Ruth's invitation to visit. And it appeared that Flo was relieved to have one less damp body in their wagon. "Gets mighty close in there," Flo said when Elizabeth stopped her horse by their wagon to say hello. "We sure appreciate the offer."

Mahala, the oldest girl, stuck her head out of the wagon and grinned at Elizabeth. "And you tell that brother of yours that if he needs any company, I'd be more than happy to oblige—"

"Mahala!" her mother scolded. "Mind yourself."

Elizabeth looked at Ezra as he checked the harnesses on the mules. He was sixteen and a fairly responsible young man. "But perhaps Ezra would like to ride with Matthew," she suggested. "I'm sure Matthew wouldn't object to some company since Brady's driving for me."

"I'd be much obliged to ride with your brother." Ezra looked hopeful.

"I'll ride over and ask him," Elizabeth said.

Matthew was happy to have someone ride with him. "I even asked Jess," he told her. "But he said he wants to ride. Try as I might to befriend that boy, he sure keeps to himself."

"Well, at least he borrowed some books from Father. Maybe you can get him to talk to you about what he's reading sometime."

Elizabeth pulled her hat lower on her brow and rode back to the Flanders to tell Ezra that Matthew was glad for some companionship. Ezra hopped from the moving wagon and ran back toward Matthew's wagon. Elizabeth nudged Molly, moving her well away from the wagon train. Despite the foul weather it felt good to be out of the wagon seat and in a saddle again. And Molly seemed relieved to be away from trailing behind the wagons. Perhaps they both were in need of some freedom.

"I know this isn't an easy trip for you animals." Elizabeth patted Molly's damp neck. "But it'll be worth it when we get there." Now she noticed the lone figure of Jess riding up ahead. With his head bent down and his coat soaked with rain, he looked even more forlorn than usual. Her heart went out to the young man, and she wondered if any of Gertie's vicious rumors had made it to Jess' ears. She hoped not.

She gently heeled Molly's middle and clicked her tongue, hurrying to catch up with Jess. "Hello," she called out as she came alongside him.

Startled, he jerked his head around so fast that his soggy wide-brimmed hat slid off the back of his head and was held around his neck by the rawhide strings. Jess looked stunned, but it was Elizabeth who nearly fell off her horse.

"*Jess?*" She stared at the long brown hair that was secured into a tight bun, taking a good long look at what she had previously assumed was a young man but upon closer inspection was clearly a young woman.

Jess fumbled to get the hat back in place and then, tightening the strings around her chin, looked defiantly back at Elizabeth. "Yes. So now you know."

"You're a woman." Elizabeth still could hardly believe her eyes.

"Please, don't tell," Jess pleaded.

"But why—"

"It's just easier this way," Jess told her.

"I don't understand."

"No...you wouldn't." Jess let out a long sigh. "You have a nice normal life with a nice normal family. You wouldn't understand!"

Elizabeth didn't know what to say.

"I'm sorry." Jess looked at her from beneath the big hat. "You and your family seem like truly good people. And I appreciate how you've been so helpful to us. I truly do. But even so...you wouldn't understand." Jess glanced over to where the wagon train was rumbling along, slogging down the muddy trail.

Suddenly, as if a light had come on, Elizabeth thought maybe she did understand. And yet she couldn't quite believe it. "Gertie Muller has been saying some things," she began carefully. "About Ruby and Doris and Evangeline. Some not very kind things." Elizabeth looked into Jess' face, which was actually very pretty. Much more becoming to a woman than a man. "Is there any truth in what Gertie has been saying?"

Jess pressed her lips tightly together, looking down at the reins in her hands.

"You can trust me, Jess."

Now Jess just nodded. "I suspect there is some truth to it."

Elizabeth felt slightly sickened by this. Still, she wanted to get to the bottom of it. "I know you want to be a farmer," she said slowly. "But why is your aunt—is she really your aunt?"

Jess nodded again.

"Why does your aunt want to go out West?"

"She and the others plan to start up a dance hall," Jess said plainly. "There's big money in that sort of thing in the mining towns."

"Oh..." Elizabeth glanced back toward the wagon being driven by Ruby.

"It's what Ruby did in Saint Louis," Jess explained. "How she supported me."

Elizabeth frowned at Jess' wet clothes. "Is it why you pass yourself off as a boy?"

"I reckon it's just easier this way." Now she looked up at Elizabeth with hopeful brown eyes. "But it'll be different in Oregon. I can be myself out there. A fresh start and land of my very own to farm."

"What about your aunt?"

"Doris and Evangeline are trying to talk her into stopping before Oregon. They heard there's big money in silver mining in Colorado, and they're already tired of traveling like this."

"You really think Ruby will let you go on to Oregon by yourself?" Elizabeth wasn't sure about too much regarding these strange women anymore, but she was fairly certain that Ruby loved Jess.

Jess shrugged.

Elizabeth chuckled.

"What's so funny?" Jess looked hurt.

"I was so shocked just now—finding out you're a woman." She laughed even harder. "And here I've been pushing my brother to befriend you."

Jess looked embarrassed. "Matthew has tried to be kind to me. He seems like a good man."

"He felt sorry for you. You seemed so lonely." Elizabeth shook her head. "You were even lonelier than we realized, trying to pass yourself off as a man."

"Makes it real hard to have a conversation." Jess lowered her voice to the gruff tone she usually used to answer people. "Having to talk like this." Now she giggled. "It's not easy."

"But I still don't completely understand. What would it hurt for the people on this wagon train to know you're a girl? And wouldn't it be a whole lot easier for you if they did?"

Jess got a thoughtful look. "I reckon. Except that I've gotten so used to being like this, I'm not sure I even know how to act like a girl anymore. I started dressing like this about the same time I started to look womanly. I figured if I could pass myself off as a boy, I'd get by with less trouble." She shook her head. "Because I know about the troubles women have. I've seen it all in my aunt's dance hall over the years."

Elizabeth shuddered to think of it.

"And Ruby seemed happy for me to dress like a boy. I think it made it easier on her. She doesn't see anything wrong with running her establishment like she does. She doesn't mind all the gambling and drinking and whatnot—but she's always made it clear that it wasn't what she wanted for me. And she's been helpful to see that I got an education."

"And she was willing to go on this overland journey with you too." Elizabeth sighed. "That was something...considering."

"Ruby still can't believe I want to be a farmer. But I've always liked growing things. I had a nice big garden in Saint Louis. My happiest times have been when I've had my hands in the dirt." She smiled. "Guess that made it even easier to dress like a boy."

Elizabeth slowly shook her head. "Well, you had me convinced you were a boy, Jess. Is that short for Jessica?"

She nodded.

"But looking at you now, I wonder that I didn't see it sooner. You are actually a very pretty girl. I can only imagine what you'd look like cleaned up and wearing a dress."

Jess pulled her hat down lower. "But you won't tell?"

Elizabeth felt torn.

"It's just that I wouldn't know how to act," Jess said. "I'm so used to being quiet and out here on my own. I wouldn't even know how to talk to a woman."

"I'm a woman, and you're talking to me."

Jess smiled. "That's different. You're nice."

"Thank you." Elizabeth tightened the strap around her riding glove tighter. "But now that I know your little secret, I will probably encourage you to give it up. I do understand why you did it to start with, but it seems that you should be able to trust the good folks of this wagon train."

"You mean good folks like Gertie Muller?"

"Oh, surely you know there are people like Gertie no matter where you go." Elizabeth frowned. "Speaking of Gertie, do you have any idea how she figured out your aunt's line of work?"

Jess rolled her eyes. "Her quiet little husband, Henry, was paying visits to our camp before we set out on the trail. Seems he likes to drink and gamble."

"Oh, my."

"And he took a fancy to Doris."

Elizabeth's hand went to her mouth.

"Don't worry. Doris hasn't taken a fancy to him." She wrapped the ends of the reins around her hand. "And Ruby made both Doris and Evangeline promise not to do anything that would put our wagon at risk of being removed from the train along the way. Aside from some drinking and card playing before we set out, I think they've made good on it too." She chuckled. "The truth is they're so worn out at the end of each day, they really don't want to be bothered with any of that."

"Maybe this trip will change their lives."

Jess made a sad little smile. "I wish that were possible, Elizabeth, but I seriously doubt it will happen. Some folks can get pretty set in their ways."

They rode and talked on into the afternoon. And by the end of the day, Elizabeth realized she was quite fond of the girl. She just wished that Jess would give up this silly pretense of being a boy. Still, Elizabeth would keep her promise not to tell. She just hoped that, in time, she'd be able to convince Jess to become Jessica again.

Chapter Twenty-Two

It rained off and on for the rest of the week. The upside was that the prairie grass would be thick and lush for livestock grazing. The downside was that everyone was sick and tired of mud and the never ending dampness. At the end of each day, they hung damp garments beneath the tarp and around the fire, but nothing ever felt completely dry.

"One benefit from all this rain is that it's put a real damper on Gertie Muller's crusade to bring down Ruby's wagon," Clara said as they fixed supper in their soggy camp. "And the Lord does work in mysterious ways, so maybe this rain really is a good thing."

"And we don't have to carry water," Ruth said as she watched Matthew and JT setting up the tarp over their camp.

"According to Asa, it's going to clear up soon," Clara said in a weary tone. "I sure hope he's right."

"There does seem to be a thinning of the clouds in the west,"

Elizabeth told her. "I noticed it when I was riding this afternoon. If you get far enough away from the train, you can actually see the horizon."

"Saw you talking to Jess again," Matthew said. "How you get that boy to talk like that is beyond me."

Elizabeth just shrugged.

"Is it true that Grandpa isn't doing the church service tomorrow?" JT asked his grandmother.

"It's true," she told him.

"That's news to me." Elizabeth measured a cup of cornmeal and poured it into the bowl. "Why is that?"

"He invited Horace Taylor to lead the service," Clara said.

"I like it when Grandpa does it," Ruth said.

"So do I." Clara paused from chopping an onion. "But Grandpa thought it was only fair to let folks take turns with it."

"What if we don't like Mr. Taylor's preaching?" JT asked as he tied off one end of the tarp.

Clara chuckled. "Well then…I suppose we could have our own family service. No rule against that. But for tomorrow, let's all try to be cooperative with the Taylors. I heard that Mrs. Taylor has a small piano in their wagon."

"They brought a piano?" Elizabeth stopped from measuring the salt.

"She plans to play it for us at their church service tomorrow," Clara told her.

"If the womenfolk don't need any more help around here, JT and I would like to do some fishing," Matthew announced. "According to Eli there are some good-sized trout in these parts."

"Are you done tending the team already?" Elizabeth asked JT.

"Brady and Grandpa are just finishing up," he assured her.

"All right." She nodded. "Some trout would be welcome around here."

Next Ruth asked to go visiting at the Bostonians' campsite. "I told Belinda I'd help her make biscuits," she explained. "She says hers keep coming out flat as pancakes."

"Yes, by all means, go help them," Elizabeth told her. "Just be back here in time to set our table for supper."

"And you can spy for us," Clara said playfully. "Find out how Lavinia's faring in the kitchen."

After Ruth was gone, Elizabeth and Clara worked quietly beneath the tarp with the sound of livestock nearby and the constant dripping of the rain. "You've got me real curious about something," Clara said as she dropped chopped onions into some bacon fat.

"What's that?" Elizabeth paused from stirring the cornbread batter.

"You and Jess getting along so well."

"Oh…that?" Elizabeth started to stir again.

"Yes, that. Today, I was watching the two of you out there riding and talking together, and I'll admit you were a fair ways off, but I could swear that I was looking at two women out there just a chattering away."

Elizabeth nearly dropped the bowl. But instead, she took in a deep breath and simply continued stirring.

"You don't seem the least bit surprised by what I just said." Clara came over to peer closely at Elizabeth now.

"I'll admit that's a very interesting observation, Mother."

"You're not telling me that I'm wrong."

Elizabeth pressed her lips together and simply shrugged.

"*Jess is a girl*," Clara said with conviction. "I just knew it."

Elizabeth blinked. "How did you know it?"

"Well, I'll admit I didn't know it at first. But seeing you together, out there on your horses and talking like that…it just made me stop and wonder. Then I got to thinking about what Gertie's been saying about Ruby and the others. And it just made sense to me that Jess might want to appear to be a fella and keep her distance." Clara chuckled. "Besides that, I've watched her walk. She moves a little too gracefully for a shy young man."

"But you can't tell anyone, Mother. I promised to keep her secret."

"And you didn't tell me, did you?"

Elizabeth just shook her head as she poured the batter into a cast-iron pan.

"The problem is that if I guessed her secret, what will stop others from doing the same, Elizabeth?"

Elizabeth looked up. "That's a good point."

"Why don't you talk her into giving up her little charade?" Clara urged. "Tell Jess that God made her a woman and there's nothing on earth better than being who God made you to be."

Elizabeth set the empty bowl aside. "Now that you've guessed her secret, it might be easier to convince her that others will too."

Clara wiped her hands on her apron. "Well, it looks like we've got supper off to a good start. Why don't you go over to Ruby's wagon and have a little chat with Jess."

"Right now?"

"No time like the present."

As she removed her apron, Elizabeth wasn't so sure. On one hand, Jess trusted her. On the other hand, it seemed unwise to allow Jess to continue this pretense. What would she do when it was her turn to perform guard duty at night? Certainly Asa would put his foot down if he knew Jess was really a woman.

Elizabeth pulled on her riding jacket and hat and headed over to where Ruby's wagon was parked just a ways behind her own. She entered their camp to find two of the women, like so many of the other campers, struggling to get their damp firewood to ignite. Ruby was bent over blowing so hard she was red in the face, and Doris was fanning it with her skirt. "Greetings," Elizabeth said in a friendly tone.

"Oh, hello." Ruby stood up and shook her head. "That doggone fire is so stubborn tonight."

"Oh, look," Doris said happily. "It's starting to catch."

"Keep blowing on it," Ruby told her.

"Is Jess around?" Elizabeth asked.

Ruby gave her a suspicious frown. "I'd like to know...why are you spending so much time with Jess lately?"

Elizabeth glanced around to be sure that no one was near enough to hear. "I know that she's a girl," she said quietly.

"Oh?" Ruby chuckled. "Well, it was bound to happen. I told her as much."

"I promised Jess I'd keep it to myself. But now my mother has guessed her secret as well. I want to encourage Jess to give it up."

"Good luck with that," Doris said.

"It would be easier for everyone," Elizabeth told them. "Jess could make friends with some of the girls her age."

"You think they'll be friendly after thinking she was a boy all this time?"

"Some would be. Belinda is a sweet girl. I'm sure she'd befriend Jess."

"Even with folks like Gertie Muller spreading her poison about?" Doris said bitterly.

"So you heard about that?"

Ruby placed another stick on the fire. "Hard not to hear when all you got is canvas for walls. And some folks talk so loud."

Elizabeth took in a slow breath. "You should know," she began slowly, "that Jess told me that you ran a dance hall in Saint Louis, Ruby." This sure wasn't a conversation she'd looked forward to having. And she hadn't planned on having it tonight.

"It was a profitable venture for all of us," Ruby said defensively. "Put a roof over our heads and food on the table."

"Yes...I'm sure it did. But I doubt it was a wholesome place for a young girl to grow up in."

Evangeline stuck her head out of the wagon. "Don't you go faulting Ruby for being a good businesswoman," she said.

"Hello, Evangeline." Elizabeth gave the pretty woman a stiff smile. "I hope you're feeling better. And I'm not faulting Ruby for anything. I'm only here to speak about Jess."

"Elizabeth is a trusted friend," Ruby assured Evangeline. "And she's right about Jess. The dance hall wasn't a good place for her. And we all know that's why she goes around dressed like a man."

"One of my biggest concerns about Jess passing herself off as a man is that she'll be expected to do guard duty with the other men," Elizabeth confided to them. "And, believe me, my father would have a fit if he found out he'd put a woman on guard duty."

"Jess can shoot as good as a man," Ruby told her.

"That's not what I'm concerned about." Elizabeth frowned. "It just wouldn't be proper. It would be unfair to Jess and to any man serving next to her. Surely you can understand that."

Ruby rubbed her hands together over the warmth of the fledgling fire. "Yes, I suppose I can. And I don't much cotton to the idea of Jess out there in the middle of the night in the company of a strange man...and with firearms involved."

"So perhaps you can talk to her?" Elizabeth felt hopeful. "Tell her about my concerns and also that my mother has guessed her secret. And warn her that others might figure her out as well. Really, it would be much simpler if Jess just admitted to everyone that she's a girl and then got on with it. Certainly, folks will talk about it for a spell, but everyone has plenty else to concern themselves with. I s'pect it won't be long till they forget Jess pretended to be a boy."

"Well, I'll talk to her. But Jess can be awful stubborn sometimes."

"She's an intelligent girl," Elizabeth assured her. "I think she'll make the right decision."

As Elizabeth walked back to camp, she hoped that Jess wouldn't see this as interfering. She really liked the girl and understood that her life was complicated. But hiding behind men's clothes wasn't going to make it any easier. Elizabeth looked down at James' old barn jacket and chuckled. Really, she was one to talk!

Chapter Twenty-Three

The Taylors' Sunday morning service was just as well attended as last week's. And as promised, Mrs. Taylor sat in the back of their wagon, playing on her slightly out-of-tune piano and singing all the verses in a shrill, tinny voice with no concern that no one seemed to know the words to the somewhat obscure hymns. Then Horace Taylor preached a long-winded sermon on the seven deadly sins. Despite the cheerful sunshine that was warming their heads, Elizabeth felt quite gloomy walking back to their camp with her mother and daughter.

"I like Grandpa's church better," Ruth said glumly.

"I think we all do," Elizabeth said quietly.

"Do we have to go to the Taylors' church every Sunday?"

"I don't plan on it," Clara said. "And I'm sure we can talk Grandpa into doing a little family service for us."

"Matthew sneaked out early," Ruth said.

"I noticed." Elizabeth chuckled. "So did a few others."

"Who's that at our camp?" Ruth pointed to where someone was sitting by their fire.

"Looks like Jess," Elizabeth told her. Ruth was still unaware of Jess' true identity, and Elizabeth wasn't even sure how she was going to explain it to her. "How about if you go tend to the chickens," she said quickly. "I thought if their crates could be set out in the sun for a while, it might help their cages to dry out a bit."

"Yes, I'm sure they'd like that," Ruth agreed. "You know what they say about a wet hen."

Clara laughed as Ruth skipped away. But her expression grew serious when they saw Jess' tear-streaked face. "What's wrong?" Elizabeth asked Jess.

"I just had a big argument with my aunt," Jess told her. "She says I have to stop dressing like a man." Jess looked up at Elizabeth with defiant eyes. "And that you and your mother are behind it."

They both sat down next to Jess, and Clara poured her a cup of coffee, smiling sympathetically as she handed it to her. "We aren't trying to make trouble for you, child," Clara said gently. "We're just concerned for your welfare."

"We don't want to see you doing guard duty," Elizabeth explained. "My father would be beside himself if he knew that he'd put a girl on guard duty."

"I could do it."

Clara put a hand on Jess' shoulder. "I'm sure you could, dear. But you are a woman. And it's senseless for you to pretend to be anything else."

Jess held her chin up, but her lip quivered slightly. "I didn't bring any dresses with me. So my aunt said I had to wear some of Evangeline's things since we're the closest to the same size. And I told her I would rather wear a gunny sack and of course Evangeline got mad and then we all started to fight."

Elizabeth exchanged a quick glance with her mother. "I have extra clothes," she said quickly. "You and I are about the same size, Jess."

Jess looked alarmed. "I can't take your clothes."

"I have plenty of things," Elizabeth assured her.

"And we have fabric," Clara said quickly.

"I didn't come here to beg for clothes," Jess said as she stood.

"I know you didn't," Elizabeth assured her. "But we like you, Jess. We want to help. Won't you let us?"

Jess looked as if she was about to cry again but trying not to.

"Come on," Elizabeth insisted. "Come to my wagon. This will be fun."

"But I—"

"Come on, it's just like having a sister," Elizabeth said quickly. "I always wanted a sister."

Jess continued to protest, but Elizabeth led her to the wagon, and soon they were inside, where Elizabeth was peeling back the bedding and digging about until she found the crate marked "old clothes." "I packed clothing that I thought might be useful in Oregon," she explained. "Some of my late husband's things for JT to grow into and some of my dresses that I thought I might alter for Ruth someday. I knew at the time I was over-packing, but I figured that clothing was lightweight—you know," she laughed, "compared to pianos." She pulled out a light-blue calico, holding it up to Jess. "This was a dress I wore before having children. I'll bet it'll fit you perfectly." She pulled out a brown gingham. "And this one too."

Jess was fingering the fabric, examining the seams. "These are nice dresses, Elizabeth."

"I'd love to see them on you." Elizabeth dug around to find some petticoats and camisoles and a few other things, including a split riding skirt with a tiny waist that fit her before having children. She thrust them all toward Jess. "Go ahead and put something on now. I need to go help my mother with dinner."

"Are you sure?"

Elizabeth laughed. "I can't wait to see how you look as a girl, Jess. Why don't you wear the blue calico today?"

As she climbed out of the wagon, she saw Ruth standing on the ground with a perplexed expression. Matthew, JT, and Asa were standing behind her with a variety of emotions on their faces, everything from concern to shock.

"Ruth said that you took Jess into your wagon," Asa said solemnly.

Elizabeth couldn't help but giggle. "That's true. I did."

"But why?" demanded Matthew.

Elizabeth was suddenly reminded of Mr. Taylor's sermon against the seven deadly sins. Was it likely that her own family suspected her of being guilty of some? Surely not. "JT and Ruth," she said quietly, "come with me." Then, casting her brother and father a stern look, she ushered her children around to the other side of her wagon.

"Can you keep a secret for a little while?" she whispered to them. With wide eyes, they both nodded. Then she quickly explained about how Jess was really a girl pretending to be a boy and how she'd been helping her with some girls' clothes just now. To her relief, although they were surprised, both of her children seemed to simply take this news in stride. Now if only the adults would be as gracious. Fortunately, the men had the teams and livestock to tend to since they would be pulling out at noon.

"Remember, don't tell yet," she warned JT as he scurried off to his own chores. Then she and Ruth went back to help her mother, quietly replaying the scene with Matthew and Asa.

Clara laughed loudly. "Oh, my!"

With dinner well in hand and the table set, Elizabeth knew that the men would be coming to eat soon. "I'll be right back," she promised Clara. Then she slipped back to her wagon to check on Jess. To her relief, Jess was fully dressed in the blue calico, and it fit almost perfectly.

"Wonderful," Elizabeth told her. "I thought you were about

the same size as me—at least before I had children. Childbearing changes the figure some." Elizabeth reached for a brush and helped to comb out Jess' dark-brown hair. Long and wavy, the color of chestnuts, it was really quite lovely.

"It feels good to have my hair down again," Jess admitted as she picked up her big brown hat and sighed.

"You look very pretty," Elizabeth told her.

"Thank you." Jess smiled shyly as she held out her hands. "Thank you for everything. I don't even know how to thank you properly."

"Seeing you like this is pretty good thanks." Elizabeth was bundling up the other clothes now. "And I want you to take the rest of these with you."

"Are you sure?"

She nodded. "And you can do one more thing to thank me, if you don't mind."

"What?"

"Let me introduce you to my father and brother."

Jess giggled. "I heard them outside the wagon. They sounded rather perturbed."

"They were very perturbed."

Together they walked back to her parents' wagon, where everyone was just sitting down to dinner. "I have someone I want you to meet," Elizabeth announced. Everyone looked up, and although her mother and children were wide-eyed with bemusement, the men looked downright bewildered.

"This is Jessica Morris," she told them. "Previously known to everyone as just Jess. And some of you probably assumed that Jess was a boy. But you were wrong about that. For as you can see, Jess is actually a lovely young woman."

Now Asa and Matthew and even old Brady looked completely stunned. But after a long moment of startled silence, Asa started to laugh. And standing, he went over and clasped Jess' hand. "Well, it's a pleasure to meet you, Jessica."

She nodded, smiling nervously.

Elizabeth handed her the bundle of clothes. "You're welcome to join us for dinner if you—"

"No, thank you," Jess said politely. "I should go find my aunt and the others." She reached out and hugged Elizabeth. "Thank you so much!"

"Well, I'll be," Asa said as he sat back down. "I never saw that one coming. Not at all."

Matthew shook his head in wonder. "So that's why Jess was so quiet all this time, keeping to himself. I mean to herself."

"She's real pretty, isn't she?" Ruth said pleasantly.

"She surely is," Clara answered. Elizabeth saw Matthew nodding with a hard-to-read expression. But unless she was mistaken, she thought that Jess might have just turned her brother's head. Of course, this reminded her of Violet and how she'd broken his heart. But if ever two women were completely unalike, it was Violet and Jess. As different as night and day. Perhaps that would be a good thing.

After dinner, Elizabeth asked Ruth to go over and invite Jess to ride with them in the afternoon. "Since she's wearing that dress," she told Ruth. "It's not really suited for riding."

Ruth was happy to oblige and returned shortly with Jess and her horse in tow. "It might be interesting to ride in a wagon for a change," she told them as she tied her horse up to the back. Meanwhile JT had opted to ride Molly.

"Do you know how to drive a team?" Elizabeth asked as they climbed up into the seat.

"Ruby's been wanting me to learn, but I haven't even tried it yet."

"Well, then it's probably high time you did." Then feeling almost like she'd gained a sister, Elizabeth released the brakes and snapped the reins, and the wagon eased ahead, directly into the Nebraska sunshine.

Chapter Twenty-Four

The next week passed somewhat peacefully with mild springlike weather, and the wagon train made good progress along the trail. Rumor had it that Gertie Muller was ailing from a cold she'd gotten during the rainy week. And although Elizabeth and her family were praying for Gertie's recovery, they did enjoy this quiet reprieve. Jess enjoyed it too, and thankfully, after everyone got over the initial surprise regarding her identity, no one seemed much concerned.

Not only were they unconcerned, but Jeremiah Bramford, Will's son, seemed to have taken an interest in Jess. "Jeremiah wants to know when you folks are going to have another party with music and dancing," Belinda told Elizabeth as several of the women and girls walked together alongside the wagon on Saturday afternoon.

Elizabeth shrugged. "I don't know of any birthdays coming up."

"Augustus has a birthday next week," Lavinia said without enthusiasm. Augustus was her youngest son, just a bit older than JT.

"Let's have a party for Augustus," Belinda suggested.

"Yes!" Evelyn agreed. "But instead of waiting for next week, when everyone will be worn out and want to go to bed early, let's have a party tonight!"

And just like that, the girls were suddenly planning another birthday party. The Bostonian girls promised to handle everything. And Ruth even suggested that her grandma might help them bake a cake. "But you'll have to do most of the work," she said sternly. "So you can learn how it's done and do it for yourself the next time."

"And we'll invite everyone in our unit to come," Amelia said eagerly.

"Let's go start inviting them right now," Evelyn suggested.

"Can I go too?" Ruth asked hopefully.

"It's all right with me," Belinda said as she took Ruth's hand. Elizabeth simply smiled and waved to her daughter, and just like a small flock of birds, the girls flitted away, chirping and running back and forth to all the wagons, inviting everyone to the evening celebration.

"Oh, my," Lavinia said as just she and Elizabeth plodded along through the tall grass. "I wish I had just a portion of their energy. As it is, I'm exhausted, Elizabeth. Sometimes I feel like I can't even go on." As Lavinia complained, going on and on about all the deprivations and hardships, Elizabeth looked longingly out to where Jess was on horseback ahead of them. Wearing the split skirt and her hair in two long braids, she was cantering along in a carefree sort of way, and Elizabeth suddenly wished she were with her. But instead of riding as she'd wanted, she had agreed to walk with Lavinia this afternoon.

"I know it's hard work," Elizabeth said patiently. "But look at your children, Lavinia. They are having such an amazing adventure. This is something they will remember for the rest of their lives."

"If they all survive this trip." Lavinia sniffed. "Oh, sometimes I think I must have lost my mind to let Hugh talk me into this nonsense. I am halfway tempted to demand we turn around at Fort Kearney next week. We could hire a guide to get us back to St. Louis and be back in Boston by late April."

"Oh, Lavinia." Elizabeth could hardly believe her ears. "You cannot be in earnest."

Lavinia swatted at the gnats that were flitting out of the grass in front of them. "I am simply not cut out for this rugged life. I am a city person. I like my conveniences. I like having a comfortable home and a housekeeper and a cook. I am sick to death of making fires with wet wood and trying to cook with smoke in my face. I'm tired of being damp and cold. Tired of sleeping in a lumpy bed in the back of a wagon. My feet hurt. I am sick of everything. Every single bit of it. I hate all of it."

Elizabeth lifted her hands toward the clear blue sky. "But look at the beauty all around you. Surely you don't hate that." She pointed at some wild irises nearby. Ruth had already gathered a fine bouquet of them. "And the flowers. Don't you enjoy seeing those?"

"I don't enjoy a single thing about this trip." And now Lavinia began to cry. She sat down right on the grass and started to sob.

Elizabeth looked helplessly toward the wagon train, obliviously rumbling along. If anyone was watching this scene, which wasn't likely, they probably simply assumed that Lavinia was "tending to her business," as folks liked to say.

"Lavinia," Elizabeth said gently, kneeling beside her. "I know you're upset, but perhaps in a day or two you'll see things differently."

"I won't," Lavinia sobbed. "I just want to lie down here and die. Right now."

Elizabeth put her arm around Lavinia's shoulders. "I'm sure you feel like that, but you don't really want to die. I know you love your children. And you have fine children, Lavinia. Every one of them. Julius and Evelyn and Augustus. They are truly fine children. And just think, we're going to have a birthday party for Augustus tonight.

There will be music and dancing, and Augustus will be so pleased and surprised."

Lavinia looked up with teary eyes. "Do you really think so?"

"Remember what a grand time we had for JT's birthday?"

"That seems so long ago..." She sniffed loudly.

"Then it's high time we had another party. The girls were right." Elizabeth stretched out her hand to Lavinia. "Come on, friend, you can do this."

Lavinia slowly stood, and digging a rumpled handkerchief from her skirt pocket, she wiped her nose. "I'm sorry, Elizabeth."

"Sorry for what?" Elizabeth hooked her arm into Lavinia's and proceeded to walk.

"For falling apart like that."

"Isn't that what women friends are for?" Elizabeth asked.

She nodded. "Yes, I suppose so." Now Lavinia looked intently at her. "You know, my dear, you remind me of Will's late wife. She always had such a positive disposition too." She sadly shook her head. "How I miss her."

Augustus' birthday party turned out to be just as lively as JT's had been. Perhaps even more so. Some of the girls changed into fresh dresses, and lanterns were hung festively all about the campground. And thanks to the Bostonian girls' enthusiasm, even the captain and Eli had been invited to attend. The captain only visited briefly, but Eli brought his own guitar this time and seemed perfectly content to play with the musicians.

Elizabeth felt somewhat dismayed that Eli was distracted with the music, but Will Bramford seemed to capitalize on Eli's absence by dancing with her at every opportunity. "Lavinia tells me you saved her life today," Will told her as they enjoyed a break between dances.

"Saved her life?" Elizabeth laughed. "That's a bit of an overstatement.

"Not according to Lavinia." He took a sip of coffee. "I partially blame myself for her suffering. I'm the one who talked Hugh into emigrating like this. I hadn't even considered that Lavinia would feel overwhelmed by trying to play mother to all six of our children."

"Well, your children aren't exactly children," she reminded him. "Other than Augustus, the others are nearly grown and able to carry their own weight. I shouldn't think that Lavinia should feel terribly overwhelmed because of them. But I know this is a taxing trip for her. Perhaps it will feel easier when summer comes. That bleak week of rainy weather took its toll on everyone."

Will tipped his head toward the Muller wagon. "I've heard that our friend Gertie is feeling better now."

"Oh…?" Elizabeth had noticed that the Muller children were participating in the dancing. She didn't know what Gertie would think of that but suspected they would all get an earful before long.

"Belinda had the misfortune of inviting the Muller wagon to come to the party, and Gertie expressed her views on dancing and carrying on, as she puts it."

"Speaking of Belinda." Elizabeth waved to the friendly girl as she approached them. "I'll bet you want to dance with your father," she said to Belinda. And to Elizabeth's relief, father and daughter joined the others. Now Elizabeth found Jess, also taking a break, as she watched the musicians. "You look pretty tonight," she told her.

"Thanks to you." Jess smiled.

"I've noticed that Jeremiah Bramford fancies you as his dance partner," Elizabeth said quietly to her.

Jess nodded. "Yes, and it's posing a bit of a problem with Evelyn Prescott."

"Evelyn?"

"Yes. Her cap seems to be set for Jeremiah." Jess shrugged. "And that's fine by me. Jeremiah is just a boy."

"He's eighteen."

"Yes, but he's led such a protected sort of life. He seems quite young to me."

Elizabeth could understand that, especially compared to Jess' unusual upbringing. She followed Jess' gaze, which seemed to be settled on Matthew. "It seems a shame that the musicians don't get to dance," she said to Jess.

"Yes, I was just thinking that. Too bad."

Elizabeth grinned and then stepped up to her brother. "Matthew, I think it's high time you took a break, and Jess over there seems to be short of a dancing partner." She removed the fiddle bow from his hand, and although he looked surprised, he didn't protest. Instead he went over to Jess and, making a slight bow, took her by the hand and led her out to join the others.

"Are you going to play that?" Eli asked her.

She laughed. "Trust me, you wouldn't enjoy it much if I did." Then she simply set the fiddle down and, turning from him, walked away. But she'd barely gone a few steps when she felt someone tapping on her shoulder. She turned to see Eli looking hopefully at her.

"I'd like a break from playing music too."

She shrugged as if this was of no interest to her.

"Would you care to be my partner?"

She gave him a cautious smile. "I think I'd like that."

Then with a fluttering heart and feeling not much older than the teens who were laughing and dancing and "carrying on," she let Eli lead her over to join the group that was preparing to dance the Kentucky hoedown.

As she danced she noticed that Will Bramford had taken Evangeline as his partner. And that wasn't much of a surprise because pretty Evangeline was a lively dance partner. But unless she was mistaken, Will's eyes were on her. She simply smiled at him, but as she and Eli sashayed up and down the line of dancers, she noticed something even more disturbing. Standing in the shadows, Gertie Muller was watching the merrymakers with a dark and perturbed expression that could only spell trouble.

"We'll soon make Fort Kearney," Eli told her as they took a break from dancing. "By Tuesday if all goes well."

"That's wonderful."

"You've probably heard that Gertie has lodged a complaint against Ruby Morris' wagon. The captain plans to deal with the issue before we arrive in Fort Kearney."

"He won't send them back, will he?"

Eli sighed. "Hard to say."

"As far as I know they haven't broken any rules," Elizabeth told him.

Eli's brows arched. "Are you defending them?"

She shrugged. "I'm only saying that if they haven't broken any rules, it seems unfair to send them back."

"I've noticed how you and your family have gotten friendly with Jess." He nodded over to where Matthew was still dancing with her, and both seemed to be having a good time.

"Jess is a good girl."

"I don't doubt that. And I suspect she had her own reasons to masquerade as a man."

Elizabeth bit her lip.

"I'm not trying to pass judgment on Ruby and the others," he said quietly. "I'm just trying to give you a warning. Your father is well aware that their wagon might be cut loose in Fort Kearney."

Elizabeth folded her arms across her front as she watched Ruby and Doris chatting with her mother. "I do realize this is up to the captain...but it just doesn't seem quite fair. Ruby chose to make this trip for Jess' sake. She's sacrificed a lot. Now if they were gambling and drinking and causing trouble, I would understand and agree wholeheartedly. But..." She stopped herself from saying there were other emigrants who stirred up more trouble than Ruby.

"It's a long journey, Elizabeth. The farther along we get, the harder it would be for them to turn back. And sure, they're not breaking the rules now. But what if we're out in the middle of Blackfoot country and they do?"

She wondered why he was telling her this now. Was it simply to prepare her for the inevitable, or did he expect her to do something about it? Whatever the case, it certainly put a damper on what had otherwise been a fun evening. Feeling slightly out of sorts, she excused herself and went over to join her father. He was just lighting his pipe and dragging a chair closer to the fire, which was mostly just embers now.

"Taking a break?" she asked as she moved a chair near him and sat down.

He nodded with a thoughtful expression as he took a long pull from his pipe.

"Eli was just informing me that the captain might be making Ruby's wagon leave the wagon train," she said quietly.

He nodded again, this time with a creased brow.

"It just seems unfair."

"I know."

"Isn't there anything we can do about it?"

"The captain said I could put it to a vote in our unit."

Elizabeth was surprised. "Really? We can vote on it?"

"Since no official rules have been broken...but he warned me that putting it to a vote might just stir up more trouble for everyone. Might be real divisive."

"Gertie Muller is rather divisive, don't you think?"

He just nodded, putting his feet up on a nearby crate.

"What do you have to do? To put it to a vote?"

"I reckon we'd have a unit meeting. And we'd have to explain the situation. You see, not everyone is aware of, well, the nature of Ruby's business."

"I have an idea," she said suddenly. "A number of people, including the Bostonians, complained about the Taylors' church service last week. They don't plan to attend their service tomorrow. And some have mentioned how they'd like for you to do church like you did on the first Sunday out."

A small smile crept across his lips. "They would?"

"What if you talked about God's mercy and forgiveness?" she said with enthusiasm. "And then you could call the unit meeting for after the church service. And then you could put it to a vote." Now she scowled, tossing a small piece of wood onto the fire. "But I suppose women wouldn't be allowed to vote."

"The captain said that some wagon trains allow women to vote."

"Are you serious?"

"It's not very common. But some of the women carry as much weight and responsibility as the men, so sometimes they're given the vote." Asa pointed his pipe at her. "For instance, you are the head of your family, Elizabeth. You're responsible for your wagon and your children. I reckon it only seems fair you get to vote."

She nodded eagerly. "That does seem fair."

"Unfortunately that privilege will not be good once we get back to civilization."

She laughed. "Civilization?"

"Well, you know what I mean."

"I'd greatly appreciate the opportunity to vote on this, Father." She stood now, suddenly feeling a sense of mission. "Now if you'll excuse me, I'm going to invite our friends to join us for church in the morning." She could hear him chuckling as she walked away. He was probably already planning his sermon. She hoped he'd keep it short, like the previous one.

Asa's church service was well attended. Other than the Taylors and Mullers and Evangeline, everyone in their unit was there. As before, they started with music, singing some cheerful and well-known hymns. But when Asa said the opening prayer, Elizabeth could hear the faint twanging of the off-key piano on the opposite end of their camp.

"Some of you know I like stories," Asa began after the prayer, "and usually I like to tell farming stories. The Gospels are full of them. But today I'm going to tell you about something that's not just a story. It really happened." He glanced around the group of listeners, pausing to look down at where Ruth and Tillie were standing side by side, holding hands.

"But since we've got some young ears in this group, I will modify the story accordingly. This all happened a long time ago, when Jesus was a man walking the earth. There were some religious folks who didn't cotton much to Jesus being the Son of God, probably because Jesus had a knack for making them look bad. So one day these religious men brought a woman to Jesus—a woman who'd been caught doing something sinful. They threw this woman at Jesus and demanded that she be *killed*."

Asa paused, holding a large rock in his fist for everyone to see. "They wanted everyone to pick up stones and chuck them at her and to keep chucking them at her until the poor woman was *dead*." Someone gasped. "So Jesus picked up a stone," Asa said loudly, shaking the stone in the air. Elizabeth watched Ruth's and Tillie's eyes growing wider.

"Jesus looked over the crowd of folks, and he said, 'Whoever among you has *never* sinned, whoever has *never* done a single wrong thing, let him be the first one to throw a stone.'" Now Asa tossed his rock aside and knelt down.

"Then Jesus knelt down just like this." Asa picked up a stick that he must have set there and lowered his voice. "And he scribbled something in the dirt." Asa etched the word "lies" and then "gossip" into the dust. And then he stood and pointed the stick in the air. "And do you know what?" He looked at the group. "Everyone left. No one threw a single stone at that poor woman because they all knew that they'd committed sins too. Then Jesus told the woman that her sins were forgiven and that she should go and sin no more."

He grinned as he dropped the stick and brushed the dust off his hands. "Just like that."

Next they sang a few more hymns, and in a closing prayer, Asa invited God to teach them to be kind and merciful, "Just like Jesus." And with that, their little service was over. But before the crowd dispersed, Asa announced that there would be an important unit meeting at eleven. "Everyone over the age of twenty-one is expected to attend. Now I know you folks will be busy getting your dinner ready and wagons hitched, but this meeting will only take about ten minutes of your time."

Asa's plan was to have the vote be secret ballot, and Elizabeth had taken some pages from her own journal, cutting them up into small pieces for voters to pencil their decisions upon. But before eleven, and with her father's permission, she hurried over to Ruby's wagon to explain the situation. She was relieved that Jess and Evangeline were occupied hitching up the team. Somehow she couldn't bear to see Jess' reaction to the need for a vote.

Ruby just nodded. "I had a feeling it would come to this. Gertie's been making a lot of noise. She told me she was speaking to Captain Brownlee."

"Is that why Asa preached the way he preached?" Doris asked with sad eyes.

Elizabeth sighed then nodded.

"Captain Brownlee warned me that we might be removed from the wagon train in Fort Kearney," Ruby said quietly.

"There are twenty-two people of voting age in our unit," Elizabeth told them.

"You must be counting women," Doris said bitterly. "Surely we won't get—"

Elizabeth cut her off, quickly explaining the situation. "In my mind, that gives you a real chance."

Ruby rubbed her chin thoughtfully. "You could be right."

"Don't be too sure," Doris said hotly. "Women can turn against us so fast it'll make your head spin."

"But we have friends," Ruby insisted.

"Friends who don't know you ran a dance hall, Ruby. We might as well turn around and go back now. Why even waste a day going to Fort Kearney?"

"Don't get hysterical."

"Ruby is right," Elizabeth told her. "And if you don't mind me saying so, I'd suggest that you attend the meeting quietly and modestly. Not with any hostility or defensiveness. My father plans to state your case. You can trust him to present it clearly and honestly." She looked into Ruby's eyes. "We don't want you to leave."

At eleven o'clock, twenty-two curious emigrants gathered to hear Asa explain the situation, which he did carefully and diplomatically. Even Gertie seemed satisfied. At least she didn't blurt anything out.

"A yea vote means the Morris wagon remains," he informed them. "A nay vote means the Morris wagon is removed at Fort Kearney." Then, after everyone recovered from the shock of allowing the women to vote, they formed two single-file lines—men on one side and women on the other—and taking turns, they wrote yea or nay on the slips of paper and set them in the tins provided. Then while everyone waited, Asa and Mr. Taylor counted the votes.

"Seven votes nay," Asa announced. "Fifteen votes yea."

A few of them let out a cautious cheer and others began to murmur among themselves.

"The yeas win," Asa proclaimed. "The Morris party will remain with us for the duration of the journey. Thank you, everyone, for your votes. And now I'll let you get back to preparing your wagons for travel."

Elizabeth couldn't help but notice the scowl that now seemed etched into Gertie's forehead as she and a few others gathered around the Taylors, loudly questioning the validity of the vote. Clearly they were the naysayers and didn't seem to care who knew it. So much for having a secret ballot. Elizabeth was surprised that this group seemed genuinely shocked and dismayed at the outcome, as if they'd honestly expected the Morris party to be removed from the wagon train.

Gertie shook her fist in the air then stomped off toward her wagon with Henry trailing a few steps behind her. Elizabeth wondered which way Henry's vote had been cast, especially considering his fondness for the Morris wagon prior to their departure from Kansas. Had Gertie wielded her influence over her meek partner today, or had he voted as he wished? Thankful for the secret ballot, Elizabeth preferred not to know. But one thing she did know was that although the vote was over, the battle probably was not.

Chapter Twenty-Five

Some of the emigrants were clearly disappointed in Fort Kearney. "Why, it's not even a real fort," Lavinia declared as several of the women entered the small village of adobe and wood buildings together. "There's not even a wall around it." Now she pointed at an earthen dwelling. "And I do believe that house is made of *dirt.*"

"It's called a soddy," Clara informed her. "Not uncommon in some parts of the frontier."

"I've heard they're actually quite warm in the winter," Elizabeth added.

"That's fine if you're a groundhog," Lavinia shot back. "But I should not care to live in a dirt house. Can you imagine the mud when it rained?"

"Please, let's not speak of mud," Clara told her. "I'm still sad that my favorite white petticoat is now a dirty shade of gray." They'd finally been able to do some laundry yesterday, but the results had been disappointing. That previous week of mud had taken its toll on a lot of their clothing.

"And washing our clothes in the river..." Lavinia shook her head in a dismal way. "How would you expect anything to ever be clean again?"

"Let's just hope they get dry before it's time to leave in the morning," Elizabeth suggested as they made their way down the busy road. Emigrants from other wagon trains, Indians, soldiers, and all sorts of people were coming and going. Fort Kearney might have disappointed Lavinia, but it was clearly a bustling place, especially considering that it was in the middle of nowhere.

"I like Fort Kearney," Ruth said happily to Elizabeth. "It's exciting!"

There was no denying that there was festivity in the air in this place. With vendors here and there, colorfully dressed Indians, and a group of musicians playing on a corner, it was quite a change from their previous days of traveling over the barren prairie. And for those emigrants who'd already run short on supplies or needed to replace items, there were a number of stocked establishments ready and willing to help out—for a price, of course. Elizabeth and Clara were both relieved that their wagons were still in good, sturdy shape and relatively well stocked for the remainder of the journey. Not only that, but their men had experienced some successes with hunting and fishing, so they had enjoyed some variation in their menu.

However, Elizabeth knew that was not the situation with all of the emigrants. And although her family tried to share and help others, she knew that everyone had to stand on their own feet. Asa had taken the role of strongly encouraging some of their fellow travelers to stock themselves more adequately at the forts they'd be stopping at along the way. The problem was that a few of the families wouldn't be able to afford it.

"Can we look at the Indian things?" Ruth pointed hopefully over to where some blankets and skins were laid out with items to purchase arranged on them.

"I don't see why not," Elizabeth told her.

"Not for us," Lavinia said to her girls. "We need to get supplies. Now, you all have your lists. Let's hurry and see what we can find."

"I want to do some looking in the mercantile too," Clara told Elizabeth. "I misplaced a large spool of black darning wool. I hope it's not back there on the mud somewhere. But I do hope to find some more. Asa's socks need mending."

So it was only Ruth and Elizabeth who wandered over to where the Indians had arranged what looked like a small outdoor market alongside the edge of the settlement. Ruth smiled and politely said hello to the native vendors, and to Elizabeth's pleased surprise, some of the Indian women smiled and said hello back to her.

"Look, Mama," Ruth pointed at some buckskin moccasins. "These are like Eli's, only smaller."

One of the older women got up and came over, showing Ruth and Elizabeth the pairs of moccasins that she thought would fit them. Of course, Elizabeth had no intention of buying Indian moccasins, but the woman continued to jabber at her in a foreign tongue, showing how well the footwear were made and the intricate beading and how they would fit. She was so intent and persistent that Elizabeth began to feel sorry for her. Perhaps this poor old woman really needed some money.

"How much?" Elizabeth finally asked. When the woman named her price, Elizabeth shook her head. "Too much." But then the woman lowered the price, and Elizabeth suddenly felt caught. It actually seemed a fair price for a pair of moccasins—if a person wanted to purchase a pair of moccasins. And she did not. However, she felt a bit guilty because she'd been the one to inquire about price. Yet at the same time, she felt such a purchase was wasteful, especially considering that some of her fellow travelers were feeling so strapped for cash and supplies.

"Please, Mama?"

Elizabeth turned the child-sized pair over, examining them carefully. They did appear to be sturdy and about Ruth's size. Even if they were only used as house slippers once they got settled in Oregon, they were probably well worth the money. Besides, Ruth seemed to love them so, and the young girl had been so helpful and uncomplaining these past several weeks. Didn't she deserve them?

"They're so pretty," Ruth said quietly.

"Yes." Elizabeth nodded to the old woman as she reached into the small coin bag tied to her wrist. She removed the right amount and counted the coins into the woman's dirty palm.

But to her surprise, the woman now handed her both pairs of moccasins—the child's and the woman's sizes. Elizabeth was confused. "*Two* pairs?" she questioned, holding up two fingers then pointed toward the coins in the woman's hand. "For this?"

The woman nodded eagerly, pushing both pairs toward Elizabeth.

"But did I pay for *two* pairs?" Elizabeth patted her small purse with uncertainty, wondering if she now owed the woman more money and feeling as if she'd been hoodwinked. But the woman simply shook her head and held up her hands as if to show that Elizabeth had already paid enough. Then she giggled and stepped away.

"That seems too little for two pairs," Elizabeth said quietly to Ruth. But her daughter was oblivious as she happily admired her new moccasins, running her finger over the delicate beadwork of white flowers and green stems. "What do you think, Ruthie?"

"I don't know, Mama." She shrugged, holding the moccasins close to her chest. "But *thank you!*"

Elizabeth reached into her little handbag again, insisting the old woman take another nickel and dime. The woman didn't refuse, but she seemed slightly embarrassed by this gesture. Then she simply smiled, revealing some broken teeth, and nodding happily, she hurried over to where her friends were sitting on a blanket. They'd been chattering among themselves while witnessing the awkward transaction, and now they all laughed as if it were a good joke.

Elizabeth wasn't even sure what had transpired. Perhaps she really had been tricked. Yet the moccasins seemed well made, and Ruth was delighted. As they walked away, Elizabeth admired the red beaded roses on her own new pair of footwear. "They truly are pretty," she told Ruth as they headed back toward the busy settlement. "That was a good idea you had."

The settlement seemed to be getting busier, and Elizabeth held tightly to Ruth's hand as they pressed through the crowded street, making their way to an adobe building that housed the post office as well as a bank. As they walked, she occasionally spied people from their wagon train and waved. Mostly they seemed to be strangers, and she hoped that her father and brother were keeping close tabs on JT. Brady had declined the invitation to join them here, claiming that he preferred the quiet of the camp and tending to the livestock. However, she wondered if he was worried that he might run into strangers who would question his freedom. She hoped it would become simpler when they reached the Oregon Territory.

Just outside the post office, they found Clara with a full market basket and a flushed face.

"Let me help you," Elizabeth offered as Clara showed off some of her finds, including black darning yarn, a dozen eggs, a ham bone, and a bundle of fresh spring asparagus.

"The asparagus was a splurge," she admitted to Elizabeth. "But I think it'll be worth it. Imagine, fresh vegetables out here in the middle of nowhere!"

"Someone must have a nice garden in these parts," Elizabeth commented as she eyed the good-sized green stems.

"A wife of one of the officers," Clara explained. Now she lowered her voice and whispered in Elizabeth's ear. "Speaking of officers' wives, I have a bit of interesting news for you…later."

"You two wait here while I go and inquire about the mail,"

Elizabeth told her. She navigated her way through the crowd, waiting in line to finally ask the clerk if there was possibly a letter for her.

"Sorry, ma'am," he said after looking through the boxes behind him. "I don't see anything with your name."

She thanked him, hoping that perhaps a letter would be waiting at their next stop. However, that wouldn't be until Fort Laramie in Wyoming Country. It seemed quite plausible that Malinda would have had sufficient time to have received Elizabeth's posts and replied by now. Certainly she'd have sensed the urgency in Elizabeth's correspondence, written more than four months ago. And surely Malinda would have appreciated the need to hear some sort of response—even a short note saying all was well. Elizabeth didn't want to worry or grow anxious about what they would discover once they reached their final destination in the far West. But until she heard from Malinda and John, there was that uneasiness that came with not knowing. She hoped nothing had gone wrong with the relatives in Oregon. Not that it would change anything. For better or for worse, they were on their way. No turning back now.

While still in the crowded post office area, Elizabeth removed her carefully folded stationery from her handbag. She'd tucked it there in the hopes of needing to answer a letter from Malinda. Despite the lack of a letter, she wrote a quick note with a pencil, explaining where they were on their journey and how they were all well and how they hoped to reunite with their relatives in September. Hastily addressing and sealing this, she returned to the counter to purchase the necessary postage, and while standing in line, she silently prayed that her letter would reach Malinda and John quickly.

"Did you get a letter?" Clara asked when Elizabeth returned.

She shook her head. "But I sent Malinda a note."

"No doubt we will hear from her soon," Clara said. "And now I think we should head back to camp. "It's time to get supper started."

"Are all these people from our wagon train?" Ruth asked as they pressed through the busy settlement.

"Many emigrants pass through this fort," Elizabeth explained.

"That's right," Clara told her. "Your grandpa said that some days there are as many as a thousand travelers stopping here in Fort Kearney."

"There's Tillie!" Ruth pointed to a group walking ahead of them, and she called out to her friend. Flo Flanders and her children stopped and waited, and soon Ruth and Tillie were walking hand in hand while Ruth told her all about the moccasins.

"Did you hear the news?" Flo asked them.

"About Evangeline?" Clara said quietly.

"Yes." Flo nodded eagerly. "I heard she..." Flo glanced around to see her teenage daughters listening attentively.

Clara cleared her throat. "I heard that Evangeline has decided to, well, she plans to marry a soldier. An army officer. Anyway, that's what Ruby told me."

"She's going to marry an officer?" Elizabeth couldn't believe her ears. "How did this happen so quickly?"

Mahala giggled. "It hasn't happened. Not yet. She just thinks it's going to happen. You should have seen her all gussied up and—"

"Hush now." Flo glanced at Ruth and Tillie, just out of earshot ahead of them and then at her middle daughter, Hannah, who was only thirteen but all ears.

"Anyway, it seems that Evangeline has decided not to continue with the wagon train," Clara filled in.

Elizabeth was stunned. "Just like that?"

"I heard that she told Ruby to set her trunk out beside the wagon when we leave in the morning," Mahala confided, "and that she'll get her man friend to help her pick it up."

"For the wedding," Flo said a bit loudly.

Elizabeth studied her friend's face. "So there will really be a wedding?"

"Oh, Ma!" Mahala laughed. "We all know that there's not going to be any—"

"I think it's a fine idea for Evangeline to marry an officer in the army," Clara declared. "It will be a new beginning for her. Imagine her in a brand-new life out here on the frontier. Perhaps she'll raise asparagus and chickens." Clara pointed to the market basket hooked over Elizabeth's arm and began telling everyone about her good finds in the marketplace. And soon the conversation shifted from Evangeline's strange decision to depart from the wagon train, to food and supplies and what everyone was fixing for supper.

As they walked back to their nearby camp, Elizabeth felt a small wave of relief. Of all the members of the Morris party, Evangeline had been the one of most concern. Not just because she was the prettiest of the bunch—well, not counting Jessica—but also because Evangeline had continued to experience bouts of "sickness" that Asa had decided might simply be the result of "too much moonshine." Plus, according to some, including grumpy Gertie, Evangeline was reputed to being "overly friendly" with the menfolk. Perhaps they would all be much better off if Evangeline did remain in Fort Kearney to "marry" an officer. One could only hope...and pray. And that's what Elizabeth decided she would do.

Chapter Twenty-Six

It only took a couple of days for tongues to stop wagging about Evangeline's absence, and unless it was Elizabeth's imagination, it seemed to have quieted Gertie down as well. And now the train seemed to fall into a somewhat predictable routine, soundly moving forward at a good pace of fifteen to twenty miles a day. Everyone, including the livestock, seemed to understand their roles now. Occasional breakdowns kept Bert Flanders busy and provided food for his family because he usually traded his blacksmithing for supplies. But aside from these, everything seemed to be working fairly smoothly and efficiently. Even the weather was congenial.

"We've enjoyed some good days of travel this week," Asa said on their fourth morning out of Fort Kearney. They had just finished breakfast and were loaded and ready to go. "But today will come with its own challenges. Let's bow our heads and ask God to bless and protect us as we cross the river."

Elizabeth squeezed both of her children's hands as her father said amen. She was somewhat reassured knowing that both JT and Ruth were able to swim. Worried that they could fall in the creek behind their farm, James had insisted on teaching them when they were still small. But even a good swimmer could drown in such a cold, fast-moving river. Elizabeth wanted to take no chances today.

They'd camped along the fork of the North and South Platte Rivers the night before, and everyone knew they would spend most of the day crossing the south river today. It wouldn't be their first time to cross water, but it was expected to be the most perilous crossing so far. And a lot of the emigrants, including poor Lavinia, were understandably worried. Unfortunately, since unit five was the last unit in the train once again, Lavinia had most of the day to work her fretting into something of a frenzy. By the afternoon, when they were finally taking their place to cross over, Lavinia was quite worked up.

"At least we're fortunate enough to afford the ferry to get our wagons across," Elizabeth reminded her as they stood on the east side of the river, watching anxiously as other wagons from their unit were getting prepared to be rope-towed across the water. Everything had to be secured inside the wagons and then, one by one, they would be pulled by a rope across the water—and with any luck, they would stay afloat. Elizabeth wouldn't admit it, but it all looked rather frightening.

By now, all of the livestock and most of the teams had already been herded across the river and were waiting on the other side. That alone had been a disturbing scene to witness. Elizabeth had almost been afraid to breathe as she'd watched her beloved horses, Beau and Bella and Molly, bravely swimming against the current with the other animals. She and Ruth had cheered and danced when they saw the horses safely emerge on the other side, where JT and a couple of the older boys were waiting to attend to them.

Now they simply had to wait for their turn on the ferry. But the waiting felt nearly as nerve-racking as she imagined the actual crossing would be. She wondered how many rivers they would cross like this before they reached their final destination. And what if the rivers were wider and wilder than this one? That's when she remembered what Asa had reminded them of the previous night. "Our Lord told us not to be anxious or worried about what tomorrow may bring," he'd told them. "Each day has enough troubles for itself, so why go borrowing troubles from a day that's not even here yet?"

But today was here now, and Elizabeth could tell that many of the travelers were worried and anxious. Particularly Lavinia.

"What if their wagons leak?" Lavinia said nervously.

With a concerned expression, Ruth pointed to where the first wagon from their unit was being towed to the edge of the rapidly running water. "What if it does leak, Mama? What if their wagon sinks? Do you think Paddy and Fiona know how to swim?"

"You know that everyone was supposed to waterproof their wagons," Elizabeth calmly told her. "Just like your uncle did to our wagon. Surely they will float just fine."

"I hope everyone did as good a job as Matthew did," Clara said uneasily.

"I don't know whether I'd rather float my wagon across the river or put it on that rickety-looking ferry down there." Lavinia frowned over at the ferry landing. "That vessel doesn't look a bit seaworthy to me."

"Fortunately, that ferry isn't crossing the sea," Clara said wryly.

"But what if the ferry sinks?" Lavinia demanded. "What would we do then?"

"Swim?" Ruth queried.

"It's not going to sink," Elizabeth assured her. Of course, even as she said this, she wasn't completely convinced. The ferry did look a bit worse for wear. Already it had taken dozens of wagons across today—without problems, as far as she knew. It seemed unlikely that it would sink, but what if it broke apart and tipped sideways and the wagons rolled off? Perhaps it would be safer to float their wagons across on the rope tow just as the McIntires were doing right now.

She prayed a silent prayer of protection for the sweet young Irish couple. Paddy was such a cheerful fellow and a talented musician. And just this week, Fiona had confided to Elizabeth and Clara that she was expecting her first baby. The poor young woman hadn't even realized she was with child when they'd started out on this strenuous journey, and now, worried that her dear husband would fret too much over her welfare, she'd yet to tell Paddy the news.

Elizabeth gasped as the McIntire wagon lurched sideways when the strong, swift current swept into it. But four pairs of sturdy oxen were pulling on the other side. Asa had insisted they needed plenty of power, and Brady and Matthew were driving the oversized team. And as Matthew loudly cracked the whip over the animals' heads, the team began to tow hard. A rope tied to the rear of the wagon was being held tautly by some of the men on this side, so the wagon slowly straightened itself out and continued across.

All the women watching from the river's edge let out a collective sigh of relief as the McIntire wagon finally made it to the other side. As it emerged dripping and dark with water, they all let out a happy cheer.

"Well, there. Now that wasn't too bad." However, Clara sounded a bit breathless.

"Oh, my heavens!" Lavinia put a hand to her forehead. "I feel slightly faint."

"Why don't you go and sit in your wagon?" Elizabeth pointed to where the Prescott wagon was in line to be loaded on the ferry. "You might be more comfortable there."

"Yes, Mother, let's get you into the wagon. And if you want to keep fretting over every little thing, at least not everyone will be forced to listen." Evelyn sounded exasperated as she led Lavinia down to where Asa, Will, and Hugh had queued the wagons down by the ferry landing. Sharing Asa's oxen team, they were just starting to load the first of the Bostonians' wagons, but it was clearly going to be an arduous affair. And it would surely take a bit of time to get them secured on the ferry and across the river. The small craft could only carry three wagons at a time, one in front and two behind, so it would probably take several hours to get all six of them across. However, with Asa taking the lead in this effort, Elizabeth felt confident they would complete their task successfully. Even the captain had expressed confidence at Asa's ability to get their unit safely across.

"It's the Schneiders' turn to float the river," Ruth announced.

They all turned to watch the spectacle. Of all the people in their unit, Elizabeth knew the Schneiders the least. Other than attending Sunday services, the family of four seemed to keep mostly to themselves. Perhaps it was their language barrier—the parents spoke little English.

"They've got a good sturdy wagon," Clara said. "I doubt they'll have any problems. Did you know that Mr. Schneider was a wagon maker when they lived in Germany? And that's what he worked at in Independence too. That's what the daughter, Anna, told me. They came over from Germany before the children were born, but it was Mr. Schneider's goal to get the family out West. He's been saving for years to make this trip."

Fortunately the Schneider wagon made it safely across without any trouble. And now it was the Mullers' turn. They could hear Gertie's loud, gruff voice yelling directions at everyone around her, insisting that they needed to tighten the slack on the ropes and that the team on the other side needed to pull harder. But eventually the wagon was across, and it was time for the Taylors.

"Do you think they'll be too heavy?" Ruth asked with concern. "Because of that piano?"

"I'm sure they'll be fine," Clara told her.

"Oh, look," Elizabeth said. "The Bramfords and Prescotts are going across on the ferry now." They all turned to watch.

"Do you think Mrs. Prescott fainted?" Ruth asked.

"It might make the crossing easier on everyone if she did," Clara said.

Elizabeth chuckled, but as she watched the ferry going deeper into the water, all humor vanished. The current was strong, and water was flowing over the top of the ferry's deck. Was that supposed to happen? What if the ferry was going down? What if Lavinia had been right to be worried? Once again, Elizabeth felt she would rather be floating her own wagon than to be trapped on a sinking ferry. She took a deep breath and, as she watched with wide eyes, she prayed for their safe passage.

"They made it!" Ruth exclaimed as the ferry was tied off on the other side. They all let out another cheer.

"I suppose we should go down and get on our wagons now," Elizabeth said. "They'll be loaded next."

As they walked toward the ferry, they saw that the Flanders' wagon was just starting to get towed across. Ruth waved to where Tillie and Hannah were perched in the back of the wagon, peering out the rounded opening in the canvas covering with excited expressions and waving enthusiastically.

"Good luck!" Ruth waved happily at her friends. "See you on the other side!"

They were seated in their own wagon, which was loaded on the ferry, when they saw Ruby's wagon, the final wagon, getting ready to be rope towed across the river. All three women—Jess, Ruby, and Doris—were sitting in front. Jess waved and smiled, but the others looked a little uneasy. Elizabeth waved to them, and Ruth called out encouragingly. Then their ferry began to move.

"Here we go," Elizabeth told Ruth. "Hold on."

Ruth laughed but grabbed her mother's hand just the same. As they began to float, Elizabeth tried not to think of how heavily packed her parents' and brother's wagons were. Surely they wouldn't sink the ferry.

"Here come Ruby and Doris and Jess," Ruth sang out.

Elizabeth turned to watch their friends as their wagon first rolled into the water and then began to float. Ruby and Doris seemed to relax some, but as the ferry was about midway across the river, they heard a loud snapping sound.

"The rope in back!" Ruth pointed to the back of the wagon floating downriver from them. "It's broke, Mama." And now the wagon, no longer secured on both ends, began to be pushed sideways with the current.

"Get another rope!" Bert Flanders yelled from the east side of the river. "Someone in the wagon get another rope and toss it to me!"

Jess scrambled from the front seat and eventually popped her head out from the back, holding up a rope with a worried look. "I've got the rope!" she yelled to Bert and his oldest son.

"Tie it to the wagon and then throw it back to us," he called as he waded out into the water. "Can you do that?"

She was already tying an end of the rope to a metal loop on the back of the wagon. Then she looped the rope into a coil and attempted to toss it over to Bert, who had his hands stretched out. But it didn't make it. So she pulled it back, winding the now dripping rope into another coil, and this time, straddling the tailgate of the wagon like a horse, she gave the coiled rope an even more vigorous throw. But just as she was pitching it, the wagon was hit by a strong current, which sent it spinning completely around so that they couldn't see her. But they heard Jess letting out a loud yelp and then a big splash.

"She fell in!" Ruth screamed, pointing to the blue calico skirt that ballooned around Jess as she was swept away by the fast-moving water. "Jess fell in the river!"

"Oh, dear God!" Elizabeth gasped. "Please, help her!"

"Uncle Matthew is going to get her!" Ruth pointed to where Matthew was running along the shore on the other side of the river. He was calling out to Jess and stripping off his jacket as he ran. And then he leaped off the riverbank close to where she was struggling in the water, and suddenly they both disappeared around the bend of the river.

Elizabeth felt sickened as she grabbed Ruth's hand. "Let's go to Grandma," she said, knowing that Clara must have witnessed the whole thing as well. Elizabeth hurried to get down and carefully helped Ruth down. They rushed up to where Clara was sitting in her own wagon with tears filling her faded blue eyes.

"Oh, my. Oh, my!" Clara shook her head. "That does not look good."

"He's going to be all right," Elizabeth told her mother. "They both are. Matthew is a good swimmer."

"But the water is so cold...and the current...so strong."

"Let's pray for them," Ruth bravely declared. And in a faithful voice, she began to pray loudly. "Dear God, please help Matthew and Jess. Please help them to swim to shore and to come back to us. We know you can do that, dear God. We kindly thank you for your help today. Amen."

"Hurry and get this boat across the river," Asa commanded the man in charge of the ferry. "That's my son in the water."

Time seemed to stand still as they waited for the ferry to move like a slow turtle to the other side of the river. Meanwhile, they helplessly watched Ruby's wagon, still struggling against the current as Brady and some other men urged the oxen to tow it to the other shore. Just as the wagon's wheels finally connected with the edge of the river bank, Elizabeth flew into action. "I'll get some blankets," she told Clara. "As soon as we land, I'll run them down the shore. Jess and Matthew will need them." She looked at Ruth. "You stay with Grandma. And wait until Grandpa helps you both off the ferry. We don't want anyone else falling in."

Then she dashed back to her own wagon, where she gathered some blankets. Bundling them against her chest, she went up to stand by her father and the man running the ferry, explaining her plan. "And get a fire going as soon as you get landed," Elizabeth told

Asa. "So we can warm them up." Then, as they neared the shore, she spotted JT standing nearby, looking toward the ferry with a frightened and confused expression.

"JT!" she yelled. "Get on a horse and ride down the river and look for them."

"Yes, ma'am!" he shot back at her.

"And I'm coming too," she yelled as he took off toward the livestock area.

When the ferry was still about a foot from the landing, she took a running leap and just kept on going.

"Do you need help?" Will called out.

"Yes!" she yelled back. "Maybe so."

So now Will and Belinda were running with her. And JT, riding bareback on Molly, shot out ahead of the three of them, quickly rounding the bend. As Elizabeth ran, she prayed silently with each step. "God help them. God help them. God help them." She wasn't sure how far they'd run, but her sides ached. It felt like at least a mile when JT yelled out. "I see 'em!" he shouted triumphantly. And sliding off the horse, he ran over to a raised bank and slid down. "They're down here, Ma!"

Elizabeth and the others followed in time to see Matthew carrying a lifeless-looking bundle of dripping blue calico out of the water. He gently laid Jess onto a rocky beach area, pushing a dark strand of hair away from her pale face.

"Is she dead?" JT asked quietly as they all stood looking.

"*No!*" Elizabeth declared as she slid down the riverbank toward them. "She can't be." She knelt down, and picking Jess up, she wrapped the blankets snugly around her. Then, shaking her lifeless body firmly, Elizabeth slapped Jess' cheeks a couple of times and shook her harder. Anything to wake her. She had to wake her!

"Come on, Jess," she yelled at her. "You can't leave us like this. *Come on!*"

Suddenly water poured out of Jess' mouth, and her eyes opened with a startled expression. As she sputtered and coughed, Elizabeth put her arms around her, holding her tightly. "Come on," she told Will and Belinda. "Help me to get her up and moving. We need to get her blood flowing."

As they all helped to support Jess, who was still coughing and wheezing, Elizabeth glanced over to where Matthew was just standing and staring as if he was too shocked to even respond. Then she noticed that he too was shivering and shaking. "Come on, you get over here too." She tugged him next to Jess, and opening the blanket, she wrapped them together like two sausages and began to vigorously rub their arms and shoulders and backs. "We need to get you two warmed up as quickly as possible."

With everyone helping, they got the strange-looking blanket bundle up the riverbank and briskly walking. And then, after Matthew assured Elizabeth that he could stay on the horse as well as keep Jess from falling, they helped them both onto Molly's back and sent them on ahead.

"Father should have a warming fire going," she called out. "But you both need to get into dry clothes first thing." She let out a sigh of relief as Molly began to canter. "Thanks be to God!"

"You can say that again," Will agreed. "I really thought that was the last we'd see of both of them."

"My uncle is a good swimmer," JT told him. "I knew he could rescue her."

"That was truly amazing," Belinda said.

"How did you know Jess was going to be all right?" Will asked Elizabeth. "I honestly thought she was dead."

"I don't know." She shrugged as they walked. "I just felt it inside of me. I felt certain that she wasn't dead…that she wasn't going to die. I couldn't give up."

"You're a good woman to have around in a crisis." He turned to Belinda. "If anyone in our family needs urgent help, I want you to run and get Elizabeth."

Elizabeth just laughed. "You might be better off to fetch my mother," she told Belinda. "She knows more about medicine than I do."

Now JT told them about the time he fell out of his grandparents' hay loft and broke his arm. "Grandma knew just what to do to fix it. It hurt a lot when she did it, but it made my arm heal good and straight. Even the doctor said she did it just right."

By the time they reached the wagons, Elizabeth felt inexplicably happy. Maybe it was a result of the close call with her brother and Jess, or the fact that they'd all made it safely across the river, or maybe she was simply enjoying the company of her son and Will and Belinda.

Matthew and Jess had already finished changing into dry clothes and were huddling with family and friends by the fire, retelling their perilous story to anxious listeners, when Asa announced that it was time to go. "The captain wants us to make a few miles before we camp tonight," he explained. "He expects another wagon train might be coming through here just a day or two behind us, and he wants to keep some space between us."

"Got your wagon all hitched 'n' ready, ma'am," Brady told Elizabeth. "Mr. Matthew's too. If'n you don't mind, I'll ride with your brother."

"I don't mind a bit. And thank you, Brady," she told him. "I don't know what I'd do without you."

"And Flax is tied at your wagon. So much goings-on, didn't want him runnin' off." He nodded shyly as he walked away.

Jess joined Elizabeth as they headed for their wagons. "I want to thank you," she told her. "It seems your family continues to rescue me." She paused to hug Elizabeth with glistening eyes. "Thank you so much!"

"I'm just so very glad you're all right." Elizabeth touched Jess' cheek. "You gave us quite a scare, young lady."

"I didn't tell Ruby and Doris *everything* that happened in the river—what a close call it was." Jess spoke quietly. "I didn't want to overly worry Aunt Ruby."

"You just make sure you don't let anything like that happen again," Elizabeth said in a slightly stern tone. "We don't want to lose you, Jess."

When she got to the wagon, JT and Ruth were already in the seat, and her father's wagon was starting to roll just ahead of them. "Can I drive?" JT asked hopefully.

"I'd appreciate it if you did, son." She stepped on the wheel hub and climbed up, pausing to smile at her children as she sat down. "Well, that was an exciting river crossing, wasn't it?"

Ruth nodded eagerly. "But God did take care of all of us, didn't he, Mama?"

"He did, Ruthie." Elizabeth pulled on a leather glove and reached down to release the brake, watching as JT sat tall, clucked his tongue, and then snapped the reins. "He surely did."

Chapter Twenty-Seven

The May weather continued mild and warm, and the prairie crossing continued without any serious calamity or mishap. Certainly, it was hard work—walking for miles, carrying water, cooking on an open fire, washing clothes in the river—but so far no one had drowned, no one was sick, the sun was shining, and Elizabeth felt there was relatively little to complain about. But she'd learned by now that a number of her fellow travelers always seemed to find a reason to moan. Perhaps they would be lost if they had nothing to grumble over.

For that reason, she usually tried to avoid certain individuals, like grumpy Gertie Muller or whiney Lavinia Prescott or the preachy Mrs. Taylor. Oh, Elizabeth would never admit to harboring such strong and disagreeable opinions on these three fellow travelers, and naturally she felt ashamed over her lack of good manners, but if she saw one of those three women coming her way, she usually tried to think of some good excuse to go in a different direction. And today that excuse had come by way of the children. When Ruth invited Elizabeth to walk with her and the Flanders' girls as they collected wildflowers, Elizabeth was more than happy to join them.

But now as the three happy girls flitted about in the sunshine, thoroughly enjoying each other's company, Elizabeth felt guilty to remember how she had avoided Gertie this morning. They'd both been on their way to fetch water, and Elizabeth had purposely slowed her pace, pretending to stop to admire a prairie flower. Really, how hard would it have been to walk with Gertie or to say something pleasant? Of course, Gertie didn't seem to appreciate anything pleasant. She truly seemed to derive more pleasure from constantly faultfinding and lambasting those who didn't measure up to her high expectations. Whether her comments were about a member of her own family or Captain Brownlee (if he wasn't around to hear it), Gertie seemed to enjoy making noise. It was simply her way.

Now Elizabeth considered Lavinia. Sometimes Lavinia seemed to truly need a friend. But more often than not, Lavinia wanted someone to complain to. The previous night she had cornered Elizabeth at the campfire. She'd gotten her attention by confiding her concerns for her nineteen-year-old son, Julius, and how worried she was that poor Julius might be smitten by Jessica—even more so after her close scrape in the river. However, Lavinia had gone from there to directly complaining about how much she regretted venturing on this perilous trip altogether and how she wanted to turn the wagon around at Fort Laramie and join a group heading east. Elizabeth was well aware that the deprivations and demands were taking their toll on the city woman, and she knew it didn't help when her rambunctious and energetic children made jokes at her expense. Most of the time Elizabeth tried to be patient with Lavinia, but more often than not she found herself wanting to run. Truth be told, Elizabeth could relate better to Lavinia's young adult children than to Lavinia.

However, and it was difficult to admit this even to herself, Elizabeth had the most difficulty with the pious Mrs. Taylor. Whenever she saw Mrs. Taylor approaching, Elizabeth wanted to duck behind something and hide. And this afternoon was no different when, alerted by Flax's barking, she realized that Mrs. Taylor was striding purposefully toward them and waving. "Elizabeth Martin," she called out.

Hushing the dog, Elizabeth lifted her hand in a halfhearted wave and stopped walking.

"Tillie and I want to go pick flowers over there." Ruth pointed eagerly to where some bright yellow blooms were growing profusely to the south of them. "Can we, Mama?"

Elizabeth looked at Hannah. The girl was only thirteen and small for her age, but she was as responsible as most grown-ups. "Only if Hannah goes with you—and stays with you too."

"I will, ma'am. I promise," Hannah told her.

"And take Flax along as well." Elizabeth glanced over her shoulder to see that Mrs. Taylor was nearly there now. "And remember I'm going over by the creek to look for strawberries, if you want to join me after you pick some flowers."

"Yes, Mama."

"And don't venture too far off, and do keep an eye on the wagons," she warned.

They all gladly agreed to her conditions, and before Mrs. Taylor joined her, the three girls and the yellow dog bounded happily off into the May sunshine. Elizabeth wished she was running freely with them. Instead she forced a smile for Mrs. Taylor's sake, congenially greeting her.

"Good afternoon to you too." Mrs. Taylor sounded a bit breathless as she fell into stride with Elizabeth. The older woman was obviously trying to catch her breath.

"Isn't it a perfectly beautiful day?" Elizabeth said cheerfully. "Just glorious."

"It certainly started out fair enough, but Mr. Taylor tells me there's weather coming our way. He says he can feel it in his bones."

"Oh..." Elizabeth just nodded.

"I saw you out here walking, and I felt moved by the good Lord to come and join you."

"How thoughtful." Elizabeth switched the small gathering basket to her other arm.

"I wish to speak to you regarding our church services," Mrs. Taylor announced in an important tone. "I'm just certain you can help me."

"Oh?" Elizabeth pressed her lips together.

"Yes. It seems silly to have two church services going at the same time. Two different services in one small unit of only twelve wagons. Tsk-tsk. Such a waste, don't you think? Not to mention how it divides our unity, separating the brethren from one another. Downright sinful if you ask me. Wouldn't you agree?"

"But many towns have different denominations and churches, all living happily side by side. It stands to reason that some congregations enjoy one sort of service and others appreciate something completely different."

"That may be so. But we are not a town, Elizabeth. And what with our ability to provide fine music and my husband's excellent training as a minister, and after all, we do worship the same God, do we not?"

"I certainly hope so." Noticing a small breeze picking up, Elizabeth paused to retie her prairie bonnet strings more securely.

"So when I saw you out here, I thought perhaps you were just the one to fix our little problem."

"To fix it?" Elizabeth blinked. "How so?"

"I thought perhaps you would encourage your father to combine our two worship services into one service this Sunday."

Elizabeth paused to carefully consider her response. "I will admit that it does seem a bit silly to have two separate services, Mrs. Taylor."

The older woman nodded firmly. "Precisely my thinking. I felt certain you would understand and agree."

"And I feel certain that my father would gladly welcome your group to come and worship with us if you'd like. His sermons aren't as long as Mr. Taylor's, and our music is a bit different with the fiddle, guitar, and harmonica, but we do have such a good time. Everyone seems to enjoy it, even the young people." Elizabeth turned and smiled directly at her. "Please, do come and gather with us on Sunday, Mrs. Taylor. We would love to have—"

"Well, I—no, my dear, that's not what I had in mind. No, not at all. I thought your group would wish to come join us. Like I said, we have the piano. My husband is a man of the cloth. If anyone is fit to lead a church service, it is us. Wouldn't you agree?"

Elizabeth knew there was no easy way to put this. "I do appreciate the invitation, Mrs. Taylor, and I can only answer for myself and my children, but we so enjoy my father's services, I doubt we can be lured away." She gave her a sly grin. "And think about it, how would my own father feel if his own flesh and blood attended a different service? Certainly that would divide our family's unity."

"But I thought your father and the rest of your family would come as well."

"Of course, it's possible that others will want to come. That's not for me to say. You would have to ask them about that yourself." She held up her empty basket. "Now if you'll kindly excuse me, I heard that I might find some wild strawberries down by the creek that runs over there. I do believe I'll go and take a look." She waved and then quickly turned, hurrying off back toward the train, where she ducked behind her own wagon, which was being driven by Brady and JT. What she said was true. She had hoped to gather some berries, but she felt childish and guilty for her hasty departure.

And she knew that it was rude not to invite Mrs. Taylor to join her in strawberry gathering. But she also knew that invited or not, Mrs. Taylor's persistent nature might push her to follow Elizabeth in the hopes of persuading her to change her mind about attending their church service. Fortunately, she did not. Of course, she probably knew by now that gathering alongside the moving wagon train meant walking quickly and bending frequently as one kept pace with the wagons—not an easy task but very rewarding when you returned with berries or mushrooms or, even more valuable, dry firewood for the cook fire.

Walking at a fast clip westward, Elizabeth saw little sign of ripened strawberries, but she was finding some good twigs and branches, and her basket was quickly filling up with the kind of fire fuel that was always more welcome than buffalo chips. Then, just as she decided it was time to check on the girls, she noticed how the southeastern sky had darkened in a strange and sinister way. A rush of fear swept through her as she saw the tall, slender shadow of a twister moving menacingly toward them. Clutching the basket to her chest, she ran back toward her wagon, calling out to Brady and JT. "Where is Ruth? Have you seen her?"

When they both shook their heads, she pointed out toward the rapidly approaching twister moving directly toward the field of yellow flowers. "Ruth was with the Flanders' girls. Right over there."

"Whoa!" Brady said loudly.

Elizabeth tossed her basket into the back of the wagon, and as it was coming to a stop, she untied Molly.

"Want me to saddle her?" Brady yelled as she led the horse to the front.

"No time. Stay here with JT." Elizabeth climbed onto the wheel hub and rearranged her full skirt. Straddling the horse, she took off toward the field of yellow blooms. The twister had moved even closer now, not very large but dark and foreboding. She had to warn the girls. She spotted the tops of their heads bobbing in the tall grass as they continued to pick, apparently oblivious to the menacing cone coming directly toward them. Elizabeth dug her heels into Molly's flanks as she yelled out to them, trying to warn them of the impending danger, telling them to grab one another's hands, to grab anything. But before she could reach them, the air turned brown with whirling dust, and Elizabeth could no longer see the girls—or anything else.

"Ruthie!" she screamed as the horse continued to gallop through the dust. "Dear God," she cried, "help those girls! Please, please, protect them!" Then as the wind grew fiercer, she bent down, clinging to Molly's neck, still praying.

And then, just like that, it was past her. She still couldn't see very well, but she nudged Molly to continue moving forward. "Ruthie!" she screamed again. "Ruthie! Tillie! Hannah!"

The air was eerily quiet as she walked Molly toward where she felt they'd been. "*Ruthie!*"

"Mama!"

"I'm coming!" With relief, Elizabeth slid down from the horse and, leading Molly toward where she'd heard Ruth's voice, called out again. "Where are you?"

"Here, Mama!" Ruth sobbed out. "Over here."

Now the dust was settling, and Elizabeth could see Ruth and Hannah and even Flax, all coated in thick brown dust. "Oh, sweetheart!" Elizabeth threw her arms around Ruth. "You're all right."

"*Tillie!*" Ruth cried. "She got taken away."

"*What?*"

"She's gone!" Hannah had tears streaking down the dust on her cheeks. "The twister took her."

"I had hold of her hand," Ruth cried, "and we were holding on to this rock." She pointed to a boulder. "But Tillie's hand slipped out of mine, and now she's gone!"

"No!" Elizabeth declared. "That can't be. We'll find her."

Holding hands, the three of them searched the area, all of them crying out for Tillie, but Tillie didn't answer. By now some of the young people who'd been walking alongside the wagons had run over to help, and Elizabeth quickly explained the strange situation.

"Take Hannah back to the Flanders," she instructed Belinda. "And tell them that Ruth and I are out looking for Tillie." She moved Molly over to the boulder the girls had clung to, and climbing on it, she hoisted Ruth and herself onto Molly's broad back. "We'll follow the trail the twister took," she called out as she turned the horse to the south. "Send some others on horseback to join us. We're going to find her!"

"Will we find her?" Ruth asked in a shaky voice.

"We'll sure try, Ruth. You pray like you did when Jess fell in the river. You ask God to help us find her." She nudged Molly faster. "And hang on tight to Molly's mane."

She cantered the horse, following the same path that the twister had taken. Although there seemed no sign of the twister nearby, or any others, she realized it might be dangerous out here. She also knew that they'd soon be out of sight of the wagon train, but she didn't know what else to do. A little girl was out there somewhere.

"Tillie!" they both yelled again and again. "Tillie, where are you?"

Just as Elizabeth was about to give up and go back to the wagon train for more searchers, Ruth let out a scream. She pointed down to what looked like an animal cowering on the ground. "*There,* Mama!"

Elizabeth squinted at the strange-looking, bear-like brown creature. "What is it?"

"It's Tillie!"

Elizabeth blinked to see that it was indeed Tillie. She was covered in brown dust and wearing only her chemise and bloomers and a wild-looking head of hair.

"*Tillie!*" Elizabeth cried as she slid off her horse, helping Ruth down. Then they both ran over and hugged the little girl.

"I knew God would help us find you," Ruth declared.

"Are you all right?" Now Elizabeth knelt down to peer closely at the frightened child, checking her for bleeding or broken bones. But other than being filthy, Tillie seemed to be just fine.

"I flew like a bird," Tillie told them with wide eyes.

"In the sky?" Ruth asked.

Tillie nodded. "And I went spinning round and round too. Just like a top."

"Were you very scared?"

"At first I was scared. Then it was all over with. I landed right here on my behind." She rubbed her backside. "That hurt a little."

Ruth hugged her again. "I'm so glad you're all right. But what happened to your clothes?"

Tillie looked down and laughed. "The twister took 'em."

Now Ruth laughed. "You should see yourself, Tillie. Your hair looks just like a tumbleweed."

"Tumbleweed Tillie," Elizabeth said as she used her handkerchief to clean some of the dust away from Tillie's eyes. Just then she heard the sound of horses' hooves and looked up to see Jessica and Matthew quickly approaching them.

"We found her," she called out to them as they joined them. "Jessica, why don't you put Tillie on your horse and run her back to the Flanders. Poor Flo must be sick with worry by now."

"And Ruth can ride with me," Matthew offered.

Seeing his horse was saddled and probably safer, Elizabeth gladly agreed. She gave Ruth a boost, helping to hoist her up in front of him. "Thanks, Matthew. I'll meet you back there." She pointed at Ruth. "And even though it's not Saturday, tonight will most assuredly be bath night."

It wasn't until they turned and rode off that Elizabeth realized there was no handy rock or log or wagon wheel hub to climb onto and help her up onto her tall horse. And without a saddle and wearing a dress, there was no way she was going to make it up there. And so she simply walked, leading Molly back toward the wagons, which were at least a mile or two off. She hoped she'd find something along the way with a bit of height to it. However, the grasslands were flat and mostly barren. Great for wagon travel, but not very helpful when one needed something to step onto. Consequently she was greatly relieved to see the dust from another rider approaching. Perhaps it was Matthew returning to check on her and she could ask him for a boost. But she was pleased and surprised to see Eli Kincaid instead.

"I heard about your adventures," he said as he dismounted his horse.

"I forgot to ask the others whether any of the wagons had been hit by it," she said. "But I think we followed its path, and it seemed to have missed the train."

He nodded. "Most of the emigrants never even saw it. But Belinda and Amelia witnessed the whole thing."

She sighed. "I've never seen anything like it." She told him what Tillie had said about flying and spinning. "You should see her," Elizabeth chuckled. "We called her Tumbleweed Tillie."

He laughed. "I did see her. And I think she's earned that name." Now he pointed to her horse. "Why are you on foot? Is your horse all right?"

With embarrassment she explained her situation. "I should have asked Matthew to give me a boost. But with all the excitement, I forgot."

He rubbed his chin thoughtfully. "Riding bareback in a dress?"

She felt her cheeks blushing. "Well, it wasn't as if I had time for propriety—"

"No, no, I didn't mean that. It's just that I'm impressed."

She shrugged. "I've been riding horses since I can remember. Nothing to be impressed about."

"Except that now you can't mount your horse." His eyes twinkled in a teasing way.

"Yes…" She started walking again. "But at least I can still walk."

"Come on," he said. "Let me help you."

Without too much ado, he offered his cupped hands for her to step into, and once again she was straddling the horse. She felt slightly self-conscious that the tops of her boots and her stockings were showing. But to her relief, Eli kept his eyes averted as he mounted his own horse. "Maybe we should take it slow since you don't have a saddle," he told her.

She was about to challenge this, reminding him that she was a good rider. But then, liking the idea of some time alone with him, she simply agreed. "It seems nothing short of miraculous that Tillie survived that twister," she said. "And I still don't understand how the other girls weren't picked up at all, although I'm very, very thankful." She sighed. "I was so worried that Ruth was—" Her voice choked on the words.

"It must have been frightening."

She found her soiled handkerchief and dabbed her eyes, trying not to reveal that she was crying and hoping she'd soon stop. "Very unsettling."

"It's plain to see how much your family means to you, Elizabeth."

She looked directly at him. "They are everything to me. I couldn't bear to lose one of them. Not my children. Nor my parents or brother."

His expression grew grim. "I wish I could say that we'll arrive in Oregon with no casualties or deaths, but it's never like that."

She swallowed against the lump in her throat and simply nodded.

"But your family seems prepared for this kind of travel. The captain and I both noticed it from the start. You're well equipped and obviously capable. If I was a wagering man, I'd bet that your family makes it through without any serious troubles."

"I hope you're right." She tucked her handkerchief back into her skirt pocket, holding her head high again. "But I'll admit that seeing that twister and knowing the girls...my own little girl was out there in harm's way...well, it reminded me of how quickly things can change." She shook her head. "Calamity can befall anyone."

"True enough."

"It makes me want to keep my children safe at my side."

"Then how would they grow up to be strong enough to handle life's troubles on their own?"

"I'm just saying I want to…not that I will." Now she told him about Ruth praying as they searched for Tillie. "I need to remember to rely on my faith like that too," she admitted. "That's what it always comes down to…trusting God to take care of us."

"I reckon." He nodded with a sad expression.

"Have you ever lost anyone you really loved, Eli?" She was surprised at herself for asking this—and so abruptly too. But it was too late. It was already out there. And the truth was, she wanted to know.

"As a matter of fact, I have."

"Not that it's any of my business…" She looked down at the reins in her hands.

"I was married once…about a dozen years ago, although it seems like more now. Like another lifetime even. It only lasted a couple of years. Then I lost my wife and son to smallpox."

She glanced at him. "I'm sorry."

He just nodded. "Thank you. Most of the time I don't think about it too much. I hardly ever speak of it to anyone."

So she told him a bit about losing James and her unborn baby to cholera four years earlier. "It seems we have more in common than I realized."

"I reckon we do."

Now there was a long silence, and she didn't know what to say. So to lighten the mood she talked about how the three little girls had been covered from head to toe with dust. "I hope we camp by the river tonight. It will take a good amount of water to get them all clean."

"I s'pect those girls will spark plenty of conversations around most of the campfires tonight."

She laughed. "Do you really think everyone will hear about it?"

"You'd be surprised at how tales can travel on a train like this. Like a wildfire on a windy day."

"I know that's true. The stories my father brings with him sometimes…" She chuckled. "And they say men don't gossip."

"Some stories can change dramatically the more they get told. By the time the twister story makes its rounds, it might sound even more fantastic than it was."

"You have to admit, the story of a little girl being carried off by a twister is already quite amazing. And to think she's all right..." Elizabeth shook her head in wonder.

Now he leaned over and peered curiously at her. "And I heard a strange part of the story too. According to one of the Bramford girls, you leaped onto your horse and galloped directly into the twister." He whistled. "Now that's something I would like to have witnessed firsthand."

She sighed. "Truth be told, it wasn't that gallant. I suppose most mothers would face the jaws of death in order to rescue their children." By now they had caught up with the rear of the wagon train. "Thank you for escorting me back..." She made a sheepish smile. "And for helping me to get back on my horse too."

"'Twas my pleasure, ma'am." He tipped his hat and grinned. "It's not every day I get to ride with the woman who chased down a twister."

Chapter Twenty-Eight

Asa had the foresight to put up the tent when they made camp that night. It provided a private bathhouse for the dust-coated girls as well as Elizabeth, who discovered she was almost as dirty as they were. "I wish we could all just jump into the river," Elizabeth said as she peeled the dust-encrusted skirt away from Ruth.

"Can we?" Tillie asked hopefully.

"Grandpa says it's flowing too fast," Ruth told her. Just then Flo and Mahala came in with buckets of water, warning that it was cold but promising to bring some hot water to warm it soon. Elizabeth helped the girls, washing and scrubbing and rinsing. But when it came to poor Tillie's hair, she didn't even know where to begin. Even with most of the dirt rinsed out, Tillie's fine, curly locks were so twisted and snarled around little twigs and burs that it was impossible to untangle.

"I don't know what you're going to do with it," Elizabeth told Flo.

"I'm afraid it's going to have to come off," Flo said sadly. "*All* of it."

"You're going to cut *all* of Tillie's hair off?" Ruth's eyes grew wide.

"Like a boy?" Tillie's eyes glimmered with interest.

"Don't worry, it'll grow back," Flo assured them.

"I'll get my scissors," Elizabeth offered, but then she remembered that Brady had taken all their shoes in order to give them a good oiling. "Except that I'm barefoot."

"I brought our moccasins to wear." Ruth stuck out a foot to show off her interesting footwear. "They're real comfortable, Mama."

So Flo went to fetch the scissors while Elizabeth put on her moccasins. "They *are* comfortable," she admitted. "But maybe not sturdy enough for walking too much."

"Indians walk in them," Ruth pointed out.

By suppertime, Tillie's hair had been cropped so short that she really did resemble a boy. "I've been scalped," she bragged as she let Ruth feel her shorn, round head.

"Put on your bonnet," Flo told her daughter. "No one will even notice."

But Tillie liked getting attention for having survived not only a twister but also a "scalping." And after supper, everyone in their unit congregated around Asa's campfire to hear Tillie give an account of her exciting adventures. Naturally, Tillie was more than pleased to accommodate them. And then the others who had been closest to the spectacle, including the Bramford girls, told their own accounts.

"We thought all of them were going to be taken up by the cyclone," Belinda said. "Tillie, Ruth, and Hannah just vanished in the whirling wind, and then it looked like Elizabeth and her horse were going to be swept away as well."

"It was a terrible thing to see," Amelia added. "We were certain we'd never see any of you again."

Will grinned at Elizabeth. "That was quite a brave thing you did—riding your horse out there to help the girls."

Elizabeth shrugged. "I'm sure you would have done the same if your children were in harm's way."

He nodded.

"But then the twister was gone, and we couldn't find Tillie anywhere," Hannah explained. "It was so terrifying. I thought I'd lost my little Tillie." She put her arm protectively around Tillie. "What would we do without our sweet baby sister?"

"But it turned out she was just fine," Ruth proclaimed. "And when we found her, her hair was sticking out all over like this." She held up her hands with her fingers splayed out. "Just like a tumbleweed. And that's why we named her Tumbleweed Tillie."

"And then I got scalped by my own ma." Tillie proudly ran her hand over her cropped hair.

"You shouldn't speak lightly about scalpings," Gertie warned her. "We're about to come into some dangerous Injun territory, where that could truly happen, and believe you me, it's no joking matter." Now Gertie launched into a terrible tale of how some California settlers suffered horribly at the hands of Indians.

"Excuse me, Gertie." Elizabeth cut her off when the description grew overly vivid. "But we have children listening."

"Children need to know about these goings-on too," Gertie argued.

"Not in such gruesome detail," Flo said sharply.

"And not before bedtime," Elizabeth added.

"I got an idea," Asa said cheerfully. "I think we should all make up a poem about Tumbleweed Tillie."

"Yes, let's do," Clara agreed.

"And I already got the first line." He grinned at Tillie with a twinkle in his eye.

"Tell us, Grandpa!" Ruth pleaded.

He stood up. "Starts out like this:

Tumbleweed Tillie, the Flanders' smallest sister,
went out to pick some poppies and got plucked up by a twister.

"That's good!" Tillie clapped her hands. Others began to add funny lines, and after a bit, Matthew was playing a tune on his fiddle with JT strumming along on his guitar. They had just put a funny little song together when Eli and the captain walked into camp with somewhat serious-looking expressions. As usual, the crowd quieted. It seemed that everyone came to attention when the captain showed up.

"Sorry to interrupt your festivities," he said as he stepped up to their campfire. "But Eli here tells me that some of the girls in this unit experienced some excitement today."

"Here's our very own Tumbleweed Tillie," Asa told him as he patted Tillie's shorn head. "We just made up a funny song about her."

"It's a great song," Tillie said proudly.

"I'd like to hear it," he told her. "But first I need to make an announcement. As you all know, it's been acceptable for folks to wander and explore a bit while we travel, as long as you stay within sight of the wagon train. But now that we're coming into Cheyenne country, we need to be even more cautious."

"Are the Cheyenne very dangerous?" Will Bramford asked.

"All Injuns are dangerous," Gertie spouted out.

"That's not true." Eli spoke in a firm tone. "Most Indians are more peaceful than white men."

"You're telling us that *savage Injuns* are peaceful?" Gertie narrowed her eyes. "What about those stories coming out of California?" Once again she began to tell of raids and murders.

"The Indians have been here much longer than the white man," Eli explained. "But the white man keeps pushing west, pushing the Indians out. It's only natural that some Indians can only take so much."

"And I reckon you think it's only natural to murder settlers too?" Gertie demanded.

"I'm not defending criminal acts," he told her. "I'm just trying to get you to understand their situation. White men have brought hunting parties to these plains and slaughtered thousands of buffalo—not for their meat or their hides but for sport. As a result, Indians starve. Imagine how you would feel if someone came and slaughtered your herds and deprived your children of food just for the fun of it?"

The group grew quiet now, and with thoughtful expressions they appeared to be considering what they'd just heard. Even Gertie was silenced.

The captain cleared his throat. "We're not trying to make you folks overly fearful of Indians, and we're not trying to turn you into Indian lovers either," he said. "We just want you to respect them. And that means respecting what some of them might be capable of. We don't expect any trouble, but at the same time we don't want to stir up any. So for the next few weeks we'll double up on guard duty at night. And we ask people to be watchful and to stay a little closer to the wagons during the day. And if you go out hunting or fishing, you make sure that it's in groups of three or more. And don't let children go out without having an adult along." He put a hand on Asa's shoulder. "And I need you to attend a councilman meeting tomorrow morning. My wagon at sunup." The captain turned to smile at the crowd. "How about singing that song for us now?"

After they sang the song, the group began to disperse, but Asa offered Eli and the captain some coffee and biscuits. The captain had other business to tend to, but Eli opted to sit a while. Elizabeth was glad he felt comfortable around their campfire...glad her father had extended hospitality.

"Sounds like you're getting better on the guitar," he told JT. "You must be practicing."

"Thanks." JT nodded eagerly. "I practice almost every night after chores are done."

Eli pointed to Ruth's feet now. "Those are mighty pretty moccasins, Ruth. Where'd you get them?"

She beamed at him. "Mama and I both got moccasins back at Fort Kearney." She pointed to Elizabeth's feet now.

"They look like they were made by Pawnee," he told her.

"How can you tell?" Ruth asked.

"Those flowers there. I could be wrong. Might be Lakota. But I've seen work like that before, and it was done by Pawnee women."

"You know a lot about Indians, don't you?" Ruth said.

"I reckon I know more'n most folks." He shrugged. "But that's only 'cause I lived with a tribe for a while."

"You *lived* with the Indians?" Ruth's eyes grew huge.

He chuckled and nodded and then took a slow sip of coffee.

"How long did you live with them?" JT asked.

"A few years."

Elizabeth was too stunned to speak. Eli had actually lived with Indians? How was that even possible? A white man cohabiting with Indians?

"Which tribe?" JT asked with interest.

"Crow."

"Where did you live?"

"We'll be near their territory when we're in Fort Laramie. They're mostly north of there. But they don't stay in one place. They're nomadic."

"What's nomadic?" Ruth asked.

"It means they move around," he explained. "They follow the buffalo herd or where the fishing is good or where the berries are ripe. In a way it's not so different from what you folks are doing. They take their homes with them."

"You mean teepees?" JT asked.

He nodded. "You'd be surprised at how quickly they can put one up or take it down. The women help each other, and the next thing you know, they're packed and ready to go."

"The women are responsible for putting up and taking down their teepees?" Clara asked with a creased brow.

"Aside from hunting and fishing, which is done by the men, the women do most of the work related to their survival. It's hard work being an Indian woman."

"It's hard work being a farmer's wife too." Clara exchanged a knowing glance with Elizabeth.

"In a way, you emigrants are living similar to the Indians, traveling in a group, taking your homes with you. Except most white folks don't know how to travel light."

"I suppose if we wanted to live in teepees and wear buckskins, we could travel more lightly." Asa sighed. "We might have to travel more lightly when we start climbing those mountains."

"Did Indians make your clothes?" Ruth asked.

Eli nodded.

"Mind if I ask how it came to be that you lived with the Crow?" Asa bent down to light his pipe.

"It's not a story I usually tell, but since you folks are friends…" Eli wrapped his hands around the tin cup. "I had an uncle who was a fur trapper for Hudson Bay Company. He'd come visit us in Virginia once in a while, always telling us all sorts of tall tales. I was about Matthew's age, and both my parents had passed on, when my uncle made one of his visits. He invited me to journey out West with him, and I saw no reason to say no. We left in the spring, and I discovered that I loved the traveling and living off the land and seeing new places. But it didn't take long to realize I wasn't overly fond of the trapping business. Still, I loved my uncle and knew he appreciated my companionship. Unfortunately, he drowned in the Bighorn River the second winter I was out there. That's when I decided I didn't really care to be a fur trapper at all."

"I'm sorry for your loss, son." Asa refilled his coffee cup.

Eli just nodded. "I'd decided to head back to Fort Laramie to spend the rest of the winter, but along the way I ran into a party of Sioux. I thought they were a hunting party at first, but they had a young woman with them, and something didn't add up. After spending a day with them, I suspected the girl was being held against her will. My uncle had been friends with some Crow Indians, and I'd learned a few words—enough to figure out the girl was Crow. And I also knew there was bad blood between Sioux and Crow, so I figured that whatever their plans for the girl were, they couldn't be good. As a matter of fact, I didn't feel too safe myself."

Everyone was listening intently now, and Elizabeth felt worried that this story might turn out to be as unsuitable for young ears as the one Gertie had been telling earlier. But Ruth and JT were so enthralled that she knew she couldn't send them to bed early. Besides, she wanted to hear the rest of his tale too. Just then Eli glanced over at her, and almost as if reading her thoughts, he barely tipped his head before continuing.

"So I asked the girl, as best I could, if she'd been kidnapped, and it turned out my hunch was right. So that night, after the Sioux were asleep, I snuck the girl out of their camp, and we took one of their horses and got away from them. We rode long and hard all night and throughout the next day. I wanted to distance ourselves from the Sioux and get back to Crow territory." He slowly shook his head as if the memory of fleeing those angry Sioux was an unpleasant one. "And when I returned her to her people, they were so thankful to have her back that they made me feel very welcome. So welcome that I stayed there for quite a while."

"Do you speak their language?" JT asked.

Eli nodded.

"Were the Crow Indians nice?" Ruth asked.

He smiled. "Very nice. They were like family to me."

"Thanks for telling us your story," Ruth said politely. "It was almost like reading an adventure book."

"A good bedtime story for you." Elizabeth picked up her lantern. "How about if you bid everyone goodnight?"

Ruth looked disappointed but didn't argue as she told everyone goodnight. As Elizabeth walked her back to their wagon, she could tell by Ruth's lagging steps that she was more tired than she'd admit. "We've had a long and exciting day," she said as she hung the lantern on the side of the wagon and helped Ruth climb into the back. "And tomorrow will be here before we know it."

After getting Ruth tucked in and hearing her prayers, Elizabeth excused herself. "I want to make sure JT gets to bed too," she told Ruth. And that was true, but she was also curious if Eli was telling any more stories about himself around the campfire. However, when she got back, Eli was gone, and it appeared that everyone else was heading for bed too.

"Time to call it a night," she told JT. She bent to pat Flax's head. "You too, old boy. Tomorrow's another long day."

"Eli is truly an interesting person, isn't he?" JT said as they walked back to their wagon together.

"He most certainly is," she said a bit crisply. She was just beginning to put two and two together regarding Eli. Remembering how he'd mentioned losing a wife and child to smallpox about twelve years ago, which was probably about the same time he'd lived with the Crow Indians, had gotten her to thinking. She'd heard scandalous tales of rough mountain men who'd married Indian women out West. She also recalled hearing reports of smallpox epidemics in the previous decade and of thousands of Indians dying as a result. Yes, she decided as she checked on the chickens, it all seemed to add up. In all likelihood, Eli had been married to an Indian woman.

She was just about to go inside her wagon when she heard something rustling on the other side of Matthew's wagon. She froze, listening intently, and knew that she was hearing the sounds of footsteps. But not normal footsteps...more like someone trying to be quiet...sneaking around. She wanted to alert JT, but he was already safely tucked into his hammock beneath the wagon. And so she tiptoed to the front of the wagon, and reaching beneath the seat, she quietly slipped out the gun that was wrapped in an old shawl.

Unwrapping the Colt Dragoon her father had given her, she

shivered at the feel of the cold metal. She knew the gun was loaded, and holding the wooden grip with one hand, she cradled the barrel in front of her and crept around to peek on the other side of the wagon. Her hand trembled slightly, and she wondered if she really had the grist to shoot another living soul if she had to. But one thought of her sleeping children and she knew that she would do anything to protect them.

But to her surprise, barely illuminated by the lantern inside Matthew's wagon, she saw two people—a man and a woman embracing. She blinked and then peered hard, trying to determine who these clandestine lovers might be. And then, recognizing the shape of her brother's hat, she realized it was Matthew! And he was kissing Jess!

Elizabeth let out a quiet gasp and backed up, worried that they might see her spying on them. But as she wrapped the Dragoon back in the shawl, slipping it beneath the seat, she felt anger toward her brother. Certainly, she had suspected that he was attracted to the girl. But to meet her in the night like this? What did Matthew think he was doing? And why was Jess sneaking around like this in the middle of the night? Tomorrow Elizabeth would have to give Matthew a big-sister scolding. Perhaps she would have a word with Jess as well.

Chapter Twenty-Nine

When Elizabeth found Matthew the next morning, he was just coming back from the river with a pail of water in one hand and a bundle of branches and twigs in the other—and he was whistling a happy tune.

"I need to speak to you, little brother," she said in a stern tone.

His eyes widened. "Something wrong?"

She nodded, placing a hand on his forearm. "I want to keep this private."

"What is it?"

So she confessed to having spied on him last night. But when she finished, he simply laughed, as if such displays of impropriety were perfectly acceptable. "Matthew Dawson!" she scolded. "What if someone else saw you? Can you imagine what Gertie would say? And Jess is such a nice girl. At least I thought she—"

"Jessica is a *very* nice girl!" He scowled.

"Yes, yes, I'm sure she is. And that's exactly why you should respect her more than to sneak around at night like that."

"I *had* to sneak like that, Lizzie. Otherwise someone would see us and start gossiping. I asked Jessica to meet me behind my wagon because I really needed to speak to her—in private." He glanced over his shoulder to where the Bostonian girls were carrying water from the river and giggling. "Do you realize how hard it is to have a private conversation around here?" he said quietly.

"But it looks bad, Matthew. And what about JT and Ruth?" She lowered her voice too. "What would they think to see you and Jess, well, behaving like that? Can't you see, it's just not right?"

He frowned. "Then how else was I going to ask her to become my wife?"

Elizabeth blinked. "You asked Jess to marry you?"

He nodded with an expression that reminded her of when he was a little boy—right after he'd gotten away with something big.

"Matthew, are you serious?"

"Dead serious. And Jessica has agreed to be my bride."

Elizabeth was stunned speechless. How had this happened so quickly? How could he be so certain? He'd only known her for a couple of months, and part of the time he'd assumed she was a boy.

Now he looked slightly dismayed. "Don't tell me you don't approve."

"No." She shook her head. "I'm just shocked, Matthew. Genuinely shocked. Are you truly engaged?"

"I asked and she accepted. She still needs to tell Ruby, and I want to tell Ma and Pa."

"So you honestly plan to marry her then?"

"Of course I do. I already told Brady, and I planned on telling the whole family this morning—unless you've already tattled on me."

"No, no, of course not. I haven't told a living soul. I wanted to speak to you first."

"So now you've heard it from the horse's mouth," he said as they walked back to camp.

And then Elizabeth admitted to how frightened she'd been last night. "I heard that rustling sound back between our wagons and started to imagine I might have to shoot an Indian," she said quietly. "Do you know how unsettling that is?"

His expression grew grimmer now. "I've done guard duty a few times. Trust me, sis, I've given that some thought myself."

"It would be awful, wouldn't it?"

He shrugged. "Not if you were protecting your family. You'd do what you had to do, Lizzie, especially if you thought your children were in danger."

She sighed and nodded. He was probably right. But now they were in camp, and Clara and Ruth looked to have breakfast well under way. Brady and JT had just finishing hitching her team.

"Where's Pa?" Matthew asked Clara.

"Still meeting with the captain." She shielded her eyes from the smoke as she turned the sizzling bacon.

"Here, Mother, let me do that for you," Elizabeth offered.

"We might as well start to eat without him," Clara told them. "I'll save him a plate."

As usual, because the wagons were already loaded and set to roll, they ate their grits and bacon and cold biscuits standing. They were just finishing up when Asa arrived. "Here's your plate," Clara told him.

"Sorry to be late," he said. "The captain was a bit long-winded this morning. But he said he'll give everyone an extra thirty minutes before starting today."

Elizabeth filled a cup of coffee for her father and then glanced over at Matthew.

"I, uh, I have an announcement to make." Matthew's tone was serious enough to get everyone's attention.

Clara looked worried. "Is something wrong, son?"

Elizabeth couldn't help but smile as she began washing the breakfast dishes in the water they'd heated earlier, but she didn't say a word.

"Nothing whatsoever is wrong," he assured them. "In fact, something is very right. As you know I've gotten quite found of Jess—I mean once I figured out she wasn't really a boy." He chuckled. "And Jess—I mean Jessica—is quite fond of me as well. Probably even more so after our little dip in the river. Anyway...last night..." He cleared his throat and paused. "Well, last night I asked Jessica to be my bride, and she has agreed to marry me."

"Oh, Matthew!" Clara clapped her hands. "That's the most wonderful news ever!"

"Jess is going to be part of our family?" Ruth was dancing around the campfire. "Kind of like a big sister?"

"She'll be an aunt to you," Elizabeth clarified. "Now come over here and help to dry these dishes, Ruth."

Everyone, including JT and Brady, took turns congratulating Matthew.

"Jessica and I decided that we'd like to be married as soon as possible," he explained eagerly. "We talked about it last night. After that day in the river, we both realized how time and life is precious. We don't want to waste a single day not being together."

"How soon do you mean?" Asa asked.

"*Soon,*" he said urgently. "We know we love each other, Pa. We know this is right. Do you think this Saturday is too soon?"

Asa rubbed his chin. "If you're certain this is what you both want...that it's the right thing to do. And as long as Ruby is agreeable to this news. Is she?"

Matthew's forehead creased. "I don't see why she wouldn't be agreeable. It's not as if she and Doris have done much to help Jessica prepare herself for life or marriage."

"Ruby left everything behind just to accompany Jess on this trip," Clara reminded him.

"And Ruby loves Jess like her own child," Elizabeth added as she rinsed a tin cup and handed it to Ruth.

"I know," he admitted. "But Jess has told me some things...well, the kinds of things that make me question Ruby's sensibilities."

"Best not to pass judgment, son." Asa winked at his wife. "Especially when it comes to your in-laws." He chuckled. "They come with the package...even if they turn out to be outlaws."

Clara laughed. "Yes, you can't blame your bride for her family, Matthew. There's always the chance you'll find a horse thief somewhere, even in the finest of families."

He nodded. "I suppose you're right."

"What matters most is that you love each other," Elizabeth told him. "That's what counts. Besides that, you know your family is very fond of Jess too."

He brightened now. "So, do you think it's all right then, Pa? I mean if we plan to get married this coming Saturday?"

Asa shrugged. "If Ruby approves, I don't see why you two can't be married whenever you like, son. Frankly, I've never understood long engagements myself." He grinned at Clara. "As I recall, we got married just a few weeks after I asked your Pa for your hand."

"Three weeks to be precise," Clara told him.

"You could probably get married in Fort Laramie," Elizabeth suggested to Matthew. "It's still a week away, but surely that's not too long to wait."

"I reckon we can wait a week," Matthew agreed.

"But I've heard Fort Laramie is a lot like Fort Kearney." Clara frowned as she handed Elizabeth an empty plate. "I'm not sure a busy settlement like that is the best place for a nice wedding. Of course, you might not want a *real* wedding celebration. Maybe you just want a justice of the peace for this, Matthew."

"No, I want a real celebration," he declared. "I think Jessica does too. Something like this is worth celebrating, don't you think? But why couldn't we hold a nice wedding right here on the Oregon Trail? It would be something to tell our children about someday."

"We could have a gathering similar to the birthday parties." Clara put Asa's plate in the dishwater. "Only better."

"And since Mr. Taylor's a preacher man, we thought maybe he could marry us," Matthew said. "I mean, legal-like."

"I don't see why not," Asa agreed. "And if Mr. Taylor can't, I expect the captain can since he's the law around here."

"But you need to discuss these details with Jess and Ruby," Elizabeth told him. "They might have ideas of their own."

"You're right," he conceded. "I don't want to take over."

"Tell Jessica I'll do anything I can to help," Clara said. "And let her know that we think a real wedding would be nice."

"I'll gather flowers for you," Ruth offered.

"And if you waited until after Fort Laramie, perhaps the Saturday after that...then I might be able to get some eggs for a cake," Clara said hopefully. "And maybe we'd find some other things to make it more festive too. Surely a two-week engagement wouldn't be too long, would it?"

He shrugged. "I'll talk to Jess—I mean Jessica—about it."

By the end of the day, it was decided that Matthew and Jessica would be married on the Saturday following their stop in Fort Laramie. Ruby and Clara were in charge of the wedding plans, and Jessica asked Elizabeth to help her put together a wedding outfit.

"Aunt Ruby offered to let me go through a trunkful of dresses she brought with her," Jessica told her as they walked to the river together the next evening. "I didn't want to hurt her feelings, but I want something more proper than a dance hall dress. Do you think I'd have any luck finding a decent dress in Fort Laramie?"

Elizabeth dipped a bucket into the water, waiting for it to fill. "If it's much like Fort Kearney, I'd be surprised if you could find anything appropriate for a wedding there. Well, unless you care to wear a buckskin dress. I noticed a pretty one when Ruth and I bought our moccasins from the Indian woman. It was white and fringed, with ornate beadwork."

"It might make for an interesting keepsake, but I don't think it's what I want for my wedding. And really, I don't think it matters so much whether I have a fancy dress or not. Marrying the man I love is what's important. Don't you think so?"

Elizabeth set the full bucket aside and turned to Jessica. "I'm so happy that I'm getting a sensible sister-in-law." She didn't know whether Matthew had told Jessica about his previous fiancée, Violet Lamott. But compared to that silly flibbertigibbet, Jessica was like a breath of fresh air.

Jessica dropped her bucket in the river and then pulled out the skirt of the blue calico dress Elizabeth had given her. "I think I'll be married in this dress. It's certainly pretty enough." She chuckled as she pulled the filled bucket back up. "It's a sight better than the men's trousers and jacket I used to wear."

Elizabeth pursed her lips as she dropped her second bucket. "But what if we can do better than that?"

Jessica tilted her head to one side. "I can't let you give me any more of your dresses, Elizabeth. Someday you'll want them for Ruth. Really, what would be wrong with wearing this dress? I truly do love it. And it's what I was wearing the day Matthew rescued me from the river." She sighed. "It will always be special to me."

"As my future sister-in-law, do you think you could trust me on this?"

Jessica shrugged. "Of course."

Elizabeth grinned as she waited for Jess to pull out her second pail. "Then let me see what my mother and I can do." As they began to walk back to camp, she got an idea. "Would you mind if we invited your aunt and Doris to help with the dress too?"

"My aunt's not too handy with a needle, although Doris is. But I'm sure they'd both love to be involved."

"Maybe Flo and some of the others would like to help too. If everyone did a bit of the sewing, sort of like piecework, we might get it done in time."

Jessica laughed. "Even if my gown ends up looking like a quilt, I will wear it proudly."

They parted ways at Ruby's wagon, which was nearer the river, but to Elizabeth's surprise, Will Bramford joined her now. "Can I help with that?" he asked, and before she could say no, he'd taken one of the buckets.

"Oh, that's not necessary," she told him. "Besides, that puts me out of balance with just one pail to carry."

So he took the other bucket. "Is this better?"

Now she was embarrassed, keeping her gaze straight forward as they walked past the other wagons because she sensed that others were watching with interest. "To what do I owe this unexpected help?"

"Just being a good neighbor," he said lightly.

"I truly don't mind carrying water," she admitted. "It took some getting used to. But now that my hands are good and calloused, it's not so bad."

"I know how much Lavinia appreciates it when I give her a hand with things like this, although I do try to get my girls to do their part in bringing water to camp."

"Your girls are wonderful at helping," she told him. "Belinda and Amelia are both such dears."

"Thank you." He smiled. "Well, I suppose by now you've heard that the announcement of Matthew and Jess' engagement is breaking a few hearts."

She laughed. "I do hope you're jesting."

"Only partly. In some ways it's helped a bit too." He lowered his voice. "At least Evelyn isn't feeling jealous that Jeremiah was pining for Jess. And Julius will probably start paying Belinda more attention again."

"I heard that those two are expected to get married someday." She paused by her wagon now, waiting for him to set down the buckets.

"That was something Belinda's mother and Lavinia cooked up when the kids were babies. After that they paired off Evelyn and Jeremiah. But I think that since these kids have grown up together, they probably think of themselves more as cousins by now."

She reached for a bucket. "Don't be too sure."

"Yes, I suppose you're right. What with Jess and Matthew's announcement, I'm guessing romance will be in the air for all the young people." Now he gave her a shy smile. "Perhaps for some of us older ones too."

She felt her cheeks blush as she reached for the other bucket. "I thank you for your help, Will." Then with the bucket in hand, she turned too quickly, sloshing some of the water out, but she continued moving toward the holding barrel on the side of her wagon, determined to gracefully empty it. But struggling to heft the bucket high enough to pour it out, she knew it was futile without a stepstool. And now even more water slopped out, dousing her boot.

"Here." Will reached over her shoulder to take the bucket. "Let me help. That's too heavy for you to lift that high, Elizabeth."

"Brady usually does it for me," she admitted as she stepped back and watched, noticing how tall Will was and, for a city man, fairly strong. But life on the trail did that for a person.

"And I'm sure I distressed you just now," he said as he poured the second pail into the barrel. "My apologies for being so forward." He turned and smiled. "Don't know what got into me."

She wiped her damp hands on her skirt and shrugged. "No apology necessary."

He tipped his head politely. "Then you won't mind me saying that I find you to be an interesting and intelligent woman and that I enjoy your company?"

Too flustered to speak, she just stared at him.

He simply laughed. "There I've gone and done it again. Overwhelming you."

"Well, I…I'm not sure how to respond."

He waved his hand. "As you know, I'm a lawyer, and some people, including my own children, believe that I'm inclined to speak my mind far too freely. Please, forgive me, Elizabeth."

"Of course." She smiled in relief as JT, Ruth, and Flax came into their camp. "And thank you for helping with the water."

"My pleasure." Now he tipped his hat. "Good evening, all."

"Why was Mr. Bramford helping you with the water, Mama?" Ruth asked curiously.

Elizabeth shrugged. "I'm not sure why."

"I know why," JT said soberly.

"Why?" Elizabeth asked him.

"I heard Augustus Prescott saying that Will Bramford has set his cap for you, Ma." JT frowned.

Elizabeth just laughed. "Oh, JT, that's just silly wagon train gossip."

JT didn't look convinced.

"Grandma said she needs more kindling for the supper fire," Ruth said. "But JT's going fishing with Grandpa and Brady. And I'm not supposed to go out alone because of the Indians."

"That's true," Elizabeth said a bit sadly. She knew that caution was a necessity right now, but she missed the freedom the children had enjoyed before. "What about Matthew?"

"He's helping Jess with something, and then they're going fishing too."

"Then I guess it's just you and me," Elizabeth told Ruth. "But let's hurry so we can get back and help Grandma with supper. And remember, we need to stay close to the wagons."

They sang songs as they walked toward the river, where the best chances of finding small twigs and branches would be. Elizabeth tried to keep a watchful eye, but since a number of other emigrants were out getting water and wood or fishing, it seemed relatively safe. Besides, with the sun shining and birds singing, it was hard to imagine trouble could be about.

"Look, Mama." Ruth pointed to some splotches of red and green downriver. "Strawberries!"

"Good eyes," Elizabeth told her as they hurried over and began to pick.

"They're nice and sweet too," Ruth said with her mouth full.

Elizabeth sampled a big red berry and nodded. "Yes, but let's not eat too many now. What a nice surprise for the others." Seeing more plants, they continued a bit further down the river, eagerly gathering more and more berries.

"*Mama!*" Ruth hissed in a frightened tone. Still kneeling, she pointed toward a clump of willows not far from them.

Still squatting, Elizabeth turned to look and then took in a frightened breath as she spied a pair of tan moccasins through the greenery. Leaving her basket on the ground, she stood to her full height and moved protectively in front of Ruth as if she could shield her child with her skirt. What should she do?

"*Eli!*" Ruth exclaimed as she pushed past Elizabeth's skirt and out into plain sight. "I thought you were an Indian!"

"Eli?" Elizabeth felt a rush of relief as their friend stepped out from the willows. "What are you doing out here?"

He chuckled. "I thought I was about to snare a rabbit for supper, but he just got away."

"I'm sorry," Ruth told him. "Did I scare him off?"

Eli tucked his snare back into his possibilities bag and shrugged. "I'm not really hankering after rabbit anyway."

"We found strawberries." Ruth held her basket out for him to see. "Go ahead and have some. Maybe they'll make up for the rabbit."

Eli plucked up a couple of her berries and popped them into his mouth. "Delicious," he said. "Thank you, Ruth." Now he looked around and frowned. "Did you know that you ladies have wandered a fair ways from the wagon? Did you forget the captain's warning?"

Elizabeth nodded guiltily. "We were supposed to be gathering kindling, but I'm afraid we got caught up in berry picking and I lost track of our whereabouts. We'll head back right now." She put the basket over her arm and grasped Ruth's hand. "My mother is probably wondering where her kitchen help has run off to."

"I'll walk you back to camp," Eli told them.

"Oh, I'm sure we'll be perfectly fine. We don't want to trouble—"

"It's no trouble."

As they walked, he inquired about Matthew and Jessica's impending wedding plans, and she confirmed that the rumor was true.

"You'll come to the wedding celebration, won't you?" Ruth asked hopefully. "Grandma is going to bake a cake, and I'm going to help get lots of flowers. And there will be music and dancing—a real party!"

He chuckled as Ruth continued. "And Grandpa is even going to roast Brownie." Now her smile faded a bit.

Eli looked confused. "Who's Brownie?"

"Brownie is one of our steers, although we don't usually name them," Elizabeth grimaced. "But Ruth is a farm girl." She patted the top of her daughter's bonnet. "She understands that some livestock are meant to feed people." She pointed at Eli. "Like the rabbit you were trying to get."

He nodded. "We eat to survive."

"Even my chickens," Elizabeth said a bit sadly. "They might not make it all the way to Oregon. Although I hope they do."

"I hope they do too," Ruth agreed.

"Anyway, Ruth is right. I know Matthew and Jessica would love to have you come to their wedding celebration," Elizabeth assured him. "And the captain too."

"Well, we always do enjoy a wagon train wedding," Eli told her. "I'd be pleased to come."

"And you can wear your buckskins," Ruth told him. "It's all right."

He laughed. "Well, thank you, but I do have some white man clothes too."

"You do?" Ruth seemed surprised.

"The buckskins are better suited for life on the trail," he explained to her. "They're comfortable in all kinds of weather, but they're tough and protective too. It's a hard habit to break."

Suddenly Elizabeth was thinking of what he'd told them about living with the Crow. By now, after having considered it more than she planned to admit to anyone, she felt fairly certain that Eli had indeed been married to a Crow woman, that they'd had a child together, and that smallpox had taken both his wife and child from him. It just seemed to make sense. And although it was sad and she felt true empathy for Eli, it was also very disturbing to her.

To complicate matters further, she felt irked at herself for reacting like this. It seemed bigoted and small-minded on her part—like something Gertie Muller might do—but for some reason she couldn't get past it. The idea of Eli with an Indian woman...being married, having a child, living like that for several years...well, it just made her extremely uneasy.

For the most part, she had been trying not to think about him anymore, at least not in a romantic sense. And she had been avoiding him. But now as he walked with them, chatting comfortably with her daughter, smiling easily, and pointing out a beautiful red cardinal for them to see...well, that only made it all the more difficult for her.

"I have a perfect idea," Ruth said eagerly when they reached their camp. "Since I frightened Eli's supper away, I am inviting Eli to eat with us tonight." She looked hopefully at Clara as she handed her some kindling sticks. "Do you mind, Grandma?"

Clara peered into Elizabeth's basket to see the strawberries and then grinned. "Not at all, seeing as how you come bearing gifts."

Chapter Thirty

Between the fabric that Elizabeth and Clara had brought with them and a few pieces from Ruby's rather strange collection of dance hall dresses, a wedding gown for Jessica was slowly taking shape. And Elizabeth felt it was going to be truly beautiful when it was finished—if only they could finish it on time. Similar to the making of a patchwork quilt, she and Clara had asked the women from their unit to work on various parts of the dress, and except for Gertie Muller and Mrs. Taylor, everyone had happily agreed.

"I don't know why you bothered asking those two," Flo said when Elizabeth dropped off the bundle of fabric needed for Flo's contribution.

"We felt it was right to include everyone," Elizabeth explained. "And to be fair, Gertie wasn't even terribly rude about it. She almost seemed to appreciate being asked. She simply admitted she wasn't a good seamstress."

"Well, that's something." Flo examined the fabric and lace in the bundle. "And what was Mrs. Taylor's excuse? Surely she knows how to sew."

Elizabeth wasn't sure she wanted to answer. However, she suspected that Mrs. Taylor would freely share her reasons with anyone interested in listening. "She told me that she doesn't approve of the marriage."

Flo frowned. "I'd wager that's just because Mr. Taylor wasn't asked to perform the wedding. Simple case of sour grapes."

Elizabeth sighed. "Is that what folks are saying?"

Flo nodded as she wrapped the wedding dress fabric back up in the tea towel to keep it clean. "But I must say Bert and I were rightly relieved to hear that Captain Brownlee is officiating. I'm sure everyone will be glad about that. Well, everyone 'ceptin' the Taylors."

"The truth is, Mr. Taylor *was* asked to conduct the ceremony, but he didn't approve of the marriage either. At least that's what Mrs. Taylor said when she answered for her husband. I almost got the feeling he would have done the ceremony if she hadn't intervened. Anyway, it's of no matter now."

"What is wrong with those people?" Flo shook her head. "Why on God's green earth do they not approve of a sweet couple like Matthew and Jess getting hitched?"

Elizabeth sighed. "As you know, they have some preconceived notions about Jessica and her aunt. Apparently it didn't help matters when they found out that young Jess wasn't a boy but a girl. According to Mrs. Taylor, that was an abomination to womanhood and an insult to God. Both my mother and I have tried to talk sense into her, but she's awfully stubborn. According to my father, the Taylors have even asked to be transferred from our unit."

"I heard about that too. But I also heard it's only because they want to hold a bigger church service with a different unit. They even asked the captain if they could hold a church service for the whole wagon train."

"They did?" Elizabeth was surprised.

"That's what I heard. I also heard that they want to take offerings."

"Take offerings? On a wagon train?" Elizabeth looked at Flo in wonder. "How is it that you hear all these things?"

"That's what one of the Schneider children said. Seems they went to one of the Taylors' services." She chuckled. "But only one."

"I don't know how you manage to hear all the wagon train gossip." Elizabeth stood to leave. "But I do hope you take it with a grain of salt."

Flo cupped her hand around one of her rather oversized ears. "God didn't give me these big old flaps for nothing." She laughed loudly. "And believe me, I know that gossip is like a hotcake—there are two sides to everything."

"Well, we really appreciate your help with those sleeves. And Fiona is eager to work with you on the trim. She's very good at tatting lace."

Elizabeth continued making her deliveries, doling out the pieces that she and her mother had cut out during the past couple of evenings. Doris and Ruby were in charge of the skirt, which would have some intricate tucks to make it seem fuller at the bottom. Mrs. Schneider, who had actually worked as a seamstress for a lingerie company in Germany, was working on the bodice, which would have inlaid pieces of lace. The Bostonian ladies had offered to sew the petticoats, using pieces from Ruby's trunk. And Flo and Fiona would complete the large puffed sleeves. When all the pieces were finished, it would be up to Clara and Elizabeth to assemble them together in time for the wedding.

As some of the women and girls walked into Fort Laramie together, they discussed the progress of their community project.

"Fiona's tatted lace is so delicate and lovely," Flo reported. "But her fine stitches make mine look like Tillie stitched it. Fiona even offered to tear mine out and redo them."

"Surely that's not necessary," Elizabeth told her.

"The petticoat is turning out to be rather fluffy," Lavinia told them. "The girls insisted on adding more layers."

"Trust us, it'll be very elegant with the full skirt over it," Evelyn assured Elizabeth.

"I hope the gown won't look like patchwork when we're done," Clara said with concern.

"Don't worry," Ruby told her. "Jess keeps telling us she'd marry Matthew in a potato sack if need be."

"I'm sure it'll be much nicer than that." Elizabeth looked at the settlement before them. Like Fort Kearney, there was no actual wall or fence around the fort, just lots of adobe and wooden structures. And lots of people. "Looks like a busy day here."

"Asa told me there have been three wagon trains through here in just the past few days," Clara said. "Now if only I can find a few eggs, I might be able to make a real wedding cake next week."

"Well, Mother, if anyone can find eggs here, I'd put my money on you." The group of females paused now, everyone deciding which way to go. People and animals were everywhere—emigrants, Indians, soldiers, livestock… Unless Elizabeth was mistaken, this place was even busier than Fort Kearney.

Clara put a hand on Elizabeth's shoulder. "And you and Ruth are going to look for what I suggested?"

"That's our intention," Elizabeth confirmed. "Although I'm not feeling terribly hopeful. Especially considering how busy it is here." Her mother had asked her to be on the lookout for bedding of any kind. She thought it would make a good wedding present from the family, especially since she was worried that Jessica might not cotton to sleeping in a hammock beneath the wagon.

But after an hour of searching several places in Fort Laramie, and after purchasing only one Hudson Bay blanket—with some moth holes in it at that—Elizabeth was inclined to give up. However, she had already set a few pieces of bedding aside, things she planned to give to the newlyweds. "Let's go to the post office," she told Ruth as they made their way through a group of trappers congregated on the street. "I want to see if your Aunt Malinda has written me back."

After what seemed a long wait at the crowded post office, Elizabeth was disappointed to discover that once again there was no word from their relatives in Oregon. She only hoped this didn't mean that some harm or misfortune had befallen them. Since embarking on this journey, Asa had heard rumors of Indian troubles in the same area they were headed to. Although he'd tried to dismiss them or play them down, Elizabeth had felt concerned then, and she was even more concerned now that she still hadn't received a letter. John and Malinda would have had plenty of time to respond by now. What if something serious had happened to them? Something Elizabeth and her family wouldn't discover until they arrived there—until it was too late?

"May we go look at the Indian crafts?" Ruth asked hopefully.

For some reason, Elizabeth bristled at this suggestion, uncomfortably switching the rolled-up Hudson Bay blanket to her other arm.

"They have some blankets." Ruth pointed to some small woven goods laid out on the ground and covered with dust.

"I don't think those are exactly what your grandmother had in mind." Elizabeth frowned over to where the Indian women, just like in Fort Kearney, had their wares spread out in hopes of trading or selling. But truth be told, Elizabeth had no interest in dealing with Indians today. Just seeing those bareheaded women of all ages, shapes, and sizes sitting in the bright afternoon sunshine and chattering among themselves reminded her of Eli. More specifically, it reminded her of Eli's questionable past. And that was something she didn't care to think of at all. "Come on, Ruth, let's go look for Grandma."

"But I brought my own money," Ruth pleaded. "I thought I could buy my own wedding present for Matthew and Jess. I want to get them something that's made by the Indians. They both like my moccasins. Maybe I can find some for them too."

"Oh, they probably don't want—" Elizabeth stopped herself. What was she saying? Why was she imposing her fears and prejudices upon her child? "Well, I suppose you can look a bit, if you really want to. But don't take too long. I promised Grandma we'd be ready to return to camp by three. There's lots of work to be done. Besides our usual chores, we have all the wedding preparations to consider as well."

This time Elizabeth stayed back while Ruth strolled along, examining the wares and picking up various items, carefully examining each one as if she were a seasoned trader of Indian goods. Finally Ruth seemed to latch onto an intricately made basket. With an interesting design in the basket's weave, it also had a woven lid with some large glass beads on the top. "Isn't this pretty, Mama?"

Elizabeth simply nodded. "Yes, it is." Then feeling guilty for letting Ruth haggle over the price on her own, Elizabeth finally stepped in and listened. But assured that the old woman was asking a fair price, she decided not to intervene. After all, it must have taken many hours to weave such a basket. However, Elizabeth watched as Ruth carefully counted out her money and paid the woman, who seemed satisfied with the trade. Then with a pleased expression, Ruth walked proudly with the pretty basket cradled in her arms. And Elizabeth was glad she'd allowed her to shop there.

"That's a lovely wedding gift," Elizabeth conceded as they went over to join some women from their unit. "I'm sure Matthew and Jess will appreciate it. It will be a wonderful keepsake of this journey."

"And I bought it all by myself," Ruth proclaimed.

With much to be done in preparation for the wedding, as well as the chores that came with daily living, the next couple of days passed all too quickly. And the June weather had been as pleasant as could be, each day prettier than the one before with tall green prairie grasses, tinged with occasional patches of wildflowers, blowing gently in the breeze. Temperate days and warm sunshine made the hardships of travel highly endurable. In times such as these, Elizabeth thought she could continue on like this indefinitely, and she said as much to her family as they were packing up to leave in the middle of the week.

"Enjoy it while you can," Asa warned as he knocked dust from his hat and secured it onto his head. "According to the captain, it's all about to change."

"To change?" Ruth looked concerned. "What's going to happen, Grandpa?"

"We start climbing higher tomorrow," he explained. "Bound for South Pass in the upcoming week."

"What's wrong with that?" she asked.

"Nothing's wrong with it, Ruthie. To get to Oregon we have to get over some mountains first."

Her eyes lit up. "I can't wait to see the mountains, Grandpa. I think it'll be real exciting."

He nodded as he tapped his pipe onto a rock to empty the ashes. "It *will* be exciting. But it's also a big challenge. Towing a heavily loaded wagon uphill is extra hard on the teams. And it's hard on the people too. We're coming to the part of the journey where our grist will be truly tried. The strength of our wagons and our livestock and even the emigrants will all be sorely tested." He glanced at Clara. "It's fortunate we've had plenty of time to toughen ourselves up, my dear. I doubt we'd have fared too well if we'd started out as greenhorns at this stage of the trip."

"But we'll be all right, won't we, Grandpa?" Ruth looked at him with wide eyes. "All of us? And the animals too?"

"With the help of the good Lord, we will all make it just fine. But it'll be hard work." He cleared his throat. "All I'm saying is, enjoy these next few days because the easy part of this journey is about to end. And now it's time to load up and get moving."

Elizabeth asked JT to drive so she could sit beside him and sew. Meanwhile, Brady would ride with Matthew, and Ruth had invited Tillie to ride with her and her grandparents. But just as the wagons were starting to roll, JT grew alarmed.

"Ma, we forgot Flax."

"Forgot him?" She looked around their cleared-out camp. "Where is he?"

"I don't know," he told her. "Now that I think of it, I haven't seen him all morning."

"Wasn't he here last night? At bedtime?"

JT bit his lip. "He kept fussing in my hammock," he told her. "So I put him out to sleep."

"Oh, well, that's to be expected." She glanced around. "Maybe he's riding with Matthew or Grandpa. Why don't you run and check before we start moving?"

JT hopped down and ran up ahead, but when he returned, his expression was even graver. "No one's seen him, Ma. Can I go call for him?" he asked.

Now the wagons were just starting to move, and Elizabeth was unsure of what to do, so she pulled her wagon out of the line and then ran up ahead to explain to her father. "Flax is probably just over by the river," she called out as she walked alongside. "Do you mind if I stay back until we find him?"

Asa looked perplexed and then glanced over his shoulder. "Since our unit is last this week, it won't be as if you're holding others up. But don't take long, Lizzie."

"Don't worry, we should be along shortly," she promised. "Flax never goes far. Besides, you know my team can move faster than the others anyway."

He grinned. "Beau and Belle might like a chance to kick up their heels."

She nodded, pulling James' old barn jacket more snugly around as she stepped away. She knew she resembled an old farmer's wife whenever she wore this coat, but it was just the right weight to keep off the morning chill.

"Don't let the train get out of your sight," Asa yelled out at her as he popped the reins and his team started to move faster. She nodded, waving, and then turned back to join JT. "We have to hurry," she told him. "Do you think Flax might be down by the river?"

"I'm sure of it," JT said.

Together they hurried down to the river, calling and whistling all the way. But once they reached the water, there was no sign of the beloved yellow dog. "Do you think he fell in?" JT asked with fearful eyes.

"I doubt it. And even if he did, Flax is a good swimmer. And the river's not too deep or swift right here."

JT looked all around, calling and whistling some more. Still, there was no sign of the dog. "JT, I hate to say it, but we have to go," she told him. "I promised Grandpa."

"Let me just run downriver a little ways," JT said. "Back to where I went fishing with Grandpa and Brady last night. Flax had been real interested in an old stump. Maybe he went back there."

"You can't go alone," she told him. "I'll go with you, but we're going to move fast."

So they ran and walked downriver, calling and whistling all the while. Still no sign of the dog.

"JT, that's it. We have to go *now*," she insisted.

JT nodded, but Elizabeth could see the tears gathering in his eyes. And the lump in her throat seemed to grow bigger with each step. Still, she couldn't allow them to keep looking. She'd promised her father.

"Flax was the best dog ever," she said sadly as they trudged back toward the wagon.

"Don't say *was,* Ma. He's still alive. I just know it."

"Well, yes, I'm sure he is alive. Why wouldn't he be? It's just that… well…" She couldn't think of one single comforting word to say to her brokenhearted son.

As they reached their wagon, which looked strangely forlorn with all the other wagons a good distance up the trail now, JT whistled and called some more. Then he begged to go back down the trail a spell. "Maybe he smelled something back there," he told her. "Like a fox or something. You know how he loves to chase critters."

She peered at the tail end of the wagon train, still within sight, but getting smaller by the minute. "I don't know."

"Please, Ma. Flax has been my best friend ever since I can remember. And I didn't let him sleep with me last night, so it's my fault."

"It's not your fault, JT. Flax just ran off. You can't blame yourself."

"But how can I just leave him behind like this? You know what'll happen to him out here on his own, don't you?"

She looked at the train and then back at JT as he used the back of his fist to wipe a stray tear. "We can only go a short ways back, son. And while you call and whistle, I'm going to pray. God has gotten us through some other predicaments. If he wants us to find Flax, I'm sure he can do that too." So as they walked and as JT whistled and called, she prayed, begging God to send their dog back to them. She felt a tiny bit silly, not to mention doubtful, but at the same time the thought of losing Flax out here was more painful than she would have imagined possible.

Goodness gracious, she told herself, he was only a dog. And yet James had picked Flax out as a pup. Flax was going to be James' hunting dog. But the children had fallen in love with the fuzzy yellow pup, and before long he became a house pet. And then after James passed, he became a trusted watchdog. "Dear God," she prayed out loud, "we don't just love Flax, we need him too. Please send him back to us."

Still there was no sign of the dog, and she knew they couldn't continue. Already she knew she'd have to push the team hard to catch up with the others before her father got worried.

"JT," she insisted. "That's it. We have to go. I promised Grandpa." She turned around, and to her surprise, they'd gone a fair ways from their own wagon. Worse yet, she could barely see the end of the wagon train. "Hurry, JT. I'm sorry, but we've got to get moving and rejoin the others."

They walked and ran back to the wagon and were just climbing up when JT spoke out in an unsteady voice. "*Ma…?*"

Worried that he was about to break down into real sobs over the missing dog, she turned to him, ready to comfort him as she reached for the brake, but then she noticed he was pointing to the north with a worried expression. She leaned over to see past him, and there coming directly toward them was what looked like a small band of Indians. With her hand still on the brake, she was tempted to let it go—and go fast. But although she knew her horses were swift, she also knew that they couldn't pull a fully loaded wagon faster than the Indians coming directly toward them. Plus there appeared to be at least a dozen of them. Maybe more.

"Should I get the gun?" JT started to reach beneath the seat.

"No," she said quietly. The riders were so close and so many, she knew that to shoot would be not only useless but dangerous as well. She took her hand off the still-locked brake. "You stay in the wagon, JT."

"Are you getting out?" he asked with concern.

"Yes. I want you to stay put," she said firmly.

"But, *Ma*."

"Let me handle this, JT."

Her knees were trembling as she climbed down and began to walk directly toward the party of Indians. As she walked she silently prayed, begging God to help her and JT. Then as she got closer to the Indians, to her astonishment, she noticed a yellow dog running alongside the horses.

"Flax!" she cried out.

In that same instant, JT had jumped down from the wagon and was bounding straight for their dog. Elizabeth gasped to see one of the Indians lifting up a bow, slipping in an arrow and taking aim.

"Stop!" she screamed just as JT and Flax united in a happy scuffle on the ground. She wasn't sure if she was talking to JT or the warrior, but she kept her eyes pinned on the shirtless Indian with the drawn bow, the arrow still aimed at her son. Then taking a deep breath, she continued to walk calmly toward the Indians, strategically placing herself between the warrior and her son.

"You found our dog," she said slowly and as pleasantly as if she were speaking to a neighbor. "Thank you so much." She continued to stand between the Indians and JT, wondering what she should do next. If only she could give them something to show her gratitude for returning the dog—although she seriously doubted that was what they were doing. The Indian with the raised bow seemed proof of this.

A breeze wafted past, causing her to notice something red dangling from her coat pocket. Ruth's hair ribbon. She'd asked Elizabeth to tie a bow into her hair this morning, but they'd gotten too busy. Now Elizabeth slowly pulled the ribbon out, allowing the length of it to flutter in the breeze. Then, continuing to walk toward the Indians, she held the scarlet ribbon before her, almost like a truce flag.

She was only a few feet away from them when someone spoke out. Surprised that it sounded like a female voice, Elizabeth peered past some of the men to spy a young woman seated on a horse. Holding a young child in front of her, she appeared to be addressing the Indian still wielding the raised bow. She was speaking passionately in quick, unintelligible words. Then suddenly, to Elizabeth's surprise, the brave lowered his bow and actually laughed, almost as if the woman had told him something funny.

Now, just standing there and wondering what to do next, Elizabeth locked eyes with the young woman for a long moment. Was it her imagination, or did she see compassion in this woman's eyes? Then, with the red ribbon still fluttering in her hand, Elizabeth continued to slowly approach the man with the bow. She held the bright shiny ribbon up to him.

"Thank you," she told him. Then she nodded back to where JT and Flax were still behind her. "That's our dog. Thank you."

The brave looked at the ribbon still fluttering in her hand and then over to JT and Flax. And then, almost as if he understood, he slipped his bow and arrow behind his back and reached down to take the ribbon. In a swift movement, he wrapped it around his wrist several times, securing it like a bracelet. And then he held it up and nodded with satisfaction.

"Thank you," Elizabeth said again, slowly backing away and hoping that the party would continue on their way.

But the Indians remained put. And now they were talking among themselves, almost as if they were arguing. She imagined that some of them were suggesting they should kill both her and JT, burn their wagon, steal the horses, and run. And perhaps some of them, like the woman, were saying, "Let them be." She wasn't sure. All she knew was that she wanted to get JT out of harm's way.

"Come on, son," she calmly told him. "Get Flax and yourself into the back of the wagon, and I'm going to drive—fast."

"Yes, ma'am."

Seated in the wagon, she had just put her hand on the brake when she saw the Indians were moving too—directly toward the wagon. As tempted as she felt, she knew it would be futile to reach for the gun. She'd seen how quickly the one brave had nocked his arrow and taken aim. Surely the others could do the same. They were only about ten feet away when the woman yelled something, this time to a different man. And now he rode his horse right up to her wagon.

With his eyes on her, the brave reached behind him. Elizabeth took in a quick breath, expecting another drawn bow to appear. Instead, he pulled out something reddish brown and about the size of a water bucket. Then, with a loud thump, he dropped it in the dirt right next to her wagon. And with no further ado, all of the Indians eased past the wagon and continued south without looking back. Elizabeth watched in astonishment as the group traveled gracefully across the prairie, getting smaller and smaller.

"What happened, Ma?" JT stuck his head out from the covered wagon. "What did they do?"

"They dropped something," she told him, cautiously climbing down to see what it was. "It's a big piece of meat." She bent down to pick up what felt like a ten-pound roast or better.

"They gave us meat?" JT asked in wonder.

"I'm guessing it must be buffalo." Still feeling shocked, she placed the meat inside the game box beneath the water reservoir. Then she climbed back into the wagon and tightened the straps on her driving gloves. Releasing the brake, she flicked the reins and yelled, "Gid'up!" to the team. "We've got to catch up with the wagon train," she told JT. "Before your grandpa sends out a search party."

"The Indians gave us meat?" JT said again.

"They did." She slowly shook her head, still trying to figure the mystery out for herself. What a strange encounter.

It wasn't until they were in sight of the wagon train and steadily gaining on them that she said what was on her mind. "JT, I don't think we should tell your grandpa about what happened back there."

"You want me to lie to Grandpa?"

"No, no, of course not. I'm just not sure I want him to know everything. I'm afraid it would worry him unnecessarily." She gave JT a sheepish smile. "Also, he'd know that I messed up."

"You didn't mess up, Ma."

"I didn't do as he told me, JT. I never should have let the wagon train out of sight like that."

"It was my fault, Ma."

"But I'm in charge," she reminded him. "I should have known better."

"But you were great, Ma." JT's eyes shone with pride. "You handled everything just right with those Indians."

She shook her head. "No, JT. I got lucky. Or more'n likely, God was helping us. But the fact of the matter is, we were where we shouldn't have been. It could have turned out so much worse." She shuddered to remember the sight of that drawn bow and the razor-sharp arrow.

"But it didn't, Ma." He laughed nervously. "Not only did the Indians bring Flax back to us, they gave us *meat* too."

She felt perplexed. "Why did they do that…I wonder?"

"Was it because you gave them Ruth's ribbon?"

"It was all I could think of to give them…to thank them for Flax."

"Maybe they thought we were poor and starving," he said.

Elizabeth looked down at her worn-out barn jacket and sighed. "I suppose it might look like that. But what about our horses…our livestock?"

"Maybe it was because we were out here by ourselves," JT continued. "Without a man. Maybe they thought we were all on our own, Ma."

"Maybe so…" She nodded as she remembered the look in the woman's eyes. It had felt like compassion…or pity. "Maybe they felt sorry for us." Whatever it was, she felt certain of one thing—she did not intend to put herself in that situation again.

Chapter Thirty-One

Somehow Elizabeth convinced JT not to repeat their strange story to Grandpa or anyone else in their family. She knew he was bursting to tell someone, but she also knew that his respect for her had grown some during that strange encounter. And that was reassuring in itself, especially because he seemed so bound and determined to become a man on this journey. It was a comfort to know that his mother still wielded some influence over him, even if only temporarily. As for the meat, Elizabeth had simply told her mother that one of their neighbors had donated it to them. Then, to avoid further questioning, she told Clara she needed to hurry. "I promised Ruth we'd go berry gathering before it's time to help with supper."

"Someone on this train is a good hunter." Clara nodded with approval as she rinsed off the dust-coated meat. "Mighty good hunter."

In the next couple of days, Elizabeth continued to wonder about the incident with the Indians. She even wrote about it in her journal in hopes of understanding it better. By now she suspected the group had been a hunting party, not a war party, as she'd originally assumed. After all, why would a woman and child travel in a war party? Yet it also seemed strange that a woman and child would travel in a hunting party. Or that a woman would have as much influence as that young woman seemed to have. Perhaps she was related to a chief. Even so, Elizabeth still couldn't understand the unexpected gift of meat, which turned out to be bison. They could have easily killed Elizabeth and JT and stolen their valuable livestock. Instead, they gifted them with the meat. Why would they do that?

By Friday, and thanks to the impending wedding the following day, Elizabeth put her ponderings over the Indian incident behind her. Now her most demanding task was to get the last of the wedding dress pieces sewn together, which was why JT was driving and she was sewing. Meanwhile, Ruth and the Bostonian girls were collecting as many wildflowers as possible. And everyone in their unit was looking forward to the next day's celebration.

By the end of the traveling day, Elizabeth was nearly done. With most of the gown carefully protected in a linen sheet, she was just stitching the last sleeve into the bodice when the wagons stopped. She didn't even look up as JT got the wagon into place for the night. Instead, she focused on her stitches. She wanted every seam in this gown to be secure enough to endure all the dancing that was sure to follow the wedding.

And so she remained in the wagon seat while Brady and JT proceeded to unharness the team, taking them over to the picket line for the night. JT joked to Brady that she had accidentally sewn herself to the wagon seat and would be sleeping there tonight. Brady chuckled and promised to come back to help free her if she needed it.

"Tell Grandma I'm finishing up here," she told JT as they were leading the team over to the picket line. "I'll be over to help her with supper as soon as I'm done with this." She threaded the needle for what she hoped was the final time, pulling a good length of white thread out and then cutting it with her teeth before she tied a knot.

"Evening, Elizabeth."

Surprised, she looked up to see Eli, seated on his horse, looking directly at her with a curious expression. "Oh, hello," she said.

"Did you not notice that your wagon has stopped and that you're in camp now?"

She gave him a tolerant smile. "Yes, I had noticed." She held up her sewing. "But the wedding is tomorrow, and this is the bride's drcss."

He nodded with what seemed appreciation. "You are indeed a woman of many talents."

"What?" She peered up at him, but feeling uneasy for the way her heart fluttered with interest, she turned back to her stitching and promptly stabbed her finger with the needle. Without flinching, she put her finger to her lips, thankful the blood hadn't spotted the gown.

"JT told me about your encounter with the Pawnees the other day."

She considered denying the whole thing. However, if JT had told him, there seemed little point. "How did you know they were Pawnees?" she asked.

"He described them to me. That boy's got a good eye for detail."

She frowned at him. "He wasn't supposed to tell anyone in the family."

Eli smiled with amusement. "So I'm in the family now?"

She pressed her lips together, sticking the needle safely into the cloth this time and then looking evenly at him. "I'm sure you think I was very foolish to put myself in that position—"

"Not at all," he said easily. "According to JT, you handled yourself in the best way possible...especially considering the circumstances."

"The circumstances?"

He made a half smile now. "Well, being that you put yourself into a dangerous position."

"But I thought you said the Indians were peaceful."

He shrugged. "It seemed that would be true...for you anyway, and at least for that one instance."

"So what are you really saying?" she challenged.

"You were fortunate, Elizabeth."

"I know." She nodded sheepishly.

"I'm sure you learned a valuable lesson."

She nodded again. "Did JT tell you about the warrior—or maybe he was a hunter..." She lowered her voice. "Anyway, did JT tell you about the brave who drew his bow at him?"

Eli nodded with a somber expression. "But he said that was only after JT had jumped from the wagon and started running at them. I'm sure they were simply being defensive."

"They perceived a twelve-year-old boy as a threat?"

"Anyone can be a threat, Elizabeth."

"Yes, I suppose that's true. And JT does know how to shoot."

"But I do commend you on not reaching for a firearm in the heat of the moment. That's what some unfortunate emigrants have done. I'm fairly certain that if you'd done that...well, both you and JT and even your dog probably wouldn't be with us now."

She sighed. "That's what I felt in that moment."

"Those were good instincts."

Now she looked directly into his eyes. "Something happened out there, Eli. I wasn't going to tell anyone, but seeing how you already know most of the story..."

"What do you mean?"

"Something happened out there. I don't know if JT noticed or not. But it's something I'm still trying to figure out."

"What is it?"

She described the moment when she'd looked into the woman's

eyes. "I was so scared, but I was trying hard not to show it. And that woman, just sitting there on her horse with her child...somehow she seemed to understand. I may have imagined it, but I really felt as if she had compassion for me and JT."

"And why shouldn't she?"

"I don't know." Elizabeth looked down, suddenly feeling ashamed.

"I know not all white people would agree that an Indian would have feelings like that..." His brow creased. "But you're traveling with a freed slave, Elizabeth. From what I can see, you treat Brady as your friend—almost like family. Certainly not all white people act like that. So I should think you would understand."

"Understand what?" She looked back at him.

"That Indians are people too. Just like you and me. They have the same needs, the same emotions. They are simply different."

She sighed then slowly nodded. "I know..."

He looked surprised. "Really? You *know* that?"

"I don't know," she confessed. "But I think I'm beginning to understand. I *want* to understand."

He tipped his hat now. "Then you are an even more amazing white woman than I thought you were, Elizabeth Martin."

She blinked, and then, noticing that Gertie Muller was standing nearby with water buckets in hand, Elizabeth forced what she hoped looked like a neighborly smile and waved. "Hello there, Gertie! Nice day, isn't it?"

Gertie barely nodded and, without saying a word, turned away and hurried off toward the river.

"What was that about?" Eli asked her curiously.

Elizabeth chuckled, mostly at herself. "I don't know...But I think poor old Gertie is kind of like an Indian. She's different, and I don't fully understand her...and as a result, it's easy to dislike her. I suppose I'll just have to try a bit harder."

Now Eli looked at her with a very intense expression, almost as if seeing her in a whole new light. "I can see you are busy, Elizabeth, and I know you need to finish Jess' dress in time for the wedding tomorrow. But I do have one more question for you."

"What is that?"

"May I reserve a dance with you? I mean for tomorrow night, after your brother's wedding? Would you save a dance or two for me?"

An unexpected thrill of happiness rushed through her as she smiled directly into his eyes. "I most certainly will, Eli Kincaid."

He tipped his head. "Thank you. I am most appreciative."

She watched in wonder as Eli deftly turned his horse, slowly walking away. Such a fine figure of a man, broad shouldered and sitting tall in the saddle, dressed in his usual fringed buckskins. She couldn't deny that her cheeks felt flushed and her heart was fluttering like a caged sparrow. And she knew, as greatly as her brother anticipated the morrow, it was possible that she looked forward to it with even higher expectations.

The wagon train made good travel time Saturday, and Captain Brownlee was in good spirits about the upcoming wedding, so everyone stopped earlier than usual on Saturday afternoon. While JT and the men were tending the teams and Ruth and the Bostonian girls were out gathering wildflowers, Elizabeth went back into her wagon and began to forage through some deeply packed crates and trunks. Perhaps it was a fool's search and a waste of time, but she was looking for an old gown that she wasn't even sure she'd packed. If memory served, it was a robin's-egg-blue taffeta. A dress she'd worn only once—for Ruth's fourth birthday party, shortly before the cholera epidemic.

For some reason Elizabeth had remembered it the night before and thought perhaps she'd packed it. To her surprise, she spotted a patch of the pale-blue fabric, and happily but carefully extracting the gown from the bottom of a trunk, she gave it a good shake and then laid it next to the clothing she'd already set out for the children to wear at the wedding. Then she went outside to help set up camp.

Everyone was busier than usual this afternoon, but it wasn't long before Asa and Brady got the big tent set up. The plan was to use it both as a bath house and as the women's dressing room before the wedding. But Elizabeth hoped to make it feel even more special than that by carrying out one of the carpets she'd packed to lay on the floor. And with JT's help, she also brought out a couple of chairs, a table and mirror, and some lanterns for when it got dark.

"Thank you for helping with that," she told JT as they stood by the wagon. She pointed to the water buckets. "Now if you can just get us set for bathwater, I'll let the menfolk keep you busy for the rest of the afternoon. And I'll leave your wedding clothes in the wagon for later."

As JT left with the buckets, she gathered up the wedding clothes for her and Ruth, carrying them back to the tent.

"Very nice setup," Clara told her as she came in with a washbasin and towels, placing them on the table. "Jessica will be pleasantly surprised."

"I want her to feel like a princess," Elizabeth said. "I hope that's not silly—out here in the wilderness."

"This should be a day to remember for always." Clara poured water into the washbasin.

Elizabeth set a bar of lemon verbena soap on top of the towels. "I found this in a trunk," she explained. "I thought Jessica might appreciate it more now than when we get to Oregon."

"Good thinking." Clara paused from arranging things to touch the blue taffeta gown still in Elizabeth's arms. "Oh, my. I'd nearly forgotten this dress. Are you going to wear it tonight?"

"It's not too fine, is it?" Elizabeth held up the dress, frowning doubtfully. "Maybe it's too fancy."

Clara firmly shook her head. "I think it's perfect. And I think

Jessica will be honored to have such a fine lady standing beside her when she makes her vows this evening," Clara went over to where they'd hung Jessica's beautiful white dress in the center of the tent. "And after seeing how well Jessica's gown turned out, and knowing how happy she is, I doubt anyone will outshine her today."

"Unless it's Matthew." Elizabeth draped the blue taffeta over the chair near Jessica's gown, pausing to finger one of the puffy white sleeves that Mrs. Flanders and Fiona had sewn, examining the inlaid lace and tatted trim with approval. "It truly is lovely. Jess will be as pretty as a picture in it."

"I've got more flowers," Ruth announced as she burst into the tent with an armful of colorful blooms.

"Oh, my!" Elizabeth laughed. "Here comes our flower girl."

"Look at these red and orange ones," Ruth said happily. "What are they called?"

"Those are Indian paintbrush," Clara said as she filled a pitcher with water from the bucket JT had just delivered.

"And you found bluebells too," Elizabeth declared as she spied the delicate blue blossoms. "Perfect."

"And columbine," Clara exclaimed. "Let's get them into water quickly."

"Looks like you found something else too." Elizabeth examined the red spots on Ruth's bare arms, trying not to show her concern. "What happened to you?"

"Mosquito bites," Ruth explained. "They're thicker than molasses down by the creek."

"We've got plenty of those around here too." Clara swatted the air.

Elizabeth pointed to the soap. "Maybe that lemon verbena will help with those bites. Why don't you wash up right now, Ruthie?"

"And I need to go put the finishing touches on the wedding cake," Clara said. "As well as a dozen other things."

"I want to help put the flowers on the cake," Ruth called as she vigorously scrubbed her hands and arms in the washbasin.

"We want to save that for last," Clara told her. "So they look nice and fresh for the wedding."

"Grandpa and Brady already got the calf roasting," Ruth informed them as she dried her hands on a towel. "The Flanders boys promised to help with the turning of it. And while I was at your camp, Mrs. Prescott brought over some real pretty platters to use for serving tonight. And a stack of china dishes too."

Elizabeth pulled a list from her skirt pocket, going over the various chores that still needed to be finished in time for the wedding. So much to be done...so little time.

Several hours later, Elizabeth wasn't sure that all the chores on her list had been completed, but as the women all clustered in the dressing tent, she was convinced that it no longer mattered.

Ruby had just given Jessica a string of pearls that had belonged to Jessica's grandmother. And Doris had pressed a lace-trimmed handkerchief into her hand.

"We'll go out and join the others," Ruby told them. "I think some of the men are starting to get antsy."

"We'll be out there in just a few more minutes," Elizabeth assured them as she tucked another bluebell into Jessica's hair. "As soon as we complete all the finishing touches."

"Yes," Jessica called out, "it won't be long."

"Oh, Jessica!" Elizabeth stepped back to survey her soon-to-be sister-in-law. "You are the most beautiful bride I've ever seen."

Ruth pushed up close to Jessica, beaming up at her with glowing admiration. "You look just like a fairy princess in a picture book," she said.

Jessica giggled as Elizabeth slipped a few more flowers into her hair. "Thanks to all of you. You've all been like precious fairy godmothers to me." She looked down at her magnificent dress, with its gathered skirt fully puffed wide due to the layers of petticoats sewn together by the Bostonian girls. She held out her bouquet of wildflowers. "I never could have done any of this without you."

"Matthew is going to faint when he sees you," Ruth told Jessica.

Jessica laughed loudly. "Oh, dear, I hope not."

"Let's hope no one faints," Clara said as she stepped toward the door.

Elizabeth sniffed the air. "And judging by that smell, I'm guessing that calf will be perfectly done by the time the wedding is over. Good thing because I'm sure we're all as hungry as wolves."

"We've probably got enough food to feed the whole wagon train," Clara assured them.

"But they're not all coming, are they?" Ruth asked with concern.

"No, of course not," Elizabeth told her. "Just our unit…and a few special guests."

"But everyone in our unit has been very generous with food today," Clara said as she opened the flap of the tent. "After the wedding, we shall eat like kings."

"Can you hear that?" Ruth suddenly cupped a hand to her ear. "That's Paddy playing his penny whistle. It means they're starting."

"Oh, my!" Jessica got a startled look. "Is it really time?"

Ruth nodded eagerly, dancing over to where Clara was standing. "Let's go!"

Jessica's hand went up to her throat, and she looked truly frightened now. "What if I do something wrong? What if I fall on my face?"

"We won't let you." Elizabeth wrapped an arm around her. "Don't worry. You're part of our family now."

"I know just what you need," Clara said as she rejoined them, taking hands with Jessica and Elizabeth. "Come on, Ruthie. It's time to pray for Jessica." And just like that, the four of them circled together in the kerosene-lit tent, and bowing their heads, they listened as Clara led them in prayer. "Dear heavenly Father, we pray that you will bless our dear Jessica as she is joined in union with our own dear Matthew this evening. We pray that you would grace us with your holy presence and with your gracious love and abundant joy as we celebrate this wonderful event with our loved ones." She paused.

"And please, dear Lord, don't let Jessica fall on her face," Ruth said quietly.

"Amen," Elizabeth added, trying not to giggle.

Clara and Ruth led the way through the camp, followed by Elizabeth and finally Jessica. With Paddy, JT, Brady, and several others contributing to the music, they all walked between the standing guests. The processional was short and sweet, and no one fell on her face. Soon they were all in place, standing with Jessica and Matthew beneath the arch of wildflowers that Ruth and the other girls had worked hard to assemble. The wedding couple, sweetly holding hands and gazing into each other's eyes, listened as Captain Brownlee led them in their short, simple wedding vows. This was followed by Asa reading some appropriate scriptures and finishing with a prayer.

"I now pronounce you man and wife," Captain Brownlee said triumphantly. "You may kiss the bride, Matthew Dawson." The unit let out a cheer as Matthew soundly kissed Jessica, and the musicians began to play with energy and enthusiasm as the happy couple led the way over to the area that had been cleared for dancing.

The audience circled around the happy couple, clapping and stomping to the time as the newlyweds danced. Before long, others were joining in, and the general feeling in the air was of festivity and joy.

Or at least it seemed that way. Elizabeth happened to glance over to where Captain Brownlee and Asa were talking together with serious expressions. Curious as to the topic of their conversation, Elizabeth went to join them.

"Excuse us, ma'am." Captain Brownlee tipped his hat. "We don't mean to talk business at such a happy occasion, but it's essential."

"Is something wrong?" she asked.

Asa rubbed his chin with a frown. "A Shoshone war party was spotted about a few hours north of here."

"A war party?" Elizabeth kept her voice low.

The captain nodded grimly. "The Shoshone are not normally aggressive toward emigrants. But it's possible they're having trouble with another tribe."

"But we still have to be ready," Asa told her.

She glanced back at the merrymakers as they started up another dance. "Does that mean the celebration must end?"

"No," Captain Brownlee said quickly. "Not at all. It's just that Asa needs to make sure the men in the unit are all informed and that they have their weapons ready to use in the event of an actual attack."

"An attack?" Elizabeth tried not to look alarmed.

"It's highly unlikely," the captain said. "But we'd rather be safe than sorry."

"Of course." Suddenly Elizabeth realized that she hadn't seen Eli in the crowd. "I assume Eli Kincaid is on guard duty tonight."

The captain nodded absently. "He's the one who spotted the war party this morning."

"Oh..."

"But I don't want this to put a damper on the celebration," the captain told Asa. "You folks carry on as usual. If anything goes wrong, just be ready to follow orders."

As the captain was talking, Elizabeth noticed a strange man walking into their camp. At least he seemed strange at first glance, but peering more closely, she noticed that it was actually Eli. Instead of his usual fringed buckskins, Eli had on dark pants and a charcoal-gray jacket. "There's Eli now," she told the men.

The captain waved, and Eli joined them. With his crisp white shirt and cleanly shaved chin, he almost looked like a different man, and although he was strikingly handsome, Elizabeth wasn't sure whether she liked this look better than when he was attired for the trail. He tipped his hat to her and smiled at all of them. "Evening, Elizabeth, Asa, Captain. I'm sorry to see I missed the wedding."

"That's all right," Asa told him. "Under the circumstances, we understand."

"The captain was just telling us about the Shoshone," Elizabeth told him, feeling her heart flutter slightly as she looked into his eyes.

"I don't think we have much to be concerned about," he said. "I ran into a Shoshone hunter this evening, and without saying anything definite, he insinuated that their problems are with the Sioux and not the white man. Let's just hope that's right."

"Even so, we'll be ready," Asa told him.

"In the meantime, we have a wedding to celebrate," Elizabeth said.

Eli held out his arm. "And you promised me a dance."

She smiled as she tucked her hand around his elbow. "That's right. I did."

She nodded to the captain and her father, pretending not to notice the glint of amusement in both their eyes as she let Eli lead her back toward the festivities. "You look very handsome tonight," she said politely.

"Thank you." He paused, turning to look more closely at her, almost as if really seeing her now. "I cannot even find the words to describe how lovely you look tonight. I know it might sound trite, and I've had a long day on the trail. And don't get me wrong, the trail is beautiful, especially in these parts, but Elizabeth Martin, you truly are a sight for sore eyes. Prettier than a high mountain meadow on a clear June morning."

She laughed lightly. "Thank you, Eli. That's high praise indeed."

Without taking his eyes off of her, he guided her to the edge of the dancing and gently placed his right hand in the small of her back. Clasping her hand in his left, he led her toward the others. And as they danced, gazing directly into each other's eyes, Elizabeth felt that either she had wings on her feet or they were dancing on clouds.

Whatever it was, she wished it would go on forever. And despite the unknown hardships that she knew surely lay ahead, whether grueling mountain crossings, wild impassable rivers, or even frightening Indian attacks, she knew that the second half of their journey held even more promise than the first—and that she would be ready.

Discussion Questions

1. Elizabeth Martin is in a dark place when the book begins. Aware of how much sharper her grief feels in the middle of the night, she longs for morning. Can you relate to this in any way? Why does the dark of night make problems seem worse?

2. Elizabeth considers living out her deceased husband's dream by taking her children to Oregon on the Oregon Trail. Did you see her as brave? Foolhardy? Unrealistic? Adventurous? How would you have advised her?

3. Were you relieved when Matthew, her brokenhearted brother, decided to go to Oregon? Describe a time when you took on a big challenge thanks to someone who was willing to go alongside you.

4. Initially, Asa and Clara both solidly oppose Elizabeth and Matthew's plans to go west. What do you think made them change their minds?

5. Can you imagine restarting your life with only a wagonload full of goods that you need to survive? What items (beyond food and clothes) would you not be able to leave behind?

6. Were you surprised to discover that Ruby used to run a "dance hall"? How did you react to the way that Asa handled this potentially explosive situation?

7. Many things about life, although challenging, seemed simpler back in the 1850s. What one characteristic of that era do you wish you could incorporate into your own life today?

8. Did you suspect that Jess was really a woman? What did you think when you realized she was? Have you or someone you know ever pretended to be something different? Describe.

9. Many lessons have been learned on the Oregon Trail, and many more are coming. What lesson do you think would have the most impact on your life?

10. Both Eli Kincaid and Will Bramford seem to have their eye on Elizabeth. Which one do you think would be the best match? Why?

11. Gertie Muller is a difficult person for many of her fellow travelers. Why do you think she's so cantankerous? Do you have a difficult person like that in your life?

12. What is your general impression of the Taylors (the missionary couple)? Do you think they're sincere in their claim to be serving God? Why or why not?

Join Elizabeth Martin and her family as they continue their journey to the Oregon Territory in book 2 in the HOMEWARD *on the* OREGON TRAIL *series...*

Chapter One

Mid June 1857

For the third time in one morning, the wagon train came to a complete halt. With reins held tightly in one hand, Elizabeth used her teeth to tug one of her leather driving gloves up higher before she firmly pulled her wagon's brake handle. Listening to the creak of wood grinding against wood and the squeak of the straining harnesses, she was thankful that her father had insisted on giving her wagon and team a complete inspection earlier in the morning. He'd urged everyone in their unit to do the same, but the Mullers hadn't taken his suggestion to heart. Consequently they had been the first breakdown of the day. As councilman of their unit, Father had not been pleased.

Shading her eyes from the sunshine with her prairie bonnet, Elizabeth peered upward at the intensely blue sky. Maybe it was the elevation or the time of year, but she couldn't remember when she'd seen sky this shade of blue. The position of the sun indicated that it was nearly noon, but she suspected they'd only traveled a mile or two, maybe less. Although she was relieved to give her weary team another chance to rest, she couldn't help but feel concerned about the travel time they were losing.

Elizabeth understood these delays were due to overly burdened teams and mechanical breakdowns. The stress of driving heavily laden wagons up this rugged trail was taking its toll on many of her fellow travelers. As a result, a number of bulky items had been abandoned alongside the trail in the past few days. Most had been large pieces of furniture, and some appeared to be family heirlooms. But no material goods were valuable enough to threaten the lives of people and livestock. And seeing the Taylors' wagon up ahead and their worn-looking team, she figured Reverend Taylor and his wife would soon be forced to leave their beloved piano behind as well. The way Mrs. Taylor clung to that instrument mystified Elizabeth. It was out of tune and was obviously putting a severe strain on their mule team. To risk injuring an animal for a piano made no sense.

Captain Brownlee had warned all the units that ascending the treacherous South Pass would be slow going this week. He'd strongly cautioned a number of wagons to lighten their loads before beginning their ascent. Some, including the Prescotts from Boston, had heeded his advice—even leaving Lavinia's solid cherry bedroom furniture behind. Others, like the Mullers and the Taylors, had not listened.

Several days back, Eli Kincaid, the wagon train scout and Elizabeth's good friend, had shared the good news that they were nearly in Oregon Country and were more than halfway to their final destination. "Of course, the hardest part is yet to come," he had said lightly.

"So I've heard," she admitted. "But at least the landscape is beautiful."

He nodded, looking up toward the foothills. "Beautiful...and treacherous."

Elizabeth looked past her sturdy pair of mules to the glistening black backs of her Percheron horses, Bella and Beau. So far this team combination had worked well together. However, it had been relatively easy crossing the prairie. She hoped that with the flat plains and weeks of travel behind them, they would be accustomed to each other and continue to pull their weight. She also hoped that she hadn't been mistaken not to go with oxen teams like the rest of her family.

"What stopped us this time, Mama?" Ruth poked her head out from the covered part of the wagon. "Another breakdown?"

"I'm not sure. I hope it's not Grandpa or Uncle Matthew." Elizabeth peered up the trail to where Brady and JT were walking back toward them. She had offered to take the morning shift of driving the wagon.

Brady and JT would take over in the afternoon. JT removed his hat and waved it high as if to signal that all was well.

"It's someone up in unit four," JT explained to her as he paused by Beau, stroking the horse's glistening black flank.

"Your ma and pa and brother and his new bride are all jus' fine," Brady told her. "No problems there."

"But the Mullers' team is looking poorly," JT said quietly. "Grandpa is talking to them right now. I heard him telling Mrs. Muller that if they didn't unload some things, he didn't want to see her or her children riding in the wagon."

"Oh, dear." Elizabeth shook her head. Gertie Muller was a big woman, and she did not enjoy walking along the trail. "Hopefully they'll lighten their load before it's too late."

"What'll they do if'n their team does give up the ghost?" Brady asked Elizabeth with concern.

"I honestly don't know, Brady." She sighed. "I suppose we'd all have to take them in or try to replace their animals with some of our extra livestock."

"That don't seem fair, Ma." JT scowled. "Would you really let the Mullers use one of our cows to pull their wagon?"

She pressed her lips tightly together. The truth of the matter was that she would resent this as much as her son would. But she was the grownup here, so she'd have to hide her emotions. "I reckon it'd be our Christian duty, JT. It's not as if we could just leave the Mullers all behind, could we?"

"As contrary as they've been toward us?" JT looked unconvinced. "I don't see why not."

Elizabeth forced a smile for the sake of her children. "Jesus said we need to love our enemies, son. Besides, don't you think Gertie needs friends as much as anyone else?"

JT's brow creased as if he was considering this. "You want us to take over driving for you?" He brightened as if the prospects of driving were better than walking.

"Don't you think we'll be stopping for dinner soon?" she asked.

"Grandpa said we're not supposed to stop for another mile."

The idea of stretching her legs was appealing. She glanced back at Ruth. "What do you say? Want to walk now?"

Ruth nodded. "I think Flax wants to walk too."

Elizabeth handed the reins to Brady and JT, relieved to get down from the firm wagon seat, and she and Ruth and their energetic yellow dog made their way up the trail. They soon reached her parents' wagon, but only her mother was with it, and her head was bowed as if she was praying.

"Everything all right?" Elizabeth called up.

Clara blinked in surprise. "Oh, Elizabeth, you caught me unawares."

"Were you sleeping, Grandma?" Ruth giggled.

"I reckon I was." Clara gave them a sheepish, tired smile.

"How are you doing?" Elizabeth asked.

Clara's smile strengthened. "I'm a little worn out but no more than the rest of the travelers. Your father is checking on our unit, trying to talk some sense into certain emigrants."

"Like the Mullers," Ruth offered.

"Ruth." Elizabeth gave her daughter a warning look. "Remember your manners."

Clara pointed to a large wooden dresser alongside the road with vines growing over it. "Look at the poor old thing. It appears to have been sitting there for some time."

"Do you think there's anything in it?" Ruth asked curiously.

"I'm sure others have already gone through it," Clara told her.

"But you go ahead and have a peek if you like," Elizabeth said as she climbed up in the wagon to sit next to her mother. Then as Ruth and Flax hurried over to investigate the old dresser, Elizabeth turned to peer at her mother, looking into her eyes. "You look extra tired today. Is everything all right? Have you been sleeping well?"

"I'm sure I sleep better than most." Clara shook her head. "When I think about some of the mothers, like our friend Flo, sleeping with all three of her girls in the back of one crowded wagon...well, I can't help but feel a mite selfish."

"Well, if you're that worried, you could always invite a couple of the Flanders girls to come over and sleep with you and Father." Elizabeth laughed. "For that matter, I'm sure Ruth would willingly join you."

Clara chuckled.

"Do you want to walk with Ruthie and me a spell?"

Clara pursed her lips then shook her head. "No thank you, I think I'll stay here with Asa until we stop for dinner."

Elizabeth reached over and squeezed her mother's hand. "Go ahead and grab a few more winks while you can get them," she said as she climbed down.

She continued up to Matthew and Jess' wagon, which was just one ahead of her parents'. She still felt a little awkward around them. She supposed it wasn't easy being newlyweds on a wagon train, where privacy was hard to come by.

"Hello there, Jess," she called out when she saw that her new sister-in-law was the only one seated in the wagon. "Is Matthew off helping his fellow travelers?"

Jess nodded and smiled. "It seems only fair after our recent breakdown."

Elizabeth climbed up to sit next to her. "It makes me glad we're in a big group. More hands to help out when someone is in need." She had watched the men working together to replace Matthew's broken wagon wheel the day before. Not only did it look extremely difficult, it had appeared dangerous as well. It was one thing to make wagon repairs on flat ground, something else altogether on a hillside. Still feeling like a protective big sister, she was relieved that Matthew hadn't been forced to deal with it on his own.

"I think we should be good from here on out," Jess told her. "It helped to move some of the load into your father's wagon."

"Yes, now that our food supplies are diminishing, it was time to redistribute some of the weight."

"And with Soda Pass only a day or two ahead..." Jess pulled out a book with a map, pointing to where they were on the trail. "And with an elevation of seven thousand feet, we need to take it as easy as we can on the animals." She stuck the book back under the seat. "Which is why I'm going to get out and walk after Matthew returns."

"Maybe you can walk with Ruth and me later." Elizabeth hopped back down. "In the meantime I want to go see who broke down up there."

"Yes, I'll be curious to hear about it too."

"Find anything in the dresser?" Elizabeth called out as Ruth and Flax came over.

"Nothing but dust."

She grasped her daughter's hand, quickening the pace. "Well let's go see what's wrong up ahead. We'll find out what's holding us up."

They discovered the trouble about ten wagons up. The Spencers in unit four appeared to have broken an axle. Not only that, but unless she was mistaken, Elizabeth thought they had team trouble as well. She knew enough about livestock to recognize a mule was seriously injured. With his big boxy head hanging straight down and one hoof lifted off the ground, the poor animal was clearly suffering.

"It's a shame," Belinda Bramford said as she and her sister came over to Elizabeth and Ruth. "We've been watching for a while, and it's not good at all."

"They're going to have to put the mule down," Amelia informed them.

"Mr. Spencer is getting his gun," Belinda said quietly.

"They're going to *shoot* him?" Ruth asked with wide eyes.

"Look at that front left leg," Elizabeth told her daughter. "You can see it's broken. He must have fallen when the axle broke."

"But can't it be fixed?" Ruth asked.

"Oh, Ruth..." Elizabeth sadly shook her head. "You're a farm girl. You know the answer to that. There's no way that poor animal can go on. The only kind thing to do is to put it down."

Ruth turned to face her mother, covering her eyes with her hands. "I don't want to watch it."

"No," Elizabeth told her. "Nor do I."

"Me neither," said Amelia.

"Let's keep walking," Elizabeth told them.

So now with the two teen girls joining them, they hastened on ahead. But they'd only gone about fifty yards before they heard the gunshot. Ruth's grasp tightened on Elizabeth's hand, but she said nothing. Her head hung down as they walked up the rutted wagon trail. Because of their fast pace, they soon caught up with the slow-moving wagons. Naturally, there were questions regarding the gunshot. Fortunately the Bramford girls didn't mind sharing the sad news. Meanwhile, Elizabeth and Ruth continued walking.

"Grandma said we have to go a mile before we break for dinner," Elizabeth told Ruth. "Maybe we can get far enough ahead to go off trail a bit to look for wildflowers or strawberries or gather firewood." She knew Ruth still felt confused and saddened over the injured mule and its untimely demise. And although it would be easy to sweep this under the rug and speak about something else, Elizabeth decided to use it as a teaching moment, and she silently prayed that God would help her.

When All My Dreams Come True

Bobbie McIntyre dreams of running a ranch of her own someday. Ranch owner Jace Kincaid figures the Lord is testing his faith when a female wrangler shows up looking for work. It doesn't take long, though, for Jace to have dreams of his own where the lovely cowgirl is concerned.

When Love Gets in the Way

Grace Bradley is running away, fleeing the man her father chose to be her husband. Cade Ramsey, her new employer's best friend, tries to render assistance in the matter. After he wins her heart, will Grace be free to choose Cade, or will another groom await her at the altar?

When Two Hearts Meet

Rachel Garrett finds that becoming a nurse is fraught with peril when she's attacked by an unknown assailant. As Deputy Sheriff Luke Mason hunts for Rachel's attacker, he finds she has snared his heart. Rachel's need of Luke's protection just might be the force that sends the wall around his barricaded heart crashing down around them.

HARVEST HOUSE PUBLISHERS
EUGENE, OREGON